Mehendi Tides

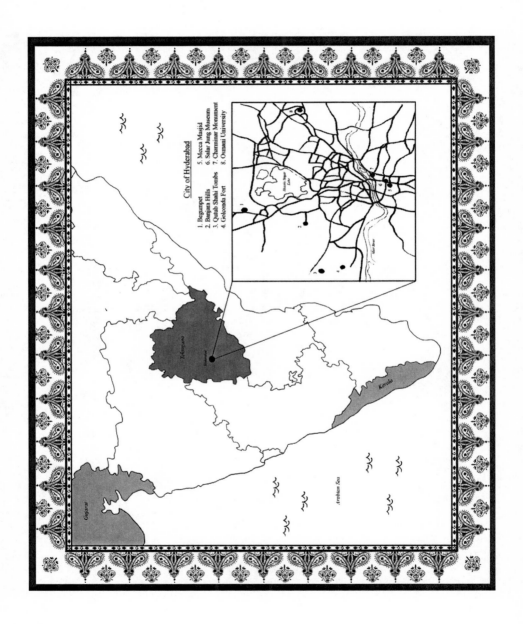

City of Hyderabad

1. Begumpet
2. Banjara Hills
3. Qutub Shahi Tombs
4. Golconda Fort
5. Mecca Masjid
6. Salar Jung Museum
7. Charminar Monument
8. Osmani University

MEHENDI TIDES

A NOVEL

To Kellie
Take a Journey
Siobha

SIOBHAN MALANY

NEW YORK

NASHVILLE • MELBOURNE • VANCOUVER

Mehendi TIDES

A NOVEL

Published in New York, New York, by Morgan James Publishing. Morgan James is a trademark of Morgan James, LLC. www.MorganJamesPublishing.com

The Morgan James Speakers Group can bring authors to your live event. For more information or to book an event visit The Morgan James Speakers Group at www.TheMorganJamesSpeakersGroup.com.

ISBN 978-1-68350-400-9 paperback
ISBN 978-1-68350-401-6 eBook
Library of Congress Control Number: 2017900290

Cover Design by:
Rachel Lopez
www.r2cdesign.com

Interior Design by:
Bonnie Bushman
The Whole Caboodle Graphic Design

In an effort to support local communities, raise awareness and funds, Morgan James Publishing donates a percentage of all book sales for the life of each book to Habitat for Humanity Peninsula and Greater Williamsburg.

Get involved today! Visit
www.MorganJamesBuilds.com

To my parents—
For giving me the gift of international travel in my youth,
and with it the confidence and compassion to discover.
I love you.

CONTENTS

ACKNOWLEDGMENTS

Mario, my husband, my best critic and supporter, for your insight into the characters' development and for the many weekend outings you took with our boys that gave me precious time to write. I could not have written this book without you.

Lucas and Lennox for inspiring me everytime I look at both of you.

Arshia, my forever friend, for taking me with you.

Indira for your friendship, visits, and inspiring conversations.

Safia and Mohammad for being my family away from home.

To all of the families and friends that shared their homes and lives with me while I was traveling overseas in the countries of India, Pakistan, Australia, Wales, Germany, Croatia, and Macedonia.

Caitlin Perry for your editing and patience through many, many versions of this story.

Shae Vasile for your wonderful illustration of India.

To my family for their love and support.

Principal Characters
(In Alphabetical Order)

Anees	Nasreen's cousin and brother to Rahim and Tariq
Arwah	Nasreen's cousin
Aunty Samina	Nasreen's aunt; mother to Hari, Max, Yasmine, and Azra
Aunty Zehba	Nasreen's aunt; mother to Rahim, Anees, and Tariq
Azra	Nasreen's young cousin; sister to Hari, Max, and Yasmine
Dean Rowbottom	Dean of Kate's graduate college
Dr. Crone	Kate's new graduate advisor
Dr. Khan	Neighbor of Nasreen's family
Dr. Schwitz	Kate's PhD advisor
Dr. Elber	Chair of the biochemistry department
Faiz	Haseena's cousin, who is attracted to Nasreen
Haroon	"Hari," Nasreen's cousin; brother to Max, Yasmine, and Azra
Haseena	Rahim's bride
Ian	Kate's father
Kate McKenna	Protagonist; Nasreen's and Krishna's childhood friend
Krishna Desai	Protagonist; Kate's Hindu-American friend
Laila	Nasreen's mother
Mamujan	Nasreen's eldest maternal uncle
Maqsood	"Max," Nasreen's cousin; brother to Hari, Yasmine, and Azra
Marah Bahri	Nanima's sister-in-law

Mona	Nasreen's neighborhood friend
Mumanijan	Nasreen's eldest uncle's wife
Mustafa	Nasreen's husband
Nanima	Nasreen's grandmother
Nasreen Abdel	Protagonist; Kate's Muslim-American friend
Neil	Kate's ex-boyfriend
Nishi	Raji's brother
Rahim	Nasreen's eldest cousin
Rahmsing	Nanima's servant
Rayah	Anees's fiancé
Sameer	Nasreen's twin brother
Sana	Nasreen's younger sister
Sara	Nasreen's friend; Shabana's sister
Saritha	Krishna's mother
Shabana	Nasreen's friend; Sara's sister
Suneel	Krishna's father
Tariq	Nasreen's cousin; brother to Rahim and Anees
Yasmine	Nasreen's closest cousin; sister to Hari, Max, and Azra

"Nobody can discover the world for somebody else.
Only when we discover it for ourselves does it become
common ground and a common bond and we cease to be alone."
—WENDELL BERRY, American novelist and poet

Chapter 1

BUTTERFLy WALLPAPER

Chicago 1987

Sixteen-year-old kate hurried in the chill of the afternoon, past the blue Chevy Malibu in the driveway, gave a quick rap at the door to her best friend Nasreen's house, turned the knob impatiently, pressed her shoulder against the door until it opened, and scuffed across the shag rug. Warm scents of marsala and cinnamon immediately enveloped her senses.

She kicked off her shoes in the foyer and left them among the mound of sneakers and *chappals*.[1]*

Sana, Nasreen's intuitive younger sister, was the first to greet her.

"Hi Kate," she said, excited. "Will you play with me? Nasreen is crying again."

"She is?" Kate asked. "I'll see what's up and then I will play with you."

"Promise?"

Sana was holding a ragdoll and brushed the yarn hair from its face.

"I promise."

---

[1] *See glossary for definitions of italicized words throughout text.

3

Sameer, Nasreen's twin, was on the phone, pacing and speaking *Urdu* and English, switching back and forth rapidly between both tongues. As twins, Nasreen and Sameer had the same walnut-shaped eyes and brown-black wavy hair, and both were tall, but Sameer's lanky shape and gaunt face resembled nothing of Nasreen's full, curvy figure. Sameer noticed Kate as she reached the top of the stairs and gave a quick arrogant nod in her direction. She dismissed him and followed the spiced aroma into the kitchen.

Nasreen's mother, Laila, pushed plump meatballs coated with mustard seeds and red chilies around in sputtering grease with the tip of a spatula. She removed the lid from the large copper blackened pot on the back burner. The pot, dented from years of use, was probably passed down through generations of Indian wives. Steam and scents of South Indian cuisine billowed forth, covering the spice rack on the shelf above the stove. Laila leaned forward to peer into the pot.

"*As-salaam-alaikum*," Kate said, smiling.

"Oh!" Laila, startled, looked up to see her daughter's closest friend in the doorway. "*Wa-alaikum-salaam*," she returned. "I did not hear you come in."

She wiped her glistening brow with the back of her hand, her fingers smeared with bits of beef and spices. Several strands of black hair and sprigs of gray had escaped her bun and stuck out in a thick wave across her forehead.

"There is a moving van in front of Dr. Khan's house," Kate said, attempting small talk.

Dr. Khan, a slight-framed, attractive Indian doctor fresh out of residency, had just moved into the neighborhood with his young wife a few months ago, right before the holidays. He worked at the cancer clinic in the city. Two weeks earlier he had been attacked walking to his car after late-night rounds and suffered cuts, a broken nose, and bruised ribs.

"Oh, the poor man!" Laila exclaimed. "It is no wonder he and his young wife do not feel safe here. It is a shame. Such random violence in our city! They are moving to Michigan. We liked them very much."

Kate nodded, not sure what to say.

"Is Nasreen in her room?" she finally asked.

"Yes. She will not talk to me," Laila said, rocking her head side to side in a pendulum motion. "I do not know what is wrong. She is being very, very difficult."

She motioned with her greased hand as a kind of surrender. "First she cuts off all of her beautiful long hair. If I did that when I was her age, my *Ammi* would have locked me in my room for two weeks!"

Kate knew Laila would never lock Nasreen in her room.

"Now she will not stop crying," Laila continued. "She says she is ill and cannot go to mosque. You go, please," she urged, replacing the lid on the dented pot and picking up the spatula again, signaling an end to their small talk.

Down the yellow striped wallpapered hall, Kate knocked on Nasreen's bedroom door.

"It's Kate," she whispered, placing her head against the door.

A classic tune played softly inside. She opened the door slowly and scanned the familiar white and pink bedroom with butterfly wallpaper.

"Nasreen?"

"Here," Nasreen answered. "I thought you were my mother."

Kate peered over the bed. Nasreen was sitting on the floor, hugging her long legs, glancing through the soft chiffon curtains through raw, puffy eyes.

"Why are you crying over listening to the musical *La Bohème*?" Kate asked.

Nasreen looked up at her friend in the doorway and glared. Kate recognized the pained look of bygone love on her best friend's face.

She closed the door behind her and lunged across the bed. Her chin rested on her fists, elbows sinking into the soft white flowered comforter.

"Your hair is growing out. I think it looks sophisticated," Kate said cheerfully.

"Tell that to my mother," Nasreen quipped. "She acts like I have summoned the evil spirits by cutting my hair so short. I have been covering my hair with a headscarf to calm her nerves. On the plus side, my mother has bought me several new scarves." She smiled cheekily.

"I was talking to your mom about Dr. Khan. He's moving!" Kate exclaimed.

Nasreen shrugged. "Yes. It is for the best. Considering what happened…that he was beaten. He should take his wife and move to a safer city."

"Do you think it was a hate crime? Because he is Indian? Why didn't they steal his wallet?" Kate asked, still baffled by the troubling event.

"How can you rationalize the madness? He should have known better than to walk in that area late at night."

Kate thought that Nasreen seemed strangely indifferent, even mean-spirited as if Dr. Khan deserved it.

"What is wrong, Nasreen? Sana says you have been crying, and I can see that look in your eyes. Tell me!" Kate demanded.

"We are going to India and Pakistan."

"India? Pakistan? When? How long?" Kate asked excitedly.

"June. Eight weeks. We are going for a visit. And a wedding," Nasreen mumbled.

Kate sucked in her breath. Her mind rattled with thoughts of Nasreen married off to someone strange, someone old. *She is not yet seventeen. What about the rest of high school? No! It's too soon!*

"Rahim is arranged to be married to a girl in Karachi," Nasreen announced.

"Oh thank God!" Kate sputtered, releasing her breath.

"What?" Nasreen shot her a look of annoyance.

"Nothing. I just thought…never mind." She shook her head.

"You thought it was me," Nasreen said matter-of-factly. "I am not getting married. Not now, anyway."

"I don't get it," Kate said. "Why are you crying over your cousin Rahim getting married or that you are going to India? Both seem exciting."

"Aunty Zehba arranged Anees's engagement too. While shopping for one son's bride you might as well find the other son a bride," Nasreen remarked caustically. "Rahim's wedding is first because he is the eldest, and Aunty Zehba expects everyone to attend. Anees's wedding will be sometime next spring. She is planning a large engagement party when we are in Pakistan."

"I'm sorry," Kate said shyly. "I'm sorry Anees is engaged."

"What is there to be sorry about?" Nasreen snapped.

She gazed out the window again. There was, so it seemed for Nasreen, something deeper than teenage heartache.

"It was never in our fates to be together. He is twenty-three now and needs a bride," she said after a pause. "He always told me he would marry whoever his mother chooses. I respect that."

"Why doesn't she choose you? She is your aunt. Why not ask her? I mean, if it is what you both want?" Kate asked awkwardly.

She had never fully grasped the depth of Nasreen and Anees's infatuation, if that's what it was—the close bond between cousins whose difference in age spanned adolescence and young adulthood.

Kate was jealous of Nasreen's maturity when it came to romance and intrigued by her power to attract the attention of a man—not a boy, but a man. Kate learned about love from conversations with Nasreen, a girl forbidden to date and whose matrimonial fate would soon be arranged in accordance with Indian culture.

"Aunty Zehba would never choose me," Nasreen snapped. "And she will never know!" She flashed Kate a look of warning.

"Why? Because you and he are cousins?"

"Cousins get married all the time in our culture," Nasreen said firmly. "But no! Anees is her favorite son. Only a wife from Pakistan is suitable. Not someone who grew up in America," she added defensively. "I just wish he had the courage to tell me himself, you know? My mother told me!"

Kate did not reply. She listened instead to the soundtrack streaming from the tape deck on the floor. Vinyl records and cassette cases littered the pink speckled rug.

"I know it hurts, but there is time for you," Kate said. "Just promise me you will not run off and get married our senior year and leave me here alone in stuffy, cliquey Rockfield High. You're my best friend!"

Suddenly, Nasreen broke into violent tears. She rocked back and forth still hugging her knees, heaving.

"Nasreen! What is it?" Kate shouted in panic. "Should I get your mother?"

"No!" Nasreen said, a look of apprehension in her eyes.

"What is going on with you?"

"I'm late!"

Kate was shocked.

Nasreen wiped her nose with the back of her hand.

"What? You and Anees were having…sex?" Kate's mouth fell wide open.

"It was a mistake," Nasreen blurted.

"A mistake? He is twenty-three! And now he is engaged!"

"It's not his fault," Nasreen said breathlessly. She started to say more but did not.

"Why are you defending him?" Kate was visibly angry now.

"I shouldn't have told you," Nasreen snapped.

Nasreen had too much religious conviction to be so careless. It didn't make sense, Kate thought. Her head was pounding. Then she realized someone was pounding on the bedroom door.

"Go away!" shouted Nasreen.

"Krishna is on the phone," Sameer's muffled voice said from the hallway.

"Ugh," Nasreen moaned. She got up and swung the door open to find Sameer leaning against the doorframe.

She grabbed the white phone and receiver, grayed by fingerprints. The phone cord snaked down the hallway from their parents' bedroom. Nasreen yanked the cord. Sana stood in the hallway singing a lullaby to her ragdoll.

"Will you and Kate play with me now?" Sana pleaded.

"No!"

"You're mean," Sameer snapped. "What are you listening to?" he said, poking his head into his twin sister's bedroom.

"None of your business," Nasreen barked as she pushed the door closed, causing Sameer to jump out of its path.

"Hello," Nasreen said hoarsely into the receiver. "Yes, I'm fine. Just have a slight cold."

"You're going to India?" Krishna's voice shrieked loudly through the phone line.

Nasreen cringed and lifted her head away from the receiver.

"Wow. So are we!"

Krishna's long, piercing pitch filled the room, shattering the melancholy tone diffusing from the tape deck.

Kate watched Nasreen pace across the bedroom.

Krishna tended to be overzealous at times. She lived a few streets over from Maple Street and often pedaled her powder-blue Schwinn bike to Nasreen's, her long black braid swinging as she rounded the block. Nasreen had known Krishna since they were toddlers and their emigrant Indian mothers met in the middle of the afternoon pushing the little brown-eyed girls in strollers.

"Really?" Nasreen asked, returning the receiver to her ear. "July? Yes, we are going in June to India and then Pakistan. I know! I know! It has been six years since I have visited my grandmother, my aunt and uncles, and my cousins."

Partly listening to the one-sided conversation between Nasreen and Krishna, Kate rolled onto her back and lay on the bed staring at the ceiling, praying that Nasreen wasn't pregnant and utterly dismayed that she might be. To distract her mind, Kate thought about the first time she had meet Nasreen and Krishna freshman year.

Nasreen's and Krishna's families did not share the same religion, language, or customs, yet the two girls were bonded on the neighborhood playground in a middle-class neighborhood by their "India-ness." Although both of their mothers were from South India, Laila was from Telangana and Saritha was from the coastal state of Kerala, making their daughters culturally divergent in a sense but both bound by their epochal duties to define their parents' legacy in America.

Krishna's parents, Saritha and Suneel Desai, each came from different Indian states divided by geography and dialects. They met in America, landing on the same college campus surrounded by Illinois cornstalks. After a peek through the library stacks, Saritha was drawn to Suneel's long jawline and thoughtful intensity as he sat studying; he was intrigued by her wide-eyed curiosity. Suneel was from the western state of Gujarat, making his marriage to Saritha a marriage never bechanced in India, only in an American college town. "A love marriage," Krishna called it with a hint of defiance in her voice. "About the only thing they had in common was that their home states shared the same Indian coastline!"

On the other hand, Nasreen's parents were born, reared, and married by arrangement in Hyderabad, their consummation blessed by ancestral order and progeniture prosperity. Her father brought his new wife to the Midwest in search of a promising engineering career.

Both sets of parents arrived in the same American neighborhood in the mid-1960s to start new lives. Their American-born daughters found friendship in hopscotch, running through the malls holding hands, and prancing around the dinner table dressed in colorful *salwar kameezes*.

In high school, Nasreen met Kate, a freckle-faced redhead, and the only other girl in her computer class. Kate and Nasreen listened to music, passed the time in mindless chatter in the pink and white bedroom, giggled about boys, and complained about home economics class. Laila often set a place for Kate at the evening meal, something fried, too spicy, peppers soaked in cumin and *turmeric* in a spiced bubbling *ghee*.

On weekends, Kate spent the night at Nasreen's and attended family gatherings—feasts at dusk during the holy month of *Ramadan*, and *Eid* parties signaling the end of Ramadan that lasted through the night. On these occasions, even in the middle of August, the house, strung with bulbs, danced in the wondrous light on an otherwise dark and quiet Midwestern street, the walkways decorated with luminary candles guiding the women in flowing *saris* bursting with color and outlined with gold diamante trim, all hours of the night.

At every wedding ceremony celebrated in traditional stages—the *mehendi*, the *nikah*, and the *walima*—in the Rockfield Muslim community, Kate was the fair girl beside Nasreen. The women were always separate from the men on these occasions during meals and prayer. Kate found comfort sitting cross-legged on the floor among a sea of veiled women, hips touching hips, so close she smelled *henna* dye in the women's hair. It was an earthy smell of the dye mixed with camellia-scented hair oil.

Kate imagined her mother's face under each veil, a beautiful face fading in her memory over the five years since she had passed away. There among the mothers and girls waiting to be mothers, she could feel her own passions in the waves of soft murmurs and prayer hymns.

Nasreen placed the phone gently against its base after saying goodbye to Krishna.

"What are you going to do?" Kate asked. "When you go to India, you will be…" She wiggled her fingers as she counted the months in her head. "…Showing!"

"Shhh," Nasreen warned. "I am just late a few days. Maybe it's nothing."

"Nothing? Nasreen, this isn't like you!" Kate exclaimed. "You're shaking!"

"Come with us."

"To India?" Kate asked astonished, eyeing Nasreen suspiciously.

Nasreen lowered her head. "I'm tired," she said. "We are supposed to go to the mosque tonight. I can't go. I told my mother I'm ill. It's not really a lie."

Kate pictured Nasreen, her cropped hair wrapped underneath a *dupatta*, kneeling on her prayer rug, a baby growing inside her.

Yes, she thought, *best to stay here surrounded by the butterfly wallpaper.*

Chapter 2

WRAPPED IN FAITH

Ten Years Later • Chicago 1998

Café Trois Oeufs on Chicago's north side was beginning to quiet down as breakfast business meetings came to an end. Clients glanced critically at their watches, while morning procrastinators prepared for their mundane Midwestern jobs.

The wooden chairs moaned loudly as patrons pushed them forward, allowing others to pass with an "excuse me," "pardon me," and "have a nice day."

Beneath shuffling feet, the hallowed floorboards of the renovated Victorian house—now a French restaurant and bakery—creaked with patrons glancing at the bright showcases of gleaming pastries and handmade glazed bread swirled in knots or twisted in ropes.

A little bell on the door mantel rang as Kate entered. The January cold drifted in and skirted across the floorboards. Kate searched among the tables and spotted Nasreen and Krishna, sitting at a table in the corner of the bakery.

Nasreen had just returned from visiting family in Pakistan with her husband, Mustafa, and called Kate and Krishna to meet at her favorite café.

"Hi. Sorry I'm late," Kate apologized.

She gave both women a quick hug, dropped her backpack on the floor, and plopped into the French wicker chair.

"I am so glad we could finally get together. It's been months!" Krishna said.

Krishna had shoulder-length straight, black satin hair that hung down along her face covering her right eye. She hardly wore makeup and didn't really need it. She had full lips, deep dark eyes, and a slight nose that was challenged to support a set of square spectacles. Krishna was constantly pushing the spectacles to the bridge of her nose with one finger. She looked critical at times, particularly when she didn't have the patience to explain what it meant to be Hindu, who Lord *Ganesha* was, what her family did during *Diwali*, if she wore Indian clothing at home, or what language her parents spoke. At other times, she was excitable, and her voice rose to a high pitch.

"How was your trip to Pakistan?" Kate asked Nasreen as she pulled off her coat and draped it on the back of the wicker chair.

Nasreen inhaled soulfully before responding.

"Mustafa and I had a great time. Karachi is very romantic at night. The buildings and marriage halls light up the evening sky. Even the bazaars glow like magical tents." She smiled, her lips glistening soft brown. "The city has changed so much since you have been there, Kate." Her walnut eyes widened with emphasis. "Can you believe it has been ten years?"

Ten years? Kate tried to comprehend the time, a void from then to now. The thought of how a decade had passed since she had traveled to Hyderabad, India, and Karachi, Pakistan, with Nasreen and her family as an inquisitive sixteen-year-old was incomprehensible.

"I visited *Mamujan* and *Mumanijan* in Karachi," Nasreen continued, referring to her eldest uncle and his wife. "Mumanijan threw a large dinner party in my honor. You remember her parties. Nothing has changed. Anees and Rayah were back visiting from Sacramento with their two boys. Aunty Zehba was ecstatic to see them. A wonderful thing because she was in a good mood!"

Kate laughed picturing Nasreen's overbearing aunt nagging everyone about something.

"And my cousin Azra! Azra is engaged!"

"Little Azra?" Kate's interest was piqued.

"And Yasmine!" Nasreen exclaimed. "It was so great to see Yasmine. She has the most adorable three-year-old boy."

Nasreen hesitated.

"Anees told me that Tariq is living in New York."

At the sound of his name, Kate felt a ripple through her heart—the same ripple she had felt every time he looked at her with such intensity, his slate-blue eyes searing through hers.

She had been enraptured by Nasreen's cousin, Tariq, during their summer in Asia, but the hope for anything more dissipated into summer dust once they returned to the US and dissolved with Nasreen's words: "Don't be foolish. My cousin will marry the Muslim girl his mother chooses."

"New York?" Kate asked, intrigued.

"Anees says he is getting his MBA then returning to India."

"Tariq said there will be jobs in India. The telecommunication industry is flourishing, and he wouldn't have to come to America for work," Kate stated flatly. "Good for him."

Nasreen slowly sipped her tea. "Everyone remembers the red-haired girl, Kate McKenna."

Kate tried to envision herself as the girl of ten years ago transplanted for eight weeks in a foreign place—the girl who walked by slums, past architectural wonders, alongside a bombed bazaar, and through stone fortresses and glorious mosques. The teenage Kate had learned customs, gestures, Urdu words, prayer times, how to eat with her hands, how to wrap a sari around the curves of her body, and squeeze glass bangles over her knuckles without breaking them.

As strange and alien as she had felt on the streets, Kate felt the opposite in the homes of Nasreen's relatives. She joined the cousins sitting on the floor, listening to the elders, singing to the pounding *dholaks,* and watching Indian movies over several days. She had embraced what she didn't understand, absorbed it with an unbiased faith, wrapping it around her like a veil.

Kate was jealous now of that girl who had wandered through a land of virtuous domes and arched walkways, rising from the heat and sand, unfettered and uninhibited.

"You would not believe the places we went in Karachi!" Nasreen exclaimed, bringing Kate back to the present.

The right side of Nasreen's mouth curled in a seductive half-grin. She tousled her hair. The red of her fingertips peeked forth from her thick dark brown waves tinted with bold maroon-colored highlights.

Kate had noticed the red highlights now fully illuminated by the light from the hanging Tiffany lamp.

"Did you dye your hair with henna?" she asked, reminded of the henna paste that had decorated their hands and palms with intricate mehendi designs during the wedding ceremonies in Pakistan.

"Yes. I just felt like a change of color."

Nasreen often changed her hairstyle, adding highlights or straightening her curls with a flat iron. Kate remembered the time in high school when Nasreen had chopped her long wavy hair severely short so that the ends wisped under her earlobes. Nasreen's mother was distraught for weeks and insisted her daughter cover her head with a dupatta when they went to the mosque, at least until the hair grew to shoulder length. Nasreen was going through a rough time then, confronting the possibility that she was pregnant.

"The nightclubs are dazzling," Nasreen continued, her voice lowering to a whisper. "Mustafa and I are treated like royalty when we go out with his friends."

"Nightclubs?" Krishna was adding sugar to her tea and looked up above the rims of her glasses clinging low on her nose.

"I tell you, Karachi has changed," Nasreen said.

Kate had read articles on the new Pakistan. Beyond the conservative streets was a pulsing other world of young businessmen and entrepreneurs armed with an imperious aura. They exuded independence and carried money shoved in silk-lined suit pockets. The "new" business professionals prayed toward *Mecca*, fasted during the holy month of Ramadan, and danced and dined in upscale clubs bestowing largesse upon their beautiful wives clad in heavily filigreed saris and wrapped in diaphanous veils.

Nasreen's husband, Mustafa Abdel, was from Pakistan as were most of the young couples he and Nasreen associated with. Their friends had married in Pakistan and were now settled in Pepperwood Grove and the surrounding northern Chicago suburbs. Nasreen claimed Pakistan, at least in part, as her family's place of origin even though her parents grew up and married in India.

The house in Hyderabad, India, where Nasreen's mother was reared was gone, demolished by bureaucrats and investors. Nanima, Nasreen's grandmother, stayed in the house as long as the developers would tolerate. Then she went to live with Nasreen's aunts Zehba and Samina in the adjacent neighborhood of Jubilee Hills. The Banjara Hills neighborhood was transformed into a high-priced hotel district with shopping areas and swanky restaurants catering to tourists and professionals in the growing telecommunications industry.

Kate visualized Nanima clutching the tin full of ingredients to make traditional *paan* and the stack of old photos from the armoire. She wondered what happened to Rahmsing and his family who had lived in the mud shack at the end of the driveway; his sole income was earned tending to Nanima and the house in Banjara Hills. Even the intertwined *tamarind* trees that had sheltered the corrugated-roof house from the city's commotion were, as she imagined, ripped from their roots.

Nanima died last July from pneumonia, and Aunty Zehba and Aunty Samina no longer lived on Old School Lane in Jubilee Hills. Nearly all of Nasreen's cousins had migrated with their families to Karachi, Pakistan. Sadly, there was now no reason for Nasreen to return to India, no reason to claim Hyderabadi lineage. Kate felt that Nasreen had all but banned India from the conversation, pushed the country aside like parsley on a plate.

Kate looked down into her tea of swirling herbs and took a slow sip, wishing she had decided on the raspberry tart with glazed kiwi instead of a plain croissant. She was on a graduate student budget and the croissant was the cheapest item on the menu. She counted her monthly finances in her head: $900 received for teaching; $400 went to rent, $200 for car expenses and insurance, and $150 for student fees. That didn't leave much for raspberry tarts served on a doily.

900, minus 400, minus 200, minus 150.

"I told my family you are getting your doctorate in biochemistry."

"What?"

"You are always daydreaming," Nasreen said, sighing. "I said that you were working on your PhD in biochemistry. Aunty Zehba was impressed, and nothing impresses her as you know!"

"Well, let's see if I do eventually get that PhD," Kate said.

Graduate school was like stumbling through a dark cave, she thought.

"Of course you will," Krishna remarked emphatically.

Nasreen changed the subject. "Mumanijan asked if you were engaged yet. She is still playing matchmaker."

"Engaged?" Kate asked as though the question were absurd. "Hardly."

Kate had no intention of revealing that she and Neil, whom she had been dating, had broken up last week. She didn't need the pity. She did not want to admit the mistake she made in dating her closest friend on the Master's swim team. Neil had provided sanity to her day, as they rendezvoused many mornings at the university union for coffee after swim practice. He was a graduate student in the English department and a good listener. He let her spill out all the demons in her head to eventually soak into the residual coffee grounds at the bottom of her cup. He made her laugh at the absurdities and the demands of professors. But he had broken off their relationship, stating that he needed to focus on graduating like it was his New Year's resolution.

"How is married life, Nasreen?" Krishna asked after a long pause.

"Married life is great." The corner of Nasreen's mouth curled coyly as she answered Krishna's inquiry. "The information technology company Mustafa works for is opening a branch in San Francisco, and he just got promoted to senior specialist. He has to travel more, but no matter how busy he is we always go to mosque on Fridays, and every Saturday we get together with a few Pakistani couples, go to dinner, or stay home and play games. Seems every weekend there is a wedding, baby shower, birthday, kids running around everywhere, it's crazy! Oh, gosh…" Nasreen paused distracted by a thought.

"What?" Krishna looked around nervously.

"I just remembered! Mustafa's siblings and their families will all be here for the month of February for my niece's wedding. The entire Abdel clan! Come for my niece's wedding!" Nasreen exclaimed.

"I can come," Krishna said.

Kate narrowed her eyes. "Umm, I…" she stammered, trying to find the right words to decline the invitation.

Kate had by far attended more Indian weddings than traditional American weddings in her youth, thanks to Nasreen. She found Indian weddings to be more entertaining, rich in textiles, tralatitious music, and rituals that transported her to a different place.

"I would love to attend the wedding," she began, "but it is a really busy time, you know." Kate looked away from Nasreen's gaze. "Undergraduates have exams coming up so I will be swamped with grading, and I am trying to finish my thesis."

"Let me know when you are free then," Nasreen responded impatiently.

Free? Kate thought. For four years she had been secluded in a lab. She had been trying to be free forever it seemed.

As teenagers, she and Nasreen had similar ambitions. Nasreen had been accepted to the top schools for pre-law. But instead of enrolling, she attended the community college to be close to home before getting married.

Now, as twenty-seven-year-old women, their lives were diverging.

Which was the better path?

Nasreen had a life of luxury filled with friends, extended family, and travel. She had a freelance gig with a financial magazine that provided flexibility. She had never been alone and continued to walk from one life event to another under a veil of family tradition, embracing faith.

Kate, in contrast, poured her soul into obtaining a doctorate in biochemistry. Besides casual relationships, human touch seemed as remote as graduation. She was driven to understand the breast cancer that took her mother's life when she was eleven years old, design the drugs that would have saved her, or change her own fate if she unluckily inherited the same misguided genes.

Was getting a doctorate her heart's desire, or was it to prove something? Was she driven by her father's pride or her mother's legacy?

"At least come for Eid in March!" Nasreen demanded.

"Definitely, I will come for Eid. I never miss it."

Kate tried to sound upbeat. March seemed eons away. March seemed yellow and warmer compared to the gray cold of January.

"I have exams in March. I doubt I will make it to Eid," Krishna said, disappointed. "Kate, are you job searching? You could find a position in Chicago. You will have a PhD. That is really incredible, Kate!"

"No!" Kate replied vehemently. "I haven't looked anywhere."

She was supposed to emerge out of the shadows of inconclusive philosophies and failed experiments into the brightness of scientific achievement, but she was still trudging through the academic tunnel.

Kate took an abrupt drink and set her cup down with force, crashing it against the saucer.

"Maybe I will quit," she snapped.

It was a matter-of-fact statement, as though she were deciding to forgo coffee every morning in an effort to cut down on caffeine, not deciding her future.

"You won't quit," Nasreen stated firmly.

"I might!"

"Why?" Krishna questioned.

"Because he is a…a control freak!" Kate blurted defensively.

"Who?"

"My advisor!"

Kate looked at Nasreen, searching for acknowledgment and emotion.

"My advisor is such a micromanager. How am I supposed to become an independent researcher, for Pete's sake!" Kate exclaimed angrily. "He has ultimate control, you know? Maybe he will sign my thesis and maybe he won't. Some days I just want to give up."

"You won't give up. Quit being cynical," Nasreen said as she reached for another pastry. "I should not eat this," she grimaced. "I ate so much in Pakistan and gained five pounds." She sighed and bit into the glistening tart anyway.

Kate stared numbly across the room. She knew Nasreen was right. She never quit anything.

"I think I would rather study genes that cause cancer," Kate said, raising her voice. "Maybe I have cancerous genes like my mother."

"You do not have cancerous genes," Nasreen said, savoring the tart.

"You don't know that!" Kate retorted.

"Stop!"

"Scientists have linked mutations in genes with breast cancer like the cancer my mother had. They have tests now, you know? I can have my DNA tested. Know if I have mutated genes. I have been reading the papers on DNA testing."

"We studied genetic testing in medical school," Krishna stated proudly. "But those tests are really, really expensive, Kate."

"If I am part of a study, I won't have to pay for the test. I don't know what to do." Kate stared into her teacup still hearing the doctor's voice in her head explaining the procedure and the potential outcome.

"Kate!" Nasreen said firmly. "Look at me!"

Kate stared into Nasreen's brown eyes for a long, intense moment.

"You are stronger than your mother was. You will not develop cancer like her and die. You won't," she said with resolution.

"Okay," Krishna interjected. "Change of topics!" She swallowed her sentence along with a mouthful of chocolate éclair.

"More tea?" Nasreen breathed deeply and smiled as she poured more herbal tea into Kate's cup. "A cup of chamomile always helps."

"Yes, as simple as that," Kate responded cheekily.

Kate blew at her freshly poured tea. She listened to the ring of the door that brought in the cold, the creak of the floor as customers departed, and the click of dishes being cleared. The place was emptying. The tables were littered with lipstick-stained cups, pastry wrappings, and a few half-eaten macaroons and custard tarts, abandoned by those too busy to finish or dieting. An older couple sat at the table in the corner.

"And med school? How's that going?" Kate's tone was biting as she focused the attention to Krishna. "Besides learning about genetic testing."

Krishna wiped chocolate from the corners of her mouth, pushed her straight hair out of her face, and leaned back in the French wicker chair.

"Tolerable," she said, unenthused. "I just need to finish this rotation, then I will be in the program. Still 'on probation,' as they call it." She bit off another piece of éclair.

Kate understood the pressure Krishna endured, and she felt slightly guilty for prodding. The pressure came from Krishna's mother, Saritha, who poured all her faith and future into her only child, desiring above marriage that Krishna become a doctor in America. Saritha at twenty years old had done the unthinkable. She had left her upper-middle-class family in Kerala to come to America in pursuit of a career in nursing. She had worked her way up through the years to head nurse at the medical school and used whatever credibility she had to convince her superiors, filling their ears during rounds, with her persistence to accept her daughter Krishna into the program. The best was acceptance, "on probation."

"If I don't pass this rotation, I'm out of the program," she confessed and looked carefully at the two of them. "I am *out*." She emphasized the word *out* in case it wasn't clear. "I can't tell my mom."

"Maybe you will pass. Then you won't have to tell her," Nasreen stated.

"Do you wish to be a doctor?" Kate asked.

Krishna straightened, a little surprised by Kate's sudden directness.

"It doesn't matter," she said defensively. "My parents want me to be a doctor. If I grew up in India, my fate would be dictated by marriage, as they so often remind me," Krishna remarked, rolling her eyes. "I would never have had the opportunity to pursue a career and be successful as a doctor in America, helping people, saving lives," she stressed. "My parents arrived in America for the opportunity to better themselves, and they expect me to achieve even more. I should be grateful they don't just want to marry me off!"

Nasreen shifted in her chair. "We do what makes our parents happy. Just try your best."

Kate glanced at her watch.

"I saw Sara and Shabana last week at mosque. They were in town, visiting. You remember them from my wedding?" Nasreen said.

"Of course," Kate responded, shifting in her chair.

"Sara is pregnant with her third child, and Shabana has two girls and a baby boy. Can you believe it?"

Nasreen had always envisioned having many kids, so three or four seemed reasonable. But Nasreen didn't have any children, not one; she had struggled with getting pregnant. Nothing happened. Kate searched Nasreen's face for any hopeful sign for mentioning Sara's pregnancy, but Nasreen was looking into her tea perplexed, and after a few moments, looked up and stared blankly toward the far side of the café.

"I can't get pregnant."

"I'm sure it will happen, Nasreen," Krishna reassured. "For some couples it just takes time."

"No!" Nasreen said loudly.

With a thump, she dropped her forearms onto the table, upsetting the cup and saucer pair, causing a terrible crash. The remaining patrons turned their heads toward the commotion. The waiter paused in clearing the dishes. For a moment, Café Trois Oeufs was still except for the echo of crashing porcelain.

"I can't get pregnant," she said again, quieter. "My doctor says I suffer from endometriosis."

"Nasreen, I am so sorry!" Krishna gasped and placed her hand over her mouth.

Nasreen righted the empty cup and carefully, soundlessly placed it on the saucer. The waiter came to her aid and wiped up the spill.

"We studied this condition in our OB/GYN rotation," Krishna said. "Endometriosis occurs when tissue grows outside the uterus. It causes scarring and lesions and a lot of pain."

"Thanks for the diagnosis," Nasreen said in a low whisper as the waiter walked away. "Anyway, my doctor says my chances are very slim of ever getting pregnant."

"It explains so much," Kate realized. "The pain every month. The missed classes and the…moods. I am so sorry too."

"It's not in Allah's will," Nasreen sighed.

Allah's will? The words hung in Kate's mind. "It's in your will!" Kate surprised herself by speaking.

"Mustafa and I have been married nearly eight years. Our anniversary is coming up in April," Nasreen said, letting the statement hang stale in the air. "I don't think it will happen."

Thoughts flashed before Kate's mind: thoughts of sitting cross-legged on the sea-green carpet among the crowd of relatives at Nasreen's pre-wedding ceremony. The women, in tradition, clasped their hands together above Nasreen's bowed head bestowing spiritual blessings of fertility to the marriage. The sound of cracking knuckles rang in her ears. The more cracking, the more blessings bestowed. All Kate could hear now above the beating of the dholak drums and the sound of popping knuckles was the pulsing of an empty, fibrous womb.

The bell resonated as someone pushed open the door to the outside; a trail of dead leaves carried by the winter wind swirled across the wood floor and tickled Kate's ankles.

"Eight years?" Krishna remarked. "Seems like we were just celebrating your nikah, Nasreen."

"It does," agreed Kate, regaining her composure. "I can still feel how heavy the wedding dupatta was draped and layered around you." She raised her hands pretending to carry the traditional matrimonial garb. "And the red and white sweet-smelling garlands in layers, so many layers. We all tried to support the material so you wouldn't break from the sheer weight." Kate attempted a smile.

Nasreen gazed at some random place, reminded of her younger self under the layers of fabric, jewels, and blessings.

Kate noticed the older couple in the corner, their hair the color of milk. The man reached across the table, precariously picked up the French Provence-patterned creamer, and poured cream with a shaky hand into his wife's tea. They exchanged a simple, timeless smile.

"There is still time, isn't there?" Kate asked rhetorically.

"What time then?" Nasreen questioned, refocusing on Kate. "By the time my 'slim' chance of becoming pregnant may happen, I will be an old woman when my kid goes to high school, or I will just be old."

"Well, I will be an old woman by the time I get my PhD."

"I will be older than old by the time I get out of medical school!" chimed Krishna.

"We can just sip tea together as old crabby women," Kate joked.

The three of them looked at each other sympathetically and then broke out in laughter—tension-relieving, watery-eyed laughter.

"To being old women who will finally get what they want!" Nasreen raised her teacup in the air.

"Before I get too old, I'm thinking of freezing my eggs," Krishna blurted.

Nasreen choked on her tea and began pounding her chest.

"What?" she exclaimed with a cough.

"I have been reading about it—about freezing eggs," Krishna said pointedly. "Talking about being old…I thought if I didn't get married but wanted to have children, I could freeze my eggs, you know, as an option."

"But you are not old," Kate said, flabbergasted.

"Why do you think you won't get married?" asked Nasreen.

"I'm not really interested in any men."

"We're not even thirty yet!" Kate erupted.

"Soon we will be! In a few years!"

"You haven't met the right person," Nasreen rationalized. "Don't you think, Kate?"

"I think I'm glad I didn't order the poached eggs."

Nasreen snorted her tea for the second time. She clasped a hand over her mouth to keep the liquid from spewing forth. She swallowed hard, shutting her eyes in brief agony, then opened her mouth and laughed loudly.

"I'm done with my tea. It's dangerous to drink around you guys."

The waiter finished clearing tables and approached them.

"Glad you are enjoying yourselves, ladies," he said. "May I get you anything else?"

"Yes. A baby, a PhD, and an MD, please. And hold the eggs," Kate deadpanned.

"Hold the eggs at Café Trois Oeufs!" Nasreen bent over in a bout of laughter. "See, good thing I wasn't drinking tea. I would choke to death."

Krishna scowled. "Okay. Okay. Forget I said anything."

Kate breathed deeply and watched the old couple as they prepared to leave. The man helped his wife with her coat, wrapped his scarf around his neck, and tucked it into his long coat, then neatly pushed the French chairs toward the table. He looped his wife's arm in his. They nodded to the waiter on his way to the kitchen, his arms full of the dirty dishes, then smiled at Kate, Nasreen, and Krishna, admiring their youth as they strolled to the door arm in arm. The door chimed as they exited.

Chapter 3
ROCKFIELD TO BOMBAY

1987

Nasreen lay in fetal position on the white and pink comforter, her arms wrapped around her abdomen. Her cropped hair stuck against her cheeks. She moaned in response to a searing cramp. She had gotten her period a week late and with it came the excruciating pains.

"India would be amazing," Kate said sitting next to Nasreen on the bed. "I am going to swim camp this summer and working as a lifeguard at the Y. But you are going to Asia!"

"I'm being punished," Nasreen said, bracing against another cramp.

"You should see a doctor. I get some cramps every month, but, jeez, you can barely get out of bed for days. It's not normal."

"I can't see a doctor for obvious reasons," Nasreen snapped. "I will have to tell my mother everything."

"Maybe you *should* tell her," Kate advised, still concerned for her friend.

"No!" Nasreen braced again then took a deep breath. "It will shame my parents. I can't do that. Not to mention what will happen to Anees!"

Kate contemplated Nasreen's rationalization, but the thoughts weighed too heavy on her mind. At least Nasreen wasn't pregnant. She wasn't going to India with a swelling belly. No one would know.

* * * * *

IN MAY, NASREEN prepared for the family trip to South Asia. Her parents visited India every year as newlyweds and after the birth of Sameer and Nasreen to stay connected to their family, and to ease the loneliness of being transplanted in America away from their culture and traditions. But after three children, the family visits to India grew less frequent. Nasreen was ten years old the last time she visited relatives halfway across the world, a child then, a woman coming-of-age returning.

Nasreen's maternal grandmother, Nanima, owned a homestead in the neighborhood of Banjara Hills in Southern India where she had raised Nasreen's mother, Laila, her two aunts, Zehba and Samina, and three uncles. Nasreen spoke of Nanima often, so often that Kate pictured her as a petite woman with horn-rimmed glasses and weathered by years. Between her aunts and uncles, Nasreen had so many cousins Kate could not remember all of their names except for Aunty Zehba's eldest sons, Rahim and Anees, who attended the University of Chicago on student visas and shared an apartment close to campus. Rahim was getting his MBA and Anees was finishing a degree in engineering. The only other cousin Nasreen ever mentioned was Yasmine, Aunty Samina's daughter.

"Here is my mother and Aunty Samina together," Nasreen said, showing Kate a photo from an album covered in paisley pink material she had dragged from underneath her bed. "They are very close. My mother must write to her in India every week. Aunty Samina keeps her up to date about Nanima."

"Here is Yasmine and I together!" Nasreen exclaimed.

"Look at you!" Kate remarked, studying the young Nasreen with two overly large front teeth and her hair tied back in a bushy ponytail. "I like the polka-dotted salwar."

"Be quiet. It was the beginning of the eighties! This is Maqsood and Haroon." Nasreen pointed to two boys, maybe thirteen and fifteen years old, with their arms wrapped around each other, smiling broadly at the camera. "Yasmine's brothers."

"You didn't mention Yasmine had brothers."

Nasreen shrugged. "I was ten. I didn't pay too much attention to the boys." She smiled.

"I hope you do not expect me to remember their names," Kate remarked.

"Maqsood goes by Max and Haroon by Hari."

"That's better."

"Yasmine has a little sister too, Sana's age. Her name is Azra. She was a toddler the last time I was there, an 'oops' baby."

Nasreen flipped the pages of the photo album. A few photos had come unglued and slipped off the page. She shoved them in the crease of the binder.

"These are my three uncles." Nasreen pointed to an old family photo. "They all live in Karachi. All us cousins refer to the eldest uncle as Mamujan and his wife Mumanijan," Nasreen said. "Mumanijan is the matriarch. She is always entertaining and never seems to tire. She never had children. I don't know why. Maybe that is why she fills the house with people, so many people. I miss her the most."

Kate smiled. "She is very pretty. What about Aunty Zehba?"

"I don't think I have a picture of her. She never liked her photo taken," Nasreen said.

"Her sons are Rahim and Anees. I got that right!"

"Aunty Zehba has three sons, and she acts like a queen for having three sons!" Nasreen rolled her eyes. "The youngest is Tariq." She pointed to the smallest of the three boys in the photo. "He is eighteen now."

"His eyes are blue!"

"Maybe his eyes turned brown now." Nasreen shrugged. "Anees told me that last summer Tariq went off backpacking in Nepal with some buddies for weeks."

"Cool," Kate said, intrigued.

"Or not," Nasreen quipped. "Anees and Rahim tried to cover for him but he was gone so long. Aunty Zehba found out and she was furious. She didn't know if he was dead or alive. When Tariq came back, Anees said, Aunty Zehba confiscated his motorbike, and he wasn't allowed anywhere except school for the entire school year!"

"Well, at least I will remember the one named Tariq," Kate mused.

"Don't get any ideas," Nasreen warned.

"What ideas? He lives in India," Kate huffed. "He sounds adventurous."

Nasreen shut the album.

"That is a lot of cousins. I have only two," Kate sighed.

"And that is just on my mother's side! It will be amazing to see them all after six years. I'm sure everyone has changed so much! Max is twenty-one now."

Kate opened the photo album again and found the picture of Yasmine and Nasreen as ten-year-olds.

"If this photo is how they remember you, well, they will be amazed!"

"What will I pack?"

"Pack?" Kate questioned. "Buy new stuff. It's India after all! Better than Chicago's Devon Avenue!"

Nasreen's eyes lit up, thinking of a new wedding wardrobe.

"Bring me something silk and exotic," Kate pleaded.

Nasreen smiled her devious smile.

"Come with us," she said enticingly. "You are practically family. You know our customs; you know our lives. Come with us!"

It was the second time Nasreen asked her to go to India with her, but things had changed. Nasreen was not pregnant.

"I need you, Kate," she said. "How will I survive Anees's engagement party? Ask your dad. Just see what he says. Please!"

Kate imagined for a moment what that part of the world might be like. Colorful and chaotic? She wondered.

✳ ✳ ✳ ✳ ✳

KATE BROACHED THE topic with her father, Ian, one morning after breakfast as he flipped through the local *Rockfield Times*.

"They invited me, the whole family. I know her cousins, Dad. The oldest is getting married and the other one is getting engaged," she explained.

She thought for a moment about Anees and how it angered her that he had a relationship with Nasreen and was now engaged to someone else even if his mother chose the girl for him. She needed to go to Asia to support Nasreen!

"Her cousins go to school in Chicago. Rahim, he is the oldest, and has a new wife waiting in Pakistan. They have only met once. Can you imagine? The wedding ceremonies will last for weeks! Can you believe it?" she said again, overly excited. "It would be amazing. Really amazing, Dad!"

Kate looked at her father in wonder a few evenings later as she lay reading in her bed. She figured he had forgotten that she had asked to travel to India. But he sat beside her on the purple paisley sheets and placed an envelope on her lap.

"It would be an opportunity of a lifetime," Ian said in a serious tone. "It is part of your college fund. I figure it's an early start to college. If you want to go, you should go. You have my blessing."

For Kate, the dream of joining Nasreen halfway across the globe and traveling through two countries she knew nothing about sat in the form of a ticket floating lightly on her lap.

But she could see the weight of her father's decision, his desire to keep her close but his decision to let her go. For the second time, he was letting go of the woman in his life. He had let go of his wife five years ago when her eyes, succumbed to cancer, told him it was time. Kate was eleven then, and now at sixteen, she was about to embark on the journey of her life—but away from her father.

✳ ✳ ✳ ✳ ✳

SPRAWLED ACROSS THREE seats in the belly of an airliner, Kate listened to the rumbling of the aircraft adjusting to turbulence as it seared through the clouds, her ear pressed against the seat. She couldn't get a seat on the same flight as Nasreen and her family and instead flew to India solo two weeks later. Feeling excited and alone, Kate drifted in and out of sleep flying over Kuwait. Foreign voices whispered through the slots between seats in front and behind.

The plane refueled in Dubai. Kate remembered the exclusive duty-free shops and Arabic men strolling across the tarmac, their bleached robes whipping around their ankles and black burqa-clad wives and numerous children who waddled after their mothers like ducklings following the robed men. The only thing she could see for miles was the sandy horizon.

Kate landed in Bombay in the early morning. Her mind was fuzzy. Something smelled stale. Oddly, no one seemed to take notice of her as she pushed the cart with her luggage through the vast room full of conveyor belts. The wheel of the cart buzzed as it vibrated along the concrete floor.

Kate followed a slender figure in a bright orange sari. She was mesmerized by how the skirt of the sari flicked against the woman's heels as she walked, causing the silver trim to dance under the fluorescent lighting. Suddenly, Kate halted at the line of soldiers forming a barricade in front of the sliding exit doors.

With long rods, inspectors poked through personal items strewn across the long white tables. Those past the inspection point hastily shoved colorful articles of clothing and gifts from America back into suitcases and pulled at the zippers.

A man pushed his cart toward the exit. The doors slid open to reveal a sea of dark faces behind the railing. Kate heard the commotion of the city outside, voices yelling. The heat seeped through the doors and blew against her face. The man disappeared in the crowd, and the doors slid shut. The sounds muffled. But then she had heard something, a faint familiar voice.

A couple moved toward the doors, triggering them open again.

"K-a-a-a-t-e."

She heard the voice clearly this time. She smiled at the expressionless soldier waving her forward, never so thrilled to hear Sameer's voice calling her.

She was in India...

Chapter 4

VISITOR AT EID

Chicago 1998

"Guess who is coming to our home for Eid! You will never guess," Nasreen exclaimed.

"Five hundred of your friends and family?" Kate remarked sarcastically.

"Well, yes. True. But, seriously."

"I give up. Who?"

"Tariq!"

The sound of his name sent a prickle through the hairs on Kate's arms.

"Did I mention that he was living in New York?"

"Yes, you did. When we met in the café."

"Well, he is coming for the weekend and staying with Sameer. I'm looking forward to seeing him."

There was a pause.

"My mother said that Aunty Zehba is insisting he marry one of the girls she has chosen for him. He is turning twenty-nine, after all."

Nasreen's words felt like a kick in her stomach.

"I just wanted to let you know he was coming so it won't be a surprise."

Kate wasn't sure how to respond or even how she felt about seeing Tariq. Maybe she would not be attractive to him. Maybe it was nothing, just a teenage lust now faded with time and dispersed like a mystical dream.

She remembered the day she met Tariq when she awoke from a heat- and jet lag-induced nap, and he was standing over her looking at her with his sky-colored eyes. Tariq was different from anyone she had ever met. He filled her ears with his journey to Nepal and how he had separated from his group but luckily stumbled upon another group of hikers.

"You can't stop from discovering the world," Tariq had said to her. "There was a time I feared for my life, but I had never felt so alive," he told her. "Look at you, Kate, you have the courage to come to India. I admire that about you."

He admired her. She smiled remembering his words in her ears. She felt there was something between them during the daily excursions to the Hyderabad city sights and countryside. The feeling seemed to grow stronger each day she saw him during the endless dinner parties and wedding ceremonies in Karachi. He had even kissed her one night in the moonlit shadows of the *Neem* trees.

But he had never responded to letters she sent to him after she had returned home, and eventually time pushed thoughts of him from her mind, probably for the best. If his mother, Zehba, only found Muslim Pakistani-raised girls suitable marrying material for her sons, then Kate's Celtic origins and non-affiliation hardly fit the profile. So there was nothing. Nothing to anticipate. Nothing to be nervous about.

* * * * *

"*EID MUBARAK*, KATE!" Sara, Nasreen's close friend, said as she flung the front door to Nasreen and Mustafa's home wide open. "So great to see you!"

Her swelling belly rubbed against Kate as the two embraced and kissed respective cheeks.

"Congratulations," Kate said, putting on a cheery smile. "Nasreen told me you are expecting."

"Thanks. We are very joyful. After two boys, we are hoping for a girl. But as long as the child is healthy, that is all that matters, right?"

Kate nodded in response.

Sara looped her arm around Kate's and led her along the hall toward the commotion of guests. Sara's arm felt silky, and she had the scent of sweet peach.

As the pair walked past the photographs of Nasreen's family and friends that hung in the front hall, pictures taken in various places in Pakistan, Kate was reminded of Tariq, and her heart filled with anxiety. Part of her had to see Tariq after all this time, and the other part of her was still heartbroken.

"Just place your coat in there." Sara unlinked her arm from Kate's and pointed to the small bedroom off the front foyer. "Nasreen is in the kitchen. She will be excited to see you."

In the bedroom, long button-down cashmere coats lay neatly on the bed, scarves tucked into the collars, and sequined purses were slung across it. Even in the early weeks of March, the northern winds brought more cold weather. It appeared as if the coat owners had rested among the paisley pink and gray covered pillows and slithered out from under their coats. High-heeled shoes and leathered boots, on the other hand, were precariously flung across the floor. Gift bags with large bows and glittered paper were stacked in the corner.

Kate cringed. She hadn't brought anything.

She removed her faded blue jacket and tossed it into the closet out of sight. The coat landed next to something familiar lying on its side with its hallowed metal rim sinking into the shag cream carpet.

It was Nanima's vase!

Kate pulled the piece upright and sat back on her heels admiring the brass work. The three-foot vase had stood magnificently on a simple block altar at the entrance to the main room of Nanima's house in Banjara Hills. It was one of the first items Kate laid eyes on in the mornings when she followed the garden path from the back bedroom to the kitchen for a cup of chai.

On the belly of the vase exploded a full rose, its petals created by tiny etched fragments that Kate recalled made the vase dance in the natural light of the doorway. The curved base was patterned with gold and red inlaid diamonds. Kate traced the fluted top with her fingers then followed the hourglass shape of the vase, letting her fingers fall into the deep-cut etchings.

Kate left the vase and went to announce herself before Sara came back to find her sitting on the floor in the dark among a heap of shoes.

The house smelled of entertainment—perfume and candle scents mixed with marsala and curry. Kate heard the zestfulness in Nasreen's laugh even before entering the kitchen. A circle of guests surrounded her, many whom Kate had never met.

"Eid Mubarak," Kate said as she gave Nasreen a quick hug.

"Kate! You made it."

"The vase in the closet…" Kate started to say.

"Do you recognize it?" Nasreen asked gleefully.

"Of course. It was Nanima's."

"Mamujan saved it from the house in India and took it back to Karachi with him but said I should have it. I tried to argue with him that he should keep it in Pakistan, but he and Mumanijan insisted. So I packed it in my suitcase and brought it back with me."

"Nanima's soul is in that vase," Kate mused. "You need to find a special place for it."

"Nasreen, got any more of the *gulab jamun*?" Sameer interrupted as he sauntered into the kitchen. "The men are hungry."

Nasreen picked up the tray of Indian sweets from the counter.

"Take them away. I have already had too many."

"Hi Kate," Sameer said. "Have one." He presented the tray to her.

Kate thanked him and took one of the deep-fried balls of dough bathed in cardamom syrup.

He leaned over and whispered in her ear. "Tariq is here, Kate." He motioned with his head in the direction of the den.

Kate's heart quickened. She followed Sameer and the sound of a sporting match to the room where the men were gathered. The gulab jamun was sticky and too sweet, and she wished she could get rid of it. In her nervousness, she shoved the sugar ball into her mouth.

The den furniture—a loveseat and two oversized armchairs in light green with white stripes, and a glass coffee table—were left over from Mustafa's bachelor days when he lived in an apartment near the University of Chicago where he obtained a degree in computer programming. Kate knew that Nasreen never particularly liked the furniture style. Thus, she was surprised the pieces managed to survive the upward societal shift to the suburbs.

The men—husbands of Nasreen's girlfriends—were consumed by the cricket match on the analog TV screen with gripping emotion. The cricket bat cracked as the player whacked the ball, and the men erupted in cheers.

"Hi Kate."

Kate spun around. A man clasped both her hands, still sticky from the sweet.

"Tariq!" She nearly choked on the remaining bit of gulab jamun.

He lightly kissed her on both cheeks.

His scent was enticing, spicy. She trembled.

"It has been a long time," Tariq said in his English-Indian accent.

Her eyes met his and a flood of memories returned.

"When Nasreen said you would be here, I was really looking forward to seeing you again."

"I'll let you two catch up," Sameer said as he slid away to join the men watching the match.

Kate noticed Tariq's elegant watch. The light of the room flashed across its accordion band. His shirt was perfectly pressed. No longer a slight-framed teenager, he was broadened by maturity, a twenty-something man of the hour. The thought of her not being attracted to him vanquished the moment his eyes engulfed hers.

"Yes. It's been a long time," Kate said, struggling to form a sentence. "Nasreen says you…you live in New York?" she asked as nonchalantly as she could manage, but her uneven voice deceived her.

"Yes. I am working on my MBA. I did some traveling through Thailand, Cambodia, Malaysia, and Singapore. Truly amazing!"

"You went alone?"

"Yeah. I did. For three months! Cambodia was the most interesting. You have to go sometime. There is beauty, hardship, adventure, poverty, all of it," he said. "I thought about how you must have felt, a young visitor in India, an observer in a place you didn't belong. I felt that way."

Kate didn't respond. *He thought about her?*

"Anyway, I ran out of money," he laughed. "I decided it was time to get a degree and a job. I will return to Hyderabad in a year. The city has transformed since you were there."

"Like you said it would."

"You must come back…to visit."

Kate wasn't sure how to respond. An invitation to coffee at a café in town would have been more appropriate, she thought. A trip to India, or Cambodia for that matter, was a little out of her price range.

"It's nice that you are still traveling about, carefree," she mocked.

"I always wondered how you have been all this time," he said, seemingly oblivious to her sarcastic tone.

Kate blinked as though the statement were intruding. She felt a flash of pain and anger flush her cheeks.

"How I have been?" she questioned. "You are asking now?"

A look of shock covered his face. He took a step back.

"Kate!" Mustafa called, finally noticing her at the edge of the room. "Thanks for coming!" he greeted jubilantly.

Mustafa had gained some weight. He sported a checkered button-down shirt that accented his round midsection. His face was fuller since the last time Kate had seen him before his and Nasreen's trip to Pakistan. His German-style lenses seemed too small for his face and accentuated his cheeks, making him look boyish and studious.

"This is an epic game!" Mustafa exclaimed. "England vs. Pakistan, huge rivalries. Winner plays in the final."

Kate didn't understand the game of cricket but nodded cordially.

"Sorry, was I interrupting something?" Mustafa eyed Tariq. "Kate, have you met Tariq, Nasreen's cousin?" he asked, extending an arm in introduction.

"Yes. In India ten years ago."

"That's right!" Mustafa slapped the top of the mahogany bar excitedly. "Wow, it's been ten years, has it? This guy has become quite handsome after all." He punched Tariq playfully on the shoulder.

Tariq shrugged off the jest and winked at his cousin-in-law.

"So doc, how is the PhD coming?" Mustafa asked, planting his hands on his hips. Tariq continued to look at Kate intensely.

"It's hard."

"If it were easy, we would all be getting our PhD," Mustafa laughed. "Me, I am just an information technology guy. But our company is opening an office in San Francisco, did Nasreen tell you?"

Mustafa readjusted his glasses and tugged at the bottom of his shirt. His skin was starting to glisten with perspiration.

"Yes, congrats."

"Thanks. It means I have to travel some, but you gotta be in San Fran. Lots of dot-com companies popping up everywhere over there. It's dot-com country! Hey, can I get you a drink?" Mustafa clasped his hands together.

He walked around the bar. "Sprite, Fanta, wine cooler?" He held up a bottle from the small fridge below the bar. "I stock these for American guests. Everything else is nonalcoholic, of course," he said, grinning. "So, what will it be?"

"A wine cooler, please," Kate answered.

He snapped off the top and placed it on a napkin in front of her. The cooler tasted like sweetened strawberry juice with fizz, but it washed down the gulab jamun that still felt stuck in her throat.

Suddenly the men roared as the batsman hit the ball and scored six runs. Mustafa joined his jubilant friends jumping up and down and celebrating with high fives all around.

Kate felt Tariq's gaze. He remained standing in the same place and never turned his eyes away from her despite what was surely a monumental sporting event on TV.

"I will, uh, let you get back to the game."

"We will catch up later," Tariq said cautiously.

"Yeah. I would like to hear about Thailand and Malaysia," she said, giving him a demure half-smile. Turning away, she walked out of the room shaking, feeling him watching her as she quickened her step across the pearl tile that extended from the husband hideout to the formal living room.

Kate squeezed her eyes shut, succumbing to the fact that she had barely survived the encounter with Tariq.

Suddenly, from above came a thunderous sound. Kate looked upward at the open staircase that spilled onto the tile like a Victorian wedding dress. Three children clambered down the stairs so fast their little feet missed the steps. The boy reached the bottom first, slipping on the tile. Two girls chased him, the first screaming as she leaped over him, and the second tumbling into him as he tried to stand, sending him sprawling again.

Kate skated out of their path as the boy, back on his feet, chased the girls squealing into the living room.

The children darted into the room, crashing into Sara's sister, Shabana, sending her off balance as she held a baby. Sameer's wife steadied Shabana and swiftly took the baby from her arms. Sara immediately grabbed her son sternly by the arm, and Shabana bent down to unwrap the two girls clutching her legs.

"*Bas*," Shabana hissed, giving the youngsters an earful of scolding in Urdu.

"I was nearly in the path of destruction," Kate announced as she stepped into the room.

Shabana's face turned from stern to glowing as she glanced up recognizing Kate. She relinquished her hold on the girls, who lost no time in escaping into another room.

"Oh, Kate. Hello." Shabana stood upright, repositioning her dupatta over her shoulder with a single bracelet-clinking swoop.

She gently tugged down on her salwar, smoothing the pleated material across her full bosom and extending an arm in a friendly embrace.

"Sorry, the children are a little wild. They didn't run you down, did they?"

"No. I was just kidding," Kate responded.

Sara kept one hand on her son's shoulder. The boy pouted, not having escaped with the girls.

Kate noticed Mona, who had grown up three houses away from Nasreen, curled up on the chaise lounge.

"Hi, Mona. You look comfortable. May I sit?"

"Of course." Mona shifted to make room for Kate.

Mona was single and lived in the same house in the old neighborhood. At the age of thirty-two, Mona was by most accounts too old for marriage and motherhood. As an unmarried woman, she still lived with her parents, helping them with life's daily routine, waiting for her own to begin.

"It's a really beautiful house," Kate remarked. "I have not been here since Nasreen redecorated."

"It's lovely," Mona responded and took a sip of water. The ice cubes clinked as she twirled the straw in the liquid.

It wasn't that Mona never received proposals; she had had several inquiries from noteworthy men. She was naturally pretty with charming eyes and thick black lashes. One beau in particular stood out. She had discovered the man she thought embodied her future. He was an immigrant from Pakistan, a family friend of a family friend with business prospects in America. Mona was full of life. But like many other proposals, this one ended in rejection.

Mona went back to work as a bank teller. Nasreen said Mona's parents continued to consider proposals, but there was always something unsuitable.

What was suitable in love? Kate thought. She noticed Mona had put on weight from idleness and a broken heart. Kate thought about her swim partner and ex-boyfriend, Neil, and how similar she and Neil were to each other. He was suitable but their relationship had been lackluster. She thought about Tariq in the next room and how, even now, he awakened every sense in her. But she and Tariq were from different cultures, different worlds.

"So what has kept you away?" Mona asked.

"I've just been busy," Kate said with some guilt. "And my car is on its last leg."

Mona finally smiled. "Mine too."

Kate recognized a photo on the table and picked up the frame. It was a golden frame of interlaced half-moons inlaid with tiny red rhinestones.

"Wow, what a photo," Kate admired. "Look at us!"

The half-moons framed Nasreen and Mustafa in full wedding garb. In the photo, younger versions of themselves, Kate, Shabana, and Krishna, stood to the right of Nasreen, and Sara and Mona stood to the left of Mustafa, who stood tall in pure white *sherwani* and pleated salwar pants. From his headdress across his forehead extended a golden fan that appeared so tall it touched the red, gold, and white streamers decorating the wedding stage. Nasreen, despite her height, was dwarfed by her husband's tall stance. She was hunched over, countering the weight of her body-length diamante covering made entirely of ruby stones and a border of green sequins. Thick as a cobra, a garland made of strands of white and red carnations hung from her neck, reaching down to her red iridescent *kurta*. Nasreen was clenching the edges of the covering to keep it in place and glanced unsmiling nowhere in particular. Quarter-sized medallion clasps covered the backside of her fists, and gold chains looped around each finger like a jeweled glove.

Kate studied herself in the photo and thought she appeared confident, smiling straight at the camera. Her long red hair hung across the sash of her silk sari that she'd bought that day at the fancy cloth shop in Hyderabad.

"You look radiant in that picture," Mona stated.

"We all look stunning, I think," Kate remarked as she placed the photo in its original place.

"My niece is getting married in November," Mona said softly. "Hard to imagine my brother's oldest is already eighteen. Where did the time go?"

To Kate, time seemed to be suspended. She leaned her head back and scanned the room. On the wall behind the chaise hung a large copper-encased mirror bordered by candle sconces. In the mirror, Kate could see the bold flower arrangement that sat on the mahogany console on the back side of the yellow settee. The arrangement was a blooming protea with broad leaves and long twigs that extended and curved to mimic the wooden curvature of the settee and matching armchair. The furniture and style were both luxurious and exotic, capturing a sense of Colonial India.

Compared to this luxuriously decorated house, Kate's living environment was flat and colorless. Having moved three times in college and twice while in graduate school, she filled each apartment with whatever she could afford or was left by others, simple and sparse. There was always the somber stacks of novels and science textbooks, a few framed pictures, a set of pillows with Indian embroidered pillowcases that Aunty Samina had given her, the brass cat from Sheela's Brass Shop, and her road bike used for both commuting and escaping along the lakeside.

In India, Kate had purchased brass and silver vases, and gold plates with images of India. One plate had painted on it the majestic Taj Mahal on a turquoise background surrounded by a wreath of flowers, and the other piece displayed the Salar Jung Museum, gold embossed on wood. Kate had bought resplendent bowls and handloomed pieces of silk and shimmery textiles that she had tailored into pillowcases, table coverings, skirts, dresses, and scarves. All these items from her trip to Asia were packed in a closet in her dad's house—no need for the frills of color and majesty in graduate school. No need for the magnificent colors of India and Pakistan in an apartment of gray.

"Food is served," Nasreen announced as she made her gracious entrance into the sunken room.

Nasreen held her arms out to Shabana's baby.

"Come here. Come to aunty," she chimed.

The child smiled and fell forward into Nasreen's open arms. She swayed and cooed as the small child kicked her feet with glee. Kate watched as Nasreen twirled the baby.

"I am so glad they are looking to adopt," Mona said to Kate in a low voice.

"What?" Kate replied, completely shocked.

Mona drew her chin in, a perplexed look on her face.

"Nasreen and Mustafa are adopting. Didn't you know?"

"I saw Nasreen six weeks ago. She mentioned she had endometriosis, and the chances of having a baby were slim to none, but she never mentioned adopting."

Mona remained silent for a moment, then began tentatively, "She is hoping for a boy."

Kate sat stunned, watching Nasreen coo at the baby.

"Her uncle has a lot of connections in the Pakistani government, and they are helping them through this process," Mona explained. "I thought she would have told you." A touch of pity seeped into her voice.

"Nasreen deserves to be a mother," Kate stated matter-of-factly.

She sipped the peach strawberry wine cooler. The sweetness of the drink was beginning to make her head feel fuzzy. She left Mona and headed to the dining room.

Throughout the evening, Tariq made sure to check on Kate in a chivalrous, but salacious, way: a simple bow to let her pass, an offering of dessert with daring eyes. This evoked both annoyance and desire in her. He told her tidbits about his travels in Southeast Asia, and she remembered what she found so intriguing about him—his curiosity about the world, his desire to explore it, and his defiance of any restrictions.

When he tried to start a conversation with her, she felt awkward, especially in the presence of Sameer and his wife. The two seemed so much in love. Sameer looked at his wife as though she were the only one in the room. Despite having lived in the country for only five years, his wife moved with poise and confidence, knowing that she was her husband's sole affection. Who knew Sameer would be so lucky in love, Kate thought.

"No kids for now. It's just the two of us," Sameer said as he looked intently at his wife and she looked back at him ravenously.

At some point in the evening as Kate and Tariq passed each other around the buffet table—he drizzled chutney on a fried potato and she took a piece of melon—Tariq asked for her number, mentioning that maybe they could meet for coffee in the morning before his flight back to New York. To talk.

Maybe.

Midnight passed, and the women appeared as fresh-faced as they had when they first arrived at the door, swaying in crisp chiffon salwars and striking jewelry. The men were just as exuberant, and the children were still wide-eyed and overly excited, their little bodies oblivious to bedtime come and gone.

Nasreen offered Kate the guest room, and she happily obliged. She was delirious with sleep by the time she was alone in the room after all the guests had left, sometime after two o'clock in the morning. She hadn't yet found the right time to ask Nasreen, constantly surrounded by guests, about the adoption and vowed to ask her in the morning.

Kate lay across the still taut and tucked mint sheet she didn't have the strength to untuck and crawl under when she finally dropped into bed. Surrounding her head were several pillows in mint and peach striped shams she had not bothered to move out of the way, still arranged three layers thick.

She stared at the ceiling wanting to think of nothing in particular, but her mind drifted to thoughts of Tariq. He had changed in many ways, but she was reminded of the eighteen-year-old young adult. He was refined and more serious, but also timorous at times around her. She liked how his brow creased when he looked at her, and he clenched his jaw when he spoke about his travels, and then the seriousness faded from his face and his mouth erupted in a full captivating smile.

Chapter 5
Sister Cities

Hyderabad-Secounderabad 1987

Kate was aroused from her jet lag stupor with thoughts of being kissed as she lay on the warm sand. Then she was dancing, her toes kicking the sand as she twirled, holding his hand, the boy in her dreams. Through her lashes, she glimpsed his silhouette and dark hair. She opened her eyes to the blue sea.

"She is alive," the boy with sea-blue eyes called out.

Sana's face appeared above hers, and then another little girl of the same age peeked at Kate. Her long, soft braids hung down and tickled Kate's face.

"Oooh," the little girl said, her wide eyes staring into Kate's.

"Wake up," Nasreen said brightly. "These are my cousins Azra, Yasmine, and Tariq! They have been waiting for you to wake up!"

"Give her space, Azra," Yasmine said, nudging her little sister away.

Kate was staring again into Tariq's piercing blue eyes. A fuzz of hair covered the tan skin above his wide lips. He helped her to her feet and steadied her before letting go of her hand.

"Thanks. Guess I am still getting used to the heat. It makes me tired," she said demurely. "You must be Tariq, Rahim and Anees's younger brother."

"Yes. But don't hold that against me. I am nothing like my brothers," Tariq laughed.

"That's a relief," she remarked under her breath, reminded of her distaste for Anees. "You're the one that went backpacking in Nepal," she said quickly.

"Shhh." Tariq held his finger over his lips. "You will get me in trouble for that one. I will tell you about it another time," he whispered.

"Pleasure to finally meet you," Yasmine interrupted, placing a hand on Kate's left shoulder and kissing her softly on the cheek.

Warmness spread across Kate's face.

"We have heard a lot about you."

Yasmine had full lips that curved like a half-moon when she spoke with a wispy English accent. Her eyes were deep-set under high round cheeks.

"Yasmine," Kate replied. "It is so great to meet you. Nasreen talks about you all the time. And you too, Azra."

Azra wore a satin pink salwar kameez. Matching satin ribbons tied the ends of her braids together. She held onto Sana's hand and smiled shyly at Kate.

"Is the girl awake?" boomed a voice.

"A-u-n-t-y Z-e-h-b-a," Nasreen accentuated without sound to Kate, a warning that Aunty Zehba was approaching.

Suddenly, Aunty Zehba's large frame filled the doorway. Her unkempt bun was the color of ash, and out sprung sprigs of hair going every which way. She waved her brawny arms and hurled through the room like a bad storm, wrapping her arms around Kate in a strong embrace.

"Welcome to India, child!" Aunty Zehba's raucous voice jolted Kate from her lethargic state.

She let go of Kate but not without pinching the girl's cheeks with firm manicured hands.

"You mustn't sleep during the day. You must adjust to India time."

"You have barely met her, Ammi, and already you are telling her what to do," Tariq complained to his mother.

"*Khalajan*," Nasreen said respectfully to her aunt. "This is my school friend, Kate."

"Very pretty, child," Aunty Zehba said. "I am so happy you have come for Rahim and Haseena's wedding!" she exclaimed with an open smile that revealed a row of angled, paan-stained teeth.

Now that Kate could focus on Aunty Zehba standing in one place, she saw the resemblance between Laila and Aunty Zehba, particularly in their height. No wonder Nasreen was taller than most of the girls in their class.

"Now that you are awake, come meet my other cousins in the front room." Nasreen tugged on Kate's shirt and led her away from Aunty Zehba.

In the front room, Nanima sat dressed in a white sari in the corner of the patterned sofa next to Laila. When Kate arrived at the Banjara Hills house, Nanima had been waiting outside for her and Sameer to arrive. She was just as Kate had pictured her, a petite woman with a wise and weathered face.

Nanima reached up to touch Kate's cheeks and pursed her lips together in a smile.

Yasmine's brothers, Maqsood and Haroon, sat in the Victorian armchairs that matched the sofa print.

"Hi. Call me Max," said the eldest, standing up to greet Kate.

"And me Hari," said the other, jumping up from the chair.

To Kate, they resembled nothing of the early teenage boys in the family photos from Nasreen's paisley-covered photo album. Max had a round face and full mustache that matched his thick brows and dark lashes. Hari was tall and lanky with large ears and a pleasant smile.

The front door swung open and a stout woman much shorter than Aunty Zehba and Laila, her jovial face flushed from heat, rushed into the room.

"You have come!" Aunty Samina shouted, flinging her gelatinous arms wide.

She embraced Laila, having to stand on her tippy toes, and the two sisters cried tears of reunion.

The only time Kate had seen Laila cry was when she cooked onion curry chicken.

"Oh, Nasreen!" Aunty Samina exclaimed as soon as she spied her niece. "You have become such a beautiful young woman! So tall and lovey as our Laila."

"As salaam-alaikum, Aunty Samina," Nasreen greeted warmly.

"Laila! Your daughter is absolutely stunning."

Laila gave a modest nod confirming the beauty of her nubile daughter.

"You must be Kate," Aunty Samina said, her eyes now on the new guest. "Oh, what lovely red hair. So wonderful that you have come to India."

Kate smiled, liking Aunty Samina immediately.

"Shall we go shopping?" Aunty Samina asked, clasping her hands together. "We have a wedding to prepare for! Kate, you will find shopping in the city to be an adventure. We will find you wonderful silk and jewels to wear that will make you feel like a princess!" She let out a boisterous laugh that displayed a wide space between her front teeth.

* * * * *

SHOPPING WAS THE authentic experience in India. Hyderabad enjoyed many of the fashions of Bombay, with less congestion of the capital city. The women and girls visited bustling bazaars, fashion houses, and secluded jewelry dealers in the quest for materials for the wedding ceremonies to take place in Karachi in the weeks following. The women purchased cloth for salwar kameezes, silk for saris and *lehengas*, and georgette for the flowing dupattas that embraced every Muslim woman's outfit.

Kate adjusted, as much as one could adjust, to the heat and stares of India and accompanied Nasreen, Laila, Nanima, Aunty Samina, and Yasmine to the shopping areas of Hyderabad. Kate enjoyed Yasmine's calm, sophisticated demeanor and Aunty Samina's animated, joyful style.

Aunty Samina did not like to drive her lime green Fiat to the city, so instead they hired three-wheeled motorized "bubble cars" as Kate called them because of the cars' spoon-like shape. As they sped along the thoroughfare over the railroad tracks, the curtain of the bubble car flapped in the wind. Kate glimpsed the changing scenery beyond the blurry faces of pedestrians and bikers. The car motored over the Afzalgunj Bridge. Water buffalo roamed in the muck under the bridge at the shallow edge of the Sagar River that separates Hyderabad from its twin city, Secunderabad.

After much weaving and circling roundabouts, they reached the heart of Hyderabad. They dodged rickshaws, motorbikes, and bull-drawn trailers, and halted for gaudy buses with gold trim and tassels. In the middle of it all, the women jumped from the bubble car and hurried to the sidewalk, clasping their saris around their legs to avoid tripping in their rush to safety.

Nasreen and Kate trailed after the older women in a beeline for the shops. Kate struggled to read all the signs—vertical, horizontal, some swinging, others flashing. People bumped her or stepped around and stared.

She hustled, keeping the women in view, following the white of Nanima's sari. Suddenly, she jumped to the side to avoid tripping over a man who sat cross-legged on the sidewalk, a green turban wrapped around his head. A pair of worn sandals, two mangoes, and a small pouch sat in front of him. Strands of beads hung underneath his grayed beard. Kate could barely see his dark eyes peering out from under the turban and dreads of gray hair.

Suddenly, a beggar child on a cart grabbed her pant leg. She stopped and three more children blocked her way, hands out and faces starving.

With a swift tug, Nasreen pulled her through a narrow doorway.

"Don't stop walking," she warned.

Kate recovered from the stumble and reoriented herself; the street sounds became a numb buzz in her ears. The interior of the shop came into view revealing glorious colors of fabric. The older women were already surrounded by flowing waves of silk and chiffon as the shop owners spun bolt after bolt in a fly-fishing motion. Each bolt of material streamed in a wave of illuminated elegance. Aunty Samina rubbed the material between her fingers critically, then moved onto the next sample and the next as fast as the men could unroll the bolts.

Kate was drawn to the most lustrous emerald-colored material. She tugged the neatly folded piece from a stack. Gold embroidery adorned the edges.

"You like?" the man asked as he began unfolding each piece, displaying them along his arm, over his shoulder, and down the other arm until he was shrouded in shimmering cloth.

Nanima was by her side and gently took the piece Kate admired, handed it to the merchant, and motioned the other pieces aside. The man threw the unwanted cloth in a heap. He wrapped the chosen piece, including a square of sheer georgette of matching green for the dupatta, and handed Kate her purchase with a slow, respective nod.

"That's beautiful," remarked Yasmine. "The color will look great on you."

"Thanks," Kate said, proud of her first purchase.

After the fabric shop, Nanima led them to a gift shop several blocks away and across a side street, a line of beggars following. They stopped at the corner to buy guava fruit from two men squatting on the curb. The man split open one, sprinkled salt and chili powder over its pink center, and offered it to Kate. The spiced-candied taste burst in her mouth.

The tattered sign above the gift shop door read in English, "Sheela's Brass Shop."

Kate milled among the open shelves of all things brass. There were plates, vases, and bowls, each with its own unique design. She chose a large brass vase with blooms the color of peacock feathers encircling the middle, and two smaller vessels, one silver with a fluted top and one copper with gold etchings. From the wall hangings, she carefully removed two gilded plates with embossed iconic pictures of the Taj Mahal and the Salar Jung Museum. Lastly, she chose a solid brass cat to place on her dresser at home.

Nanima again shooed her aside and bargained with the shop owners until they surrendered, frustration and disappointment filling their eyes. They began to wrap the pieces one by one in brown paper.

After a few more shops, faring better at maneuvering through the crowds, Kate followed the women and ducked into a small stand with a large Pepsi advertisement on the yellowed, stained wall. Aunty Samina ordered drinks and fried snacks, and the seven of them squeezed together on the bench and fanned themselves with napkins that hardly did anything but help Kate imagine that she were cooler.

Kate hugged her shopping bag and futilely tried not to let her sweaty hips and shoulders press against Nanima on one side and Aunty Samina on the other. Despite her discomfort, Kate was thankful to rest her hot, swollen feet. The stall was a haven after the crowds of the streets, the stares, the eager vendors and persistent beggars. She sipped the orange cola.

"Don't drink directly from a bottle, ever," Aunty Samina warned. "Always drink from a straw."

Stepping out of the snack stall, Nasreen, Kate, and Yasmine discovered a display of patterned textiles hanging around the outside of a parked truck trailer. The truck vendor eagerly showcased the skirts as the girls approached.

"The one with the elephant motif!" Kate exclaimed.

"Ooh, the blue one there is pretty." Nasreen pointed over the seller's head at the one hanging at the very top corner.

"The yellow one is my favorite," Yasmine added.

The cloth seller grabbed the blue one off the hanger and tried desperately to keep pace with the girls' oppositely pointing fingers and changing expressions. The rejects lay in a growing heap.

Pedestrians and bicyclists detoured into the streets to get around the truck. A crowd of spectators curious about the girls haggling over swatches of silk in the back of a truck created a bottleneck along the roadside. This was the case in India; one shift in space caused a chain reaction in the dense movement of people and vehicles.

"Make a decision! You are making a scene," pleaded Laila. "*Chelo!*"

"Okay, okay," Nasreen said, turning to Kate. "It's enough. They will make beautiful skirts for school," she added and paid the gleeful truck-shop man and left him to restack the rejects.

The sari shop was the last stop for the day. Kate was starting to drift off to sleep, sinking into the back of the bubble car as they sped through the side streets so narrow that pedestrians pressed themselves against the walls as they passed. Even the stench of the cattle carts, roaring buses, and beeping Nissan cars did not keep her head from falling forward.

Aunty Samina nudged her awake as they came to a halt in a busy shopping district. Kate followed Aunty Samina through an opening to the "Saify Stores." The door was off a narrow street so dense with shops and signs that had Kate not kept her eyes glued to Aunty Samina's long braid, she may have been forever lost to the city.

The moment Nanima and Aunty Samina stepped inside the sari shop, the store men scrambled to their feet to assist her.

Salaam. Nod. *Salaam.* Nod. *Salaam.* Nod.

"My family has been coming to this shop for decades," Nasreen explained to Kate as they watched the dance of respect the men gave to the elder women. The owner was a small man, very animated in his joy to show his patrons his collections of cloth. He led them upstairs to a private unfurnished room and motioned with a sweeping bow for them to take a seat on the floor. As soon as they arranged themselves, the store men appeared with a steeping teakettle and teacups.

Nanima cocked her head side to side as she spoke to the owner in Urdu.

"Ah, yes. Yes, of course," the cloth store owner responded, clasping his hands together in enthusiasm as if a large production were about to begin.

The man swung open a large cabinet with a fervency to reveal an impressive assemblage of silk pieces neatly folded and stacked in an array of compartments. One by one the store helpers snapped the pieces open with wild elegance. The silk rippled in a shimmering wave, hovered midair, and then slowly floated down to rest on the women's laps. As soon as Kate saw a piece she admired, it was buried by the next wave of silk and so on until the women were nearly drowned in fabric.

"Bas!" snapped Nanima, signaling it was enough.

As quickly as the men flung out the silk, they swooped the pieces through the air like retracting spinnaker sails and meticulously folded each again and placed them back in the cabinet.

Nanima spoke again to the owner in Urdu. He motioned to his helpers and suddenly seven-foot-long extensions of sari material rolled out across the wood floor. This material was heavy with gold embroidery. Nanima placed the end of a richly red and navy colored silk sari across Kate's shoulder. Filigrees of threadwork created a thick border of intertwining long-stemmed flowers and leaves that hung across Kate's chest like a royal sash.

"It's beautiful, but a sari? I don't know how to wear a sari," Kate fretted.

"Not to worry," Yasmine declared. "We are experts."

Nanima smiled, her eyes creasing nearly shut and her silver-rimmed glasses riding up her nose. Kate caressed the embroidery and imagined herself wrapped in its graceful embrace. The shop owner looked from Nanima to Kate.

"This is the one then! Excellent choice!" The sari was folded to perfection, and the storeowner placed it into Kate's open palms with a formal bow.

On the way back to Banjara Hills, the driver pulled over at a stall on the side of the road. "Ghani & Sons Tailors" read the sign above the one-window booth.

Aunty Samina greeted the shop owner with a hearty smile and handed over the bundle of textiles from the day's shopping spree.

There was just enough space in the shop for two worktables. Hunched over antique-looking sewing machines, the two tailors worked intently, the machines' needles bobbing furiously as the workers pushed the material through the machine at such speed that any mistake in rhythm could prove disasterous.

Aunty Samina requested the design and style of each tunic and salwar. The owner was a small man who stood not much taller than the ledge of the booth. He listened intently and eyed each woman long enough to guess their dimensions but not too long as to be inappropriate.

Nanima held up the emerald piece Kate had chosen from the first shop. She moved her hands over the applique and then over Kate's neckline and across her chest describing with few words what should be done. The owner scribbled on his writing pad, rocked his head side to side, and placed a notch on the cloth, a little reminder, like string around a finger.

*****

IN THE FOYER of the Banjara Hills home later that same day, Nanima waved her arms above Kate's head in a swirling motion and kissed her gently on her head.

"It's a custom when a girl buys her first sari," Yasmine had explained to Kate earlier as the car rattled among the potholes on the drive back to Nanima's house, preparing her for what she was about to experience.

Laila and Aunty Samina continued the ritual. Kate's skin warmed to the touch of each kiss. Her head became light and her body swayed from heat and exhaustion and the emotion of this feminine moment she had not experienced since her mother was alive. She squeezed her eyes shut and clenched the plastic bag that contained the coming-of-age sari and matching crimson *choli* and petticoat.

"You are a woman now," Nasreen whispered so only she could hear. "Let's hope they don't marry you off while you are here."

Kate's eyes opened wide in shock.

Chapter 6

A SACRIFICE

Chicago 1998

The click of a door woke Kate the morning after the Eid festival. She figured it was Mustafa leaving for work. Even on Sunday, Nasreen said he provided technical support for the computer company he worked for.

The house remained silent. Nasreen was probably still asleep, having happily played hostess until the early morning.

As she lay in the dimple of the comforter and pillow shams, she retraced the encounter with Tariq the night before. *He had thought about her during his travels. How often did he think about her now?* It felt as if no time had passed since they were teenagers, and yet so much time had passed that they both kept a cautious distance.

There wasn't an opportunity to ask him all the things she wondered about over the past years. Had he read her letters? Why hadn't he responded? But still, he had asked for her phone number. Would he call her? Why did he want to talk now? He was heading back to New York today, then Hyderabad after graduation or some other country to roam about. Aunty Zehba was arranging his marriage back in India, so if he didn't call her, she would survive. There was really no point in meeting anyway.

She stared at the ceiling, the questions floating around her head.

Reluctantly, she rose and dressed in the same clothes she had worn last night. She started down the stairs but stopped when she heard whispering coming from the foyer. Kate crouched down on the stairwell landing to peer through the railing. All she could see was Nasreen's pretty pedicured feet.

"You will do whatever you want, Nasreen," Mustafa said harshly.

"Keep your voice down! Kate is still sleeping," Nasreen hissed. "I don't want her to hear us arguing."

"Why do you even ask what I think?" Mustafa lowered his voice but the harshness remained. "Somedays I wonder if you care at all. I can see the resentment in your eyes. Why, Nasreen?"

"That is not true. I do care."

"Is it because we can't have children of our own? Is it because I married you, and you wanted someone else? Is there someone else, Nasreen?"

Kate could visualize the desperation that must exist in Mustafa's eyes. She had never seen him upset or frustrated by anything. He was uncomplicated, gullible at times, and had a relaxed view of the world, as if everything at some point would work itself out.

Last night, Kate noticed that each time Nasreen and Mustafa passed each other among their guests, they smiled cordially at one another, respectfully, a soft glance and simple touch. Nasreen and Mustafa seemed comfortable enough as a couple of nearly eight years. Perhaps this was a normal disagreement between husband and wife. Kate knew she should return to her room, give them privacy, but she continued to listen from her place on the stairs.

"There is no one else," Nasreen said steadily.

"Why do you cry out at night? I try to comfort you, but you push me away. You always push me away."

"They are just bad dreams."

"So many bad dreams? You can tell me, Nasreen. I will understand. I have never judged you."

What did he mean he had never judged her? Did he know about Anees? Kate questioned. *That was a decade ago.* Her face contorted listening to the pain in Mustafa's voice.

"You are my best friend, Nasreen, and I love you. But I can't go on like this. I have always been honest with you, but there is so much you are not telling me. I see it in your eyes, and it makes me feel like I don't know you at all. I can't bring a child into our lives like this," he justified. "I can't."

Kate held her intruding breath.

The door creaked and shut swiftly as Mustafa exited.

Kate dodged back to the hallway and tripped over the top step. She landed with a thump on the upper landing, her heart pounding against her chest. In between the railings, she spied the top of Nasreen's head appear from the foyer and disappear as she walked in the direction of the kitchen.

Kate stood up and hovered in the hallway shadows a few moments longer to regain her composure before coming down the stairs and making an appearance.

"Good morning," Kate said as she stood at the kitchen entrance.

"Oh!" Nasreen spun around, a coffee craft in hand.

She clutched her chest and breathed deeply.

"You startled me. I thought you were still asleep. How long have you been up?" Nasreen asked nervously.

"Not long. I heard the door shut."

Nasreen turned to face the sink and filled the craft with water.

"Uh, yeah. Mustafa had to go into work for a bit."

"Are your in-laws here?"

"No, out shopping. Macy's is having a sale." Nasreen looked over her shoulder at Kate and rolled her eyes. "My mother-in-law loves to shop."

Kate said nothing, still disturbed by the argument she overheard in the foyer. Why was Nasreen crying at night? Kate was reminded of the time when Nasreen learned Anees was getting engaged and thought she might have been pregnant. She had cried nonstop for weeks even long after she knew she wasn't pregnant.

Nasreen continued making the coffee, scooping grounds from the large tin into the filter.

"What do you want for breakfast?"

"The coffee is fine. I ate enough last night to last the week. Besides, I have to get going. I have to go into the lab for a bit today," Kate mumbled.

"You don't sound too excited. Maybe you need a day off," Nasreen suggested.

Kate thought about a day off as she glanced out the French doors at the barren maple trees waiting for spring.

"Okay. Stop your pitying," Nasreen teased, reading Kate's expression. "Have a bagel."

Nasreen lifted the lid off the bread tray then opened the refrigerator door.

"There is cream cheese in here somewhere," she said, her head stuck in the fridge.

Kate heard the sound of crisper drawers opening and closing, something tipping over on its side.

"Are you thinking of adopting?" Kate asked suddenly.

"Wait a sec. Can't hear," Nasreen said as she continued to rummage through the fridge searching for cream cheese.

"Here are leftover samosas and chutney," she said, bringing forth a plate wrapped in plastic wrap along with the tub of cream cheese. "Better than bagels. Would you like some?"

"No thanks."

"What was it you asked?" Nasreen set the samosas and chutney on the island countertop.

"Are you adopting? Mona mentioned you were."

Nasreen turned to face Kate and cringed. "She did?"

Kate nodded.

"I was going to tell you. I was," Nasreen said apologetically.

"When? From Pakistan?"

"I haven't seen you in months!" Nasreen snapped back. "You seem so distracted. And...sad, really. What is up with you?"

Nasreen's words pinged guilt and hurt.

"I looked into adopting when my doctor confirmed I had endometriosis severe enough to cause infertility. I think I knew all along," Nasreen said, brushing back her hair from her face. "I didn't want to get my hopes up so I didn't tell anyone...

except Mona. Mona is easy to talk to about disappointments, and she encouraged me not to give up and to find a different path."

Her voice was empty. She paused for what seemed a long time.

Kate couldn't find the words to fill the silence between them. If Nasreen could keep going, find another path, what was so difficult about getting through graduate school and moving forward with life, Kate wondered.

"My uncle is very connected in Pakistan. He can help us. You have to know someone in the government to adopt in Pakistan…if you are American," she stressed.

Nasreen began slicing the multigrain bagel down the middle. "I think I will just have a bagel after all. Sure you don't want one to go?"

She looked at Kate, then placed the knife down.

"Look, I meant to tell you and Krishna that Mustafa and I started the process to adopt. Just didn't seem the right time. All of us appear to be going through our own life phases," Nasreen explained.

Phases? Kate thought. Was she just going through a phase?

Nasreen dropped the bagel halves into the toaster and flicked the lever.

"This is a big thing," Kate remarked, "adopting a baby. I don't know quite what to say."

Kate glanced out the French doors again.

The bagel popped from the toaster. Nasreen grabbed each half, and as it started burning her hand, she flung the toasted bagel halves on a plate and blew profusely on her fingers.

"Do you want a girl or a boy?"

"Both," laughed Nasreen. "Maybe a boy first. Always good to have the eldest be a boy. There is an orphanage in Islamabad, one of the better-off ones," Nasreen sighed. "The conditions aren't great. Similar to the village we visited in India, you remember."

It was not a question but a statement. One never forgets images of impoverishment. Nanima took them once to visit a woman, and the only way to get to the woman's house was to walk through the outskirts of a village of tin-roofed, handmade huts. Women cooked in open pits, cleaned clothes, and flattened them with the charcoal-filled rusted irons. Children ran along the sewer streams, others sorted trash, pounded rocks, and played cricket. A city within a city. Babies were born, babies died, and sometimes the lucky ones were taken to orphanages for the slim hope of something better.

"You will be saving a child," Kate stated with honesty.

"That is a good thing to say."

"When will you hear something about adopting?" Kate asked.

"I don't know," Nasreen said as she spread cream cheese on the bagel, licking her fingers to cool them. "I may have to pick up and go as soon as we know something."

"How does Mustafa feel about all this?"

As soon as she spoke, Kate realized her question didn't sound the way she intended.

Nasreen's smile vanished. She wrinkled her forehead.

"Of course he is as excited as I am. This is what we want," Nasreen said defensively.

"I didn't mean anything. I should get going." Kate took a step back.

"Were you eavesdropping?"

Kate's heartbeat quickened. She heard it vibrating in her eardrums, growing louder and louder.

Then a piercing sound startled them both. It was the coffee maker beeping, flashing its green light. Nasreen, astonished, turned away. The coffee cups rattled loudly in the cabinet as she fumbled to grab two. The cups clanged against the countertop; a little more force and they would certainly have split into pieces. Nasreen reached for the coffeepot, held it for a moment, and then placed it back into the holder with force. She slumped over the counter, bracing as if she had been thumped on the back.

"I admit, the process of adopting from another country has been a bit of a strain on the marriage, but Mustafa has been very supportive despite the pressure he has been under with work and from his parents."

"What do you mean pressure from his parents?" Kate asked.

"They are from a different generation."

"They don't want you to adopt?"

"Mustafa's parents are not completely accepting of raising 'someone else's child.' That is what they said." Nasreen's fingers made quotation marks in the air.

"It's okay. I'm sorry," Kate apologized.

"It's not okay," Nasreen objected. "Mustafa is the eldest, and his role is to care for his parents in their senior years. I completely respect my in-laws living with us. In Pakistan, things are different. The mother-in-law generally rules the house. This is America and this is our house," she stated confidently. "If I want to bring a child into my house, I will! I'm not asking for help," Nasreen shouted.

"You have every right to feel that way," Kate said. "I'm sure it isn't easy for the two of you."

"What did you hear?" Nasreen asked suspiciously.

"Nothing."

Kate backed out of the kitchen soundlessly and walked past the foyer, empty now except for the echo of Mustafa's words. She reached the front door.

"Kate!"

Kate turned to face Nasreen.

"Okay. I overheard everything," she confessed. "What did Mustafa mean that he has never judged you?"

Nasreen shook her head, annoyed.

"Never judged you for what?"

"For not being a virgin at eighteen when I married him," Nasreen said reluctantly.

Kate was taken aback. She felt a strong distaste in her mouth and swallowed hard.

"I knew Mustafa would keep it to himself when he realized I wasn't pure. In our culture, most husbands would reject their wives and bring shame on the family. I knew Mustafa wouldn't do that."

Kate blinked in astonishment. "You married Mustafa because he was safe?"

"You don't understand," Nasreen said.

Kate folded her arms across her chest. She thought for a moment of the times in Hyderabad and Karachi. The two of them explored together, climbed the rocky cliffs, stomped through the murky river, and rode a camel on the beach. She thought of them dressed in silk and sparkling head to foot and moments later sharing the same heart-wrenching sympathy for the crippled and poverty-stricken children on the street. Even in the most foreign place she would ever be, the comfort and connection with Nasreen was there, always there. Now in Nasreen's home, Kate felt like an awkward stranger on unfamiliar ground.

"I do understand, Nasreen," she said, angry now. "It was a mistake. Anees was weak! He should have known better than to have sex with you when you were sixteen! Now you're paying for his mistake ten years later in your marriage!"

Kate took a breath. Nasreen said nothing, waiting for Kate to finish.

"All these years, I regretted saying anything. Revealing how horribly wrong this all was! I have hated feeling this way, Nasreen. And what is really maddening is that Anees has always acted as though it was nothing." Kate stressed the word "nothing," her face contorted in pain. "He even had the nerve to say to me, ten years ago at Rahim's nikah, that I shouldn't jump to conclusions! Like, what the hell did that mean?"

"I should have told you the truth," Nasreen said calmly.

"What truth, Nasreen?"

"It wasn't him," she said with clenched teeth. "Yes, I had a crush on him. It's true! I was fifteen the first time he visited, a college man of twenty-one. I looked forward to his visits. The relationship was forbidden, but it was innocent. Really it was!" she shouted. "It wasn't Anees. It wasn't Anees!"

Nasreen squeezed her eyes shut and doubled over as if she had suddenly become nauseated.

"I was...raped!"

Kate stood in shock.

Then Kate pictured him, the young doctor who had moved in across the street! Memories flooded her mind, his confident air and salacious smile at Nasreen as she poured him a cup of tea. At first, Kate thought he was charming, and Nasreen's parents were so hospitable and welcoming, she ignored any awkward thoughts she had of the doctor. But she had felt something was not quite right. Kate closed her eyes and scanned her mind. The moving van was in his driveway the day Nasreen revealed she might be pregnant!

Suddenly, Kate's jaw dropped in horror. She covered her mouth. Her stomach ached. It was a pain that wrapped around all of her and crept upward, tightening around her lungs, making it difficult to breathe.

"Dr. Khan? It was Dr. Khan!"

Kate's head felt muddled and pounded from lack of caffeine.

Nasreen didn't speak.

"Nasreen!" Kate's eyes welled with tears.

"His wife had to go to India to visit a sick aunt or something," Nasreen began slowly with a shaking voice. "My mother felt bad that he was working so hard at the clinic and had no one to cook for him. She made her famous meat patties, a platter full of vegetable samosas, and a tray of baklava. I was just across the street," she said.

Nasreen's gaze went through Kate to somewhere beyond.

Kate's breathing became erratic, the anxiety rising again and making her face flush. The tears streamed down her face as she listened to Nasreen's story.

"I took over the food. He was inviting. Attractive. We flirted." Nasreen's lips twitched. "He showed me around the rooms in the house. It was like a dream. I couldn't wake up, I couldn't move. I was immobilized as if rods anchored me to the bed in a guestroom."

Kate wiped the tears from her cheeks.

"When it was over, he looked as shocked and horrified as I must have. Then he asked me if I wanted baklava," Nasreen said angrily. "I found that so odd. How could he ask me that after what he did to me? I was sixteen! To this day baklava makes me sick! I ran from the house. Anees came that weekend and I told him. It just came out."

"Who attacked Dr. Khan?" Kate still held her hand over her mouth. "His attack wasn't some random act of violence, was it? But Anees?"

"Anees couldn't stand up to his own mother," Nasreen sneered. "It was Rahim who attacked that creep. Rahim has old India tradition in him, an eye for an eye. He sent him to the hospital with a bruised face and broken ribs. It might have been worse if Anees hadn't stopped him. It was enough to scare that bastard into moving away."

"All this time," Kate choked. "How could you make me believe it was Anees?"

"Think about it, Kate," she asserted. "It would have been my word against his! My mother would have suffered so much for having sent me there. Not to mention having a 'ruined' daughter. Anees and Rahim would have been arrested for sure," Nasreen said rationalizing, trying to make sense of something senseless.

Kate couldn't see Nasreen's face, blurred by her tears.

"Too many sacrifices," Nasreen sternly defended.

Abruptly, a key in the door sounded.

Kate gasped, blinked the tears away, and smeared the evidence of sorrow from her face.

"As-salaam-alaikum," Nasreen's mother-in-law sang from the foyer. Shopping bags rustled. Her mother-in-law appeared, arms decorated with brightly colored boutique bags with roped handles.

"Wa-alaikum-salaam," Nasreen greeted cordially, smiling. She instinctively reached for the packages, kissing her mother-in-law's cheeks and nodding to her father-in-law as he was in the process of removing his shoes.

"As-salaam-alaikum," he said in a hoarse tone.

"Everything okay?" her mother-in-law questioned, catching her breath. "You look a little pale," she said to Kate.

Nasreen set the packages carefully on the hall table.

"Oh, we're just tired. Late night," Nasreen said cheerfully, covering for Kate. She waved her now free hands in disregard. "Good sales today?"

Her mother-in-law nodded. "Very, very good sales at Macy's today." She eyed Kate hesitantly. "I will make something to eat."

"No thank you," Kate said as she cleared her throat, squelching the rising dread in her chest. "I was just leaving."

Nasreen's father-in-law appeared in his stocking feet behind his wife. He nodded in silent greeting, seemingly exhausted from the shopping spree.

"Please stay for tea at least. I will make chai."

Her mother-in-law did not wait for an answer but turned and headed into the kitchen.

"I would love to, but I...I have to run." Kate sounded panicked.

"Oh," Nasreen's mother-in-law said, dejected, standing at the entrance to the kitchen. "I will make tea for us then. Nasreen, *bahu*, will you help me?"

"Yes. Of course."

Kate fumbled with the knob of the front door and quickly slipped out. She hurried down the front steps, nearly stumbling, and around the corner to her car where she had parked it among the parade of cars the night before, her eyes filling with fresh tears as her mind flooded with images of the young doctor.

Had she always known it was Dr. Khan and not Anees?

Chapter 7
BANJARA HILLS

Hyderabad 1987

In the back of Nanima's house was a detached mud-brick room with a toilet and a large metal tub for bathing. A crooked trail of fragmented rock, buried under earth and dense moss, led from the bathhouse to the back bedroom Kate shared with Nasreen. The trail continued from the bedroom through the garden to the main room of the house.

Kate traversed the path every morning in search of Rahmsing, Nanima's longtime servant, to prepare for her a cup of chai.

Kate was dressed and already sweating.

"I'm going for breakfast," she whispered.

"It's too early," Nasreen moaned, still curled up in the cot.

Leaving Nasreen to doze, Kate leaped across the stones through the sprawling, wild garden full of blooming succulents, evergreens, and water lilies to the main house, balancing barefooted on the rock. This was Kate's favorite time of day, standing in Nanima's garden, a sanctuary from the city. It was the only time of day she was not overstuffed with food, overheated, or plain overwhelmed by India.

The fallen white blossoms from the wild chickweeds crushed under her weight as she continued along the path, the stones warming her feet. She ducked under the laundry line extending from the corrugated roof to the trunk of the large native *banyan* tree. Nanima's white saris, undergarments, and linens hung limply in the still air, soaking in the scent of earth and sassafras.

In addition to the banyan tree, two bushy tamarind trees guarded the untamed garden. The trees produced pods of fruit that Rahmsing blended into juice and jams for breakfast. Among the many strange new fruits Kate tasted in India, she found the tamarind to be quite tangy and not as sweet as the guava fruit they bought on the street.

The tranquility of Nanima's garden was intruded upon by the construction of a six-story, five-star hotel. The shell of the hotel towered over the one-story sectioned house. Kate peered through the entangled tamarind trees and watched the women high on the open floors. The trees' pulpy hanging fruit blocked the sun's rays, gaining strength in the early morning, and allowed Kate a better view.

The women working at the construction site knelt in their thin saris and soaked up rainwater with a sponge then squeezed the water trickle by trickle into a pail while the men pounded and drilled. Engulfed by construction dust, the women workers seemed oblivious to the screeching noises, focusing only on the murky water, filling the pails, soaking and wringing, soaking and wringing.

Under the canopy of Nanima's garden, the moist leaves of the banyan and tamarind trees collected a grayed outline from metal and stone. "Nanima will put up a big fight to keep her house," Nasreen told her. Kate hoped she was right and that the construction would not break the tamarind trees' embrace and convert the property into a parking square or café garden.

Continuing toward the house in search of Rahmsing to serve her chai, Kate tiptoed past the row of potted ivies sitting on the kitchen windowsill. The ivy strands followed the trails of rust extending from the corrugated gutters of the house down to the dusty earth.

A dingy red ball rolled to a stop in Kate's path. In a moment, Rahmsing's barefooted children—a girl and a boy—appeared from behind the trees. The girl, maybe five years old, stared at Kate, frightened. She wore a loose white dress so sheer Kate could see the outline of her thin legs beneath. Her younger brother hovered behind her, holding his worn trousers up with one hand. Kate swooped up the ball, startling the girl who promptly grabbed her brother by the arm and scurried under the laundry line and disappeared into the stalks of the lily plants and under the shadow of the banyan tree.

Kate stood holding the red ball. She knew that her pale complexion and red hair was a strange sight in India, the country that pulsed with the color red. Red shone in the silk of saris, and glittered in golden tassels and trim that outlined headscarves and hung across buses. Red richened foreheads and earlobes in rubies. Mustard red was the color of Indian spices, curried lamb, turmeric powder, and *masoor dal*. Brides in India were adorned with garlands of red and white flowers, painted in dark mehendi dye, and draped in flaring maroon dupattas.

The red of Kate's hair, in contrast, was an anomaly—alien, mutant. At home, her hair color brought smiles and compliments from passersby. But in India, her coloring made all unforgiving eyes on the street turn her way.

Kate gently rolled the ball toward the place the children had disappeared and continued to the house. In the doorway, she found Rahmsing's wife sleeping. Stepping over the woman, Kate entered the house and her eyes adjusted to the natural light of the large room. Inside the door stood a large vibrant red etched vase on a pedestal, one of the few items presented as a display in what was a simple but inviting dwelling. The etching in the vase reflected the bit of light that seeped in through the door. To Kate, the house felt like she had always been its natural guest.

Kate spied Nanima, in a cotton sari as white as the chickweed blossoms, standing in the shadow of a large antique armoire at the end of the dining table. Nanima looked up at the girl and voiced a command, and in the next moment Rahmsing was standing in the kitchen doorway as though he had been waiting all along.

"Chai whona?" Kate said shyly.

"I want chai" was the only way she knew to ask for tea, and by making her request into a question, she hoped it sounded more polite.

Rahmsing nodded and disappeared.

Nanima brought forth a metal box beaten by years from a small drawer in the armoire next to a stack of old photos. She extended a gesture for Kate to sit at the long oak table. The woman placed her hand on the box's hinged cover and squinted through her horn-rimmed glasses at Kate, who could barely see the woman's eyes from beneath the thick rims.

"What are you doing?" she longed to ask, but Nanima did not understand a word of English.

Kate watched every meticulous movement as Nanima began an ethnic preparation made from *betel* nuts. From inside the silver betel nut box, the betel leaves lay lush in foil, still moist with rose water.

First, Nanima smoothed a lime paste around the leaf. Her tin box was divided into sections. Red round nuts and yellow and green fennel seeds, all separated into sections, were like threads and buttons in a sewing kit. With a miniature spoon, Nanima scooped each type of nut and sprinkled them on the lime paste. She created a pattern of nuts and seeds, a perfectly balanced, harmonious *supari* mix.

Next, she added flakes of coconut, cardamom, mint, cloves, and various other dried spices. Last came a spoonful of red thick chutney to suspend the areca nuts and dried powders together.

Nanima wet the edges of the leaves with a tiny brush and folded it all into a compact triangle. Then, piercing the loose end of the leaf with a clove, she presented the wrapped delicacy to Kate.

"Paan," Nanima said in a hoarse voice.

She passed the paan to Kate, who held it carefully like it was a fragile bundle and waited for Nanima to finish wrapping her own.

As Nanima took a bite of the paan, Kate noticed the remnants of betel nuts lodged between the older woman's teeth, stained from years of chewing. Kate bit the tip of the paan. The rose-mint aroma drifted up her nose and exploded as the cloves and cardamom scents diffused over her tongue. She did not care much for the taste of paan, overpowered by the acrimonious sweetness, too culturally distinct for her American tongue. But sharing paan with Nanima was a spiritual event.

Rahmsing reappeared with two cups of chai and set one before Kate and left the other for Nasreen. The cinnamon in the wondrous liquid warmed her senses, and the pinch of chili powder tickled her throat.

Nanima brushed a hand across the teenage girl's shoulder as she headed into the kitchen to plan the daily meals. Rahmsing had disappeared again to attend to the chores. His wife was awake and sweeping the front step with a handful of bristles. The girl and the boy, holding the retrieved red ball, appeared at their mother's side, but in a single motion their mother waved her handmade broom, an order for the youngsters to play elsewhere.

Kate's quest for chai had started the household caste in motion.

Chapter 8

LETTERS

Chicago 1998

A s soon as Kate entered the front room of her apartment, an aching sickness crept over her in the stale heat of the closed-up space. She sank into the sofa and picked up one of the decorative pillows. Aunty Samina had given her the set of pillowcases embroidered with white-beaded elephants adorned with gold-threaded sashes prancing on a bed of velvet and silver-sequined trefoils as a gift the night she left Karachi and returned to the US. They looked entirely too ornate against the brownish-green hand-me-down sofa.

Her mind went through the events of the morning and the night before, Nasreen's confessions, Tariq's attention, and all the things said and not said.

The phone rang, startling her.

"Hello, may I speak with Kate, please?"

"Tariq?"

She was surprised by his voice. He called!

"We didn't get to talk much at Eid," he said.

There was a pause.

"Have you had breakfast?"

Kate had to think about the question, and then realized that despite watching Nasreen pull out several items from the refrigerator, she had not eaten.

"No."

"Neither have I. There is a place close to you called Harvest Moon. Sameer recommended it."

"It's one of my favorites," Kate responded.

"Will you join me?"

She was intrigued.

"My flight to New York is late afternoon. I'd love to meet you before I leave," he urged.

Kate looked at the clock on the microwave. The morning was slipping into noon.

"I'll meet you there," she said and hung up.

Kate showered quickly and chose an outfit, casual and light. She freshened her face with a brush of powder and mascara to hide the shadows of her troubled thoughts about Nasreen.

✶ ✶ ✶ ✶ ✶

A LARGE CROWD hovered in the cool morning under the awning outside Harvest Moon.

Kate looked around for Tariq but didn't see him.

"Kate!" Tariq called to her from the doorway, motioning for her to come inside.

"I'm sorry, I should have warned you," she said. "This is a very popular place on Sundays. The wait is at least…"

"I have a table, here," he said, placing his hand on the small of her back and leading her to a table for two by the window.

Tariq was dressed in a dry-cleaned oxford shirt, sharply creased pants, and smelled like fragrant sea salt.

"Can I help you with your coat?"

"Thanks," Kate responded. "But how did you get a table so fast and by the window?"

"I talked to the waitress. Said I had to catch a flight and was meeting someone special." He smiled charmingly.

Kate glanced around the crowded breakfast joint and caught the waitress eyeing her from across the room. The waitress quickly flipped her head around as soon as Kate spied her.

"How suave," Kate said, smirking.

"Is that a compliment?"

She laughed and didn't answer him.

"I am still trying to figure out a few things in America," he said. "Especially American women."

"Oh, I wouldn't try to figure that one out," Kate said sarcastically.

"Indian women are less…mysterious," he commented, as he attempted to push her chair in, but Kate scooted her own chair to the table. "More predictable."

"Is that better?"

Tariq sat across from her, wrinkeld his brow, and looked probingly at her.

"Should we order?" she asked.

"We should," he said, glancing at his watch and sitting back in his chair.

"Do you have time?" she quipped.

"Yes. Thanks for meeting me."

Kate ordered what she always did: eggs florentine with house potatoes. Tariq ordered plain eggs.

"Bacon or sausage with that?" the waitress asked.

"No pork, thanks."

"Okay. How would you like your eggs?"

"Beaten with spice," Tariq responded.

"Scrambled, and I'll bring you some tabasco sauce," the waitress remarked impatiently as she gathered the menus.

Tariq frowned.

"That," Kate said as the waitress hustled away, "was predictable."

He shrugged. "I have a few things to learn apparently."

"I am sure living in New York will teach you a few things."

"It's a crazy city," Tariq laughed. "New York drivers are as aggressive as Indian drivers."

"I don't know about that," Kate teased. "I'm sure they honk as much though. I recall I almost fell off the top of that van on our way back to Banjara Hills from Mamujan's farm."

"I caught you."

"Yes. You did." Kate smiled.

"I was hoping to see you," Tariq said seriously.

Kate's smile faded. She nodded.

"You seem the same as I remember," he added.

"Not sure I feel the same. Time has passed," she responded. "Graduate school is tough. It's not so much the science that is hard but the life. It's quiet and dim, the opposite of India."

Tariq laughed. "It's impressive. Anees is the one that told me you were here in Chicago getting your PhD."

Thoughts of the morning clouded her mind at the mention of Anees.

"You never seemed to like my brother. But Anees has always spoken of you like a sister because you are so close to Nasreen."

"I was wrong about Anees," she confessed. "I'm sorry."

"Wrong about what? Why are you sorry?"

Kate shook her head. "It's complicated."

"Hmm. Mysterious," he said smugly.

"Anyway. I hope Anees and Rayah are doing well."

"Yes, very. It's a good marriage. I have two amazing nephews who ask me a million questions," he laughed.

"Nasreen says your marriage is arranged," she blurted. "Speaking of marriages."

Tariq looked at her, stunned.

"Nasreen mentioned that?" he sighed.

"Yeah, she did."

"My parents have been wanting me to get married. They are getting impatient. I'm the last of the three sons. My parents want to retire," he laughed, a hearty carefree laugh. "As soon as I'm finished with my master's. It was part of the deal."

"The deal?" Kate questioned.

"That I could come to New York for a degree then return to India and get married. My parents have someone in mind."

"Have you met her?"

He shrugged. "Yes. She is from Hyderabad. She is very pretty, smart, and nice."

"Is she predictable?"

"Maybe," he responded, sounding slightly annoyed. "I look at Sameer and his wife and they are so much in love and very happy together. It makes me think that things will work out."

"Leave it to fate."

"I leave nothing to fate! You should know that about me."

"Okay," Kate retracted. "Will you stay in India, or will you bring your wife to America?"

"I know a few people in the telecommunications industry in Hyderabad. We will see. I'm not even married yet."

Tariq paused.

"You're grinning," he said, intrigued.

"I remember you stood atop that hill in Hyderabad overlooking the Hassain Sagar Lake."

"Naubat Pahad! My favorite place!"

"Out of all the places you have traveled to in the world, that hill is your favorite place?" she questioned.

"I always come home," he said.

"Well, when you stood on your favorite hill," Kate continued, "you said, 'All of this will change, you will see. There will be business, and we will not have to go to America for jobs.'"

"You remember that?" Tariq asked, his eyes drawing her in.

"I remember a lot of things about India."

"Do you remember we climbed that boulder…"

"And you dropped me at the top to grab Nasreen's hand?"

"I felt bad about that."

"I got over it," Kate laughed. "It was a beautiful view and worth the climb… and the fall."

"It was…beautiful," he agreed, looking at her in earnest.

The waitress came by, momentarily interrupting their conversation to deliver their food.

"Do you remember the tombs?" she asked him, unrolling the silverware from the thick cloth napkin.

"And how you almost sat on an ancient royal bath and then nearly fainted? Yes, I remember," he teased.

She smiled. "You caught me then."

"I did," he said, grinning back. "One time out of two isn't bad. Oh"—Tariq slapped the breakfast table—"and the van we just mentioned that you almost fell off when we swerved to avoid the oncoming truck. So two out of three times I saved you." He smiled proudly.

They gazed at each other for a moment, and then Tariq's expression grew serious.

"Are you dating someone?"

Kate poked at her eggs florentine with her fork.

"Yes," she lied. "I'm seeing someone. We met on the master's swim team. He is a graduate student too. We have a lot in common."

"What is his name?" he asked.

"Neil."

Technically she had not told anyone they had broken up, so for the record they were still dating, she rationalized. But she couldn't meet Tariq's eyes.

She sighed then, realizing time was running out.

"Tariq, why didn't you ever…"

"How are we doing here?" the waitress intercepted and abruptly started stacking the plates. "Can I get you anything else?"

"No, we are good," Tariq responded.

"Here is the check," she said, slapping the receipt down in the middle of the table. "When you are ready. Our credit machine is down at the moment. Cash only. Unless you want to wait."

Tariq looked at his watch.

"Gosh. I have to get going!" he exclaimed. "I need to return the car and get to O'Hare to catch my flight."

He stood up and grabbed his black European-style coat.

"I'm sorry to cut it short. Time went fast! Here is my cell number," Tariq said, scribbling his number on a red napkin and handing it to Kate.

"You have a cell phone," she said, impressed. "I have an answering machine."

"I know. I called it several times this morning hoping you would pick up."

"Oh," she said.

"Call me if you come to New York. It's an amazing city. I'll show you everything. I have another year in the MBA program."

"I'm sure you will be back to Chicago at some point," Kate said, meaning her statement to be a question, but Tariq didn't confirm or deny.

"It was great to see you, Kate. Ten years and now I am rushing," he laughed nervously as he slid his coat over his broad shoulders, digging in his pocket to throw a wad of cash on the table.

"Thanks for breakfast," she said, trying not to sound disappointed that their time was coming to an abrupt end.

"Oh," Tariq said. "I have something for you!"

"For me?"

He pulled a gift out of his coat pocket.

It was a hand-carved wooden box tied together with a red satin ribbon.

"I found it in a village in Cambodia near the Laos border. It's a jewelry box to hold your rings and things," he said, a little embarrassed.

"I don't wear rings—finger or toe ones," she joked.

"Earrings?"

"Yes, I wear those. Thank you. It's very pretty," she said sincerely and pulled at the ribbon.

"Open it later. At home," he urged.

He led her out the door and onto the sidewalk. A sizable crowd of patrons still waited for tables.

"Good luck with everything, Kate," he said then kissed her on each cheek. "I hope to see you again."

"Tariq!"

He turned around and looked at her with anticipation.

"Enjoy New York," she called.

He hesitated. "I will."

She watched him hurry around the corner and disappear.

She looked down at the red napkin with his phone number scrbbled on it and the jewelry box with the ribbon partly untied in her palm, then shoved both into the pocket of her faded blue coat. She jaywalked across the street to her car to drive to the lab. Anything was better than going back to her apartment to be alone with her befuddled thoughts.

* * * * *

THAT NIGHT, SLEEP hovered but never came. Kate stared at the shadows in her room. The shadows parted and she saw Dr. Khan socializing with Laila and teenage Nasreen over a cup of tea, his charming smile, lingering looks, and overconfident air. How could she have missed so much? Why didn't Nasreen tell her any of it? She felt angry, betrayed, and at the same time she pictured Nasreen's truthful, raw stare the moment before she fled the house this morning.

She thought of Tariq and their meeting at breakfast. He seemed unaffected by the weight of the world and unfazed by the future. What did his gift mean?

The gift!

Kate jumped out of bed. Her coat was hanging across her desk chair. She took the jewelry box from the pocket, leaving the napkin with his phone number on it. The ribbon had completely untied and the lid was separated from the base. She rubbed her thumb across the deep carvings in the wood and looked inside the empty box with silk lining.

What do I have that is valuable to place in such a box? she thought.

Would the box hold a girl's desires or a woman's ambitions for safekeeping? Would the stone encase troubled thoughts to be sorted out another time, or harbor thoughts never to be thought again?

What did Tariq want? Did he expect her to come to New York? For what? To be his lover before he returned to India to get married, a mistress in America, or worse, did he just want to be friends?

She turned the box over in her hand. It fell from her open palm, crashed to the floor, and flipped under the nightstand.

She was on the floor reaching for the box. She grabbed it along with grit and lint. She noticed the corner of a pink paper sticking out from the bottom drawer of her nightstand. She placed the box on the nightstand, wiped the grit off her hand,

and pulled open the drawer. It was full of letters, papers stashed and forgotten. Pink paper and yellow paper, written front and back.

Kate rummaged through the stack and scanned the pages of the collection of letters Nasreen wrote to Kate the summer they returned from overseas and Kate was away at swim camp. Nasreen had enrolled in political science at the community college in Rockfield to stay close to home and wait for a marriage proposal.

Kate shuffled through the crumpled stack, matching pen color and paper type, and read hungrily, frantically, searching for teenage Nasreen's secrets within the handwritten lines.

"*I think I have gotten some proposals lately,*" Kate read. "*My mom hasn't said anything to me because I don't believe they are 'suitable.' But I can tell she is searching and probably put an ad in some Muslim Chicago Journal. I don't ask her these things,*" Nasreen wrote.

"*Pre-law classes are killing me! Calculus II, Poly Sci, and Economics are impossible. Did I tell you I am head of the debate team? I probably told you. I feel like I write to you all the time. Anyway, between all that and serving on committees that will supposedly help me get into law school, there is just no time for marriage proposals!*"

Kate skipped a few lines and continued reading. Despite the exhausting pace, Nasreen seemed to grow restless waiting for her future to begin in a small Midwestern town.

"*I wish you were here, Kate. Most days, I don't feel like getting up and going to class because there are so many things that are more important to me now. Sara told me all the plans for Shabana's wedding. I'm jealous. I want to get married and get on with my life!*"

Kate wondered what pressure kept Nasreen running. Was it the pressure of career and independence in one direction, and tradition and marriage in the other?

Between calculus problems, debate team, and planning committees, Nasreen escaped to the city.

"*I went to International Night at the university with Shabana. Dozens of good-looking Pakistani guys were there. But you know, Kate, all of them are dating an American girl or worse living together. Shabana thinks many of them drink also. Are there no decent Pakistani guys left?*"

Kate flipped to the next set of letters.

"*Aunty Zehba was here for the weekend.*" Nasreen's handwriting appeared as if she had written in a rush. "*She bragged about Rahim and Haseena and how happy they are. She expects Haseena will be pregnant by the year's end. Good for her. Aunty Zehba showed pictures of Anees's wedding too. He's married now, a relief really. I am happy for him. Aunty Zehba's pictures from India made me feel like dropping everything and flying back. I miss our time there so much, Kate! Oh, but do I have gossip for you! Do you remember the pretty dancers at Rahim's wedding? Well, Faiz (you remember, Haseena's cousin (jerk) who seemed to be in love with me?) is secretly dating the younger sister. Her father is a prominent businessman in Karachi and very religious. When he discovers his daughter is dating Faiz, he's finished! Aunty Zehba gossips about all this; can you believe it? She seems much more relaxed. Probably because she has two sons married off. One to go! Well, I am sure there won't be anything more exciting to write about. Love, Nasreen.*"

Still one to marry off. Tariq.

Kate must have asked Nasreen about Tariq as she addressed him in her next letter.

"*Aunty Zehba mentioned Tariq is enjoying school in Chennai and doing well. That is all she said. He hasn't sent any letters. I am sure he is busy.*"

During the summer of '88, Nasreen had become infatuated with a man called "M." Kate couldn't remember his full name. In all the letters, the object of her affection was always referred to by the initial "M."

"*I saw M in Chicago,*" she once wrote. "*We barely spoke.*"

Their misinterpreted relationship was a series of run-ins at Muslim Youth events, weddings, and gatherings. Nasreen stole away to Chicago whenever she had an opportunity with the hope of meeting him at approved places for the proper amount of time and surrounded by the appropriate group of people. She cursed the bad weather and family duties that kept her in the small town.

"*Kate, I am going to this wedding in Chicago. Shabana is friends with M's sister and she said M is going too! What am I going to wear? What if he doesn't go, or worse, what if he goes and ignores me? I am going crazy right now!*"

In the letter dated a week later, Nasreen wrote, "*I didn't see M. Men and women were separated. I did not see a single male over the age of five the whole time! If I do not lose my mind to Calculus II (I am the only girl in the class, by the way), then I will lose* it over M. Shabana tells me I am living in a fantasy world, but I cannot give up, Kate. When are you coming back? I wish you were here!"

Another trip, another chance to meet, and another letter to Kate:

"He was polite, yet distant and aloof. We didn't really talk, only small talk. Ugh, why are things going so slow? I cried to Shabana and she told me to be patient. (Easy for her to say. She is engaged!) She said guys have a lot more pressure on them about school because they are the ones who must support the family. Like I don't know that? She talked to M's sister about me and his sister said that their mother is very preoccupied taking care of an ill relative and about getting the eldest son married first. Maybe it's not me, Kate!"

There was a several-week lapse before the next letter. Kate flipped the pages to make sure she had the dates and page numbers sequenced correctly.

"Bad news! M wasn't happy that Shabana spoke to his sister about me. I think I totally screwed things up. What am I supposed to do? Kate, are you listening? I couldn't stop crying (No, I didn't cut my hair again in case you are wondering! Just dyed it neon pink—just kidding!). My mom tried to get it out of me but what can I tell her? M no longer exists in my life! Do you hear me? I am screaming right now! You should stop asking about Tariq. He hasn't written. We both just need to move on from these men!"

Next letter…

"Kate, why have you not written? I am sorry. I didn't mean to snap about Tariq. I hope you are enjoying camp and meeting new people. I hope it is more exciting than this stupid town. I want to live in Chicago because I want to be a part of the Muslim Youth movement. It is impressive what the group is doing in the city!"

Near the end of the summer, the stress was evident, and with frenzied anticipation, Nasreen's body and soul were summoned to marriage.

"Kate, I have the most exciting news! Aunty Samina called. Yasmine is engaged! I am so excited for her. I want to go back to India so badly but I cannot miss Shabana's wedding. They are getting married in the same month! Can you believe it? Why can't we both just jump on a plane again and go back just for a week? I told my mother that all the decent Muslim men live in Chicago and I plan to move next semester and transfer to U of C. I think she got the message that I am ready to be engaged!"

The "Official Eligible List," she called it. She seemed more excited by the thought of being on it than having been inducted into Phi Beta Kappa. Three acquaintances had asked for her picture in one week.

"Kate, they have been sending my pictures to friends and family in the U.S., India, and Pakistan. Aunty Samina wrote that I had gotten a proposal in India. But I want a Chicagoan! Some days I worry about who I will end up marrying. Will he be a strict Muslim? I'm so frustrated that I cannot go to Chicago this weekend (my mother is making me attend a wedding for a family we do not even know, but it will be disrespectful if we do not attend!). M is back from Pakistan, and I wish I could see him. I have these stupid dreams, Kate, that maybe M has come to the realization that he doesn't want any of those girls in Pakistan, that they are not the right girls for him. Then I think that it is me who is not the right girl."

Chapter 9

WHITE MOSQUE, BLACK STONE

Hyderabad 1987

The rotary telephone, faded black circa 1950, rang and rattled Nanima's house early. It was Krishna calling. She had finally arrived in Hyderabad.

"Let's go to the Salar Jung Museum," Krishna shouted over the static of the large receiver.

She was staying at an uncle's home in Hyderabad for a few days and then traveling to Gujarat to her father's home.

"My uncle will drive us. Be there in thirty minutes," she said and hung up.

"Chelo," Nasreen said with sleepy eyes to Kate as she headed through the kitchen toward the back bedroom to get ready.

An hour later, the girls stood waiting outside for the car.

Kate was still unaccustomed to the meaninglessness of time in India. From among the large lily plants and cactus trees in Nanima's garden, they watched the women work at the hotel construction site as they waited. The women shoveled rocks onto large flat plates. In one rhythmic motion, they lifted the plates onto their heads and walked steadily to the far end of the site, disappearing behind concrete blocks. The women returned to refill the plates with rocks, starting the cycle again.

Nearly two hours late, the car with Krishna's uncle driving rolled down the dirt drive rocking side to side over the water-filled potholes toward Nanima's house.

"Sameer! They're here. Come on!" Nasreen called to her brother.

She wasn't keen on her brother tagging along, but her mother insisted that Sameer escort them to the old city.

"The city is not safe for girls unescorted," Laila warned.

Sana wailed at the doorway wanting to come too. Laila led the crying child back inside.

The gravel crunched under the tires' weight as the car rolled to a stop.

"Nasreen! Kate!" Krishna jumped from the car. Her hair was neatly braided. "I'm so glad to see you. I cannot believe we are all here in India together. Last month, we were sitting in the hall at Rockfield High eating cheese sandwiches!" Krishna exclaimed. "Kate, look at you! You're in India!"

Rahmsing's wife looked up momentarily from her sweeping, curious about the new guests. The working hotel women paused too and stared down at the scene for a fleeting moment and then resumed the sound of scratching dirt against twigs and of tumbling rocks.

"We're so late! We had relatives stop by, and everyone had to eat, and then, well, you know how it is. It's India!"

"It's okay," Nasreen consoled, amused by Krishna's animation. "We don't have much of an agenda." She smiled.

The girls squeezed in the back of the sedan, and Sameer sat in front next to Krishna's uncle.

The ride toward the old city was the most serene sitting inside the plush vehicle with its motor whispering. With the windows sealed, they sat in glorious air conditioning. The typical clangorous world as heard tucked inside a bubble car or in Aunty Samina's roaring Fiat with the windows down diminished to a sequestered hum. The dank and soggy street smells that regularly pounded her face and soaked her hair were sealed outside. Kate inhaled the smell of vinyl and Nasreen's and Krishna's fresh body scents.

"Where are you going, *chaachaa*?" Krishna shouted into her uncle's ear, grasping the leather headrest, realizing her uncle was veering off-course to the old city.

A plump cheek and large round eye appeared in the rearview mirror. He answered her sharply in Hindi.

"Very close. Take no time," her uncle said in broken English.

Krishna slumped back against the seat and grimaced.

"My uncle has to go to the bank first," she said. "Sorry it's taking so long."

"I'm fine," Kate confirmed, attempting to get used to the way things flowed in India.

This was the first car ride that hadn't felt like a death wish. Kate continued to watch the scenery change as they drove along the Musi River, making a series of turns that seemed to take them full circle. Several minutes later, Krishna's uncle stopped in the middle of the street.

"I go there," he said, pointing to a narrow opening among the street vendors and shops. "Bhilwara Bank," he clarified.

"This is why Indians show up two hours late for everything," Nasreen laughed.

Kate wondered if they would make it into the city before the museums closed, but who knew what time they did close for the day.

"Hurry please!" Krishna urged.

Her uncle nodded, jumped out, weaved through the crowd, and disappeared into the bank.

Horns suddenly blared, the bubble cars beeped short beeps, rickshaws rang out, and the buses moaned a deep pitch as angry drivers deviated around the stalled car blocking the roadway. Kate turned around to look out the rear window at the commotion.

"Wow, look at that!" she exclaimed. "Get out, I want to take a picture."

"We should stay in the car," Krishna said anxiously, but Kate and Nasreen had already piled out of the car followed by Sameer.

The full sounds of the street crashed into Kate's ears. The heavy pulse of the city streets spewed forth a gritty sheet that clung to Kate's perspiring skin. A white marble temple loomed in the background, and the congested street seemed to converge at the stately landmark.

"It's absolutely beautiful!" Kate exclaimed as she angled her Olympus camera, trying to fit the mosque into the frame of view.

"Careful," Krishna warned as the noisy traffic weaved around her.

Kate quickly moved behind the car and rested the camera on her chest. A man holding a rickshaw stopped in front of them, having lost his place in the flow of traffic. His lips parted, revealing dark spaces between his teeth, and a bewildered wrinkle stretched across his ashen forehead as he watched Kate photographing.

"Okay, you two sit in the rickshaw. I'll take your picture. Let's do this quickly," Krishna said, relinquishing to the moment and removing the camera's strap from around Kate's neck.

Kate hesitated, scrutinizing the rusty contraption and the rickshaw driver. The sleeves of his linen shirt were rolled up, and he wore a simple cloth skirt that covered his grasshopper-like frame.

"Come on," urged Sameer.

Nasreen and Kate climbed into the bucket seat. The footstool was so high their knees pressed into their chests. The thin seat of the rickshaw sagged downward; the wheels angled inward, struggling under the girls' weight.

Huddled together in their jeans and collared striped shirts, Nasreen and Kate were superimposed into this foreign place. Men lingered under a yellow sign advertising bus routes to places like Nagpur and Karimnagar and watched the scene unfold. They leaned against the concrete wall of an office building littered with tattered film posters displaying Bollywood stars. Others watched from among the rows of bicycles and powder blue mopeds that lined the dirt sidewalk in front of the Bhilwara Bank.

"Ready?"

From behind the camera, Krishna's tension melted away. She became animated and maneuvered to get the best shot, forgetting the increasing crowd.

"You guys look great. Just one more." Krishna lunged forward and cocked her head to one side. Her braid swung down.

The best friends clasped their hands around their legs and smiled at the camera. Nasreen's hair, now grown to shoulder length, blew softly across her tanned face, and Kate's crimson red strands billowed around her ivory skin.

"Okay, got it!"

The girls jumped down, and Sameer placed a few rupees in the rickshaw *wallah's* eager open palm. The coins clinked as he quickly dropped them into the dingy bag that hung at his waist.

Another rickshaw wallah crossed in front of Krishna. She jumped away like a startled cat. Kate was acutely aware that many more rickshaw drivers had stopped to see what the commotion was about. Lethargic-looking men loitered on the sidewalk, alleyways, and street and watched, bemused. The beeping became incessant; the crowd grew with more pedestrians and rickshaw wallahs.

Kate spun 360 degrees. *Why are the men staring?*

She tried to breathe. A policeman ran across the street directly toward her, and she froze, terrified. He waved his hands hysterically. Despite his short stature, Kate backed away to stand beside Sameer.

"What is he saying?" Kate gave Nasreen a pleading look as Sameer approached the stout policeman.

Sameer spoke Urdu, apparently apologizing for the commotion, but the policeman yelled "Away! Away!" swinging his cap before securing it back on top of his head.

"We have no driver," Sameer explained loudly, raising his shoulders, unwilling to oblige.

"In. Get in!" The furious officer flung his arms high and wide, desperately trying to increase his stature and presence.

"Okay, okay," Sameer said, thrusting his hands forward in protective surrender.

The girls had already ducked inside the car. Krishna's uncle stepped out of Bhilwara Bank, saw the chaotic scene around his stalled vehicle, and hustled toward the car in a side-to-side waddle.

"Very sorry, very, very sorry," Krishna's uncle apologized, bowing to the policeman while still hurrying in full waddle.

He reached the car door and swung it open for Sameer and nearly pushed him into the car. He continued to bow and apologize to the policeman.

"What is this matter?" he asked angrily, out of breath, taking his seat in the sedan.

"We just wanted to take a couple pictures," Krishna explained apologetically.

Her uncle frantically attempted to steer out of the crowd. He edged the car aggressively into traffic, waving to the policeman, now blowing on his whistle in the middle of the street trying desperately to unravel the chaotic gridlock.

"Okay, now! Go! Go! Go!" Sameer pointed to an open break in the crowd.

The car lurched forward, and Krishna's uncle began to weave through traffic before swerving sharply down a side street.

Sameer swung himself around to face the girls.

"Kate, you stopped traffic!" Sameer bantered.

"All I wanted was to get a picture of the temple," Kate blurted. "It was your idea to sit in the rickshaw." She looked accusingly at Krishna and then back at Sameer.

Krishna's bewildered uncle peered annoyingly at Sameer then Krishna through the rearview mirror.

"No word about policeman to *chaachii*!" her uncle warned and sped off in the direction of the museum.

✳ ✳ ✳ ✳ ✳

THE SALAR JUNG Museum stood a brown geometric building, adjacent to the State Library on the south bank of the Musi River.

Inside the galleries, eyes shifted from the worldly treasures of wealthy Salar Jung III to Kate if she hovered too long in one area. In the silent open light of the furniture gallery, she felt raw, uncloaked, especially after the scene on the street.

"I'm enjoying the coolness in here." Nasreen lightly brushed a few strands of hair from her brow.

"The clock room should be just down there," Krishna reported, her head hidden behind a museum map.

"Gosh, put that away," Nasreen scorned.

Krishna, unsuccessful at folding the map correctly, crumpled it into a wad.

The girls descended the staircase that opened into the magnificent clock room. Tones struck the air from a variety of deep heavy bongs from the grandfather clocks, clicks from swaying pendulums, and light whistles and tinny chimes from miniature, ancient timepieces.

"It's quite a crowd," Kate said, pausing to marvel at the array of clocks from her vantage point on the stairs.

"Look at the clock over there on the wall." Krishna pointed across to an ornate small square piece set on a high shelf, a tiny palace fit for a Lilliputian prince.

Four miniature gold columns supported an arch and framed the golden face of the clock. Atop the columns perched glorious tiny birds with their wings outstretched.

"Wow," Kate remarked in awe.

"I believe the crowd is now staring at us," Nasreen noticed.

Kate descended the last several steps and ducked into the crowd in a futile attempt to blend in. She felt a gentle tug on her hair. A bewildered child, his pudgy chin nestled on his mother's shoulder, stared with high intensity at Kate. In his tiny hand he firmly clasped a lock of her red hair. A thick line of *kohl* outlined his dark wide eyes, making the whites of his eyes almost haunting. The baby seemed on the verge of howling, his kohl-rimmed eyes widened in reverence. Kate sucked in her breath and slowly tried to back away, but she felt the painful pull of his grasp. Her hair looked like copper coils wrapped around his clenched fist.

The palace clock suddenly played a wondrous tune. Out popped the princely timekeeper.

"Awe," murmured the crowd in unison.

The startled baby stirred in his mother's arms. With one quick yank, Kate was free, leaving a few strands behind, twisted around the baby's chubby knuckles.

"Ping. Ping," went the clock as the toy man struck a bell twice with his tiny mallet, signaling two o'clock. Then the figure retreated. The hinges snapped shut and the clock stood silent. Children clapped and women giggled softly, covering their mouths with the end of their dupattas.

Kate spied Nasreen, reached wide through a gap in the crowd, and grabbed the corner of her shirt as the crowd started to move.

"I'm ready to go."

"Yes, Sameer is waiting for us. Chelo."

✳ ✳ ✳ ✳

ON THE STREET in front of the museum, they found Sameer buying roasted nuts wrapped in paper from a street vendor with a rusted cart. The nuts sizzled on the grill. Sameer juggled a hot nut in his hand before popping it into his mouth and munched happily on the partially blackened mixture smelling of honey, cloves, and hazelnut.

The girls followed Sameer along the street from the stately columns of the Salar Jung Museum to the white stone minarets of Mecca Masjid. Kate was enthralled by the city. From the gray and dust of the streets arose something so pure white, an architectural marvel. She paused and allowed her eyes to adjust to the sun reflecting against the albescent granite of the mosque.

The girls strolled through the long passageway leading to the high arches of the glorious Mecca Masjid. The covered stone offered coolness and a haven from the intense afternoon sun. Light from the reflection pond poured in through the many temple windows, creating a row of hands-in-prayer shadows along the opposite wall.

"Ten thousand persons can offer prayer at a time," Nasreen read from a plaque on the side of the central archway. "Wow. Our mosque at home holds about fifty," she joked.

"That is twenty thousand shoes!" exclaimed Kate, staring at the pile of sandals marking the entrance. "I will pray that I will find my shoes."

Nasreen flashed her a look of disapproval.

Kate removed her white and pink canvas shoes and placed them to the side of the mountain of brown worn chappals.

"I don't think you will have a problem finding yours among the thousands," Nasreen said. "There are not so many pink ones."

"Hopefully this place is welcoming to Hindus," Krishna added, kicking off her sandals.

"Just be a tourist, Krishna," Nasreen remarked. "Are we ready to go in now?"

Inside the vast open area, tapestries depicting Islamic art from the times of the Deccan Kings hung from the high walls. Rows of men prayed in one section and a large group of women stood near the back. Kate meandered through the group of women while admiring the awesomeness of the mosque. The mosque was silent except for the simple shifting sounds of the women's saris, so different sounding from the rugged whisper Kate's jeans made as she moved.

The girls passed through the open archway and stepped into the sunken courtyard. Hundreds of double-fluted minarets lined the top of the mosque, and at each corner stood giant columns elevating enormous cupolas that rounded to a point extending into sky-piercing spires. A man handed flower petals to Krishna, who refused to take them. He motioned to throw the petals inside the ring of a stone block.

"It's a grave," explained Nasreen. "Throw them in," she said as she accepted the soft leaves and sprinkled them into the ring.

Kate accepted the petals and let them fall from her fingers, thinking of her mother and roses raining down on her.

"You will have good karma."

The flower man lightly touched Kate's head and shoulders with a small brush, and repeated the same ritual to Nasreen. Krishna flinched and scooted away from the man's brush.

"No good karma for you," Kate joked to Krishna.

"Well, you know. I'm Hindu," Krishna said.

"Come look at this stone," Sameer said, leading the girls to the western wall.

"There," he said, pointing to a small whitewashed stone. "It's the only one of its size in the whole building. The plaque reads that this particular stone was carried here all the way from Mecca during the Qutb Shahi dynasty in the late 1600s. Amazing."

Kate sat on a large black stone in the courtyard feeling exhausted but enthralled. The girls joined her, and the three friends sat on the black stone bench, framed by the arches of Mecca Masjid, their bare feet dangling.

"Tourists who sit on the stone will return to Hyderabad once again," Kate recited from an inscription in the stone.

Nasreen grinned and placed her arms around Kate and Krishna as Sameer snapped a photo.

"We mustn't break the ritual."

Chapter 10

ARE YOU LISTENING, LORD GANESHA?

Chicago 1998

Τ he entrance to the science building at the university resembled the Salar Jung Museum in Hyderabad. It was Sunday, two weeks since Kate ran from Nasreen's house the day after Eid. Two weeks since she had met Tariq for breakfast.

Regret had hardened around Kate's heart, making each step feel weighted as she trudged along the wide-open barren walkway, the daffodil bulbs still dormant underground, toward the front door to the building and the lab.

Like the museum, the science building had hard, long lines and an overpowering dominance with two concrete wings that expanded out from the block entrance. Three rows of equally spaced windows, too small to filter more than minimal light, lined each side. But unlike the museum in India, the science building lacked a central dome atop the front entrance, and smaller domes perched at each end of the two wings like the Salar Jung's Persian architectural influence.

Kate was not enlightened within the concrete wing of the science building, dimly illuminated by flickering fluorescent bulbs, as she walked the quiet halls. The corridors were empty except for freezers, centrifuges, and liquid nitrogen tanks, pushed out in the hall as lab space became scarce. The objects cast eerie shadows in the low light, their motors intermittingly hissing and moaning as Kate shuffled from one lab to the next.

She was suspended, suffocating in the vapors of organic solvents, the fuzzy pungent stench of reagents, and the sweet stale odor of molecules that she was supposed to transform into disease-fighting medicines for her PhD thesis, her life, before the wings of the university threatened to flap shut and engulf her.

Dr. Schwitz, her graduate advisor, was half Venezuelan and half German but had not inherited the tall German genes. He was a small man with dark hair, a square jaw, and hard eyes. He never answered his students' questions about growing up in South America, as if revealing his origins would present an inequality he could not allow.

"Many students would love to work in my lab," Dr. Schwitz said to Kate during a weekly one-on-one meeting. "I am very well-funded at this university and can't jeopardize my position. You understand, Kate," he said in a condescending tone.

Dr. Schwitz spoke four languages, but Kate always felt lost in translation. *What is he saying?* she thought. He had a habit of bringing his hands together in a temple and hunching forward so that his lips pressed against his fingertips. His neck disappeared beneath his shoulders, and he stayed like that looking intently at her, one brow raised. From behind his enormous desk, piles of papers neatly stacked to the side, he gave the impression that he was shrinking into his high-back leather chair.

The meetings were intended for her to share her progress and gain guidance; but instead, the time quickly degenerated into a schizophrenic session of manipulation and mistrust. She stared at the marble clock fountain pen stand on the corner of his desk. She wondered if the writing tablet had ever been written on or if he tore off a sheet every morning to give a pristine appearance. She had to think of anything to keep her mind from derailing.

Their last meeting was particularly excruciating because all she could think about was Neil and the sting of their breakup. She had quit the master's swim team to avoid him, but she desperately missed his friendship and their daily rendezvous over coffee and his entertaining stories such as the one he told her about the writer.

"A mate of mine in the English department writes the most amazing poetry," Neil told her one morning. "His writing is genius, but he only writes when he is high on meth. Can't write a single word sober."

"What?" Kate looked at him astonished.

"It's true. A friend in the chemistry department made the meth out of his farmhouse. One day the feds came and took him away. He got nine years."

"You make this stuff up," Kate said in disbelief.

"As far as you know." Neil grinned a mischievous grin and sipped his coffee.

As absurd as his stories were at times, Neil had empowered her. He'd introduced her to rowing on Lake Michigan and taught her the basics of maneuvering a rowboat in the swirling north wind. Being with Neil eased the dimness of graduate school. But his passionate nature had suddenly turned stoic. He was focused on graduating and obtaining a university teaching position in English somewhere.

Now all she missed were the talks over coffee.

Kate brushed the thoughts of Neil and her advisor aside and tried to focus on her work. Except for the clinking of spinning stir bars against the sides of flasks, the lab was quiet.

The lab phone rang. The abrupt sound startled her, and she inadvertently drew a thick line of ink across the page of her lab book.

Who would call here on a Sunday?

"Kate?"

"Nasreen?"

"I called your apartment all afternoon. Finally called your dad, and he gave me the number of the lab."

Kate was surprised to hear Nasreen's voice. They had not spoken since that horrible morning after Eid. She felt guilty for not calling and longed to unload her mind about Tariq and tell her about the old letters she'd found.

"Nasreen, look, I'm…" Kate began to apologize.

"Krish's mom had a…a stroke," Nasreen blurted, distraught.

"What?"

"Stroke!" she shouted into the phone. "She's in the hospital. Kate! Krishna's mother is in a coma!" Nasreen breathed heavily into the phone as if it were exhausting to say that much. "Krishna and her dad are with her. It doesn't look good," she cried.

Kate heard the fear in Nasreen's voice.

"Are you there? Kate?"

"Yes." Kate cleared her throat. "I'm here. I don't understand. A stroke? A coma? How is that possible? Her mother is so healthy, so holistic!" she rambled, trying to make sense.

Kate visualized Saritha in the kitchen, standing on a stool to reach inside the cabinet, spinning the lazy Susan stacked with herbs and supplements searching for the neem oil. "The special oil comes from the neem tree in India," she explained to Kate one humid afternoon when the girls had come inside. Kate remembered that Krishna had a stomachache that day. "It is very good for the digestive system," Saritha said. "And it makes your hair so shiny. Here it is!" She beamed. "My daughter, you will feel better with a few drops, trust me!" she had explained as she squeezed three drops into a cup of tea.

"They say it was an embolism," Nasreen said.

Her voice was fading. To Kate, it sounded as though Nasreen said "symbolism," which made her visualize the large embroidered framed picture of a Hindu symbol that hung in the foyer of the Desai home and greeted each guest.

"The family is coming from India. They arrive the day after next," Nasreen said, speaking to fill the void. "I pray that she will be okay, that she will come out of the coma. I can't believe this is happening!"

Nasreen's tone changed from sadness to bewilderment.

"She needs us."

Kate waited until after she heard the click at the other end of the line before placing the phone down. She visualized her own mother's face, young and unscarred by disease. She tried to hang onto that image of her mother. She squeezed her eyes shut, but the image dissolved and all she could see was dark and light. Opening her eyes, Kate stared at the receiver for a long time, feeling haunted by shadows in the lab and echoes in the hall, half thinking the phone would ring again and Nasreen would say it was all a mistake. *Have faith.*

* * * * *

A PORTRAIT OF Krishna's mother as a young woman hung in the center of the wall. In the photo, Saritha's head was turned to the right and she gazed off somewhere in the distance. Her long black hair cascaded across her neck and shoulder. She wore a white collared blouse. The photo appeared to be her graduation photo from nursing school, perhaps the only photo the family had of her alone. Garlands were looped on each corner of the frame, the kind of frame sold by the pack, pre-matted for framing documents and certificates. The garlands were tied together below the portrait, interwoven with pearls and prayer beads. The room was cleared of all furniture except for a cloth-covered cardboard table decorated as an altar.

Kate sat on her knees on the floor and stared at the elephant-headed idol on the altar. Purple beads and white garlands with fluorescent pink bows hung under his trunk, covering his round protruding belly. She tilted her head and squinted, trying to view Lord Ganesha on his green satin altar from a different angle. Still she found his multiple hands—each grasping a golden object—a little unnerving with fingernails painted white and wrists bound with gold bands. The flamboyant plaster god of wisdom and prosperity paraded a coronation headdress made of white and pink carnations. Even his elephant eyes were pink.

The family from India had arrived and gathered around Saritha's hospital bedside. The nursing staff, many of whom were Saritha's subordinates, gave the family space and grieved in the hospital corridors as the machines kept Saritha alive. Eventually, Suneel abided by his wife's wishes and released her soul. "Never let my body be kept alive by a machine," she had told him. "Promise me, Suneel! Let my soul float into the sea."

"When all the relatives were here, my father and I…" Krishna began.

Kate looked over at Krishna kneeling beside her on the floor and waited in the shadowed silence of the room for her to continue speaking. It had been a few weeks since her mother's death, and Krishna's relatives had returned to India.

"We decided to make this a prayer room. A room for meditation," Krishna continued. "Hinduism is about connecting mind and soul to God." Krishna's voice cracked when she said the word "God," as though mentioning the name of the Almighty took more strength than she could muster. "I pray every morning just as my mother and I used to do together."

She was saying the words, but they sounded surreal to Kate's ears. She continued to study the altar. Small offerings sat on each side of Lord Ganesha: a bowl of fruit, silver trays of spices, *japa mala* beads. Wreaths of red, white, and yellow daisies lay at the base of the son of Shiva and Parvati. Among the flowers, incense burned from candleholders. The pencil-thin smoke line snaked upward and diffused below Saritha's portrait.

"We kept the room this way even though my relatives left. It's just my father and me," Krishna said, then paused. "We can come here to be with my mother. Talk to her. Just haven't figured out what to say."

"Krishna," Kate said, breaking her silence, "maybe you don't have to say anything…right now."

Krishna sat stiff and motionless with eyes shut, a pained expression shadowing her brow.

Kate bowed her head and closed her eyes, willing herself to pray. She didn't pray to a Christian God. She was not baptized. Sometimes she attended Sunday school with friends, but church to her felt like wearing heavy shoes that clomped and dragged loudly against the floor with each slow step.

Sometimes Kate lay on the basement floor in the dark, wrestling with contradictive thoughts about the logic of Christ versus the logic of science, a curse of choice. She wanted to believe that her mother was somewhere comfortable, floating timelessly in the mist of a cloud, or that her spirit hung in the everyday objects around her. The more she understood about religions, the more agnostic she became, carrying the burdens of the world upon her shoulders—and the more challenging it became for her to commit to any one religious sect without self-sacrifice. A commitment to one was a rejection of others; a commitment to all was hypocrisy, a belief in nothing. She was quite simply in a state of religious limbo. Why would Lord Ganesha hear her now?

Are you listening, Lord Ganesha? Kate thought.

Pink eyes looked back at her.

She never asked Nasreen or Krishna the difference between mosques and temples, growing up Muslim or Hindu. She visualized the Birla Temple that overlooked the twin cities of Hyderabad and Secunderabad and how it filled the sky out the rear window of the speeding car as they headed north along the Hussain

Sagar Lake. It was the Hindu temple, the white marble wonder on the hill, that was the object in her camera lens that day they waited outside the Bhilwara Bank for Krishna's uncle to return, the photo she had taken that caused such ruckus on the city's main roadway.

To Kate, the temple with its multiple levels and ample girth looked plump and soft with billowing domes reflected in the lake's drifting crescents. The temple had lovely white staircases leading to many smaller temples. She imagined sitting in an enclave, whispering privately with a deity about nothing in particular, or about things that concerned her, thoughts that weighed too heavily.

So unlike the temple, the Mecca Masjid mosque had twisted spires, embedded rows of spades along the flat rooftop, and endless passageways lined with pointed arches. In the vast open spaces of the mosque, she felt her own judgments reflected in the reflecting pond. The space was a tribute to Allah's omnipotence, a place to join the masses in prayer.

The ring of the doorbell jarred Kate from her thoughts.

Krishna remained still beside Kate with her eyes closed. Her head was bent forward and her hair hung down across her cheekbones. Beguiled in *Sanskrit* and meditation, Krishna flicked each sandalwood mala as her lips moved in mumbling recitation.

Not wanting to disturb Krishna, Kate closed her eyes again.

Lord Ganesha, she prayed. *Let Krishna's mother's soul find peace. Give Krishna the strength to find what makes her happy. And, Lord, remover of obstacles, please help me finish graduate school. Help me persevere and know where to go from here, I pray.*

Kate breathed deeply. The sweet incense and warm spices massaged her nostrils. She was reminded of India and felt the caressing hand of Nanima across her hair.

Krishna's hand was patting her shoulder.

"Kate," she said softly. "Kate, I don't want to disturb you, but Nasreen is downstairs."

Kate followed Krishna down the staircase and to the door.

"I'm glad you are both here," Krishna stated.

"Grab a coat, you two. Let's walk," Nasreen urged.

A short trek out the back of Krishna's house, down the hill, was Deerfield Park. Nasreen marched ahead like a soldier. Krishna and Kate followed reluctantly.

"Why are we out here?" Krishna asked. "It's chilly."

"I thought the fresh April air would feel good," Nasreen announced.

Nasreen spun around and jogged backward.

"Come on!" she urged to Kate and Krishna, both shuffling along the path, hands in their pockets. "We have to move faster, get some exercise."

Nasreen had on Mustafa's oversized gray university sweatshirt, sweatpants, and pink gloves that matched the pink trim on her jogging shoes. Pumping her arms as if she lifted imaginary weights, she stomped ahead along the trail. The trees were still bare, the thawing ground a bluish gray. Canadian geese huddled underneath the deck at the edge of the pond with their beaks tucked under their puffy wings. They soon would paddle in the water, making v-shaped ripples behind them as they darted to feast on bread thrown by spring's first visitors. But today the Canadian geese stayed huddled and warm.

The girls followed the path across a bridge. The ducks rustled their feathers, hearing the girls' feet above.

"Any news on the adoption front?" Krishna asked Nasreen, trying to be positive despite her raw grief.

"Yes," answered Nasreen, excitedly. "I might be going back to Pakistan very soon."

"Really?"

"We jumped to the top of the adoption list thanks to my uncle's connections in Pakistan. We may have a baby soon."

Kate and Krishna stared blankly at Nasreen. After Saritha's death, the announcement of a baby took time to seep through the layers of clothing and into their skin.

Nasreen's tone grew serious. "Well, this walk isn't about me adopting a baby. It's about you, Krishna."

"What about me? I am sad, can't you see?"

"I know," Nasreen sighed. "Do you want to talk about anything?"

"No, not really."

Kate and Krishna kept pace with Nasreen's marching speed, warming their bodies in silence until they had rounded the opposite end of the pond.

The path around the pond inclined a short distance. At the crest of the slope, the carillon tower peeked into view rising above the maple trees. During town festivals and in the summer evenings, Kate listened through the open bedroom window of her childhood home to the faint chromatic octaves of the sixty-seven cast bronze bells played from the carillonneur's cabin.

"I love this view," Kate said breathlessly. "You can just see the top row of bells. They look so tiny from here, like bells you can ring in your hand."

"I will always remember the carillon as part of my childhood," Krishna reminisced. "My mother and I walked this park almost every summer evening, and my parents took me up to the observatory when I was a kid. On a clear day, you can see the city."

"That's a nice memory," Kate said.

Krishna stopped walking and stared ahead. "It's just me and my dad," she said faintly, suddenly peering through the grief and confronted with the future. "We pace through the house, through two thousand square feet of memories too painful to share with one another."

"Krishna, I know it has been just a few weeks," Nasreen said, treading carefully, "but are you going back to medical school? Maybe getting back into the program will help get your mind…"

"I'm not going back to medical school!" Krishna shouted, still staring ahead. "I'm out! I failed my exams!"

"Krish. Why didn't you tell me?" Nasreen looked helpless.

"I didn't tell anyone," Krishna cried. "I couldn't tell my parents. And then… and then my mother was in a coma!" She heaved and clutched her heart.

In the background, one of the female geese, apparently disturbed from her nap, stretched her black neck lithely in the air and honked long and fiercely.

"While she was in the coma, I kept thinking, how could this be happening?" Krishna began. "There was time for my mother and me to become best friends. I always imagined we would achieve that closeness, eventually."

The goose quieted. Kate and Nasreen stood motionless, listening.

"I remember when I used to go around the house with my Nikon Zoom camera," Krishna continued, "recording the eighties in our wood-paneled home, focusing on the tin and gold trinkets from India lying all around that my mother had brought back from Kerala along with murals of the sea. She would snap at me, 'Put the camera down, Krishna! That is not what I mean when I say focus! Are you listening? You must think about your career and your future.'"

Krishna pretended to be her mother and planted her fists against her hips.

"My mother had the slightest South India accent, and even when she was angry her voice purred. My father would always take her side even though he had given me the camera one year for Diwali, and honestly, he would rather have been reading an article in *Applied Physics* or preparing notes for a class he was teaching in…thermodynamics or whatever. 'Dat is why we came here. To A-mey-ee-ka!'"

Krishna mimicked her father's ways and thick Gujarati accent by pinching her fingers together and striking the air with each syllable.

The pain seeped into Krishna's voice. "We had time, my mother and I, to understand each other. I wanted her to open her eyes one last time to see me." She pressed her hand to her chest. "Then I was just going through the steps…for my family's sake. They still held out hope; but I knew…I knew she would never open her eyes."

Krishna covered her face with her hands.

Nasreen galloped toward Krishna, catching her.

"It will get better, I promise. You need time." Nasreen drew back and clutched Krishna's hands in her pink-gloved ones.

Krishna broke Nasreen's grasp and backed away.

"My father wanders the house in a daze. I don't think he knows what to do with me," Krishna sighed. "I'm not the person my parents wanted me to be. In so many ways, I'm not!"

Her words descended through the air to lay a cloak on the cracked earth.

Nasreen looked confused. "What do you mean, 'in so many ways?'"

"Nothing. I just don't meet their expectations."

"Screw medical school!" Kate blurted. "It's not for you. Go travel. Go to India and visit your mother's family!"

Nasreen and Krishna blinked at Kate.

"Well, that is what I would do," Kate added.

Nasreen shrugged. "Traveling with your dad could be very therapeutic."

"Or a disaster. My mother's family never quite accepted him."

"Maybe they will think differently now. For your sake."

Krishna started walking again. They had almost completed a single circuit around the pond. Just ahead was the path up the hill to return to the house. The walk of fresh air was nearly over.

"I don't know much about my mother's childhood. She said she came to America because it was her dream. But I still wonder how she had the courage to leave and travel alone to a country she knew nothing about."

Krishna looked in the distance across the pond. The aroused goose strutted to the lake's edge and plucked its black beak against the thawing, thick mud, awakening its senses to the changing season.

"When I traveled to India," she continued, "I was a visitor, the cousin from America. It wasn't until I was nearly twenty that I began to see things differently. When the weather was nice, my mother and I knelt together on the back porch in the warm sun and meditated sitting side by side. There was no one else around, and it was the one time I felt close to her. I understood finally what being Hindu meant to me," she confessed. "I never told my mother that I was proud of her but I was. And I am proud to be a Hindu-American."

The awakened goose suddenly opened her wings in full span and fluttered them repeatedly. The bird's beautiful neck arched sensuously as it prepared to soar.

"Maybe you are both right," she said. "Maybe my father and I should go to India for a while and visit relatives. I would like to understand why my mother left the Arabian coastline for Middle America. Maybe the trip will help me figure out where to go from here."

"It's a great idea," Nasreen said, satisfied.

Kate nodded and breathed in the cool air.

Krishna's gaze followed the goose's flight over the pond until it disappeared beyond the trees.

Chapter 11
GARDEN AT THE TOMBS

Hyderabad 1987

The bubble car drivers went on strike.

"The strike could last a day, a week, who knows," Aunty Samina remarked. "That is India." She smiled broadly.

Kate was secretly thankful for a break from the untamed streets of Hyderabad's city center and the incessant stares at the color of her hair.

She bathed in the dilapidated outhouse adjacent to her bedroom to wash away the grit of India trapped deep in her pores mixed with night sweat.

The mosquitoes flying in through the warped spaces of the rotting wood boards were ready to attack. She had to be quick about it. She leaned over the basin of cloudy lukewarm water. The coils wrapped around the basin glowed menacingly like a cobra ready to hiss. She grabbed a bucket, scooped, and dumped the cool water over her head with a gasp then swirled a slippery ball of soap against her body. The soap escaped and landed with a splatter on the concrete floor in a pool of floating mosquito corpses.

Dropping the metal bucket, she ripped the tail of the electric snake from the socket of its bellowing belly. With a gurgling sizzle, the hot coils faded to black. With a towel loosely around her, Kate bolted from the bathhouse to the bedroom, her hair dripping wet and soaking the stepping-stones.

She appeared for chai donning a light blue salwar kameez. Nanima smiled approvingly.

"Look at you," Nasreen grinned.

"It's more comfortable than jeans," Kate explained. "And entirely less hot."

"That salwar is one of my favorites."

After breakfast, the cousins arrived at the Banjara Hills house. Kate emerged in the front room already sweating in the cotton salwar kameez. Yasmine looked bright in a yellow pinstriped salwar kameez. Her hair was neatly braided. She stood and kissed Kate's clammy cheek with feathery lightness. Kate was still getting used to the intimate greetings in India.

"We have a great day planned for you," Yasmine said. "To the countryside!"

"I thought the auto rickshaws were on strike."

"Who needs auto rickshaws?" Tariq said. "We have a van. You can't let the ways of India slow you down. You won't get anywhere!"

"Chelo!" Max shouted from the door. "Hari and Azra are in the van."

The five cousins and Sana, Nasreen, Kate, and Sameer piled into a rented baby blue Suzuki van with rusted wheel hulls.

Max drove a long distance through the sprawling city until they reached the city limits marked by decaying archways. The van's engine smoothed to a hum. Kate's seat bones ached against the jostling of the Suzuki bunker, but she sensed lightness, the void of urban toil. She heard it in Nasreen's carefree laugh: to be out in mixed company, no concern, and no suspicions to be talked about at the mosque on Fridays.

They drove along the Musi River through ancient gateways to the picturesque old city and to the massive fort surrounded by crumbling stone walls.

"First stop, Fort Golconda," Hari announced as he stretched across Yasmine and Azra, impatient to exit the van.

"Hari!" Yasmine yelled, smacking him on the back as he crawled over her.

"These walls used to stand fifty feet high," Hari said, standing at the entrance to the fort and stretching his neck upwards. "Can you imagine?"

Kate looked up at what remained of the blocks of granite and mortar. She admired the iron knobs protruding from the archways. The pointed knobs, once sharp, were now blunted and shiny from visitors rubbing them over the years.

"The knobs were to stop the charging elephants," Hari explained.

"Really?"

"The Mongols attacked while riding on elephants, so the knobs prevented the animals from battering the walls. I read a lot about history," he said, grinning.

"Interesting," Kate said, as her attention drifted to three native women, their long dark braids swooped together, nearly touching as they looked toward the structure on top of the ruins.

Their skirts lifted in the breeze, the vibrant crimson and ginger colors contrasting starkly from the layers upon layers of gray granite rubble. The women's heads bent together in an intimate exchange.

Kate imagined the women transformed in time, standing in the lush courtyard among the royal palaces, gossiping about the love affairs of the nobles. She continued walking, a diminished figure, under a series of stone archways imagining the impressiveness of the fort's perimeter that protected its sultans through the ages. She watched Tariq's figure come in and out of view as he meandered among the ruins ahead of her. His eyes caught hers as he stepped around a column.

"This region was famous for its mines," he told her as he leaned against the column.

"Mines?" she questioned.

"Yes. Mines that produced the most famous diamonds," he said. "Like the Hope Diamond."

"What is a hope diamond?" Kate asked, intrigued.

"Something very rare and beautiful," he said, squinting against the sun.

"Race you to the top," Sameer shouted to Tariq, jabbing him in the stomach as he hurried past toward the tower.

Tariq doubled over from the direct hit and raced after Sameer, leaving Kate to ponder the gems once hidden away in the fort.

Three hundred and sixty steps led through the maze of walls in a zigzagged path to the top of the fort. Kate followed the others up and up. At the top were three arches and a lookout tower. Panting, she could see to the other side of the river with the sprawling new city of modern buildings and fashionable localities.

"An underground tunnel runs all the way to the city center," Hari said to Kate. "I read about that too."

His hand pointed to where her eyes focused: all the way past the Saify stores to the corner of Bangalore Road where the old man with a gray turban squatted, selling roasted nuts and guavas.

After some time, the group descended the winding stairwell from the interior of the fort. They had ascended the way of the soldiers and descended the way of the sultan and his queen.

* * * * *

THE VAN RATTLED for miles outside the city before stopping at the entrance of the military barracks.

"Quiet!" Max yelled back from the driver's seat, a finger across his lips.

The expressionless soldier at guard held out a hand, signaling the van to stop. He asked Max a question in the local dialect, peered toward the back seats, and stared intently at Kate. He said something to the other soldiers, who spied through the window at the van full of teenagers, and then nodded to proceed.

Kate felt vulnerable and leaned toward Tariq, letting his shadow hide her face. She smelled the spicy sweetness of his cologne and perspiration.

"You are a *feringhee*," Sameer remarked to Kate once they cleared the soldiers at the checkpoint. "They think you are married to one of us. That is the only rational thought to explain why you are here and wearing Indian clothing."

"Well, hopefully they don't think I am married to you," Kate shot back, annoyed.

"You are a feringhee too, my cousin!" Tariq teased.

Yasmine laughed and Sameer sneered at them both.

While Kate's Celtic coloring drew heavy stares, Sameer and Nasreen were not immune to the locals' attention with their independent air and full faces aglow from their American upbringing.

The van proceeded through the massive stone walls that surrounded the military zone. Continuing on, they passed a series of temples until the road became a rocky path. The van's struts labored along the uneven muddy ground until finally Max brought the van to a halt.

Kate peered out the Suzuki's back flap to see a lake that must have been much larger at one time but had receded, leaving a muddy perimeter of broken rock and shell. There was nothing resembling city life, only a few cows spotting the landscape.

The boys jumped from the back, stretched their backs, and helped the girls climb down the tailgate. They deserted the van and started walking, their shoes sinking into the mud.

"Oh, my sandal!" cried Yasmine as she plucked her naked foot from the earth, hobbling on one leg.

She bent to retrieve the muddied bright orange sole. Sameer, a facetious grin across his face, kicked at the ground as if he were kicking a soccer ball into a goal, and mud splattered across his cousin's kameez.

"Sameer!" Yasmine froze in shock for only a moment, and, forgetting the sandal, she grabbed a fist of mud and slung it at her cousin. Sameer grabbed Tariq, twisting him around to face the swirling muck.

"You...ahh!" Tariq huddled toward Sameer as the muck pounded his back.

Kate, Nasreen, and the two youngest, Azra and Sana, threw off their shoes and ran from the scene squealing. Chunks of mud were flung off their heels. By the time they reached the grassy marsh, they were speckled head to foot.

"Your face," laughed Nasreen, pointing to Kate.

Kate felt the cool soft mud hardening on her cheek. She wiped her face with the back of her hand, smearing muck across her cheek.

"Much better," Nasreen joked.

Boulder and fragmented rock covered the landscape to the receding water's edge as though a stone fortress had crumbled, sending pieces of towers rolling in all directions until inertia set in and earth hardened. Boulders stacked one on top of each other raised above the water level as a lone tower.

Sana and Azra were waist deep in the murky lake hanging on to each other for support. The others ran into the cold lake, splashing wildly. Yasmine's irradiant yellow dupatta floated atop the brown opaque water. Sameer grabbed the free end, unraveling his cousin as he drew the cloth in.

"Sameer, stop!" She tugged back. "You are such a pain!"

Hari heaved his lengthy body through the water to Yasmine's rescue and yanked firmly, sending Sameer stumbling.

"Tariq! Help me out!"

Tariq responded and seized the yellow cloth behind Sameer and joined the tug-of-war game.

"Get him!" Sana yelled to Nasreen and Kate, watching from a safe distance.

The girls pounced on Tariq, dunking him bellow the murky surface. He released his hold on the scarf, sending Sameer face first into the water. Sameer let go and dived into the water to avoid a face flop, causing Yasmine and Hari to soar backward with a plunge, nearly falling on Azra.

"Enough!" Max called, resting a hand on his little sister's shoulder, leading her out of the water.

Kate tried her best to wring out her hair and clean the mud off her shoes, wading them in the water.

"Well, I'm a mess, but that was really terrific," Kate said, enthused.

"We must show you the fun side of India. It is not all filth and poor people and lots of noises," Tariq said.

"Not all filth?" Kate laughed. "Look at us!"

His smoky blue eyes were even more piercing against his charcoal-grime glistening skin and ruffled damp hair.

"Take a look at that," Tariq stammered, still catching his breath.

Tariq pointed to a stretch of rocky land jutting out into the lake. A massive oval-shaped boulder teetered precariously atop a rectangular one of immensely larger size. The formation's silhouette appeared like a colossal toddler sitting legs outstretched ready to throw his bald looming head back in a howling brawl.

"We must climb it!"

"You are crazy, cousin!" Max exclaimed. "I'm not climbing that."

"I'm in!" Kate said excitedly and started trekking across the mud with Tariq, shoes in hand.

Yasmine strolled behind, hanging onto Hari's arm with one hand and clasping her soiled sandals with the other. Nasreen followed.

By the time she reached the coupled rocks, Kate was worn out from lack of exercise. The flank of rock was smooth and seemed not scalable. Tariq had already started climbing the layers of rock and was feeling for grooves on the side for footing. His sinuous muscles showed as he grappled with the rock and heaved himself upward.

Kate beat her shoes against the rock to remove the hardened mud and gravel and pushed her feet into them, spreading the remaining pebbles around with her toes. She began to climb.

"Here, give me your hand."

Tariq stood at the throat of the stone-faced toddler, extending his hand to Kate. She looked up at him.

Kate grabbed Tariq's open palm. His hand closed warmly around hers, and he heaved her upward in one steady motion. She fell against him. He wrapped his arm around her waist, and she felt the strength in his leg anchored in the groove of rock. Tariq's eyes looked into hers. The horizon spun around her, and for a fleeting moment she felt suspended in his arms.

"Uh. Hello. Help me!" Nasreen yelled from the side of the rock. "Tariq, I need a hand!"

Tariq instantly released Kate and rushed to Nasreen's aid. Kate lost her balance and tripped across his leg and landed flat on the rock, its pointed surface digging into her breastbone.

"I could have fallen to my death," Nasreen remarked after stepping on top of the rock. "Thanks, cousin," she said, letting go of Tariq's hand and dusting off her salwar. "Kate, what are you doing lying on the rock?"

"Enjoying the view," she answered smartly as she stood up and rubbed her sore breastbone.

Tariq flashed her an apologetic smile.

"It's beautiful up here. Well worth the climb," Nasreen shouted down to Max and Sameer, who remained below with Azra and Sana.

In the distant horizon, Kate could make out the diminished outline of the city, the haze caressing the spires and domes and small clusters of buildings disjointed and disconnected from the others. She sat, legs dangling over the side, feeling the wind across her face and breathing in the unadulterated air. Tariq sat a comfortable distance from her and she studied his silhouette as he scanned the landscape. A wave of hair fell across his eyes. Kate felt a momentary sense of unconditional freedom, the touch of wind on her face, and the feel of her waist where Tariq had held her.

✳ ✳ ✳ ✳ ✳

MAX MANEUVERED THE Suzuki along a half-paved gravel road. They had driven several kilometers through the barren and broken stretch of land heading back to the city. Suddenly, the graceful curves of ancient domes peered above the tree line. As the van approached, the trees parted, the rocks turned to pebble walkways and square gardens, and a stunning mosque came into full view.

"Wow!" Kate exclaimed, wiping a layer of sweat and lake silt from her brow as she stepped out of the van, the rising humidity threatening rain. "It's incredible!"

"They are tombs," Max remarked, extending his arm in a presentation of the cluster of majestic domes that served as resting places for dynasty rulers.

A small man appeared from the arched entryway, luring the group forward with his sweeping soft gestures first to the raised platform and then inside the mosque.

"Welcome to the Qutb Shahi tombs," he announced, waiting for the group to still before speaking more.

His placatory voice billowed into a cloud of whispers rising within the mortuary haven, then diffusing to a soundless spirit. He led the group down a long narrow stairway. Kate slid her hands along the damp concrete walls for guidance as the outside light faded, her eyes adjusting to the underground darkness. She was beginning to feel hungry, and the walls seemed oppressing, as if they were slowly closing in.

In the center of the dim lower chamber sat a perfectly round stone. The symmetrically painted lines curved to a point on the stone's surface creating a rotating illusion. The walls were embossed with Indo-Persian style inflections encased by arches. A crisscross pattern in the stone connected the arches, creating a continuous arcade of tunnels and dead ends. The guide switched between broken English, Urdu, and a local dialect.

Kate lowered herself slowly to sit on one of the marble squares facing the central stone of the mortuary bath, which now appeared to Kate to be spinning.

"No. No. Please, no sit, royal bath!" the guide's voice burst from a whisper to a vibrating echo trapped within the vaulted chamber.

The reverberating sounds confused Kate. Tariq offered her his hand. She faltered, and he grabbed her elbow with his free hand to steady her.

"Let's get you out of here," he whispered in her ear. "I can't understand his dialect anyway," he joked.

She could still feel his breath on her ear as they mounted the stairs and she leaned into him for support.

A slit of light opened up into a charming garden with wildflowers and miniature temples.

Kate breathed in the scent of jasmine and looked up at the balustrade-lined terrace that extended over the courtyard. The humidity caused a tingling sensation across her forehead.

"Sit here," Tariq said, pointing to a bench shaded by a blood-orange bougainvillea.

She plunked down on the bench in the garden hoping he would sit next to her. Instead, Tariq walked along the path and out of the garden. Kate closed her eyes. Her head ached. She imagined herself on the side of the rock high above the ground, stretching for Tariq's hand.

She opened her eyes; Tariq stood in front of her. She gasped.

"Here, drink some water," he said, handing her a jug.

The water was warm and tasted stale, but her mind became clearer. Tariq looked around the garden awkwardly.

"I'll get the others," he said, turning away.

"Sit with me," Kate blurted. "Tell me about Nepal. I want to hear."

Tariq looked back at her for a lingering moment, contemplating her request. She thought he would walk away again, but he returned to the bench and joined her.

They sat for a few moments and Tariq told her about his backpacking trip. At one point, he had been separated from the group. He was near exhaustion and low on food when he ran into another group of hikers. As he spoke, she could feel his euphoria over his experience, both terrifying at times and exhilarating.

"You had the courage to come to India...alone."

Kate straightened.

"I have never seen anyone with hair like yours, the color of mehendi," he said, raising his hand as though he wanted to touch her forehead, but did not.

She smiled.

"Do you feel better?" he asked.

"Much."

"I'm glad you didn't faint," he said. "I would have had to carry you up those treacherous stairs."

The thought of him carrying her, his long arms under her legs and around her back, made her skin tingle.

After sitting together awhile, they heard Sana's voice resonate from the stairwell as the group ascended from the underworld and out into the garden.

"Enough for today?" Yasmine asked.

Kate nodded.

"We came up for a bit of air," Tariq explained.

"We worried we lost you in the catacombs," Sameer joked.

"No, we didn't, Sameer!" Nasreen snapped, rolling her eyes. "Like I would leave you in the catacombs! Are you feeling okay?"

"Yes, just a little hungry, I guess."

"We will stop down the road for lunch," Max responded as he caught his breath from climbing the steps.

✱ ✱ ✱ ✱ ✱

AUNTY SAMINA HAD packed egg sandwiches, spiced beef patties, mango slices, cinnamon cookies and a thermos of tea. It was the best lunch Kate had ever tasted.

The day was perfect, she thought, just as the first few raindrops fell. She couldn't remember laughing so much with a group of teenagers; certainly not in high school. By the time the group had packed up lunch, the rain beat down, and they ran into the van for shelter.

Max had driven them to the boundaries of civilization—from Mughal ruins to a military fortress. When they finally reached Banjara Hills, they must have smelled like algae scum mixed with rain and dirt. Rahmsing gave them a peculiar look and made them chai and potato-filled samosas with green sauce that they quickly devoured.

After the cousins had left, Kate removed her soiled clothes and dressed in sweats and a T-shirt. She brushed her teeth using the water in the cooler by the kitchen sink and washed the crusty mud from her face. She fell into bed, too tired to bathe or scratch at the mosquito bites covering her body.

In her sleep, she danced barefooted in a flowing crimson and ginger gown, Tariq twirling with her through the royal fort, across the terrace, and into the gardens. She dreamt of them sitting on the bench.

This time, he touched her hair and kissed her.

CHAPTER 12

SUMMONED TO MARRIAGE

Chicago 1998

Kate paused, panting and sweating despite the cool spring temperature. She stared into the back of the halfway filled U-Haul trailer. Boxes and furniture were interlocked with engineering perfection, leaving no crevice unfilled.

She had been loading boxes all morning, mindlessly lifting, rolling, and heaving. She lifted her navy sweatshirt over her head and tossed it just inside the trailer. The crisp air tinged her warm skin.

Neil was moving, driving the U-Haul down to Austin, Texas, in the morning. She agreed to help him knowing she probably should not. Since he defended his thesis and his position at the University of Texas was set, Neil was at ease, relaxed, and offered his friendship. Kate told him about Krishna's mother's death and Nasreen's adoption of a baby in Pakistan, but not about seeing Tariq after ten years. Helping Neil move kept her distracted from sinking into her own thoughts, and she hated to admit that she was desperate for his friendship.

Krishna was on her way to India, Nasreen would leave for Pakistan any day, Tariq was somewhere in New York, and Neil was leaving for good to a job and life after graduate school. Kate closed her eyes, willing time to be still for a moment or speed forward, she wasn't quite sure which.

"You good?" Neil asked, gripping her shoulder.

The extra weight rocked her slightly off balance.

Neil sat on the edge of the trailer to catch his own breath.

"Thanks for your help, Kate."

She nodded. "Look at all the empty space. You can fit another apartment's worth of stuff in here."

"That's all it is—stuff. I should have gotten rid of everything. It will be nice to start fresh."

Kate tried not to focus on how insensitive Neil's statement sounded as she stared at the shadows in the truck.

"Come along. I'd love the company!" Neil's weary face broke into a broad smile.

"Just crawl in. Hitch a ride to Texas?" she questioned.

"I will let you sit up front in the cabin," he joked.

"It's a great offer," she said sarcastically.

"Come on, I'll buy you dinner. We're done here."

"Thanks, but I'm tired. I'm going home."

She met his eyes then and realized this would be goodbye.

"You seem lost in thought, my friend. What's up?" Neil asked.

"Just remembering," she said. "Remember we snuck onto Lighthouse Beach at night, hid from the scanning headlights, and swam in Lake Michigan?"

"You were so cold," he said, smiling.

"Because the water was freezing! But it was exhilarating. It was fun."

"You sure you don't want to have dinner?"

"No. Thanks." She backed away. "I'll be over in the morning to see you off," she lied, hurrying to her car, avoiding any formal goodbye.

* * * * *

THAT EVENING KATE heard her roommate come in late. 12:35, the clock radio mocked. Flap. 12:36. Flap. 12:37…

She switched on the lamp on her nightstand, opened the bottom door, and grabbed Nasreen's letters. She shuffled through the ruffled pages finding the place she had read last.

The man Nasreen referred to as "M" in her letters occupied the pages less and less, but the feverishness with which Nasreen longed to be engaged remained in the thickness of the print and frequency of exclamation points.

"I don't feel I belong to anyone or anyplace. Most girls would hate the idea of belonging to someone, but I really need that!" Nasreen wrote near the end of the summer in her last letter to Kate.

Kate turned the sheets back to front and held them closer to the lamp, searching for any mention of Mustafa.

"We are heading to my aunt and uncle's for the weekend. They have someone they want me to meet! I am so excited to see you next week when you get back! Maybe I will have great news, Kate!"

Kate lay back and stared at the ceiling. The "meeting" didn't pan out, she recalled. Nonetheless, Nasreen was engaged less than two years after she and Kate returned from India and Pakistan. She was eighteen and full of life, a woman seemingly in love as a young woman knows love.

Nasreen chose Mustafa from a portfolio of life offers. He looked nice. The families were acquainted, aligned, and bonded by faith. Mustafa was eight years her senior and a Chicagoan, originally from Pakistan and educated in Chicago. Sitting together in a small room with their parents on the other side of the door, summing up the many blessings that would come from the union, the two smiled at each other, consummating the engagement.

This is what she wants, Kate told herself when Nasreen broke the news one afternoon in the pink and white butterfly bedroom. Shabana and Yasmine were married now. It was Nasreen's turn.

Nasreen peeled open the intimate engagement details to Kate. Nasreen was dressed in a tailored skirt, long-sleeved blouse, and headscarf. Nasreen wore the scarf with grace and elegance, an accent to every outfit, giving a hint of the beauty beneath. As she spoke, her fingers twisted a thick bracelet.

"An engagement gift from his mother," Nasreen said, fiddling.

Nasreen as the shy, submissive Muslim bride-to-be in Rockfield had been a more foreign sight to Kate than witnessing the ceremonies joining Rahim and Haseena in Pakistan. At the wedding in Pakistan, Kate had been mesmerized by each ritual, engaging the meaning of every movement, every layer of adornment signifying the relinquishing of a daughter and the deliverance of a wife. The summer following the girls' return from Asia, Nasreen wrote about desperately and insanely seeking love, inscribing it in her letters to Kate. She conflictingly sought a permissible, contractual comittment but also a lustful, passionate love that a teenage girl yearns for at the age of eighteen, before the promise to this man, this family.

On the day of the pre-wedding ceremony, Kate crowded into Nasreen's bedroom along with Krishna, Sara, Shabana, and Mona, all childhood friends. Shabana was visibly pregnant with her first child. Nasreen sat on the floor in the middle of the room draped in yellow. Only the outline of her cheek was visible, shadowed by the metallic trim of her dupatta.

"Yellow is not my color," Nasreen whispered to Kate and grinned, causing her visible cheek to fatten.

Laila huddled over her daughter, fiddling with the shapeless material covering Nasreen's head. Nasreen was to be presented as the unadorned, natural bride. Kate peered at Nasreen's grin under the mustard-colored cloth.

"Yellow is not particularly your color, but you look naturally beautiful," she confirmed. "I actually have on more makeup than you tonight," Kate said with a smile.

Nasreen tilted her head.

"Hold still," snapped Laila.

Kate felt fashionable, adorned in the gold and rose-salmon paisley salwar kameez, one of the Pakistani wedding outfits she had tailored by Ghani & Sons in India for Rahim's wedding. The taffeta billowed from beneath the heavy embroidered salwar and rustled with sophistication as she shifted her sitting position. Her many gold bracelets clinked together. Her hair swooped together and hung loosely at the back of her head, showing off her loop earrings. Mona had helped her with makeup and hair, meticulously pinning each copper strand in place.

"Okay, enough, Mom," Nasreen ordered.

Laila stopped messing with the layers of chiffon. In one last attempt at fussing, she molded the dupatta around Nasreen's face. The material, burdened by the weight of the silver trim, fell naturally as it was.

"Everyone is here. Go!" Nasreen gently pushed her mother out the bedroom door.

As soon as Laila left, Nasreen pushed back the dupatta, which fell to her shoulders revealing her tired face.

"How awful do I look?" Nasreen pleaded to her friends circled around her on the floor.

Mona spoke first. "You look beautiful. It's your *mayoon* ceremony."

"Yes, you look nothing short of buttered cream. Like us," Sara joked and huddled against her sister, Shabana.

Both were dressed in light marigold salwar kameezes sans the metallic trim décor. The girls' smiles lit up their slender faces. Kate had never seen the sisters look anything short of stunning no matter what color they wore.

"Stop," Nasreen said playfully, enjoying the attention.

Her hands and feet were painted in henna artistry, her black hair highlighted in deep maroon. The yellow glow of her skin was still apparent from yesterday's henna fight. The girls, in tradition, hurled chunks of the wet henna clay at each other until their skin and clothing, as well as the wall, had a yellow-reddish tint.

"They are all here," Sameer's voice came from the hallway.

"Sameer, take our picture. Please."

"Okay, hurry up."

Nasreen raised an eyebrow at her twin in warning not to rush her. The girls shuffled around on the floor moving pillows and blankets out of the way to kneel close to Nasreen. Folding chairs were stacked against the pink flowered wallpaper. Handsome gifts were piled in the corner and atop her white desk with mauve trim that matched the dresser drawers and the bed frame; a child's dreamy slumber room transformed into a bride's quarters.

Kate sat on one hip, her cushioned shoulder pressing against Nasreen. Sameer snapped the photo.

"Okay, everyone out," Nasreen ordered, shooing everyone toward the door.

Outside, the party gathered. Cars lined the gutters of Maple Street. Guests spilled out of the cars into the darkened and lazy suburban road. The women each brought a platter, alight by several candles melted in a mold. The men in their traditional white tunics carried toddlers, and the older children chased each other around. The gold in the wives' outfits sparkled in the candlelight creating a festive parade to the doorstep of the bride's home.

Kate, Shabana, and Sara lined up at the door, flattening their bodies against the railing to allow the parade of flames and glittering guests to enter. In chant, women and girls flowed upstairs, men downstairs.

On the main floor, the furniture was moved and replaced by blankets and elaborately embroidered cushions for the bride. The women found places on the floor, ready for the rituals of the ceremony to begin.

Kate tiptoed back to Nasreen's bedroom. In the pink room, preserved by a girl's tears and dreams, a teenager's secrets and confessions, and a bride's hopes and doubts, she found her friend hidden behind the yellow dupatta waiting to be escorted out. The girlfriends surrounded Nasreen, and Kate fell in behind the entourage.

"Kate!" Nasreen paused. She twisted around but was too covered in cloth to see behind her.

Shabana motioned to Kate to step up and stand on the other side of Nasreen. "Brace her so she doesn't trip," she commanded.

The other girls held a corner of the decorative yellow veil like a canopy and paraded down the hallway. Kate quickly tucked a hand on the inside of Nasreen's elbow. A million times, Kate had walked along this corridor leaving a scuff mark or two on the striped wallpapered wall, and now it seemed the longest walk of her life.

The girls guided Nasreen across the living room, slowly to the cushions. The elders grabbed at Nasreen, pulling her down; Shabana and Kate resisted. Nasreen dangled, half squatting, held up by her childhood friends at each elbow and tugged at her petticoat by the elders—a pendulum between girlhood and cultural calling.

The older women eagerly arranged the dupatta over the subdued face of the bride and began adorning her with jewels. Upon Nasreen's limp mehendi-painted hand, they placed rings and massaged glass colored bracelets onto her wrists, interleaving them with rhinestone-studded ones until her forearms were covered, then decorated her painted feet with anklets and toe rings. Kate watched the transformation of a girl into a woman, a childhood friend into a traditional Muslim bride.

Kate smiled to herself remembering the summer in Pakistan, the flirtatious encounters and secret rendezvous. She recalled the afternoon at Clifton Beach. She and Nasreen had mounted a dung-smelling camel and rode the beast along the stretch of sand, their bodies rocking in rhythm to the camel's stride and their hair clinging to their gleeful faces. The waves of the Arabian Sea formed silvery peaks in the afternoon sun. They squealed carefree, remiss of small jealousies and misinterpreted affections. They did not have permission to be there unescorted and in mixed company. There was a blank page in Kate's photo album of that day because Nasreen had snatched her photos and hidden them away lest her mother should see.

Nanima clasped the *tikka* in Nasreen's hair so that the strand of uncut pearls lay along her hairline and the jeweled medallion hung on her forehead. Laila followed by clasping bell-shaped earrings that matched the choker and the medallion upon a languorous Nasreen.

Lastly, in a single motion, her grandmother placed the choker of precious stones around Nasreen's neck, cracked her knuckles above her granddaughter's head, and pressed the blessing of prosperity and fertility onto the top of her veil and down along her cheeks.

As Kate watched grandmother and granddaughter, their heads bowed together, she knew that despite Nasreen's unfaltering commitment and passion, as a first-generation Muslim-American, she was a fiercely independent, sagacious woman well aware of her own irradiant beauty and sensuality that no veil could conceal.

Chapter 13

RAIN ON THE WINDSHIELD

Chicago 1998

The morning light filtered in through the blinds casting light and dark shadows across the notepaper lying on Kate's chest. At some point while reading Nasreen's letters she must have dozed. She heard the grunt and wheezing of a large vehicle pulling to a stop. A few moments later, the buzzer sounded to her apartment. She rose out of bed and parted the faded green curtains. Down below, she could just make out Neil's white sneakers peeking out from under the awning.

The moving truck was parked in front of her apartment building. She struggled to open the sash. Finally, the window trim unstuck, cracking the paint around the seal, and the sash flew upward, crashing against the top frame. The dawn smelled of approaching rain. The streets were just beginning to sprinkle with cars, driven by students heading to the university in hopes of grabbing a free parking spot within reasonable walking distance to campus.

"Hey!" she yelled down.

Neil looked up and saw her at the window.

"What are you doing?" she called.

"You forgot your jacket." He held up the navy sweatshirt. "I'm too lazy to mail things. Do you want me to bring it up?"

"Hang on. I will be right down," she yelled, disappearing from the windowsill.

Kate flung open the dresser drawers, threw a couple pairs of jeans, shirts, a jacket, and undergarments into a duffel bag. She grabbed her backpack and threw in her wallet and a book she had started reading but couldn't finish. She dressed quickly, grabbed her toiletries, scribbled a note to her roommate, and ran out of the apartment.

Neil was checking the trailer latch when she appeared, looking disheveled with her bag slung over her shoulder.

"You okay?" he asked. "Your eyes are a little puffy."

"I didn't sleep well, but I am fine," she responded firmly. "You need a navigator, right?"

"Yes. Absolutely!" he said, giving Kate a reassuring nod.

With her sweatshirt still in his hand, he hurried over to the passenger side, opened the door, jumped up, and cleared the seat of the clutter. He folded the maps quickly and tucked them next to the seat and threw the rental paperwork into the glove compartment.

"Okay, ready. Just step up there," he instructed.

Kate lifted her duffel bag and stumbled as her backpack fell off her shoulder.

"Oh, here, I'll take those," Neil offered. "There is room behind the seats for luggage."

Neil walked around to the driver's side, stashing the bags and sweatshirt in the back part of the cabin before climbing in.

"Okay," Neil said, rubbing his hands together. "We've got CDs here, lots of snacks in the cooler. Plenty of coffee." He pointed to the large thermos in the middle console. "Maps are here. I marked the route." He paused and looked at Kate for a lingering moment as if he thought she might be joking with him and at any time jump out of the truck.

"Do you need to call your dad?" he asked in a serious tone.

"I'll call on the road."

Neil bit his lower lip, heaved on the brake, and cranked the gearshift into drive. His arm muscle popped from beneath his faded White Sox T-shirt.

From her high perch, she watched the large maple trees that lined Washington Park pass. The university quad was sprinkled with students trudging wearily to first-period classes on a Monday morning. They drove past the corner bar, The Boathouse, which had quarter pitchers of Long Island iced tea on Tuesdays, and the beatnik coffee shop, which had poetry readings on Wednesdays.

Out on Sheridan Drive, Chicago traffic was in full swing. They passed the aquarium, Navy Pier, and morning joggers beating the paths along Lake Michigan. Somewhere along Interstate 55 to St. Louis, she fell into a deep sleep.

$$* * * * *$$

"WAKE UP!"

Neil slapped Kate on the thigh as he turned the keys in the ignition. The revving engine of the U-Haul sputtered, rattled, and died. Neil stretched his foot to the floor engaging the brake.

"Some navigator you are. Pit stop."

They were somewhere in the cornfields of central Illinois at a truck stop and food mart. Kate's head ached.

She jumped down on wobbly knees and headed into the food mart for breakfast. Neil was pumping gas into the U-Haul when she returned.

"This is going to burn a hole in my credit card," he complained.

"You are no longer a struggling graduate student, remember?" Kate said with a smirk. "You have a real job."

"Good to see a smile on your face. By the way," Neil said, pointing behind her, "see that pay phone over there?"

Kate turned to see the phone box at the side of the food mart.

"You should use it."

She looked out across the spans of cornfields momentarily before confronting the calls she needed to make.

She called her dad first and told him she was taking a break and helping a friend move to Austin.

"Call me tomorrow," he said, sounding more concerned than when he had put her on a plane to India.

Then she called her professor.

"We have group meeting today. You will miss it."

Kate said nothing. The answer was obvious.

"You should tell me in advance of these things," he continued.

"It's a family emergency," she lied.

"Oh, I hope everything is okay. Can I do anything?" he asked in an apologetic tone that made Kate feel guilty for lying.

"No, I will be back at the end of the week."

For the first time in days, she felt her chest expand and lower in a deep breath. She imagined her professor sunk in his high-back chair.

"Not a missing person?" Neil asked, glancing up from studying the map laid out across his seat.

"No. But it felt good to be one, if only for a few hours."

"Sometimes it is good to let the world get along without you temporarily. It will survive. And so will you."

His direct look stung her like an open wound. She blinked back tears and jumped into the cabin.

When they began driving again, Neil probed. "You got all this open road to clear your head. What's on your mind?"

She had told him the basics but didn't know how to talk more about her confrontation with Nasreen and how she should have known what happened to her best friend. She was overburdened with disbelief and guilt. She didn't want to speak about how lost Krishna seemed trying to cope with her mother's death and failing medical school and now abandoning life temporarily to go to India. She definitely couldn't talk about Tariq or her desire for him. She wished she had been truthful and said she was single. Perhaps it would have made a difference. Instead, she shook her head with reticence at Neil's invitation for conversation.

"Later," she said.

She watched the raindrops splatter in random spots across the windshield, falling faster and faster until one splatter merged with the next and the windshield wipers smeared the rain across the windows, creating a blur of water.

They crossed through Missouri traveling on Interstate 44 and moved at a crawl's pace in traffic. The drone of the rain pounded into her head. The rumble of the truck's engine rattled through the floor of the cabin and through her numb feet, up her legs, and into the bones in her back.

"I don't understand what he wants," Kate fumed about her professor's maddening behavior. "Nothing is good enough, ever!" she vented. "I think he is really going wacko from the stress of grants and being a perfectionist. Mei defended her thesis almost a year ago, but there was always one more thing, one more thing. He promised to give her a recommendation for another position. It never happened. Then she up and left. Who knows where she is!"

"Mei?" Neil struggled to follow the conversation above the rickety cabin noise.

"Yes. She is gone."

Mei was a graduate student from Taiwan, and to Kate's knowledge, their advisor had never signed off on her dissertation, which forced Mei to continue working in the lab to keep her visa status. She was too respectful to challenge him. Last week she disappeared.

"One of the guys in the lab mentioned she had a relative in Boston, so maybe she went there. But she only had two weeks on her visa to find employment before being forced to leave the country. You have to run away to get out," she snapped. "Maybe I just won't go back."

"Are you running away?" Neil asked sarcastically.

Kate clenched her jaw.

"You can't quit," he said rationally. "Yeah, okay, you have an ass for a professor, so what? You're smart. You'll get through it. Besides," he continued, "the chair of the department won't let you quit."

"Why would he care?" she said.

"If you weren't good enough, you wouldn't be there. It doesn't look good for the department to lose students, especially female students."

His words ricocheted into her chest. Kate stared at the road ahead.

"I'm done driving. I have to stop for the night," Neil said wearily, giving up on the conversation.

On the outskirts of Springfield, Missouri, with nothing visible but a gas station, a repair shop with a stack of lopsided tires in front of the garage, a Waffle House, and a budget motel, Neil parallel parked the truck at the motel.

"I'll get us a room. Two beds or one?"

In response to Kate's glare, he said, "Okay, two. Just checking to see if you were listening anymore."

Dinner at the Waffle House and three beers later, Neil fell into a soft snore. Having slept much of the day in the truck, Kate lay on her side listening to the light drizzle hitting the pavement outside their door.

* * * * *

KATE AWOKE ABRUPTLY to a door shutting. Her shirt clung to her skin. Lying in bed, she scanned the thin, daisy-printed bedspread, the brown curtains, and the bolt on the thick door. Her mind was momentarily vacant as to where she was. The tangy odor of citrus ammonia cleaner reached her nose.

She remembered, the budget motel.

"Good, you are awake," Neil's voice bellowed through the small room.

The ammonia smell gave way to the scent of sweet aloe leaves and aftershave lotion. Neil ruffled his damp hair with a pea-green towel and tossed the towel on the floor.

"If we get an early start, we should make it to Dallas before dark, depending on traffic."

Kate sat up and leaned back against the flimsy headboard that promptly banged against the wall. She hugged her knees and watched Neil pack his duffel bag.

"Take your time. I'm just going to grab some waters in the lobby and study the map."

A quick zip of his bag and Neil unbolted the door and walked out. The heavy door closed with a bang, sending an echo down the corridor.

Lunging out of bed, Kate reached for the bolt on the door and turned it quickly, locking herself inside. With her body pressed against the door, she heard voices coming from several rooms down followed by slamming doors and roller wheels scratching along the balcony of the motel.

Somewhere, she realized, in crossing from the northern Great Lakes into the Ozark highlands, Neil was no longer leaving a place but steadily moving toward a new start, a new career.

She turned from the door and saw her reflection in the mirror above the desk. The corners of the mirror were rusted where the metallic coating had peeled off. The objects on the desk reflected in the mirror. The phone's message button was still flashing. There was a display of brochures and a brown leatherbound Bible lying next to a pad of paper and a plastic pen, both stamped with the motel's emblem.

What was she running from? A manipulative professor? A childhood best friend, wronged? A broken heart? Her scheduled DNA test?

She missed her mother more than ever. The void in her chest grew broad and ugly. She crossed her arms over her chest and slid with her back against the door to the floor. In a huddled position, she tried to suppress the void from rupturing and breaking her apart, but the monstrous space rose in her throat. She sobbed then, long heaving sobs. On the floor of the sterile, cheap ammonia-smelling motel room, she cried until the void inside her fell away to numbness.

"Housekeeping!"

The knock on the door kicked her in the back.

Kate jumped up, startled.

"Please," her weakened voice cracked. "Please come back later."

"Yes, ma'am."

Kate listened to the maid's footsteps shuffle away, followed by a knock on the adjacent door.

Kate climbed into the cabin of the U-Haul. Neil looked impatient but said nothing as he turned the key in the ignition.

The long hours on the road and the passing landscape calmed her. Kate told Neil stories of India and Pakistan.

"You never shared those stories when we were dating," Neil remarked.

Kate shrugged. "Too preoccupied with lab, I guess."

"I'm sorry if I hurt you by breaking it off," he said sincerely. "If I stayed in Chicago...I would be lucky to date you."

Kate nodded nonchalantly.

She looked out at the plains of Oklahoma moving slowly across the flat horizon.

"I miss traveling," she mused. "I think that's what's so hard sometimes about graduate school. I feel trapped, like I can't see past the next week."

"You have been to a lot of places," Neil remarked. "Most people don't get to experience such places their whole lives."

"When you travel," she began again, "you can sense your future. It's an acute awareness you gain about yourself while you are in an entirely different place. You can taste your ambitions in the grit of the streets. You can sense your soul in the architecture. You watch locals' lips move, their words are incomprehensible, but yet you have a vague sense of what they're talking about. It challenges you to the core!"

She looked over at Neil. He had remained silent, listening intently and glancing at her from time to time.

"You know what I mean?" she asked, searching his face for acknowledgment.

"Not really." He smiled. "Traveling to Austin, Texas, is about as exciting as it gets for me. But you make foreign travel sound very intriguing."

"I can't afford to travel now."

"Apply for a fellowship overseas."

She filed the suggestion away for the future.

"Someday I will write about traveling. I'll write about India."

"Why someday? Just write."

"I don't have time. I have to write a thesis." She wrinkled her nose.

"No one is asking you to tackle a whole book. Write a paragraph or a page here or there. Keep a journal. Gee, Kate, you are allowed to have hobbies in graduate school. Just begin."

He looked at the road and back at her, challenging.

"You know?" he continued. "Maybe your lab mate Mei didn't run away. Maybe she took control, took a risk."

* * * * *

AFTER TWO days of slow driving in the U-Haul, they reached Neil's apartment complex in the humid subtropical climate of inland Texas.

They grabbed a cab to Tablao Flamenco, a Spanish restaurant near an old mission, for dinner. In a corner of the cozy restaurant, a pair strummed classic guitars and a woman in a sleek red dress that ruffled around her ankles snapped her fingers and stomped gracefully in flamenco style. A crowd of boisterous locals had gathered to enjoy the music and clapped loudly. They clapped faster and faster as the dancer stomped so forcefully that the ruffled comb shook in her hair. The flamenco sounds and Latin language filled their ears and replaced the drone of the truck traveling over twelve hundred miles of road.

"I feel like I've been transplanted into another world," Kate remarked as she cautiously took a bite of paella.

"Yes, it will take some getting used to," Neil agreed. "Although this Spanish-Mexican fare," he said with a mouthful of salty black beans, "I can definitely get accustomed to."

He washed the beans down with a gulp of Modelo beer and waved to the waitress.

"Two more, please," Neil called out, not bothering to ask Kate if she wanted another.

"Okay, but this is the last one," she cried. "Three is enough for me!"

"It just feels good to be done with driving," Neil said. "Come on, hitchhiker, celebrate with me," he mocked.

"Hey!" she warned playfully.

The musicians traded their guitars for a double-headed drum and started playing salsa. Several locals rose to their feet and stomped to the rhythm. The flamenco dancer now held a pair of maracas and swung her hips. An old man with a bright smile urged Kate out of her chair. He took her wrist in his thin hand and led her in dance.

"Quick-quick-slow," he chanted as he rolled his shoulders and shifted his feet in a box step.

The man had the agility of someone half his age. Kate tried to keep pace, and when her feet stomped offbeat, the man took her wrist and effortlessly engaged the beat, pumping through her arms to her feet until she felt the groove in her steps.

Neil admired the scene until Kate cajoled him to join her. The fluid music and cheap beer eased their minds, and the dancing loosened their stiff bones.

* * * * *

THE TAXI DROPPED them off in the wee early-morning hours at Neil's apartment complex. Neil jiggled his key in the wrong lock. A dog barked. Lights flicked.

"Run!"

Kate grabbed Neil's arm, running around the corner of the stairwell and huddling together to hide. He smelled of aloe, sweat, and beer.

"You're going to be a big hit in this complex," Kate laughed.

"Shhh," Neil shushed her. "All the apartments look the same!"

Neil finally found the right door. They stumbled into the vacant apartment. Kate laughed loudly now that they were inside. She grabbed him to steady herself, and he wrapped his arms around her. She kissed him hungrily and he responded. She unbuttoned his shirt and moved her hands to his waist.

"Kate," Neil gasped for breath. "Do you have to head back to Chicago tomorrow?"

"Yes."

He threw off her shirt and fiddled with her bra.

"You can stay a few days."

They fell onto the futon, the only piece of furniture they had managed to drag inside before heading to Tablao Flamenco.

* * * * *

THE EARLY-MORNING light flooded in through the curtainless windows. Kate was entwined in the sleeping bag. Her head ached, and her back was stiff from sleeping on the futon. She tried to focus on the room's beige carpet and beige walls that smelled of fresh paint. The sounds of rhumba and salsa played in her ears.

Neil snorted. He was sprawled across the futon, his eyes shut and his mouth wide open.

No!

An alarm went off in Kate's head as she remembered them stumbling into bed in their drunken state. She slipped off the futon, gathering her clothes and bag.

Dressed and with her bag slung over her shoulder, she watched Neil sleeping for a moment, then turned and let the door click softly behind her.

She walked to the 7-Eleven store on the corner and found a pay phone.

"Yes, I will accept the charges," she heard her father respond to the operater.

"Hi, Dad."

"Kate, are you all right? Where are you?"

"I'm in Austin. Sorry to wake you."

"Are you okay?" he asked again.

The concern in his voice made her eyes swell.

"I'm fine," she said. "Nothing like a road trip to take your mind off things." She laughed nervously.

"What is on your mind, Kat?"

She could not contain the emotion welling up inside. Her body started to shake as she sobbed into the receiver.

"I don't know what I'm doing here, Dad," she cried. "I don't know what I'm running from."

Her voice quivered. She squeezed her eyes shut in anquish.

The 7-Eleven was abandoned except for the clerk behind the counter biting his nails and a truck driver who glanced at Kate as he poured himself a cup of coffee. She recoiled around the phone and tried to control her sobs and sniffling.

"Come home, Kat."

"I feel so lost."

"Just come home."

"Dad!"

"I'm here. I am always here."

"Okay," she said, taking a deep breath. "I will buy a bus ticket today."

"Forget the bus, Kat! I will get you a plane ticket. Just stay on the line."

Chapter 14
ROAd FROM BEGUMpET

Hyderabad 1987

S undays in India are reserved for visiting relatives and paying respect to elders. Most shops are closed. Aunty Samina called for a driver to take them to Marah Bahri's house in Begumpet. Marah Bahri was the sister of Nanima's deceased husband, and Nanima visited the elderly woman every Sunday. Aunty Samina and Aunty Zehba and Nasreen's cousins would meet them there. Kate anticipated seeing Tariq again.

There was no certainty as to when the driver would arrive. Kate watched Nanima mill about, expecting nothing and no one in particular to visit. Having been widowed for thirty years, she walked in her own shroud of white. She saw daughters and nieces married off and settled into their in-laws' homes, and sons uproot and move to Pakistan, neighbors disappear, and neighborhoods transform.

Nanima's sons urged their mother relentlessly to move to Pakistan. She refused to leave Banjara Hills. Only Aunty Samina and Aunty Zehba stayed in Hyderabad. Whatever loneliness or heartache Nanima endured, she buried it deep in the folds of her widowed-white sari and sauntered through the present in a peaceful independence.

In the mid-morning, Nanima went to the armoire behind the dining table and removed the metal betel leaf box to prepare paan as was routine. Today, she ruffled through old photos in the adjacent drawer. Kate glimpsed the shades of white and gray in the photos as she peered across the table and longed to ask about the people captured in time.

What caused Nanima to look at them with quiet nostalgia? Kate wondered.

To Kate, pictures were her past and her future. Only in pictures could she relive the image of her mother.

"You have her same intensity and vibrancy," her father used to say when she engulfed him with questions about her mother.

As Kate matured into her teenage years, her father discovered resemblances to her mother: the curve of her jaw, the slope of her nose, or the way she curled her mouth when she was indecisive.

"Don't fret," he told her. "Your mother used to fret."

Through adolescence, Kate studied her reflection in the bathroom mirror, watching for physical changes as her face merged with that of her mother's in the photos preserving her mother at age thirty-nine.

Nanima looked up at Kate, as if she felt the girl's focused intensity.

"Family photos?" she asked.

Nanima pursed her lips and tilted her head like she did, tick-tock, tick-tock, without speaking. She placed a photo, creased along the side, on the table in front of Kate.

The black and white photo was of a young couple taken in a different era. The woman in the photo wore a delicate sari with lace along the neckline and trim. Her light-shaded dupatta draped over her dark braid to hang at her petite waistline. The man stood stiffly beside her with a dark jacket and hat and a pleasant face. Nanima tapped lightly on the face of the woman.

"Ammi," Nanima said, pointing to the woman and then pointing to Laila, who approached the table.

"I haven't seen this photo in a long time," Laila sighed, leaning over Kate's shoulder and carefully picking up the picture.

"It is a photo of my mother and father as newlyweds," Laila explained. "See here, my mother still has the mehendi design on her hands."

"Mother?"

Kate squinted and focused on the woman's hands clasped across her abdomen. The intricate design on her wrists disappeared beneath the lace of her dupatta.

"Let me see," Nasreen interjected, appearing beside her mother and taking the photo from her hand

"But how can that be your mother?" Kate asked Laila, confused.

"My parents died about ten years after this photo was taken. I was two," Laila said with dull emotion. "Nanima raised us. My sister and brothers and me."

Kate looked at Laila with disbelief. She was Nasreen's mother who drove them to the mall, picked them up from after-school activities or the movie theaters, and cooked Indian food at any time of day whenever someone appeared at the door, expected or unexpected. Kate had never known that Nasreen's mother was orphaned as a toddler in India!

"Your parents died?" Kate questioned in shock.

"My mother was Nanima's older sister." Laila took the photo from Nasreen and handed it back to Nanima, who looked at the photo endearingly like it was the first time she laid eyes on it.

"So, Nanima is…" Kate's face contorted as she struggled to understand.

"I was the youngest and too young to know any other mother than Nanima," Laila interjected. "But I know it's hard to lose a mother so young." Laila placed her hand on Kate's shoulder. "We were lucky, my brothers, Aunty Zehba, and I. We had Nanima."

Nanima rocked her head, tick-tock, tick-tock.

Kate looked to Nasreen for explanation and reassurance.

"She has always been Nanima to me," Nasreen remarked firmly.

"How did they die? Your parents?" Kate asked cautiously.

Laila looked troubled and seemed to retreat from the question. Nanima continued to study the photograph in her hand.

"They were killed in a car crash, supposedly," Nasreen answered impatiently for her mother.

"Supposedly?"

"They were driving home from Begumpet when their car wrecked. There were no other cars involved," Laila said, but her eyes looked somewhere else.

"Their bodies were pulled from the car and left on the hillside, not far from here," Nasreen continued where her mother left off. "My father told me everything. Times were bad then after the Partition of India in 1947 from the British Empire that created India and Pakistan. I read all about it," Nasreen stated with passion. "People found themselves in the wrong place at the wrong time. No reason, no justice. My grandparents thought they were safe here—in a Hindu-majority state but with a Muslim ruler who wanted Hyderabad to remain independent. There was brutality on both sides."

Laila took her daughter's hand and finished telling her story.

"Nanima was already a widow at twenty-five and mother to Samina. Then the accident happened, a lost husband, a lost sister, no time to mourn. She became an instant mother to three small nephews and two nieces, me and Zehba. Samina was six months older than I. We thought we were twins growing up."

Nanima interrupted in Urdu; her tone was short. She placed the photo among the others in the thin drawer of the armoire and shut the drawer with as much force as a small woman could have, then took a tiny key from underneath the folds of her sari and locked the cabinet, ending the morning's tribute.

Kate was left to ponder the questions swimming in her mind as she tried to form an image of her own mother's face fading in her memory.

✳ ✳ ✳ ✳ ✳

BY LATE MORNING, a paddy wagon showed up to take them to Marah Bahri's in Begumpet, on the other side of the park from Banjara Hills. The paddy wagon drove by way of a circuitous route, clamoring over the steep inclines and around the curves, many times nearly colliding with oncoming traffic. Sana had fallen asleep, her head vibrating against the window.

The modest home set precariously perched at the end of a rubble street. The driveway sloped to one side making the home appear uneven, ready to slide down and sink into the rising road.

Aunty Samina, Max, Hari, Yasmine, and Azra greeted them exuberantly, having already arrived. Nasreen, Yasmine, and Kate sat cross-legged on the floor. Azra and Sana sat off to the side whispering together, or rather Azra listening to Sana describe elementary school life in the US. Kate tried inconspicuously to dislodge betel nuts from between her teeth, stuck there from the morning's paan.

The older women sat on the sinking sofa conversing in Urdu, Laila in a yellow cotton sari, Aunty Samina in a rose-colored one, and Nanima and Marah Bahri both in widow white.

For a while, Yasmine and Nasreen translated but grew tired of the wearisome conversation and at times broke into soft laughter at the loss in translation.

"What? What did they say? I heard my name," Kate asked in anticipation.

"I think they are arranging your marriage," Sana said, giggling.

"You should speak now or forever hold your tongue," Yasmine said, joining in the teasing.

"Whatever."

"You think we are kidding?"

Kate looked up curiously at Nanima. Behind the horn-rimmed glasses, the old woman's eyes smiled at her, but her lips remained pursed. The nerves of her jaw twitched between smiling and pursing.

Kate bent her neck forward in an awkward bow of respect to the elder decree. Nanima smiled, revealing blackened gums and red, paan-stained teeth.

With no place to go, the afternoon passed quietly. After a lunch of spinach dal, *biryani*, and *naan* and more paan, Nasreen and Yasmine flipped through Indian fashion magazines, Azra dozed on her mother's lap, and Sana colored a picture of Nanima's house and sang softly to herself as she drew lifelike figures of all of her aunties and cousins. Kate fell asleep under the spinning fan until she heard Aunty Zehba's voice fill the lackadaisical air and rose immediately lest Aunty Zehba should catch her sleeping and complain she was not adjusting to India time.

Rahim and Anees had finally arrived in India. Aunty Zehba beamed widely as she presented her sons to the family. Tariq stood off to the side while his brothers absorbed the attention and shot Kate a sly smile that made her heart jump.

Rahim had grown a beard to mark himself ready to become a married man. He wore a traditional button-down shirt and brown trousers and respectfully greeted Nanima and his aunts and gave Nasreen a warm, brotherly greeting. Anees tried to appear relaxed in a James Dean style sport shirt and jeans but shuffled nervously, seemingly uncertain about his transition into a man-in-waiting. He and Nasreen gave each other quick pecks on the cheek, avoiding eye contact, and Kate glared at Anees when his eyes met her to remind him that all was not forgotten, never would be forgotten.

* * * * *

BY LATE AFTERNOON, they were back in the paddy wagon on a detour toward the city before heading home. Aunty Samina, Yasmine, Azra, and Tariq joined them. The older boys and Aunty Zehba went separately.

The heat closed in on Kate as they walked through the shopping district, a shock after spending most of the day indoors under spinning fans. Select shops were open on Sundays if you knew what you were looking for and the right place to find it.

Kate followed the group down an alleyway and into a jewelry store with no sign. She stepped up to admire the jewelry behind the cases before realizing she was alone.

"Up here," Nasreen hissed.

Kate looked up to see the silver row of bells around Aunty Samina's ankles disappear to the floor above. Nasreen was steadying Nanima as she climbed the circular open stairwell. Kate hurried up the stairs behind them.

The floor above opened to a casino of businessmen huddled over tables, counting stones, weighing, and scrutinizing gems with dainty magnifiers strapped over one eye like a patch. Patrons crowded around as if they were watching the roulette wheel, anticipating a win.

Kate leaned close to Nasreen and whispered, "Are we supposed to be here?"

"This is how you buy jewels in India. Really expensive jewels."

A salesman waved Nanima and her entourage to his open table. Laila squeezed a chair in beside Aunty Samina and Nanima. Azra and Sana hovered next to their mothers. The man went away for several minutes and returned with large black velvet boxes. As soon as the salesman creaked open the first box, Nasreen grabbed Kate's wrist with one hand and pressed her free hand to her chest.

"Look at those rubies," Nasreen gasped. "And diamonds!" She squeezed Kate's wrist harder.

"Ouch!" Kate cried.

"They are gorgeous!" Yasmine exclaimed.

Sameer and Tariq were less interested in the jewels and more interested in the two guards who stood at a stance by the only exit, both hands on their rifles slung around their shoulders.

"Check out the AK-52," Tariq whispered to Sameer.

Kate, still immobilized by Nasreen's grip, returned her gaze to the ruby necklace and earring set. They were exquisite against the bed of black velvet. The base of the earrings was a mosaic of rubies with a diamond in the center, and from the base hung a gold half-moon of inlaid diamonds and rubies curled around a set of three pearls. The man tilted the box upright and the half-moons swung gleaming, dancing in the light.

Aunty Samina and Nanima handled the necklace and started haggling over the price.

The man snapped the lid shut and put the rubies aside and opened another case. This one was a sapphire set.

"Oooh!" the women cooed.

"I love sapphires," Nasreen squealed. "Makes you want to get married just to wear them, huh?"

Kate gave Nasreen a worried look.

"I'm kidding."

"I would like emeralds anyway," Kate said with a smirk.

After much debate and more haggling, the women decided on the ruby set for Rahim's bride, Haseena. The armed doormen scrutinized their purchase before allowing them to exit the upper-level alleyway shop.

Down the winding stairway in the store below, Kate admired a set of red bangles far more dull and artificial than the real ones tucked under the folds of Aunty Samina's sari.

"A souvenir from India," Tariq said as he pulled forth a few rupees from his pocket and spilled them onto the counter.

"May I have some too? Oh, pleeease, Tariq," squealed Sana.

"Of course, my little cousin."

The salesman scooped up the coins without counting them and handed over the bangles, the red set to Kate and a pink set to Sana.

"Thank you," Kate said happily, admiring the red bangles.

"You're welcome," Tariq responded cordially.

"Chelo," Yasmine called from the door leading to the alleyway.

They snaked through the alley, out onto a main road. Nanima purchased paan for all to share before piling into the idling paddy wagon. Tariq gently jostled the snoozing driver, who immediately shot upright, looked around, and jerked the van into traffic.

"Just one more stop," Tariq yelled over the paddy wagon's muffler. "We need to pick up some chicken."

He rolled down his window to scan the shops as the car sped along the busy street. The dust, heat, and noise poured in through the open window.

"Here. Stop here," Tariq yelled to the driver.

The driver halted mid-street, mid-traffic. Persistent honking pursued.

"Be right back," Tariq said, jumping out.

"I will go with you," Sameer called, quickly unleashing the door.

He turned back around and stuck his head in the window.

"Kate, stay in the car this time. No sitting in rickshaws and stopping traffic," he said, flashing a cocky smile.

She returned a steady glare.

"What is that about?" questioned Aunty Samina.

"Nothing," replied Nasreen. "Just hurry, Sameer."

Tariq and Sameer headed toward a shop with skinned chicken carcasses dangling under a tattered red and white striped awning. "Fine Foods," the sign read. Below the lettering, crates of empty cola bottles formed a column against the wall. A man squatted on a bloody wooden stump chopping chicken parts. He was surrounded by cages stacked one on top of the other, each filled with bobbing, squawking chickens. Some of the cages were covered with burlap. In the open cages, the chickens snapped their heads side to side, responding to the movement on the street. Underneath the table stump, a satisfied-looking feral cat lounged in the shade.

A few moments later, the boys returned with a wrapped package of chicken pieces looking proud as if returning from a hunt.

Now dusk, the wagon meandered through the crowded streets transporting the group back to Banjara Hills. A week ago during her maiden voyage through the heart of Hyderabad, she had clutched the side of the car for dear life. Now Kate watched the street life, unfazed by the chaos and congestion. The sideways rocking of the van teased her with sleep as the paan's aphrodisiac kicked in. Suddenly, the vehicle came to a screeching halt.

Thump!

Kate slid onto the floor, hitting the backside of the seat in front and landing partly on Tariq's lap. He grabbed her waist.

"What happened?" she questioned, blushing.

Tariq pushed her abruptly off his lap.

"Go! Go! Go!" he demanded, waving the driver forward furiously.

The traffic was starting to weave around the van blocking its path.

"We hit a man on a bike!" Sameer shouted.

"What?"

"Go that way, now!" Tariq was hovering over the driver pointing to an escape route.

"To the right! To the right!" Sameer called out, taking Tariq's lead and directing the driver.

"We have to stop and see if he's alright!" Kate shouted back.

"No! It will cause a riot," Tariq snapped. "Trust me! You don't know!"

She sat back, angry.

"It's better to keep going," Sameer stated in a steady voice.

"People are helping him," Nasreen consoled. "We can't stop."

Kate looked horrified at her best friend as a scene of what might be flashed in her mind. The wagon lurched forward. Tariq braced her again and continued to shout at the driver. The driver accelerated heavily away from the gathering crowd. Glancing out the back window, Kate watched a mob forming. Men waved their fists in the air. She looked at Tariq with his fists clenched, a fierce expression on his face.

Nasreen's mother looked fatigued and concerned but remained silent. Nanima sat wedged next to the window, lips still pursed, eyes squinting ready for sleep.

Despite Nasreen and Sameer having grown up in America and not India, it appeared to Kate that they both nonetheless held an intrinsic understanding of their ancestral home that subliminally dictated their actions in extreme situations. She relinquished and let her weight sink into the creaking seat springs.

The driver had turned down a side road and onto the throughway.

Tariq stared intensely out the window, his fists still clenched.

*****

KATE FELL INTO a deep sleep on a pile of pillows under the spinning fan after Rahmsing served a late dinner. Nanima placed a sheet across her.

Kate dreamt of strutting chickens, their wings arched back, white chests puffed out, displaying ruby necklaces. The chickens paraded back and forth across a ravine, the jewels sparkling as they prudently cocked their heads side to side.

Slowly, the dangling rubies turned to drops of blood.

Chapter 15

KRIShNA'S DARKROOM

Chicago 1998

Kate arrived into O'Hare at dusk carrying her duffel bag. If she took the 'L' to Evanston, she'd be home in an hour and would call her dad.

She shuffled slowly toward the exit as if her bag weighed far more than it appeared. Her eyes tracked the floor. She almost didn't see him standing there when she walked out of the terminal.

"Hi, Kat."

"Dad!"

The sight of her father was overwhelming. She froze. Travelers weaved to either side. Her father approached and circled his arms around her. Kate pressed her cheek against the breast pocket of her father's shirt. The two of them stood together as passengers formed an hourglass path around them.

"Let me take your bag," Ian finally said as he led her out of the crowd and to a water feature in the main terminal.

"Sit."

"Thanks for coming, dad," Kate said, regaining her composure and taking a seat on the edge of the fountain.

The sound of the cascading water pacified her mind.

"What's wrong, Kat?"

She pondered his question for a moment. It had been a long time since she talked, really talked, to her father. She didn't know how to start the conversation. Maybe he didn't either. But he was here now, listening.

Kate breathed deeply.

"I don't know if I will get through graduate school. Somedays, I feel I will go into the lab and the walls will just cave in on me."

Acknowledging this to her father was painful. She didn't look at him but instead watched the arcs of water flow from the top basin to the bottom basin, a sort of miniature replica of the Buckingham Fountain.

"Take it one day at a time, Kat," Ian said.

"Yeah. I guess," she shrugged.

"Hey, I happen to think you are brilliant," her father remarked with compassion. "Whatever you want to do, you will do it and be great at it. Hang in there." He squeezed her shoulder.

She nodded and gave her father a half-smile.

"Tell me, why did you hitch a ride to Texas, Kat? It was not in your nature and it was a little disconcerting."

"I was upset. Nasreen and I had a…confrontation."

"I don't quite see how that would make you run away to Texas."

"She lied to me, Dad! She kept this horrible secret from me for years," Kate revealed. "A best friend wouldn't do that!"

"Well, did she have a reason for keeping the secret? To protect something or someone?"

Kate watched another crowd of travelers flood out of the terminal dragging suitcases or cranky children toward baggage claim, taxis, and waiting families.

"Yes," Kate finally acknowledged with a heavy sigh.

"Well then what is the problem? Sounds like she is forgiven."

"It's not that simple, Dad. Part of me is angry that I didn't know," Kate said irritated. "Part of me is so amazed by her courage to overcome. I don't know if I would have had the same strength."

"You're pretty strong, Kat."

"I don't know. Nasreen and I are so different," she brooded.

"That's what makes your friendship so special," Ian said. "Yeah, you two are different, from different cultural and religious upbringings. But there is no one who knows Nasreen like you know her. You have experienced her homeland, her entire extended family! They welcomed you into their homes."

Kate looked up at her father.

"Did you ever think that maybe keeping this secret from you hurt her more than it hurt you?"

She hadn't thought about it that way.

"Am I helping? I don't know if I am making sense. I just believe your friendship goes beyond your differences," he stressed.

"You are making more sense than you know, Dad."

"You don't have to figure it all out on your own, Kat."

"Okay," she said, sounding unconvinced but relieved.

"Something tells me that isn't everything," he pried. "Come on, tell your old man. Is it about a guy?"

His insightfulness surprised her. She shook her head.

"I'll listen if you want to tell me. Otherwise, I am hungry, and we should get something to eat in Chinatown."

"Can I ask you something first?"

"Fire away."

"Why did you let me go to India and Pakistan? I was sixteen, Dad. The normal parental answer would have been, 'are you crazy?'"

"Fair question," Ian said, laughing. "In fact, I wondered why you never asked me. The normal answer would have been no," he confirmed. "But you are not normal, and neither am I. You see things in places and people like no one else, Kate. You get that from your mother. She was so insightful and compassionate."

She creased her eyebrows, intrigued.

"I knew the trip would transform you. How could I deny it? And part of me had to let you go and experience. I didn't want you to be defined by your mother's death. If I held you too close out of my own fear, I would take something away that would inhibit you from becoming you, this wonderful woman." His voice cracked slightly.

Kate sighed, touched by his words but wishing that sometimes he had crushed her just a little by holding on too tight.

"The experience overseas did transform me," she told him. "In so many ways. I have these powerful memories," Kate said, placing her hand on her heart. "Nasreen's grandmother died last summer. I remember so much about her. I remember the people, the ceremonies, and all the amazing places we visited."

Her dad listened.

"There was this guy in India," Kate said softly, looking into the cascading water again, "a cousin of Nasreen's. He was eighteen. I liked him. I liked him a lot." She smiled. "He was so carefree and interested in exploring the world. I wrote to him and thought about him over the years. He never wrote back. Then I saw him in March, at the Eid celebration at Nasreen's. He came out of nowhere. I felt like I was sixteen all over again."

She looked down again at her hands.

"He gave me this…this jewelry box. It's beautiful, but I don't know what he meant by it. I'm not sure if he really cared for me or if it was in my head. I felt foolish." She covered her eyes.

Her head felt light and dizzy from dehydration and lack of sleep.

"Well, any man who makes you feel foolish is not worth it. That being said, seeing someone after so many years, Kat, it takes time to reconnect. How do you really know he doesn't care or never cared? Was there anything in the box?"

"No. It was just an empty box. I can't help thinking that what attracts me to him may be the very thing that makes him unattainable. Doesn't matter now. He went back to New York."

Ian appeared at a loss for words.

"It wouldn't have worked, like Nasreen said."

"You are getting a little over my head," her father said.

"I have been thinking of mom a lot lately, Dad. I know she'd have the answers."

"I know I don't have all the answers, Kat. But I do know that you are strong, stronger than you think to get through everything."

Her father placed his hand on her shoulder.

"My daughter, tough as nails and soft as velvet. Now let's go grab dinner."

* * * * *

IT WAS LATE when her father dropped her at her apartment before he headed back to Rockfield. She immediately dialed Nasreen's number, not caring about the time of night.

"You missed her," Mustafa's voice echoed in her head. "She flew out last night. She said she tried calling several times."

Kate scanned the kitchen frantically. On the floor was a yellow sticky note. "Nasreen called" was scribbled in her roommate's handwriting. Kate crumpled the sticky note in her fist.

"She is on her way to Pakistan. She seemed really concerned that she couldn't reach you," Mustafa said. "Is everything okay?"

"I don't know," Kate responded vaguely.

"This has happened quickly. The Pakistani paperwork went through and there is a baby boy available for adoption at the orphanage. But that is not it! There is a baby girl too. Twins!"

"Twins?" Kate asked astonished. "Will the babies be split up?"

"Nasreen wants to adopt both! Twins!" he shouted into the phone again, this time sounding nervous. "I was still preparing to adopt one."

"Sounds like you should prepare for two," Kate said impatiently. "I'm sure it will break Nasreen's heart to split up the babies and only adopt one. She is a twin after all!"

"I know," Mustafa said, resigned. "I got Nasreen on a standby flight right away. She was stressed packing. I haven't seen her like that. Nerves, I guess."

Kate cringed remembering her and Nasreen's confrontation.

"When will she be back?"

"A few months."

"A few months?" Kate yelled into the receiver.

"At least. We do not have American papers for either baby. But she can stay with relatives. She will have lots of help with the babies. Maybe too much," he chuckled. "I should get my work done now, right?"

He sounded so lost and uncertain, traversing on foreign ground. Kate recalled Mustafa's words as she eavesdropped from the stairs, "*I can't bring a child into our lives like this.*"

And now there were two.

* * * * *

"KATE?" KRISHNA'S FATHER, Suneel appeared at the door in faded blue, wrinkled kurta pajamas.

"I'm sorry. Did I wake you?" Kate asked, glancing at her wristwatch. It was 10:15 in the morning.

"No," Suneel responded. "I was just watching TV. Please, come in." His speech was slow and deliberate.

"Is Krishna here? I really need to speak with her," Kate said rapidly.

Suneel didn't respond for a moment, still processing the question as if the words confused him.

"Yes. She is here."

Kate stood awkwardly in the foyer. The house smelled stale.

"I don't want to interrupt if she is meditating."

"Oh. No. No. You are not interrupting at all," Suneel articulated each syllable. "She is in the kitchen. You know we just returned from India?"

"Yes," Kate said, realizing she should inquire about the trip and make an attempt at small talk.

"How was India? You spent time with family, yes?"

"Oh, yes!" Suneel exclaimed. His face brightened. "It was good. We took a train to Gujarat to see my family. They are in North of India, you know? Then we spent time in Kerala with my wife's family."

"That sounds nice," Kate said.

"Yes, was very, very nice."

She followed Krishna's father into the living room. A large pillow, molded in a spoon shape, was propped against the arm of the beige couch and a blanket lay strewn on the cushion and trailed onto the floor. The coffee table was littered with several teacups, a heap of tea bags on a silver platter, a half-eaten bagel, and scattered newspapers. A stack of mail had tipped over and sprayed across the table.

Kate glanced into the kitchen. She saw the back of Krishna at the sink washing dishes. She had earphones in her ears. The cord snaked down into the pocket of her apron. Dirty dinner dishes mixed with breakfast bowls were piled on one side of the sink and clean dishes dripping with soapy water were piled on the other side. Pots with dried drops of sauce on the sides were cluttered in the middle of the stovetop waiting to be washed.

"Would you like some tea?"

"No, thanks," she answered.

Suneel walked slowly into the kitchen and tapped his daughter on the shoulder. Krishna turned and yanked the earphones from her ear.

"Kate!" Krishna's eyes widened in surprise upon seeing Kate at the entrance to the kitchen.

She wiped her hands on the apron.

"Where were you? Nasreen left for Pakistan. We called you. We were worried!"

"I'm sorry. I had to leave town for a few days," Kate said, feeling a pang of guilt. "I am back now."

"Nasreen is going to adopt twins!"

"I know. I talked with Mustafa last night. It's exciting. But she is going to be gone three months!"

"So, we have to keep busy," Krishna said, enthused. "I converted the downstairs bathroom into a darkroom. I'm printing pictures from our trip to India!"

"You're printing photos?" Kate was happy that Krishna was in good spirits after her trip.

"I was just cleaning up first," Krishna said, rolling her eyes. "I need to hire a maid," she mumbled under her breath. "Obviously, my mother did all the cleaning. I will finish the dishes later," she said, removing the apron and draping it over a chair. "Come on, I'll show you some prints."

Krishna motioned for Kate to follow her downstairs.

"I will make some tea," Suneel replied meekly as he reached for the kettle on the stove.

The basement was a large unfurnished space. Scrap rugs with fraying ends hid part of the concrete flooring. Behind a plastic curtain was a wall of wood shelving filled with aging books, board games, worn shoes, and a variety of trinkets that never made it into the display cases. There were light bulbs, linens, and tubs of outdated clothing.

"My dad plans to finish the basement. My mom wanted an entertainment space for relatives and friends when they visited from India," Krishna explained. "The idea was to corner off a bedroom on that side and finish the bathroom and tile this room, put in a stereo system, a TV, and serving area, even a pool table..."

Krishna paused, imagining the room transformed to what it should become, a place for a professor and his wife to entertain, a place to enjoy relatives visiting from the homeland.

"But it will probably stay like this forever," Krishna added, walking briskly through the utility room to the door opposite.

Kate followed and ducked under the clothing hanging from a rod between the open ceiling boards.

"Where are you taking me?"

"It will be a little tight," Krishna said, opening the bathroom door next to the dryer with stacks of folded clothes on top.

Kate squeezed into the bathroom corner between the faucet trickling over a tray of photos and a table of developing trays that straddled the toilet. The smell of silver nitrate was powerful.

"You need to wear a mask in here!" Kate exclaimed, holding a hand to her nose.

Krishna closed the door and snapped the string to a red bulb suspended from the rafters. She flipped a plastic bib over her head and tied it across her waist.

"You get used to it."

In the red glow, the sights of India were illuminated as whites and shadows. Kate drew in her breath. Freshly developed, still dripping prints of India, images similar to the ones Kate lived and breathed ten years ago, were strung like lights from one corner of the bathroom to the other. The magnificent white of a Buddhist temple exploded across the photo paper clipped to a piece of string by laundry pins. The astonishing enlargement still shimmered with wetness.

"Krishna! These are beautiful!"

In one photo, children played in mid-leap, their faces blurred and exuberant, on a rooftop terrace bounded by buildings layered with grid windows, piping, wiring, and satellite dishes.

In another, Krishna sat on a bench in a crowded market watching a man, his arm held as high as he could reach, pour a fountain of caramel liquid into a row of porcelain cups. The walls of the tea stall were constructed of recycled wooden crates with the names "Black, Darjeeling, and Assam" imprinted in black ink across the front and stacked five and six high.

"You look like you are having fun." Kate squinted at the photo, her nose just inches from it.

"I love taking a pause to watch the chai wallahs do their thing. They are very entertaining." Krishna chuckled. "I stocked up on Darjeeling tea too, my favorite. We'll have some later."

"Where was this one taken?" Kate asked.

She pointed to a tranquil setting, a simple sandstone structure with gliding platforms over a placid lake interconnected with narrow bridges.

"In a village in Kerala," Krishna answered. "It's a short distance from where my mother grew up. My aunts told me my mother was always pleading to my grandmother to take her there."

"I can see how it was your mother's favorite place," Kate said. "It's beautiful."

"Here." Krishna averted Kate's attention to the next photo. "This is in Gujarat where my father's family lives."

"Your dad said the trip was nice."

"It was," Krishna said and then frowned. "The train to Gujarat was rather long, to be honest. I didn't know what to say to my dad."

Kate looked quizzically at Krishna.

"Anyway," Krishna continued, "my second cousins are making *vindaloo* with vegetables." She pointed to the two young women in the photo, one cousin was stirring the concoction in a tall tin pot on an open-flame stove and the other was dicing vegetables so rapidly that the hand clasping the knife blurred in the photo.

In the background, tin pots hung from nails pounded into the yellowing wall and unlabeled spice jars were neatly lined in rows on the open shelving above a vast sink.

"And, here, these are my aunts and my great aunt making *roti*."

Kate strained her neck closer to the drying print, as if to hear the women's intimate talk as they sat in a circle on a floor mat rolling dough and flattening it, their backs against a barren wall. Even in black and white, Kate could imagine the vibrancy of their saris, in varied patterns and hues, billowing around them as the women leaned in. Their hands, so animated and unfocused in the camera's shutter speed. Krishna had captured them mid-laugh, the women's broad smiles revealing misshapen teeth.

"These photos are amazing, Krishna!" Kate exclaimed again. "There is so much emphasis on shadows. I feel transported to India right here in this tiny bathroom."

The side of Krishna's face was darkened by the red light, but Kate could detect pride, having been masked by stress and grief, in the way the corner of Krishna's mouth quivered upward.

"Look at this man. I can feel his stare," Kate said.

The man stood on an unpaved road in front of a bull cart stacked stories above his head with large burlap bags, the hay inside poking through the holes. His eyes, the same shade as the bull's hairy backside, bore into the camera lens.

Kate recalled the different types of stares she encountered in India. There was the stare of the idle man on the street, a look of bewilderment. The laborer and the merchant both had a stare of hope and anticipation that their limp hands would fill with rupees by a passing feringhee. The upper caste stared at her with guardedness, dressed in pressed polyester pants and shirts. They stood as street monitors with their hands clasped behind their backs. And then there were the stares of the soldiers, stares of indifference as they stood rigid, their hands grasping the rifle slung across their shoulders. These were the street stares of India—intense stares of deliverance.

"These images were taken in the village where my father and his siblings were raised," Krishna explained, pointing to the cluster of prints nearest the door.

Kate studied the rawness of the photos.

"My mother and father came from such different backgrounds," she said. It would have shamed my mother's family if they had met and wanted to get married in India. It would never have happened!"

"Well, good thing they met on the Illinois prairie. Nobody really cares where you came from as long as you cheer for the right football team and know what detasseling corn means," Kate said amusingly.

"See here. This was the dwelling where my father grew up. It was part of a complex shared with many other families," Krishna explained. "Just a place to cook and a sleeping room for all six of them!"

Kate took in the simple kitchen with a clay stove that rose just inches from the stone floor, a table, and short stool. Several tin pots, jugs of water, and earthenware bowls were stacked on a shelf next to the stove. Light seeped in through the warped wallboards.

"Off to this side"—Krishna pointed around her as if the bathroom space and her father's childhood village kitchen were one and the same—"was the main stairwell in the complex. My father told me and my mother that as a boy, he used to sleep on the platform at the top of the stairs. There was a slight night breeze that swept in from the roof and space to sleep. He told us, his presence used to irritate the building's cleaning woman, who lived on the roof, and she demanded rupees as payment for sleeping on the stairs. It was her turf! Of course, my father had no money to give to her and she never complained to anyone just stepped over him in the morning, I guess. My mother enjoyed those stories," Krishna reminisced with a half-smile. "She wasn't ashamed of him, of where he came from."

Kate stopped looking at the photos and instead turned her attention to Krishna, her face covered in a midnight hue from the shadow cast by the red bulb. She had changed since her trip to India. The grief was giving way to inspiration.

"These images are your India!" Kate exclaimed.

After several moments, Krishna said, "I really do enjoy photography. I enjoy capturing my parents' stories in the images. Photographing our trip took away some of the pain."

"Then tell your parents' story about why they both left India and how they met in America. It's interesting."

Krishna fell silent, lost in contemplation.

"What photos are these?" Kate asked, peering into the sink, the faucet still trickling a steady stream of water over one tray.

"Oh, gosh." Krishna lunged toward the sink and snapped off the flow of water.

"Those are probably well washed now," she said, laughing absentmindedly.

She poked at the floating photos in the tray with a pair of plastic tweezers.

"I took these pictures of Mustafa and Nasreen the other day before she left for Pakistan. We took them in their backyard. Great light. Nasreen was definitely nervous though. You can see it in her face."

"Mustafa looks troubled," Kate added knowingly.

Heaviness flushed over Kate's body, and she was almost too fatigued to counter the weight that felt like a cloak around her. She watched as the photos shuffled through the water, submerging and surfacing with the waves created by the tips of Krishna's tweezers, Nasreen and Mustafa's bodies and faces distorting in the ripples.

"I thought I would enlarge a couple and frame them as a baby shower gift. Last photo before they become parents, you know? This one is my favorite." Krishna held the photo up by one corner, letting it drip into the sink.

Kate tilted her head in line with the picture of Nasreen and Mustafa embracing next to the mulberry tree.

"They look happy," Krishna remarked.

"Do they?"

"What?" Krishna appeared dumbfounded by the question. "What do you mean?" she asked, confused.

"I don't think they're happy."

"Why do you say that?" Krishna asked, taken aback by Kate's statement. "Sure, it's been rough on them not to be able to bear children, but they are adopting. They're getting through it and moving on."

"Nasreen brings a lot of baggage to their marriage that she hasn't dealt with. She was raped, Krishna!" Kate blurted. "She has kept it a secret for so long!" Her voice rose to almost a shout, too loud in the close confines of the bathroom.

The laundry line of photos swung in response to the force of Kate's breath. Krishna stood rigid; a dark shadow cast over one troubled eye. She was still holding the tip of the photo. She flicked off the last of the water droplets before turning to clamp it on the line.

"You knew," Kate said accusingly. "You knew!"

The red light flashed across Krishna's face so only the tip of her nose and her round lips were illuminated.

"That is in the past," Krishna snapped. "She has gotten over it."

"How does one exactly get over it?" Kate asked, horrified.

The words left an acrimonious taste on her tongue.

"Nothing good would come out of revealing the truth. It's better to forgive and forget."

Have faith.

"It's a heavy secret," Kate whispered. "Close friends like us shouldn't have secrets."

"Everyone has secrets."

"I don't," Kate dismissed.

"Yes you do," Krishna shot back. "You have been in love with Tariq, and you won't openly admit it! Nasreen told me about Eid. Is that why you hitchhiked to Texas?"

"I didn't hitchhike," Kate defended. "I went with Neil."

"Whom you broke up with! Oh, c'mon, we could tell," Krishna barked.

"I had a crush on Tariq a long time ago. We were teenagers. I just needed a break and didn't have a lot of money to spend, and Neil was driving so I figured why not?"

In the sublevel bathroom with creaking pipes, Kate suddenly felt cloistered by the faces and scenes of India—the women in mid-laugh, the children in mid-run, and the staring eyes of the man next to the bull cart. Then she spied another photo in the series…of a woman.

"Who is she?" Kate asked, changing the subject away from talking about Neil and Tariq.

A young Indian woman with thick eyebrows and lashes and wide, effervescent eyes looked passionately at the camera.

"She's a friend." Krishna's tone was short.

"Okay. So can you elaborate a little?" Kate pried.

"Her name is Raji. She works at a photography store on Harper Street. I bought the Nikon FG camera to take to India, and I was testing it out. She was my model. We were at a park near the shop. She is always happy," Krishna explained as if it were difficult to imagine someone so happy. "Nothing ever seems to cloud her eyes."

"She has bright eyes," Kate agreed, still studying the photo of the woman.

"Anyway, we have been hanging out a bit and we have become close…friends."

The acid smell from the fixer was starting to sting Kate's eyes. She watched Krishna admire the photo and the essence of the woman in it.

"You never mentioned her," Kate said, confused.

Krishna shrugged. "She is a new friend."

"What's your secret, Krish? You said everyone has secrets. So what is yours?"

Krishna remained silent.

"You can't tell me?"

Krishna shook her head. "Not now."

"These are beautiful pictures, Krish. They really are."

Krishna seemed to be lost in thought.

"Thanks for showing me. I have to run," Kate said before pushing the bathroom door open.

The light flooded in. Krishna recoiled, blocking her eyes with her forearm.

Chapter 16

BOMBING OF BOHRI BAZAAR

Karachi 1987

S
ameer was ill. His fever rose steadily for several days. The flight to Karachi was postponed. Nanima and Laila nursed Sameer, exchanging the cool, wet cloth on his glistening pink brow and making sure he took the antimalarial pills the doctor in Banjara Hills had prescribed.

"He will make a full recovery but cannot travel until he is stronger," the doctor told them.

Karachi, Kate could imagine, would be quite different from Hyderabad. There, she and Nasreen would be more defined by societal codes of behavior and consumed by the formalities of a Muslim wedding. For now, Sameer's illness meant for Kate more time in Hyderabad and more time to spend with Tariq.

She was happy to escape with the cousins and visit several historic places that dotted both sides of the Musi River and defined the once princely state of Hyderabad. They visited the Charminar monument and its four fluted minarets that served as a gateway to the old city, several palaces and public gardens, and the massive façade of the College of Arts building at Osmania University, a symbol of Indian renaissance. In between the tourist stops, they sauntered through Saify Stores and the congested tobacco- and fish-smelling Begum Bazaar.

At night, the cousins lounged on the balcony of the Banjara Hills hotel where Kate discovered Indian ice cream. The mango flavor was divine! The fresh sweetness rejuvenated her tongue from the heavy South Indian spices. The evening breeze was cooler, and Kate wore a salwar kameez she borrowed from Yasmine. She enjoyed the camaraderie and gazed across the main road toward Nanima's house and the construction site where soon an even more opulent hotel, the rival Royal Taj, threatened to block the view.

✳ ✳ ✳ ✳ ✳

"THIS HILL IS famous," Tariq announced one afternoon as he stood atop a hill that hovered over the Hussain Sagar Lake.

He wore jeans and cowboy boots and gazed at the open span of rocky land.

"It is called Naubat Pahad," he explained. "This is my favorite place to come and sit. You can see everything from here—the beauty and the ugliness of Hyderabad, the temples, parks, and monuments, and the old railway station in this direction," he said, pointing in the distance. "And in this direction, you can see the flooded plains and the shacks along the hillside."

The wind blew across the land and through Tariq's hair. Yasmine and Nasreen clasped their dupattas as the material flapped wildly in the wind and across their faces.

"Hyderabad is changing," Tariq continued. "There will be businesses, high-rises, luxury apartments with courtyards, and terrace cafés someday."

He spread his arm wide as if he had the power to transform the landscape.

Kate imagined him standing on a peak somewhere in Nepal

Yasmine smiled. "You dream, my cousin. I hope you are right."

"We will not have to go to America for jobs. You will see."

Kate knew she had only had a glimpse of India and of a city pulsing with history, on the verge of either exploding into modernism or imploding into self-destruction, swallowed up by aimless overpopulation.

In her journal, Kate wrote feverishly about the majestic temples, the rusted corrugated shacks, and bulbous domes that hovered over a sea of burlap-tented bazaars. She wrote about the man who sold guavas on the corner, the shop owners at Sheela's Brass store, and her sari purchase at the fancy cloth store. She wrote about their mud-stomping adventure through the countryside, into the dark depths of the tombs, and to the terraces of the fort overlooking the rubble courtyard. She wrote about Tariq.

Maybe she would return to sit on the black stone of Mecca Masjid as the legend told, and she would return to a vibrant and thriving city of the future, and he would still be there waiting for her.

* * * * *

IN THE DANK, echoing airport corridor, Kate perched herself on one of the suitcases and waited. She kept an eye on Nasreen and Laila among the congestion. Extended families huddled together in masses, making it difficult to determine which line belonged to which attendant. She pressed her arm over her lower stomach, feeling the outline of her passport beneath her blouse. Sameer too sat on one of the suitcases, sweating profusely from his malaria-weakened state and from having dragged the heavy bags across the urine-smelling airport terminal.

Their flight to Karachi was in the middle of the night. They stood in line after line.

India moved on its own schedule.

"Traveling from India to Pakistan is more complicated than flying from America to India," Nasreen remarked.

Kate thought of the cousins Yasmine, Azra, Hari, Max, and especially Tariq. They had arrived at Nanima's to help her and Nasreen pack. She would see them in Karachi in two weeks and already looked forward to their companionship again. Rahim and Anees would arrive then as well, one cousin preparing to be married and the other preparing to be formally engaged. Anees's preoccupation with family and betrothal responsibilities, including frequently visiting his fiancé's and her family, was a relief to Kate. The less time Anees was around Nasreen the better, she thought.

"Come on, Kate," Nasreen urged. "We have to get our tickets approved, and then we can leave."

"Approved?" Kate asked, confused.

"I can't explain. Just come."

Kate moved from the suitcase and fought the sickening feeling rising in her stomach from heat and exhaustion.

Four hours later, their tickets finally approved, they boarded the plane for the forty-five-minute flight to Bombay.

The Bombay airport was a world of its own and seemed a far different place to Kate than it had two weeks earlier when Sameer had met her in the echoing terminal after a grueling trip from Chicago to escort her to Hyderabad. There were more lines, but things moved faster and they had first-class tickets.

"Only six bucks more for first class," Sameer explained.

His face was still pale as he struggled to stay alert.

On their way to the gate, they passed an entire waiting area filled with men in blinding white robes waiting to board a plane to Saudi Arabia. Kate knew the men in white *thawbs* were engaging in a once-in-a-lifetime pilgrimage to Mecca.

"At some time in their life, a Muslim must make the trip on their own earnings," Nasreen told her.

Kate thought of her father. She could hear his voice tell her he would pay for her trip to India and Pakistan. His face was filled with awe and weighted by a parent's burden of unpredictable politics and uncontrollable events in granting permission to a child to travel overseas alone.

This was her pilgrimage.

She thought of the children on the streets who hovered around the fruit stands, ran around the reflection ponds chasing pigeons, pulled themselves along on scooters, or begged for rupees in the bazaars. They could only hope for a pilgrimage as they listened to the distant calls of the minarets to unite them in faith.

Once on board the flight to Karachi, the first-class seats offered some comfort. An Arab with a wide girth waddled as he made his way down the aisle toward Kate. His walking cane tapped her ankle as he moved past her seat. His wives clad in black burkas followed him, some carrying sleeping babies and others hustling young boys dressed in white robes like their father. Through the slit in the burka, one of the woman's eyes, fierce and powerful, met Kate's. The woman's fury and intensity felt like a spear through her chest. Kate felt the breeze from the women's burkas wash over her as they passed.

It was four in the morning when they finally reached Karachi.

"We will be up until morning during the wedding ceremonies," Nasreen said, grinning. "Get used to the time," she teased.

She followed Nasreen through the sliding doors pushing one of the carts piled with luggage. The sweltering heat pummeled Kate like she had walked into a wall. Signs waved in front of her, some with people's names, items to buy, or places to go written on them.

"Taxi! Taxi? Ma'am?"

A man was suddenly in her face.

"No!" she yelled aggressively in her panic to keep sight of the others.

Suddenly, smiling faces encircled her. Nasreen, Sameer, Laila, and Nanima exchanged embraces with family members. Someone picked up Sana in a bear hug. Bangles clashed with bangles as the women reunited. The men slapped Sameer on the back.

The welcoming clan was dressed for a party. Pressed saris and shirts, painted lips, and bright eyes before dawn. Kate was passed from relative to relative in the dizzying introduction. Nasreen shouted out names above the excited voices and airport congestion. More cousins, more aunts and uncles...

* * * * *

IN KARACHI, THE days were long and scorching hot. The intolerable heat encircled Kate's throat until she choked and tried to spit, but her tongue felt clumsy inside her swollen cheeks. She was thankful for the air-conditioned home of Nasreen's aunt, Mumanijan, and uncle, Mamujan, even though the air would shut off intermittently.

On Wednesday, they planned to go to Bohri Bazaar. It was a dry, sweltering afternoon, and they spent a leisurely morning in the cooled home before the air-conditioning unit finally started to labor and whine.

"Chelo. Chelo," Nasreen's uncle said with urgency, his forehead glistening with sweat as the temperature rose in the house.

He shooed the women off their perch on the sofa and into the car. He drove the family to Bohri Bazaar for more wedding shopping. The day before, Kate had picked out an outfit for the wedding at the bazaar—a salmon taffeta with golden-threaded design—from a stall near the perimeter of the hustling tented city. They had meandered all day weaving through the stalls of cloth, *jutti* shoes, bangles, purses, perfumes, and dupattas. But there was still much to do before a crowd of relatives and friends would arrive for the weeks of ceremonies celebrating the union of Rahim and Haseena.

Mamujan drove along Jinnah Road in thick traffic toward the congested city circle. They were a few miles away when suddenly the motorway buckled beneath them; the car launched forward and skidded to a stop.

In the moment of shock, Kate heard a deep pounding. The sound ripped through the road, rattling the floor of the auto. She whipped around thinking a car had hit them from behind. But the car behind stopped at a safe distance.

Another explosion erupted in the distance.

Then she saw a trail of smoke rise toward the sky. Nasreen's uncle spoke in panicked Urdu and spun the car around, weaving against the heavy traffic that was slowing to a gridlock. The sound of ambulances grew closer. The car braked hard causing Kate's body to hit the seat in front. The pedestrian they had nearly hit slammed his hand against the hood of the car.

"Bombs! Bombs!" he yelled at them through the windshield.

In surrendered defense, Mamujan took his hands off the steering wheel. He stared in horror at the man. Mumanijan, sitting in the passenger seat, ripped her dupatta across her face and buried her head into her chest as if to become invisible.

"What is happening?" she cried into her dupatta.

A van maneuvered in front of them, and the driver thrust his head out the window frantically waving cars out of the way.

"Blood! We have blood! Let us through!" the driver cried in Urdu.

* * * * *

THE RADIO REPORTED two car bombs ripped through Bohri Bazaar resulting in a few casualties. By morning, the newspaper revealed a far different tragedy in the pictures of blackened ash and debris, collapsed stalls, and burned tents. The bombs ripped apart the main shopping center in Karachi, leaving nearly seventy dead.

Kate recalled the day before when she had walked past the bangle stall, the spice and tea stall, and the juice stand where Sana had a drink of mango juice. Then she had strolled onto the main street where a man sold roasted nuts that he scooped into cones made of newspaper. She envisioned the juice man handing Sana a cup. She remembered the man and his son breaking for midday tea in the middle of their beaded necklace shop. And she imagined the old man who sold her the jutti shoes in a stall in the main row of tents.

Gone. Ash.

The Pakistani government declared three days of mourning following the attacks on black Wednesday. The shops were closed, buses and taxis were off duty, and men stayed home from work.

Who was responsible? Kate didn't know, and she didn't ask for translation when the uncles spoke about it.

In America, terrorist attacks that happened overseas were reported by international correspondents whose columns appeared in *The New York Times*, not felt from a couple miles away in a crowded shopping center. Kate was like many American teenagers, relatively unaware of Asian politics. All that was clear in the stillness of the days that followed the bombing of Bohri Bazaar was that her life might have been spared by the randomness of Pakistani power cycles.

To pass the time during the days of mourning, the family watched an endless melodramatic Indian movie on a small television in the front room. Kate tried to follow the characters—the dashing hero, the pious wife, and the seductive mistress. The actors moved from stage to stage, breaking into song and dance. The actresses' perfect feet pounded to the clamor of drums, vibrating the tiny bells on their anklets, their arms layered with rattling bangles intertwined in sinuous fluid movements as their voices rose.

After long hours, the tinny chimes and high-pitched homogenous sounds made Kate's head ache. She sat on the couch and monitored the passing of time by the five daily calls to prayer and the five daily meals. Time lingered in the cracked, yellowed wallpaper with nothing to do but wait for the next spicy meal to be served. She could not get rid of the *garam masala* paste that coated her gums even after cleansing her palette with scoops of fennel seeds. The seeds only got stuck between her teeth.

"Come on," Nasreen coaxed in the afternoon on mourning day three as she headed for the back stairs. "Follow me."

"Where?" Kate asked.

"To the terrace."

The air conditioning stopped working, and the house was growing uncomfortably warm. Kate perspired as they climbed the stairs. Nasreen punched open the door at the top, and the two walked out into the sizzling open air.

The barrier around the terrace was so tall that Kate had to stand on her tiptoes to peer over the edge. She looked out at the yellow sandstone walls of adjacent homes, which resembled a maze of fortresses rather than a neighborhood. Unlike the many earthen ramshackle homes she saw in India, these homes had foundations, smoothed clay walls, high gates, and small pristine courtyards.

Women were not hanging clothes or sweeping. Boys were not playing cricket on the small dusty lot two lanes over. The fruit wallah who rolled his cart filled with fresh mangos, guavas, and coconuts through the neighborhood calling out the items for sale in a rhythmic chant had not been heard for days.

The neighborhood was still.

"Don't let anyone see you," Nasreen hissed.

"But there is no one."

"Shhh!" Nasreen placed a finger across her lips.

She moved slowly toward the utility shed at the far end of the roof, softly closed the door and locked it.

"My uncle's handyman lives up here. He would freak out if he saw us."

Nasreen laid out the towels across the terrace floor, knelt down, and removed her salwar shirt over her head then scooted out of her pajama bottoms. In her black panties and bra, she positioned herself on the towel and closed her eyes.

"Ah, this feels great. Sunbathing in Pakistan," Nasreen moaned happily. "You should write about this in your journal." She smiled with her eyes still shut.

Kate peeled off her jeans and shirt that clung to her perspiring body and looked at the locked door, nervous for the man inside.

"Won't he get hot in there?"

"It's just for a few minutes. He is probably sleeping now anyway. It's midday after all."

Kate scooted onto the towel next to Nasreen. The sun was scorching, but the air was fresh.

"I have gained weight," Kate sighed.

"I know. Me too."

"We can run up and down the stairs."

"Great idea." Nasreen fanned her dark curls across the towel. "Later."

Kate lay back and let the sun warm her thighs, midriff, and breasts until her face started to burn.

"I may be a tomato in a few minutes, you know."

"Well, it will add some color to your white skin," Nasreen teased.

"Funny," Kate said as she slid her T-shirt over her eyes and nose for protection.

Her shirt smelled like fried samosas. She closed her eyes again and imagined herself at the beach and Tariq applying sunscreen to her skin. She felt his wide hands move across her back. In her daydream, he brushed her hair across one shoulder then kissed her neck.

"I had a dream about Tariq," Kate blurted, the hairs on her neck prickling.

Nasreen made no response.

"I dreamt we were riding an elephant down Michigan Avenue, sitting high in the *howdah*. I was holding onto him for dear life, and the Chicago taxis were weaving about the elephant's legs and honking incessantly," she said, giggling.

"A bit absurd, but very funny," Nasreen remarked.

"When he looks at me, it's like his eyes pierce through me."

"Really?"

"If Aunty Samina and Nanima want to marry me off while I am in Pakistan, I vote for Tariq," Kate laughed aloud.

"Not likely."

"That's mean," Kate sneered.

"Well, it won't happen," Nasreen insisted. "I am just trying to save your feelings from being hurt."

"Maybe it can. Maybe he will fall in love with me. There is always the future. A different time and a different place."

"You are not Muslim."

"So?"

"His parents will only approve of a Muslim as his wife."

Kate peered over at Nasreen and scowled. Nasreen's words burned and hissed in her ear like sweat hitting the hot terrace.

"It's me, Nasreen," Kate defended.

"I know. So, you understand."

Kate waited for Nasreen to say something more, to say she was kidding, but Nasreen remained motionless on the towel. Her eyes closed.

"Did you talk with Anees at all in India?" Kate asked with spite. "He seemed quite preoccupied."

"About what?"

"Uh, gee, I don't know, his engagement. Isn't that why we are here, in Pakistan?"

"We are here for Rahim's wedding," Nasreen asserted.

"What does Anees think of his fiancé?"

"Rayah? I don't know. I don't think he has met with her much in private. The whole thing has been a little rushed. I guess Aunty Zehba is eager to marry both sons off."

"Did she know?" Kate asked and sat up. "About you and Anees?"

Kate's T-shirt slid off her face, and she squinted in the fierce sun. Aunty Zehba had been critical of Nasreen throughout their time in India. She complained that Nasreen's ankles showed too much, that her makeup was too heavy, that her hair should be covered…then again, Aunty Zehba was critical of everyone.

Nasreen opened one eye and looked up at Kate.

"No," she answered. "Not to my knowledge."

Kate lay back down, flipped the shirt over her face, and refrained from asking more. She stared at the orange glow under her fried-samosa-smelling T-shirt.

"Aunty Zehba would never approve of me marrying Anees. I am too American." An ugly scowl reared across her face. "She wants traditional Pakistani brides for her sons. And Anees will marry only whom his parents approve."

Kate didn't know for how long Nasreen and Anees had kept their infatuation a secret, a year maybe. Anees arrived in the US for college two years after Rahim and shared the small apartment with his brother in a middle-class neighborhood close to the university. On school breaks, Rahim and Anees drove to visit their Aunt Laila and enjoy traditional Indian meals before heading back to student life. Sometime during the visits and the home-cooked meals and fresh-smelling bedsheets, Nasreen and Anees, to Kate's disbelief, became lovers.

Kate thought how lucky Nasreen was that she had not gotten pregnant.

"You cried all the time," Kate remarked, sitting up again. "I didn't know what to say. I mean, what do I know? I've never had a boyfriend. I learned about love from a girl forbidden to date!"

Nasreen snickered.

"It's not funny." Kate looked toward the shed annoyed and wondered when the handyman would realize he was locked in a sauna.

"I'm sorry. I was depressed," Nasreen said, shrugging her shoulders. "But what's done is done. I am over him."

"What if you had gotten pregnant?"

Nasreen sat up abruptly, rage reflected in her eyes.

"It didn't happen! Don't speak of it!" she screamed.

"But Nasreen…"

Suddenly a loud pounding came from inside the utility shack.

"Out, out! Please! This will be the death of me!"

"Oh, no! The handyman!" cried Nasreen. "Hurry, get dressed!"

The girls tripped and stumbled to the door. Nasreen fiddled with the lock, covering herself with the towel.

The door swung free and opened wide, and the handyman burst out shielding his face with his salwar shirt so as not to glance at them. He bolted to the door on the opposite side of the terrace and disappeared down the stairs.

"What would be the death of him, the heat or seeing our skin?"

"Both!" Nasreen answered, the girls breaking into laughter.

"Come on! Aunty Zehba will be looking for us. Pray the handyman doesn't rat us out because she will lock us away!"

"She would do that?"

"Yes! And that will surely end any chance you have with Tariq!"

Chapter 17

SECOND CHANCES

Chicago 1998

With a whirl, Kate's body somersaulted, cutting through the water. She forced air out of her nostrils in two thunderous streams. She flipped, planted her feet against the pool wall, and sprang from the surface, her toes pointed as they left the wall and her arms outstretched. She glided long and soundlessly; the water flowed over and under her slender body, carrying her. As her lungs expanded, burning slightly, she turned her head, breaking the surface of the water and gasped, slowly drawing the air back into her lungs.

In the early afternoon, Kate had the lap lane to herself at the university pool. She lost count how many yards she had swum. With each flip turn, she crushed the stress of the morning against the tiled wall of the Olympic-size indoor pool.

After returning from her detour to Texas, her advisor seemed suspicious. During the lab group meeting, she was ruthlessly grilled about her recent results and relatively unprepared to answer the questions thrown at her like darts at a dartboard.

Her advisor reminded her, dwarfed by his office chair, that she needed his signature on her thesis to graduate. He mumbled something in German.

You're such a manipulator! she wanted to scream at him.

Instead, she stood stonily staring at the silver Mont Blanc rollerball pen set.

She ached to speak with Nasreen. But Nasreen was still in Pakistan, nearly three months trying to adopt the twins, with no set return date.

"She is having issues obtaining the baby girl's US visa," Mustafa explained.

She called him every week to get an update on Nasreen's return and got the sense that Mustafa and Nasreen were not speaking to each other very often.

"I'll call as soon as she books a flight home, I promise you, Kate," he consoled.

She thought of Nasreen playing with her adopted Pakistani babies, the aunties fussing about them, passing down the teachings to ensure the natural order of raising a son and a daughter. Most likely there was an endless stream of visitors to celebrate the baby boy and welcome the baby girl.

She thought of Krishna searching for her soul in the printed photos strung across a dark bathroom.

She thought of her father.

"You're stronger than you think, Kat," his voice drifted through her mind.

She swam alone with just her swirling thoughts. She had been to the clinic, deciding to undergo the genetic testing. She thought she saw Dr. Khan among the doctors in white coats and felt a panic attack emerging in her chest, but she had imagined it. He wasn't there. The nurses collected her samples and now she waited while the sequencing instruments printed the readout of her genes, good ones or bad ones.

The warm water rippled along her body as she pivoted her torso side to side. With each stroke, her hand slapped the surface. She stretched her right hand, curling her palm around the water, then pulled, thrusting herself through the pool. A dull pain spread through her shoulders as she pulled through the opposite stroke. The repetition of swimming released her mind to her dreams. She heard only the muffled roar of the water pushing against her and the echoes of voices at the opposite edge of the pool. No one could hear her even if she screamed into the water.

Kate stopped at the wall. She was panting, exhausted, and clinging to the pool ledge. Her limbs were cramping, and it felt as if a hot rod lay across her indecisive, heavy heart.

* * * * *

THE SIGN ON the door read "Biochemistry Office." Kate walked by the chair of the department's office every day on her way to the lab. Every day she wanted to barge in, insinuate that her advisor was insane. How does one explain the undermining manipulation? Students feared their thesis would be left unsigned, their recommendation letters for hopeful positions left unwritten. She felt she had to be obliging to his demands yet undermining to maintain control over her own destiny. She was exhausted.

She had only a few moments of fleeting courage, like that of sand in an hourglass flipped end-to-end, as she stood outside the office door. In the rippled glass pane, she could see the silhouettes of the administrators in the office as they shuffled back and forth between filing cabinets and desks. Undergraduate courses began in two weeks, and the office staff was busy.

Kate abruptly opened the door.

Karen, the head administrator, stopped typing and looked up. Her assistant swung around, causing the top folder in a thick stack she was carrying to slip from her arms and slap the floor.

"I'll get that," Kate said.

She picked the folder up from the floor, sliding the papers back inside. The assistant took the folder from Kate.

"I'm sorry, but Dr. Elber is not in at the moment," Karen said. "Do you want to make an appointment?"

Kate thought for a moment, but the last few grains of sand had slipped through the hourglass.

"No, it's fine," she responded.

Kate turned to go and opened the door just as quickly as she had a moment ago. Dr. Elber's large frame filled the doorway, and she almost knocked into him.

"Kate. Hello. Here to see me?"

"Yes, but I can come back later."

"If you have come to see me, then I am sure it is important," he said, winking. "Let's go into my office."

He stepped forward, and she had no other route but to step backward, turn, and proceed into his office.

Dr. Elber walked past her to his desk, unzipped his shoulder bag, and began pulling out its contents: a daily planner, lab book, and file folders.

"What can I do for you?"

Kate thought for a moment, turning over the hourglass in her mind one more time for another few moments of fearlessness. Her father's words filtering through her mind: "*Don't give up.*"

"I would like to request a transfer to another lab," she said, her voice shaking with adrenaline.

"What?" Dr. Elber was still arranging things on his desk. "Transfer?"

"Yes."

"Why would you want to start over in another lab, Kate? You are more than halfway through your PhD thesis."

He let out a groan as he plopped into his chair and tapped on the keyboard to awaken his computer.

"This machine gets slower by the day. Like myself," he chuckled.

"It's either that or I quit."

Dr. Elber stopped shuffling and tapping and looked up at Kate. He sat back in his swivel chair. The worn leather made a flatulent sound against his weight. He brought his interlocked hands to rest on his stomach.

"You can't quit," he said in a near teasing tone, attempting to gauge her seriousness.

She stood firm, pursing her lips to hide their quivering.

"You are a good student."

"Then I deserve a system that works for me."

"I'm not sure I follow."

"I won't be like Mei!" Kate blurted.

There were still sand grains left in the hourglass.

"She ran away just to escape the craziness! Who knows if she got a position she deserved or had to return to a country that she hasn't lived in for a decade. Because why? Because our advisor won't sign her thesis because he is...a..." she stopped.

The look of shock on Dr. Elber's face made her rethink what she wanted to say. She swallowed the words, stood firm, and squeezed her hands into fists.

Dr. Elber grew serious.

"What do you want?" he asked pointedly.

"I want to transfer to Dr. Crone's lab. I have already talked to him."

"Why Dr. Crone?"

Dr. Crone was Scottish and had a crude and rather abrupt nature. But he was honest. Crassness, Kate could fight; belittling manipulation tore at her insides.

"I am more interested in his research," she stated firmly. "It's a better fit."

"We will have to meet with the dean. Explain the situation."

There was nothing else to say. Kate turned to leave.

"Between you and me," Dr. Elber said as he stood and walked around to the front of his desk.

Kate turned back to face him. He leaned against the desk and folded his arms across his chest.

"Mei has a position out East. I want you to know. I gave her a recommendation."

He pushed the button on the intercom.

"Karen," he called into the device on his desk, "please set up an appointment with Dean Rowbottom at his earliest availability."

Kate left his office as the last few grains of sand fell through the hourglass.

*****

NASREEN RETURNED TO Chicago after four and a half months in Pakistan. The summer heat had evaporated. The leaves were turning colors and clinging to their branches, waiting to be blown away by the winter winds.

Nasreen opened the front door to see Kate on the doorstep. By the look in Nasreen's eyes, Kate could see the toll the trip had taken on Nasreen and the process of adopting not one but two babies and bringing them safely and legally home. Kate embraced Nasreen as tightly as she did when she arrived in India, sweaty, dusty, and delirious from travel and desperate for familiarity.

"I really missed you," Kate said, a sob swelling in her throat. "I'm sorry I was not here when you left. I really am. I'm so sorry I wasn't there."

"I know. I am sorry too. I should have told you more. You would have listened. You always listen."

In the time that she was away, Nasreen's editor at the financial paper suspended her employment.

"After six weeks, my editor called me in Pakistan and fired me over the phone."

Nasreen saw the positive in the situation.

"Now I can stay home with baby Mani and Sabreena."

Nasreen's in-laws had moved out temporarily and gone to live with Mustafa's younger brother and his family in Santa Fe.

"The extra space right now will be helpful," Nasreen rationalized. "Mustafa plans to work more from home now that the babies are here. Unless he is traveling," she added. "Besides, it will be warmer through the winter for my in-laws in the Southwest," Nasreen explained. "It makes sense. They will move back next summer."

The fact that Mustafa's parents were not there to welcome their new grandbabies when Nasreen returned home made Kate assume the reason was more heartbreaking, a rejection of birthright.

Nonetheless, Nasreen looked happy. She was dressed in a new salwar kameez from Pakistan, bright yellow to celebrate new life. She was softer and rounded; the aunties had fed her well.

The babies lay on a plush white blanket with blue moons and silver stars. Little Mani kicked his feet in the air and grabbed at his sister, who rolled toward her twin, stimulated by the touch. Both babies responded to smiles from Nasreen's cooing friends. Sara, Mona, and Shabana kneeled before the babies, kissing their cheeks and feet and holding a pinky finger out for each to grab ahold.

"They are both too precious, Nasreen," Sara squealed.

"Very, very cute," agreed Shabana.

Nasreen smiled proudly.

"They were spoiled in Pakistan. My aunties fed them every time they cried. But they did help fatten them up."

Kate watched Mani and Sabreena kick. They hardly looked fat and round like most babies did with chunky cheeks and rubberband wrists. The diapers hung loosely around their thin legs and shallow bellies.

"Twins are born small anyways," Nasreen explained. "The twins were born in the orphanage a little underdeveloped. But…"

"Oh, he is beautiful with his round eyes," Shabana interrupted, poking Mani's belly. "You will grow to be big and healthy, won't you? Yes, you will."

Mani showed his soft gums in a broad, gleeful smile.

Sabreena drooled and watched the women with wide, curious eyes.

"I love little Sabreena's heart-shaped lips," chimed Mona as she brushed away the drool sliding down the baby's chin.

Kate placed the gift bag she had brought full of diapers—a practical gift—against the wall.

"I need a glass of water," Kate said as she walked toward the kitchen.

Krishna was at the stove making sauce for the samosas. She looked up as Kate entered the kitchen.

"Krishna! I have been meaning to call you," Kate said.

"You have?" Krishna dropped the spoon in the sauce. "I thought a lot about what you said when you came over that day I was printing in the basement bathroom. You know, about telling my mother's story as an immigrant to America."

"Really?"

"Her story is unique. So I thought maybe through my photography, I could trace my mother's path to America. Tell her story."

Nasreen rushed into the kitchen, waving her hands. "The samosas are in the oven! I forgot!" She flung open the oven door.

"Anyway," Krishna said, ignoring the samosa emergency, "I enrolled in Columbia College's photojournalism program!"

"You did?" Kate was flabbergasted.

Nasreen dropped the tray of hot samosas on the stovetop.

"Awesome!" Nasreen exclaimed, hearing the news for the first time as well.

"Yes, really. I did." Krishna smiled. "I'll try it for a semester or two. I am going to look for an apartment near campus and stay with my dad on weekends. I hired a housekeeper to help him out."

With a nervous laugh, Krishna pushed her glasses up higher on her nose.

"Well, I am switching out of my advisor's lab," Kate announced.

"What?" Krishna looked concerned.

"I didn't quit the program. I am just changing groups."

"Oh, good." Krishna patted her chest. "I'm glad you didn't quit."

"I talked to the chair of the department. Told him what I wanted."

"Good for you!" Nasreen said, impressed, arranging the samosas on a platter.

"Guess we are both starting new paths," Krishna said, grinning.

Mustafa bounded down the stairs and appeared in the kitchen, a briefcase in hand. He greeted and kissed both girls on the cheek. Shadows hung under his eyes and dark stubble spotted his jawline.

"Our Nasreen is back!" Mustafa said. "Your friends worried about you," he told Nasreen.

"It is good to be home," Nasreen responded unemotionally.

"I'm sorry I bugged you so much," Kate apologized to Mustafa.

"No need to apologize. I missed her too." He looked at his wife longingly.

"The babies are beautiful," Krishna added. "Congratulations."

"Thanks. They both have perfect lungs too," Mustafa complained. "Especially Sabreena. She cried most of the night. Poor Nasreen, I don't think she got much sleep. I wasn't much help, I'm afraid."

"I guess it's just a matter of getting into a routine," Kate said.

"Well, I've got to meet some clients."

"You're leaving?" Nasreen said, disappointed, as she held the plate of samosas.

"I'll be quick," he responded tensely. "I'll let you girls mingle."

He grabbed his overcoat from the hall closet and left through the door to the garage.

"I guess it's hard for him to work from home," Nasreen remarked, annoyed. "He seems so eager to leave."

"It will take time to bond," Kate said.

"I think he feels a bit misplaced. I have been inseparable from the twins since they were a few weeks old. Mustafa has to spend time with them. Get to know his son and daughter."

Nasreen shifted the tray in her hands.

"I have to put this hot plate down. The heat is seeping right through the oven mitt and burning my hand!" she said as she hurried into the other room to join the others.

The samosas were savory with spiced lamb laced with fresh ginger. They smelled to Kate like the street stalls in India where the grease popped and crackled as she walked past the sweating cooks frying samosas on the open grills, the burnt smell, smoke rising in their faces.

"You made these?" Kate asked, her mouth full of the piping hot pastry.

"Of course not," Nasreen responded cheekily. "A woman at the mosque made them for me. I just heated them."

Mani started to cry, overstimulated by the constant caressing and smiling faces. The women tried to soothe him, but he clamped his eyes shut and waved his tight tiny fists in a growing rage. Shabana picked him up and bounced him in her arms. He squirmed and howled even louder. Sabreena followed her twin's cue and squealed.

"I think they are hungry," Shabana announced above his cries.

"Oh my, yes!" Nasreen glanced at her watch. "It's past feeding time!"

She hurried to make two bottles of formula. Her breasts didn't swell with milk at the sound of her adopted babies' cry. She missed the cue. She shook the bottles furiously to dissolve the powder. Shabana held Mani and took one of the bottles. The baby's mouth found the nipple, and he sucked ravenously. Mona passed Sabreena into her mother's outstretched arms.

Except for the babies' gurgling and swallowing, the room fell silent. All eyes watched Nasreen, now seated in the high-back yellow chair by the stone-mantel fireplace, feeding her daughter, the baby's eyes locking with hers. She may have dreamt of several of her own children, but now the two little miracles from an orphanage in Islamabad was enough. Soon, Sabreena's eyes fluttered like the wings of a butterfly and she fell asleep.

"I'm going to put her in her crib," Nasreen whispered. "Help me off this chair. Mani will be awake for hours still."

Mona placed a hand on Nasreen's back and pushed her up and out of the chair.

"We'll come with you," Kate whispered and she and Krishna followed Nasreen up the stairs.

Kate felt the tension as she climbed the same set of stairs she had descended nearly seven months earlier to eavesdrop on Mustafa and Nasreen in the foyer.

"I haven't had time to put anything away," Nasreen whispered over her shoulder.

Kate realized this was true when they entered the babies' room. Clothes and toys lay scattered on the floor of the nursery. Pictures of bears, puppies, and bunnies adorned the outfits, all intended to make the babies' bellies irresistible to squeeze and poke. Some had matching bibs, miniature socks, and plush shoes. Others were paired with little mittens and hats and knitted sweaters with sayings like "superstar" and "daddy's girl."

Nasreen set Sabreena lightly in the white-painted crib that looked gently used with cracked paint along the hinges. She brushed her cheek before raising the side of the crib and locking it into place.

"Shabana gave me the crib," she said. "When the twins get bigger, I will have to buy another one. My mom had an extra dresser. I'm going to paint it white to match the crib, eventually," she added. "And Mustafa bought the changing table."

Kate and Krishna nodded, acknowledging and glancing around the room. The windows were curtainless, and the walls were beige except for a section with brush strokes in various shades of sample paint color of lavender to light indigo.

"I didn't know if this would work out. You know, adopting a baby," Nasreen said shrugging, keeping an eye on her sleeping daughter. "So I avoided buying things or getting a nursery together and painting the walls. I just couldn't," she sighed heavily. "Then suddenly I was on a plane to Pakistan, and there was no time. And now there are two! Maybe I am crazy. How will I handle two?"

"You are not crazy," Krishna said. "I think it is amazing what you are doing."

"Enjoy your time," Kate added. "You don't have to go to work now so just enjoy."

"I will be busy," Nasreen added. "I need to get some curtains too. The sun makes the room too bright in the afternoons."

"I'm sure it will look beautiful."

Nasreen nodded and put a finger to her lips as the baby rustled in her crib, letting out a short whine.

"We are glad you are home," Krishna said.

"And you have beautiful twins that owe you their little lives," Kate whispered. "It's a new start for all of you."

Chapter 18

PARADE OF TRAYS

Karachi 1987

The red-painted wooden trays were arranged in two long rows on the floor. Each crepe paper-lined tray contained a complete fashion ensemble from dupatta to toe rings. Nasreen's aunts stepped carefully between the rows, adding the final accents: small perfumed sachets bound with mint-green ribbon.

Aunty Samina, Hari, Max, Yasmine, and Azra had finally arrived in Karachi and so had Aunty Zehba and the brothers Rahim, Anees, and Tariq. All the family had arrived for the nightly celebrations that would last over a span of two weeks marking the union of Rahim and Haseena. Mumanijan flowed through the rooms, dressed in shimmer and glitter, full of joy at the sounds of voices, laughter, and music that filled the two-story home. Haseena, the bride, was now in seclusion awaiting the main wedding ceremony, the nikah, to take place in five days.

Tonight, Rahim would not be present as they paraded to the bride's home with the trays of gifts. Kate sat at the edge of the room, tying the last of the sachets that the aunties had filled with dried rose petals, leaves, and fennel seeds. The three-year-old daughter of Nasreen's youngest uncle played with the netted pouches and

175

scrap ribbon. She pleaded for her mother to place the ribbon in her hair. Nasreen's aunt paused from the preparations to tie a bow at the end of the child's braid and then focused intently on last-minute stitches to the *zari* of Haseena's wedding dupatta, draped across her legs, shining in waves of red and gold crystal stones.

When the final sachets were tied, Kate scooped up the sweet-smelling potpourri pouches and placed one in each tray, admiring the fashions fit for a woman of high society.

The first tray displayed an illustrious blue and silver salwar kameez neatly folded. Kate imagined the bride slipping into the garment and sliding her dainty arms through the sparkling bracelets placed by the sleeve of the tunic just above the matching blue satin purse decorated entirely with silver rhinestones. She imagined her pulling the kameez trousers over her slim hips and placing her petite feet into the half-heeled silver pumps.

Aunty Zehba must have been watching her, as she called out to Kate to put the sachets in the center of the tray near the bodice of the dresses, not at the far corners. Kate abided. Stepping to the next tray, she placed another packet near the bosom of a deep fuchsia sari with golden threads throughout, elegant for an evening out. The sheer dupatta lay across the silk material as if it had been blown by a breeze and come to rest. Peeking from under the lower edge of the sari was the petticoat in a lighter shade of pink. Kate ran her finger along the golden embroidery trim at the neckline and there pinned at the shoulder of the choli was a sachet filled with accented jewelry.

Kate's favorite tray held a bright yellow salwar kameez, an airy outfit for a casual day complete with coordinated sequined strap sandals, designer sunglasses, and a shiny striped tote. The delightful ensemble spoke of a woman, fun and sophisticated. Kate touched the bold earring and necklace set resting atop the creamy yellow dupatta and let the thin metal ornaments dangle through her fingers.

The outfits collectively danced in the light of the room. Where would Haseena wear such fashions? It was, by all accounts, an elaborate array of attire for a seventeen-year-old. Would Haseena stroll along a shop-lined street, the trendy tote slung across one shoulder, the yellow tunic flowing above her manicured toes showcased by the pretty sandals; or would she find herself instead harbored inside Rahim's small apartment by the University of Chicago, too fearful to venture outside alone in a country so foriegn? Kate thought, just as she had traded her jeans and tennis shoes for a cotton salwar and sandals only a few days after arriving in India, Haseena would shed the coordinated dress and purse for a pair of jeans and a backpack. The gleaming gowns would hang in the dark at the back of the closet.

Kate's mind drifted to several nights earlier when she and Nasreen were guests at Haseena's mayoon ceremony which marked Haseena's transition to a bride in waiting, relinquished of all chores and daughterly duties. The girls observed from a distance as Haseena and her family sat on a decorated platform alight with gold embroidered red and purple cushions while a procession of family and friends looped strands of yellow marigolds and red roses around their necks. Sweet jasmine hung in Haseena's hair, and oil soaked into the roots of her henna-highlighted strands. Her skin glowed yellowish with the paste of turmeric and sandalwood, oozing out bad *jinn*.

The group moved in a circle to the drumbeat, clapping and chanting as the elders patted the yellow ubton cream into Haseena's cheeks and forehead. It was the night that Nasreen met Faiz, Haseena's cousin. He stared at her from across the room with his deep-set rebellious eyes. His hair was parted and long and he had a thin mustache. As he watched Nasreen, the drums resounded rapidly; in rhythm, the girls danced, slithering their shoulders and arms like cobras moving to a whistling pipe. Faster they moved, slapping their feet to the ground, lifting the spirit jinn to diffuse away.

The drums softened. The women pulled their dupattas over their hair and sang to the prophet. As the verse echoed through the room, the uncles spritzed the crowd with rose water. Kate was unsure of whether to cover her hair or not. She let her dupatta slide to the base of her head, her copper strands visible, then lowered her gaze to the mehendi-tattooed feet of the wedding party and pretended to pray.

In the days to follow, Haseena's body would be decorated with mehendi, then layered with wedding fabrics and jewelry from her ankles to the tikka that hung from her forehead. She would exist between a daughter and a wife, the nascent bride, moving back and forth like the tide across the sands before she was carried away to her husband's family.

"You should get ready," Aunty Zehba said abruptly, waving her arms, waking Kate out of her daydreaming and motioning her along.

The aunties began wrapping the trays in cellophane for the trip to Haseena's family's house.

Kate bounded up the stairs to find Nasreen grooming at the mirror, softly brushing her bottom eyelid with the edge of her nail. Each night Nasreen seemed to apply a thicker line around her eyes, making them richer, blacker.

Their room had become a dressing lounge for the cousins. Hair rollers and makeup were strewn across the small vanity that ten or more cousins huddled around every night fighting for a space at the mirror. Dresses and shoes were scattered everywhere. Nasreen's cousin Arwah was braiding one sister's hair, and the other sister was rummaging through the closet. Yasmine bounced the little three-year-old cousin in her arms. The child pulled at the ribbon her mother had so meticulously tied around the end of her braid and squirmed in Yasmine's embrace.

Kate felt that they waited only for the nights, sleeping most of the day, and rising to prepare for the next engagement. Each night the parties carried on later and later into the evenings, the drum pounding grew stronger, and the chanting of playful insults and jests flung between families grew louder.

"Kate, I brought my blue *churidar* kameez for you," Yasmine said in her delicate British English as she peeked in the room before opening the door wide, lest she smash someone behind the door.

"Wow," Kate marveled.

She picked up the iridescent dark blue dress. It was heavier than she imagined it to be. The material gleamed in fabulous colors. Thick crisscross borders of metallic thread and tassels outlined the Persian embellished neckline, sleeves, and the bottom edge of the dress. The dress reminded Kate of the metallic silver buses with yellow panels that screeched through Hyderabad's city center with passengers hanging for life from thick twisted rope that dangled in loops around the open windows.

"The trousers are here as well." Yasmine lifted the kameez to show the satin pants that did not look much wider than her ankles.

"They are supposed to fit very tight and gather at the ankles. Try it on."

Kate looked over at Nasreen, who had paused from applying mascara and shifted her attention to the dress.

"Tonight is the mehendi. It is a very colorful, lively night," she said. "The most fun evening! Believe me, you will fit right in wearing that."

Yasmine nodded in agreement.

It took the girls nearly three hours to get ready for the mehendi. Kate was ready first, wearing the churidar kameez Yasmine had picked for her. She watched the aunties meticulously wrap Nasreen, Yasmine, and Arwah in their *khara* dupattas, six yards of glittering material. The dupattas were tucked into the backside of their churidars. One end slid over their left shoulder and hung down the front and the other spread across the front of their tunics, looped again over the left shoulder, and tucked inside the right elbow. The free end swooped over their forearm.

Arwah's sisters looked young and fresh in matching vanilla-colored dupattas with yellow patterning and a border of pure silver motifs. Arwah's was lime with silver. Yasmine wore a mustard tunic and navy khara dupatta with silver embroidery and *zardozi* work. Nasreen's dupatta was the color and softness of babies' pinked feet and trimmed with gold latticework. She sported solid pink churidar pants underneath.

Both Nasreen and Yasmine completed their ensembles with a seven-strand satlada of pearls set with rows of rubies and a *kanphool* earring pair supported by a strand of pearls clasped in their hair. The younger cousins wore a modest set of jewelry suitable for their adolescent years.

Before the girls assembled for pictures, Nanima placed a choker of pearls with a gold pendant around Kate's neck, and Aunty Samina adorned each earlobe with a hanging half-moon of uncut pearls. She touched each carefully, feeling the satin smoothness of the pearls. Another hour passed for pictures and yet another hour was needed to load the rented van with all twenty-one trays.

Once they reached Haseena's, they filed out of the vans and formed a line, each carrying a tray like colorful soldiers bringing gifts to their queen. The trays were cumbersome and awkward, and Kate was thankful she did not have a khara dupatta to support in addition.

In front of her, Nasreen struggled against the weight of both her khara dupatta and the tray she carried and resorted to short quick steps. Yasmine walked effortlessly. The long line of guests moved slowly through the gate, looking like silverfish gleaming in the moonlight, past the guards hired to protect the entourage of priceless jewels.

As they reached the front doors, they began singing as the hosts placed rings of flowers around each guest's neck. Finally, Kate was able to put down her tray.

"Ah, thank Allah," Nasreen whispered before they were shooed outside again to form a circle in the courtyard.

The drums, the singing, and the dancing started again, as it had so many nights before. As was customary, the two groups grew louder and louder, chanting insults to each other that Kate did not understand. Finally, the bride's family proclaimed victory.

Haseena made a cameo appearance. Still dressed in yellow, she appeared more delicate than before, a solemn sight on a celebratory night. The trays with clothes, jewels, lingerie, perfumes, and a silver tea set and platter for serving biscuits and bite-sized sandwiches were laid out for display. There were even trays for the unborn baby's first clothes and fluffy blankets.

"The other half is locked away," Nasreen said with a gleam in her eyes. "Hence all the guards."

"No way!" Kate remarked, astonished. "Maybe I should let Nanima and Aunty Samina arrange my marriage," she said, admiring the wedding dupatta and kurta.

"Can you imagine yourself in all this stuff?" Nasreen questioned. "Covered head to foot with gold and red, the wedding dupatta weighing you down like you are drowning?"

Kate visualized herself as the jeweled bride in red. Then she was drifting in the crest of the waves, slapping the water in a panic to stay afloat. The mehendi dripped from her hands like tears…

"No," she said. "Not when you describe it like that."

"I don't approve of my cousins dating American girls," Nasreen said, shaking her head.

"I know," Kate snapped, remembering their conversation on the sunny terrace. "What if the girl they date is Muslim-American? Like you?"

"I meant white girls," Nasreen responded.

"Like me?"

"Convert to Islam. Then you can marry my cousin."

"Nasreen." Kate stomped her foot. "I have known you since we were fourteen. I have been your friend, unconditionally. Do love, religious beliefs, and marriage have to go together?"

"I have to think so," Nasreen replied.

For a moment, Kate sensed a hint of vulnerability in Nasreen. She glanced across the room and spotted Faiz looking their way. He curled the corner of his mouth in a semi-smile. Faiz had been flirting with Nasreen during the song and dance ritual. Kate looked away, annoyed.

"Oh good, dinner is served," Nasreen announced. "C'mon, let's eat. Again!"

Kate watched Nasreen disappear into the crowd of dupattas migrating toward the buffet; the men must have already been served. Something was cracking between her and Nasreen; she could feel it raw and widening like the barren wasteland separating Hyderabad and Secunderabad.

She thought of the guards by the gate, the men on the street with machine guns, the oppressive heat and provocative stares that pierced her like daggers. There was nowhere for a redheaded American female in Pakistan to escape outside, if only temporarily, so she could think, make sense of Nasreen's world and hers, and where and when they intersected and diverged.

She missed her dad. She missed going for long walks, swimming laps in the aquatics center, riding her bike around the park by her house. She raised her homesick gaze and saw Nanima standing several feet away, a shrinking woman in white. Nanima smiled at her showing her paan-stained teeth.

The night dragged on in a monotone; the drums and chanting fell flat to Kate's ears, and she became increasingly annoyed by Faiz's constant presence around Nasreen and the fact that Nasreen seemed to enjoy the attention.

Finally, they piled back into the vans. Without the trays, there was plenty of space. Kate was quiet during the drive. She sat by the window and watched her shadowed, expressionless face reflect as they passed under the streetlights and entered the darkness of the neighborhood.

When they reached Mamujan and Mumanijan's house, Rahim opened the front gate, anticipating their return. The group was full of enthusiasm. The cousins gossiped about who played the drums the loudest, who danced and showed too much skin. They teased Rahim until he blushed beneath his beard. They giggled that his bride was radiant, her skin as soft as a baby's, having bathed three days in a mask of turmeric, and her eyes shined with the eagerness of a young virgin in love.

"Just two more nights," Azra toyed. "Bring lots of rupees," she warned. "You will have to get through all of us cousins with a hefty bribe if you want to carry your bride into your love-making nest."

"Azra!" gasped Yasmine, astonished as she placed her palms over Sana's little girl ears.

Azra clasped her hand over her mouth to hide a giggle.

After the family had dissipated, Rahim, Anees, Tariq, Nasreen, Kate, and Arwah lounged on the floor. The others had already gone to bed.

Anees lay down next to Nasreen. He gently scooped her head up and placed it across his knees.

Nasreen laughed.

Kate was irritated by Anees's presence next to Nasreen, but before she could protest, Tariq coaxed her to lie down and place her head on Nasreen's knees. "Come on. It will be fun," he persuaded.

Arwah and Rahim joined the game.

"Hold still. Your big head tickles," Anees teased.

Nasreen sat up, her mouth open in dismay.

"Rude!" She slapped his chest playfully.

Hesitant, Kate lay her head across Nasreen's knees once she was situated again. Then Tariq made himself comfortable. His head felt heavy and hot on Kate's legs. Arwah giggled as she felt Rahim's weight across her legs. Like fallen dominoes, the six of them lay looking at the sparkling plaster ceiling and chatting about tomorrow's event in which they would be host to the parade of tray-carrying tinsel-clad guests.

Tomorrow, the aunties would spend the afternoon stringing gardenias, marigolds, and red roses on long strands to garnish both the guests and platters of food and sweets. The most magnificent ones would adorn Rahim's neck and wrists when he made his appearance just as Haseena had, although his appearance would be of triumph, not shyness. There would be shouting and whistling again as both sides fought for the groom's wedding finger. It was the last celebratory ritual before the solemnity and formality of the nikah.

"Last days of bachelorhood, my brother," Tariq said to Rahim. "Any confessions?"

"Nice try," Rahim responded. "You are not getting gossip from me. Anees is the one who can never keep a secret," he jabbed.

"Yes, brother, tell us about Rayah," Tariq prodded. "Three days until you are officially engaged."

"I don't kiss and tell."

"That is because you have never kissed her! Too surrounded by family watching every move," Rahim laughed.

Kate tried to see Nasreen's face, but she could only see the tip of her chin as she stared toward the ceiling.

"Okay, boys. Do we care?" Arwah remarked.

"No. We don't," Nasreen answered.

"Anyway, what do you think of all these marriage traditions, Kate?" Arwah asked. "It's insane, don't you think, the weeks of celebrations?"

"It's amazing," she answered. "It makes an American wedding seem so…boring and short," she laughed.

"Would you have an arranged marriage, Kate?" Arwah asked excitedly.

"Yes! If I got all the things Haseena received in the trays today!"

"So, you want to marry an Indian man?" Tariq probed Kate. "We are quite handsome and known for being great lovers."

"Tariq!" Arwah said, shocked.

"Ouch!" he cried in response to her reaching over and swatting him on the head.

"I want to marry who I fall in love with," Kate said, her face hot from Tariq's remark.

She stared at the ceiling praying he could not see her face.

"If he is Indian, then fine with me."

"If Kate wants to marry a Muslim man, I told her he would ask her to convert to Islam," Nasreen said.

"Would you do that?" Tariq asked. "Convert?"

"Are you Christian?" Arwah asked.

"You don't believe in any particular religion, do you?" Nasreen interjected.

"I do believe!" Kate was defensive. "I'm just not practicing. How did I become the topic of conversation? Rahim is the bachelor!"

"Oh, he will have his time. Don't worry," Tariq teased.

"I agree with you, Kate," Arwah said. "I believe in love. I want to marry my true love and go to America."

"Ah, to be young," Rahim said in jest.

"Love is maturity," Anees remarked rather boorishly.

"Maturity?" Nasreen smirked.

"Yes. Love deepens over years of marriage when a couple shares their life connected in faith, family, respect, and support, not in idealization and infatuation. Look at our parents. They have been together a long time, built a solid foundation based on faith and respect," he recited. "Everything is in its natural order in an arranged marriage."

"I want to marry someone who can understand and respect me," Nasreen stated assertively.

Tariq lifted his arm over his head. His hand brushed Kate's leg. A small surge traveled up her leg to her pelvis.

"Your turn, Tariq," Rahim prompted. "What do you want?"

"I want to build a business in India. Make it successful. And I want to travel."

"We are talking marriage, little brother of mine," Rahim teased. "Get your head out of the clouds."

"I don't want to get married. There is so much to see and do in the world."

"What if you fall in love?" Arwah mused.

"What does it mean to fall in love when your marriage is arranged?" Tariq debated.

"You are selfish, Tariq," Rahim interjected. "You had your excursion and are lucky to be alive."

"I'm not selfish!"

"Shhh!" Rahim warned.

"Yes, we don't want to wake Ammi. She would kill us if she knew we were out here lying on the floor together," Anees added.

"Still worried about what Ammi thinks?" Tariq snapped.

"Have your fun, little brother," Rahim continued, condescendingly. "Find yourself. Grow up! When the time comes, you will have an arranged marriage like us. Our parents will see to it."

"I'm not you, Rahim! I am not a traditionalist. That doesn't mean I don't believe. Faith is something I hold inside. I take it everywhere I go. It was there with me in Nepal when time was running out. It doesn't mean it dictates my life."

Kate smiled at the ceiling. She wanted to touch Tariq's hand still resting on her thigh.

"You are not invincible. Be responsible!" Rahim roared.

"Enough, you two!" Anees shouted louder than all of them.

A shuffling came from Aunty Zehba's bedroom. Then the soft pounding of footsteps and the jiggling of a doorknob.

"Up, up, up. Go!" Rahim shouted in a whisper.

The six of them scattered off to their respective rooms.

Chapter 19

RAJI'S CHARM

Chicago 1998

The gravel path through the quad was barren except for yellowed leaves turning to earth, the last ones to fall from the maple trees in late October. Kate followed the path around the university quad all the while staring at the crisp ground, her chin buried inside her jacket, her brown suede hat pushed down to the bridge of her nose. She had her father's encouraging words in her head intercepting her runaway thoughts.

"You're a survivor, Kate."

She was on her way to a meeting with Dean Rowbottom. She was finally escaping Dr. Schwitz's maddening grip. Instead of marching straight to the dean's office in Old Main, she had taken the long way around campus to clear her head. Staring only a few feet ahead, Kate pondered the possible consequence of switching labs. How long would it take her to finish now?

"Don't sweat the small stuff," her father had advised. "In the grand scheme of things, losing a year or two won't matter."

Kate thought about Krishna and how enrolling in photojournalism school brought a renewed ambition about her future career. Krishna had relinquished medical school and shed the guilt that accompanied quitting a path set forth by her deceased mother.

Why should this be so hard? Kate thought.

As Krishna set off on a new path, Nasreen's family life threatened to fall apart. For Nasreen, the dream of adopting Mani and Sabreena brought new stress to her marriage. The stronger she bonded with the babies, the more fragile the link between her and Mustafa became. Her in-laws were gone, and Mustafa became busier and more absent from home. Laila helped Nasreen with the twins as much as she could, and Nasreen's girlfriends often visited to help entertain the babies so she could rest or catch up with household chores. But still it seemed the joy of a new family brought with it a newfound loneliness.

Kate found her life suspended, neither falling apart nor moving forward. Her father's consistant presence in her life at least kept her from standing still.

She continued walking, following the hardened path as it curved toward the student union. It suddenly occurred to her that swarms of students were walking to and from the union, which meant second-period classes were about to begin.

Panic seized her chest. She was late!

Kate hurried past the engineering building and pounded up the amphitheater style steps of the old city hall converted into the university administrative offices. She barged into the dean's office.

The assistant was on the phone and eyed Kate condescendingly. She raised a finger to signal Kate to wait. After a long, agonizing moment, the administrator hung up the phone.

"Yes?" she asked, one brow raised.

"I have an appointment with the dean. My name is Kate…"

"Yes, Ms. McKenna. They are waiting for you. You may hang your coat there."

The woman glanced over her bifocals toward the coatrack.

The men were laughing when Kate cautiously opened the door.

"Come in! Thank you for joining us. Please have a seat," Dean Rowbottom greeted and motioned to the empty seat beside Dr. Elber.

"Kate," he nodded in greeting as she took her seat.

Dr. Crone sat opposite and seemed in good spirits.

"Well, now that everyone is here, we can get started," the dean said, crossing one lengthy leg over the other and clasping his hands in scholastic style.

"Kate," he addressed her.

She stiffened.

"I understand that you wish to remain in the PhD program but transfer thesis advisors." His intonation was ambiguous as to whether he was asking a question or making a statement.

"That is correct," she stated.

"Dr. Elber has indicated to me that this is the best possible solution for you. And, Dr. Crone, here"—he waved his hand methodically toward the man to his left, then clasped his hands together and rested them on his knee—"has agreed to become your new advisor."

He spoke slowly with a pedantic tone as though he wanted her to understand the difficulties she had caused.

Kate glanced over the top of the dean's head at the certificates of excellence collected over a long career. Sitting there among men in their secured careers, she felt small and vulnerable, as vulnerable as she had sitting in the clinic several weeks ago in a paper gown that scratched her nipples, waiting while the nurses took her blood, saliva, and vitals and asked pages and pages of questions. The genetic results were on her answering machine, the red light blinking, almost mocking her. She wasn't ready to know the fate in her DNA.

She could feel the tide rising inside, threatening to drown her.

She shut her eyes, feeling her dad's hand on her shoulder.

"Just so I understand you, Kate," the dean began.

She opened her eyes and stared straight into the dean's eyes.

"Why is it that you wish to transfer, potentially starting over again on a new thesis project? This is not a process to take lightly or that we wish to accommodate unless absolutely necessary."

His hands opened and closed as he spoke. His elbows were firmly planted on the arms of his office swivel chair.

"Dr. Schwitz conducts high-profile research and has secured top funding. You may be eligible to defend in a year or thereabouts; why transfer?"

His hands opened and clasped again.

Why transfer? Kate repeated his question in her head and turned to Dr. Elber.

He shifted in his chair, settled back, and raised his brow at her as if to indicate he was just as curious as to her reply.

They all waited for her response.

"Well?" the dean said impatiently.

"You go to graduate school to think independently," Kate stated.

The dean nodded, affirming her statement.

"I don't feel I can be that independent researcher under my current advisor's… direction," she said, fidgeting in her chair.

The room was quiet. Dean Rowbottom looked at her with narrow eyes.

"I want my thesis from this university to mean something," she said, more confident now. "I want my degree to be mine because I earned it, not because my advisor walked me through each step afraid I would make a mistake. I'm not interested in following his set of misguided, manipulative rules."

"Misguided? Manipulative?" the dean asked, raising an eyebrow. "These are strong words, Kate."

"Yes. They are."

"What makes you a special case?" Dean Rowbottom asked cautiously. "What if others want to change advisors because they don't feel their experience is…right, shall we say?"

"Then they should stand up and make a change," Kate said, this time without hesitation. "I am not asking to be treated special. I am asking for the same fair opportunity as any other student in this department," she said, stressing the word fair.

The dean tapped his fingers together before he spoke.

"You raise some interesting issues," he explained. "I would like to look into the situation more, but for now, we want you to be successful here. Dr. Crone has agreed to accept you into his lab, and Dr. Elber has convinced me that this will be a positive move for you. I trust it will be successful."

"I think it will be," Dr. Crone interjected in his lecture voice. "We'll make it work." He flashed a charismatic smile.

"I am in full support," Dr. Elber added.

"Great," the dean acknowledged. "Kate, as of Monday, Dr. Crone will officially be assigned as your new advisor. I will speak with Dr. Schwitz and explain the situation. You are free to go."

With a simple thank you, Kate promptly left the room, feeling their stares burning into her back as she opened the door.

✱ ✱ ✱ ✱ ✱

"IT'S DONE, NASREEN!" Kate yelled toward Nasreen as the two approached each other on Devon Avenue, an east-west thoroughfare in the Chicago metropolitan area and the heart of little India. There were no oxen on the street or butchered chickens or carcasses hanging from shop windows collecting flies and dust. There was no guava man on the corner or beggars dragging themselves along the crumbling sidewalks. The air did not make you choke, and screeching Suzuki trucks were replaced by bright yellow city cabs.

Despite these differences and the late autumn air, strolling down Devon Avenue felt every bit the same as walking through the markets in India.

"What's done?" Nasreen asked as she hugged Kate and pressed a cold cheek against hers.

"I had a meeting with the dean. I was so nervous, but it's done! I switched advisors."

"Wow! Congratulations. A fresh start," she said, smiling.

Kate breathed deeply.

"Glad to see you happier," Nasreen remarked.

"Where is Krishna?" Kate asked. "I thought she was meeting us here."

"I couldn't get ahold of her. Her father said she was on campus studying. She seems to be absorbed in photojournalism school. I haven't seen much of her, but that's a good thing, I suppose."

"A very good thing," Kate agreed.

"I need a new outfit to wear to Mona's niece's wedding next week. I have gained a few pounds," Nasreen said, slapping her hips with her gloved hands. "Seems having twins in the house has more or less eliminated my workout routine."

"You will get back into it," Kate assured.

"For now, I need bigger clothes."

They started walking along storefronts. The smells of fried samosas, curries, Assam tea, and fresh baked roti floated from the various vendors. Kate felt the warmth from the fryers. Sounds of traditional Hindustani, Bollywood tunes, and modern fusions of classic percussions mixed with jazz blared from shop speakers.

"My mom is watching the twins. I promised I would be back in a couple hours, so we don't have much time to shop. Let's head for the covered bazaar where it's a little warmer," Nasreen said.

Indian-Americans could buy anything on Devon Avenue, from traditional wedding attire to the rarest of spices exported from every corner of India, including imported betel palms and pure neem oil.

"It's busy today," Kate shouted above the street noise.

She stepped off the curb and back on to avoid running into a group of women and their bundles of shopping bags clustered around them like wings. The air was cold, but the sun was shining and the city wind was surprisingly light for this time of year.

"It's always like this," responded Nasreen.

Nasreen turned down a central aisle of the market and then made a series of turns through the mazes of stalls.

"My mother always goes to the same cloth shop. It's around here somewhere."

As they rounded the corner, there was a series of platform stalls with rows of material hanging from ceiling rods.

"Here it is!" Nasreen exclaimed with triumph.

Without so much as a greeting to the shop owner, Nasreen immediately pointed to various patterned pieces displayed on the back wall. The salesman had already unrolled two bolts of material by the time Kate plopped onto one of the viewing chairs to rest. Nasreen caught an edge of one of the pieces as it floated down across the platform. The scene was similar to the time in India when they shopped for wedding material. She remembered Laila and Samina pointing to this and that and Nanima quietly observing, her purse and hands folded in her lap.

"It will be nice to wear something new. I feel like I barely get out of my pajamas most days," Nasreen remarked as she held up a yellow silk piece to her neckline and faced Kate.

"How's this one?" she asked, quickly exchanging the yellow one for a red one. "Or this one?"

Kate twisted her mouth to one side and shook her head. Nasreen likewise shook her head at the salesman, who promptly tossed the bolts of cloth aside, walked across the platform, and pulled out three more samples.

"No. None of these," Nasreen told the man with the thick mustache. "I would like something lighter."

The man nodded and stepped across the platform and from the stacks of folded samples wrapped in cellophane, yanked off the wrappers, and unfurled a peach-colored piece and a cream one that shimmered in the overhead fluorescent lights.

"Mustafa is not going," Nasreen stated out of the blue.

As she mentioned this, the cream silk fell across her face hiding her from view. It fell softly off her shoulder and rested on the platform.

"What?" Kate responded. "You are going alone to the wedding?"

"He is traveling," Nasreen sighed heavily.

"Why?" Kate probed.

"The new company in California is requiring a lot of his time. Okay, honestly, we are taking a little break."

"A break? What does that mean?" Kate asked.

"He has been staying with a friend for the past few days. I don't know if it is that he is moving out or if he is just needing space. He says I am pushing him away. Oh, yeah, you were eavesdroping that morning; you know that already."

Kate rolled her eyes.

"Anyway, until we work out a few things, it's best if he doesn't come with me."

Nasreen lifted the cream silk; the applique in copper, silver, and light-blue thread danced in the light.

"This is nice," Nasreen remarked to herself.

"People will ask if you are alone. What will you say?"

"I will tell them something…and say I brought you instead." She smiled cunningly at Kate and tilted her head slyly to one side. "Please, come with me," she pleaded. "You can wear your red sari. The one you bought in India! It's the perfect chance to show it off again."

Kate looked up at the salesman waiting patiently for Nasreen to make a decision.

"Get that one. It's gorgeous," Kate said, touching the cream piece.

Nasreen waited.

"Okay, I will go with you," Kate agreed.

Nasreen clapped her hands.

"I'll take this one, please," Nasreen said, handing the material to the shop owner. "Now I need a matching dupatta and a few other things, and then a warm cup of tea. Thanks for coming with me."

They meandered past a purse vendor. The leather bags dangled from the ceiling rafters. Kate tapped them as she walked through the shop.

"This one is very nice," she said, twirling the purse around so Nasreen could catch a glimpse. "Oooh, it's expensive," Kate added, flipping over the price tag.

"I don't need a purse. I have too many as it is," Nasreen said.

"And I'm too broke to buy anything," Kate said.

Kate walked out of the purse shop and catty-corner across the aisle.

"Look, the shoes with the curled toes. These were so cheap in India."

"They are called jutti shoes," Nasreen reminded Kate. "But I will wear heels."

Kate laughed. "Of course you will."

Nasreen continued walking straight to the shop that sold dupattas. She showed the man her new swatch of material. He turned to the stacks of thin, neatly folded dupattas, dragged his finger along the edges of the fold, first one stack then the next, until he found the one. A perfect match!

Nasreen quickly paid, shoved the dupatta in the same sack as the sari material, and glanced at her watch.

Kate spotted a stall selling bangles and hopped up on the step. The stall was just large enough for the seller to stand and reach anything around him.

"Oh, look at these!" she exclaimed and dragged her hand across the rows and rows of gleaming, colorful bracelets arranged like stacks of poker chips.

"I could never get these past my knuckles," she laughed. "Nanima and Aunty Samina had to grease my hand to get these things on. They never broke a single bangle."

Kate's eyes darted from one corner to the other, then to the back wall of the stall where hundreds of different styles were displayed on the shelves. She remembered Tariq had bought her a set at the jewelry store the day they hit the man on a bike. The seller moved to one side trying not to block her view and tried eagerly to discover which pair was her favorite.

Nasreen lifted one of the rolls of bangles, cream and gold with stripes of blue, admired the set before pressing the roll back into its place.

"You should tell Mustafa," Kate blurted.

"Tell him what?"

"About the rape. About Dr. Khan!"

A flash of surprise and then anger spread over Nasreen's face.

"How can you be silent?" she asked desperately. "Mustafa will understand, Nasreen. He is the most trustworthy person I know. Tell him! He is dying for you to let him in."

"Why are we talking about this?"

"Because it is destroying your marriage! You are losing him."

The stall vendor, oblivious to the women's conversation, displayed a set of red and gold etched bangles from his two index fingers to Kate.

"Maybe you buried it, Nasreen. But I think it's still raw and staring you in the face. I'm trying to help you. It's not just about you anymore!"

Nasreen looked hard at Kate for a long moment. "You've changed. You have become more courageous," Nasreen stated flippantly.

"I'm trying." Kate sequestered a lump rising in her throat. "Nasreen, how will you raise twins alone if he leaves? It's not your fault! It's not his fault!"

Nasreen stared at the gleaming bangles for a long moment.

"I know it's not his fault I was raped at sixteen. I have never been able to talk about it with him. And then at some point we stopped talking altogether," Nasreen remarked. "Mustafa and I, between the craziness of his work and travel and our not being able to bear children of our own, and then going through the process of adopting two babies…we stopped talking. But maybe we never started talking."

It wasn't supposed to be like this for Nasreen, Kate thought. She wasn't supposed to be facing a future as a single mother to two orphans from the outskirts of Islamabad. What happened to faith?

Kate glanced at the storeowner still patiently holding the set of red bangles. They gleamed and sparkled in the light from a large bulb that dangled from a string from the stall's wooden frame. She chose two and twirled the bracelets in her hand.

Nasreen handed the cream and gold bangle set to the stall owner.

"I'll take these," she said. "And those." She pointed to the red and gold bracelets in Kate's hand. "For you," Nasreen said to Kate as she pulled out her wallet. "They will match your sari."

"Will you start talking to Mustafa?"

"I'll try. Congratulations on standing up to the boys' club and getting what you want," Nasreen said firmly and started walking away, leaving Kate holding the bangles wrapped in tissue.

Kate followed Nasreen through the market in silence. As they passed a fabric shop, an expanse of white cloth unfurled before her in slow motion, and she felt as if in a dream. She saw only white and then stars of light scattered from the rhinestones of the designer pieces hanging like curtains overhead.

The cloth bellowed in front of three women who reached out to catch it as it drifted. From her peripheral view, Kate imagined the three women as Laila, Aunty Samina, and Nanima. The women turned and nodded to Kate. Another white shimmering bolt unleashed outward from the man's hands. The air escaped from the rippling fabric and blew across her face.

"I really need a cup of tea," Nasreen said as she started walking in full gait. "There is this excellent place two blocks on the corner. It's very popular. The chai tastes just like Rahmsing used to make." Nasreen smiled back at Kate. "C'mon."

"Tea sounds great," she said, thinking now of Rahmsing's tea.

* * * * *

THE TEA SHOP on the corner was as Nasreen predicted, bustling with activity as shoppers stepped in from the cold to sip on golden liquid that reminded them of home. Patrons greeted one another with broad smiles and enthusiastic embraces and dragged chairs from one table to the next before wiggling free of jackets and taking a seat.

Nasreen and Kate made their way around the chairs, spying for an open table. Suddenly, Kate halted and Nasreen bumped into the back of her with an "ummpf."

"Krishna!" Kate exclaimed.

Krishna looked up abruptly. She was holding the hand of the woman who sat across the table. Startled by Kate's presence, she snapped her hand from her tablemate's grasp.

"Kate! Nasreen!" Krishna leaped up from her seated position, nearly knocking her chair backwards. "What are you doing here?" she asked in a nervous tone.

"We were shopping on the avenue. I called you," Nasreen responded, looking at the unfamiliar woman at the table and back at Krishna.

"Oh, umm, this is my friend Raji," she said, introducing the woman. "These are my friends Nasreen and Kate," Krishna said to Raji.

"It's great to meet you." Raji's voice boomed over the commotion in the teahouse. She smiled an exuberant smile. She had thick shoulder-length black hair that was slightly unkempt.

Kate instantly recognized Raji as the intriguing woman in the photo that Krishna had printed that day in the basement darkroom.

"Krishna has mentioned you," Kate responded.

Nasreen eyed Kate, confused, but said nothing to the fact that she had no idea who Raji was.

"Please join us!" Raji offered and began rearranging the half-empty cups of tea to make room for Nasreen and Kate. Krishna reluctantly sat down.

"I met Raji in a photography shop," Krishna explained, responding to Nasreen's quizzical look once she had taken a seat.

Kate acknowledged with a nod.

"She developed my black and white film from India."

"Oh, yes. The prints were very impressive, I have to say," Raji beamed.

"I saw them come to life in Krish's makeshift darkroom," Kate said. "I was transported back to India surrounded by her photos."

"She has talent!" Raji agreed. "I encouraged her to enroll in photography classes at Columbia. I'm actually a second-year master's student in the photojournalism program."

Kate and Nasreen nodded.

"Well, I haven't had the chance to see the photos but I look forward to it," Nasreen interjected.

"Nasreen just returned from Pakistan where she adopted twins," Krishna told Raji.

"Oh my gosh, how incredible!" Raji said enthusiastically. "Congratulations!"

"Welcome to Tamarind House," the waitress interrupted in a singsong voice. "What can I get you?" Her nose ring glistened in the fluorescent light.

"Uh, just a chai tea for me," Kate ordered. "Thanks."

"Make that two," Nasreen added.

"The waitress scribbled on her notepad words that seemed much longer than the words "chai" and "tea.""

"So, Krishna tells me that the three of you grew up together and even traveled to India together!" Raji continued to say after the waitress walked away.

"I've known Krish since we were in diapers," Nasreen responded. "We lived two streets away from each other. We met Kate our freshman year in high school."

"Wow! That is so great that you all have remained so close. You are so blessed to have each other."

Blessed? The word seemed to overpower the three of them as they sat speechless looking at each other around the table.

Kate noticed a small box with a red ribbon on the table next to a half-eaten sandwich. "What did you get, Krish?" she asked.

"Just a vegetarian sandwich," Krishna said quickly. She let her hair hang across her face as if she were hiding behind it.

"Not that. That." Kate pointed again to the gift.

"Oh. That." Krishna laughed nervously. "Just something Raji gave me from her mom's shop, right?"

Krishna patted her neck and avoided eye contact.

"My mom owns a boutique in Montreal," Raji explained. "This is one of my favorite necklaces."

Raji reached across the table, pushed Krishna's hand out of the way, and displayed the charm in her palm, turning it until it caught the light.

Kate and Nasreen peered closer at the violet heart charm.

"Lovely," Nasreen said.

"I like the color. Very pretty."

"It's amethyst," Raji chirped.

"Isn't that your birthstone?" Nasreen asked.

"Yes," Krishna whispered in a raspy voice then promptly cleared her throat.

"So you are from Montreal?" Kate detoured the conversation from talking about the necklace, an apparently uncomfortable topic for Krishna.

"Yes. My parents are originally from Delhi. They immigrated to Canada when I was five. I moved to Chicago last fall on a student visa to get my master's degree at Columbia."

"You speak French?" Kate inquired.

"Ah, oui," answered Raji. "I can speak Hindi too, just not as well as French. I miss Montreal a lot, but I have met a lot of interesting people in Chicago and my brother is coming next week for Diwali. Hey, Krishna, what are you doing for Diwali? I am having friends over. If you are free…"

"My father and I are having Diwali at the house with family," Krishna stated unemotionally.

Kate could see the dejection in Raji's eyes.

"Well, if you have a chance to come over later in the evening, all of you," Raji said, looking to Nasreen and Kate, "you are more than welcome." She smiled a faint smile.

The waitress approached with the tray of tea.

"Thanks for the invite," Nasreen replied, filling the pause.

"Two chai teas," the waitress announced and plunked the mugs of tea on the table while she balanced the tray full of drinks with the other hand. She grabbed two spoons from her apron pocket and dropped them with a clink against the mugs. "Enjoy."

Kate wrapped both hands around the mug of piping hot liquid and brought the cup to her lips, closed her eyes, and breathed in its sweet aroma, almost burying her nose in the cup. She sat in a huddled position, as if curling her body around the tea mug offered intimate comfort and a way to shrink from the awkwardness at the table and the unexpected meeting.

The corner café was becoming increasingly loud as customers came and went. The air filled with Asian and Middle Eastern languages intermixing.

Kate smiled and drank the creamy colored liquid that drained through her chest, thawing her veins.

"How is the tea?" Nasreen asked.

"Not the same as Rahmsing's. But good."

Chapter 20

DANCE IN THE PINES

Karachi 1987

From a platform in the Sheraton Hotel marriage hall drifted the rhythmic, mellifluous taals of classical Pakistani music. Four men and a boy sat cross-legged on the platform in silk vests the color of pink flesh. The man in center stage strummed a *lute* instrument. The boy to his side strummed the strings on an old board. One man thumped the cow-skin base of the tabla, another blew into a small bagpipe, and the other player pumped a harmonium. The melodic, saccharine sounds of the percussion rose and fell, and at times, to Kate's untrained ear, carried the whine of a goat awaiting sacrifice.

Despite the fatigue settling in Kate's bones from staying up too many consecutive nights until the early morning, she felt elated that Rahim's nikah ceremony had finally arrived. The preparations and the gatherings filled with traditions and customs had converged at this moment when Rahim and Haseena would share the wedding platform side by side.

Rahim's *baraat* had finally arrived nearly two hours past the scheduled time at the Sheraton Hotel. Haseena was in a separate room with family and friends accepting her marriage to Rahim. Four weeks of ceremonies and dinner parties and they were still apart!

Kate loved her crimson rose sari. Finally she was able to wear the sari that she had purchased during the first few days in India. The border was embroidered almost entirely with golden thread and imprinted with a paisley motif. The outline of the elliptical shapes resembled the leaves of the banyan tree in Nanima's garden.

Aunty Samina and Nanima had pleated the skirt of the sari tightly and tucked it into the petticoat, accentuating Kate's waist. The remaining yards of material were wrapped across her bosom and slung over her left shoulder. Mumanijan had lent her a necklace of gold teardrops each with a ruby eye and earrings that hung from her lobes like miniature chandeliers. Yasmine had pinned her hair in a fine loop to show off the jewelry.

Kate stood beside Rahim as Nasreen snapped a picture. Her shoulder pressed against his, crushing the cream *banarasi* silk of his sherwani suit. His head was bound in a cream and gold turban with an ornamental fan.

"Faiz, make yourself useful," Nasreen teased. "Take our photo."

Nasreen, dressed in a shimmery midnight blue sari, handed the camera to Faiz and wrapped an arm around Kate.

"You two look exquisite," said Yasmine.

"Absolutely," Arwah added.

After all the pictures, a curtain of flowers was attached to Rahim's turban. More than a hundred strings of white gardenia balls, fuchsia carnations, and gold tinsel with pieces of metallic blue hung the length of his body to the curled toes of his jutti embroidered shoes. He was a walking, sweet-smelling botanical shield.

Entirely dependent on family and friends, Rahim was guided to his place on the wedding platform. The shield of flowers was parted enough to reveal his narrow nose and beard. There he was perched for the night, a strange white gleaming bird waiting for his arranged mate.

Nanima, jewelry-less, colorless, unlike the rest of the baraat dressed for wealth, remained untransformed. She was curled in the corner of the wedding platform, sinking into the cushions and glancing nowhere in particular. Aunty Zehba fussed with Rahim's headdress that blinded him from the room.

Rahim's father sat by the band waiting for the marriage ceremony to begin. Dinner simmered in warming containers, the staff stood in the shadows. The percussion taals floated timelessly through the hall as guests mingled, and children dressed like miniature brides and grooms grew restless and chased each other through the rows and rows of chairs.

"Come on," Nasreen whispered in Kate's ear as she promptly scurried toward the door behind Yasmine and Arwah. "Follow me."

Nasreen waved urgently for Kate to join, leaving Faiz standing alone.

Kate trailed the girls as they walked quickly with purpose through the richly decorated lobby of the hotel, past elegant shops selling westernized salwar kameezes and accessories. She followed them past the dining hall filled with foreigners puffing on cigarettes and sipping cognac and aged whiskeys. Except for the turban-clad doorman, who bowed as the girls promenaded through the foyer and out the tall brass-handled doors, there was little to remind Kate that she was anywhere but the center of Karachi.

The night air breathed steamy across their faces and attempted unsuccessfully to sway their hair, heavy with aerosol, or their clothes, weighted by thick auric threads. The girls tiptoed down the steps at the back of the hotel into the grand gardens. Without hesitating, Arwah chose the path to the left that led between the rows of trees. The path to the right led to the lighted tennis courts, and the central path curved to a circular water fountain with four symmetrical arches of spray illuminated silver blue under the moon.

"Where are we going?"

"Shhh!" Nasreen spun around to face Kate. "Arwah is meeting someone."

"We don't have a lot of time," Yasmine said. "Hurry!"

Time? Kate thought. Time is what they seemed to have too much of. They were always waiting, waiting to be escorted to the next moment of their lives.

"I can't walk that fast in a sari!" Kate cried.

The path was covered by a canopy of blackened branches. The lights from the garden filtered through the manicured trees just enough to light the path. Ahead of them a figure stepped out onto the gravel. Arwah quickened her step. From behind, by the tilt of Arwah's head, Kate could tell she was grinning widely. Arwah greeted the figure with formal salaams. From the little light that sprayed across the path, Kate could see the young man's profile. He had a skinny neck that showed his protruding larynx; it bobbed awkwardly as the two spoke rapidly in Urdu.

Arwah introduced Nasreen as her cousin and introduced Kate as the "friend from America." He nodded cordially; his hands remained clasped behind his back. Kate could see he had bad skin but was otherwise very pleasant.

The two of them smiled widely at each other, and even in the shadows it was evident that Arwah was blushing. Nasreen nudged Kate and continued further down the path.

"Let them talk," she whispered.

"Who is he?

"Someone she met in school. They want to get engaged, but it has to be their parents' idea. So their parents cannot know they have met," she stressed.

"Then how do they make it their parents' idea?" Kate asked naively.

"It's complicated, but there are ways," Nasreen responded confidently. "Anyway, I am glad to get away from the party and avoid Faiz."

"I thought you liked his attention."

"He is being a nuisance lately."

They came to the end of the tree line and the path opened again into the lighted gardens.

"I'm glad we are returning to Chicago soon. I am tired of all this wedding stuff. I will be too busy in my internship for these insolent men!"

"Internship?" Kate asked, confused.

"I have to tell you," Nasreen said, her tone softened, "I got an internship at a law firm first semester."

Kate stopped. Her mouth dropped open.

When Nasreen turned around her face was in complete shadow; only her dark curls were lighted by the garden spotlights.

"I'll be around on weekends, promise. You will be so busy and…"

"Nasreen!" a male voice barked.

Nasreen spun back around, startled by the sound of a voice. It was Sameer. He was joined by Anees and Tariq.

"Where have you been?" Sameer snapped at his sister.

"Getting some air. What's it to you?"

"The ceremony is about to start. Come on!"

"Is Arwah with you?" inquired Anees. "Her mother is looking for her."

"I'm here," Arwah answered, suddenly appearing beside Kate.

Kate looked at her bewildered and glanced around, but the pimply-faced boyfriend had disappeared. Nasreen and Arwah grinned coyly.

"Let's go," Nasreen said as she hurried in the direction of the fountain.

Kate hesitated, confused by the situation. Nasreen and the others were already at the end of the path. She could no longer see Tariq. Was he avoiding her?

"Wait!" Kate cried as she gathered the sari material around her legs to avoid tripping and hurried to catch up.

As she came to the point where the path blended into the open garden, Tariq stepped out of the shadows of the trees.

"Oh!" Kate gasped.

"Shh," he whispered pressing a finger to his lips.

She looked at him for a long moment.

He took her hand and spun her around. For a brief and wonderful moment, they danced in the filtered light from the garden, the sound of cascading water from the fountain in the background. Then Tariq took a step back, releasing her hand. Kate's arms floated as if he were still guiding her.

"You can hear the music from the wedding hall," Tariq said softly. "Close your eyes and listen."

She closed her eyes and let the moment wash over her. She could hear the faint strings of the lutes and the subtle sweet harmonium. She swayed and the gravel path crunched under her feet. Then she felt his breath and his wet lips brush hers with feathery lightness. She was wrapped in warmth and the smell of him. She stood there savoring his kiss and reaching out to him before the smell of pine and sassafras returned. She opened her eyes, and he motioned for her to follow.

Kate touched her lips then grabbed the skirt of her sari and hurried along the path, following his silhouette past the fountain and through the balcony doors. She followed the sound of the drums, harmoniums, and lutes to the matrimonial hall. As soon as Kate passed through the wide decorative doors into the grand room, she saw his figure. His back was to her, and he turned toward the doors. His eyes engulfed her.

"There you are," Nasreen said quietly. "I thought you were right behind me. The ceremony is about to start," she whispered as she grabbed Kate's elbow and led her to sit next to Laila and Aunty Samina.

The music fell silent and the band players sat still, their heads bowed. Kate was certain that the room could hear her heart pounding as loud as the drums.

Aunty Zehba and Rahim's father stood on the platform next to Rahim, giving consent for the marriage of their son in the presence of a thick-bearded man who held the Qur'an.

Rahim signed a certificate and a verse from the Qur'an was read. Somewhere in another room, the bride signed herself into wifedom. Nanima sat wedged in the corner of the sofa, her forefinger pressed against her upper lip. Another wedding, another time.

Then a joyous murmur filled the room. Aunty Zehba clasped her hands together.

"*Mubarak!*" she exclaimed.

The guests followed Aunty Zehba's lead, issuing congratulations to all those around them. Rahim bowed respectfully to Nanima, careful not to bury her in his headdress of garlands. Aunty Zehba stepped down from the platform and embraced family members, squeezing the faces of little nieces and nephews. Her duty as a mother was complete.

In her mind, Kate was still dancing in the night with Tariq.

"What are you daydreaming about?" Nasreen teased.

"Nothing," Kate responded breathlessly.

"Look, here comes the bride."

The guests organized into rows once again, all eyes on the bride's procession. Haseena, in full ceremonial garb, was led down the walkway toward the platform and her new husband. Her brother, father, Faiz, and other male cousins walked as pillars at her side, supporting the weight of thousands of crystal stones scattering the lights from the multi-tiered chandeliers. Haseena's father pulled one side of the garland so the bride could see one step ahead, her head bowed.

Kate glimpsed the bridge of her nose and the red of her lips as she was slowly led to the platform, lifted slightly up the steps. Haseena, her head bowed, only a rouged cheek, the tip of her nose, and her full lips visible under the garb, sat slumped next to her husband, exploding in vibrant red like the heart of a pomegranate.

The percussionists picked up their instruments and began to play, this time with a faster tempo. The bagpipes' haunting sound filled the room. Aunty Zehba clapped her hands together. The two pretty sisters Kate recognized from the mehendi parties joined in the dance. The chimes that clasped around their dainty ankles shook violently and sounded a pitch higher than the bagpipe and harmonium. The dancers' sheer lavender dupattas twirled around their slender bodies.

Nasreen spied Faiz walking toward her and dodged away and joined Arwah, Yasmine, and several other girl cousins clustered together marveling at the dessert table.

Kate continued to watch the girls dance, fascinated by their fluid arm movements like petals of a tulip. Eventually Anees strolled over to stand next to her.

"My brother is married," he said in a deep voice.

"Finally," Kate responded, surprised by Anees's appearance at her side.

Kate had managed to avoid Anees most of the time since he had arrived in Karachi.

"And to think, the parties are just starting."

"More parties?" Kate rolled her eyes at him.

"Oh yeah. Don't you think this is all crazy?" he asked her.

"Nasreen is the one who seems crazy right now," Kate remarked, agitated.

Anees chuckled. "She will seem crazy until she is engaged."

Kate shuffled her feet and searched the room looking for a way to escape Anees's company.

"It's hard for girls," he said. "They are so…restricted. And Nasreen, she is from this world but belongs to another. She is American, raised American. She is a deeply devoted person but not someone who will sit around waiting for someone to tell her what to do, not like many Pakistani girls."

"Why are you telling me this, Anees?" Kate said, losing her patience.

"I have lived in the US for three years," he continued, "but even I have a rough time keeping both worlds separated."

"You have a rough time keeping a few things seperated!"

Anees looked at Kate, shocked.

"What issue do you have with me?" Anees clenched his jaw.

Kate looked at him flabbergasted.

"You know," she hissed. "You're lucky she is not...fat." Kate glanced around to see who was within earshot.

Anees was visibly perspiring. He looked at her with sad eyes.

"Nasreen is lucky to have you as her closest friend. I care a lot about her too. Don't be so quick to judge," Anees stated and walked swiftly away from Kate.

What? What did he mean by that? Kate thought standing alone, fuming.

"Hey. Are you okay?" Tariq asked as she approached her.

He gently touched her arm and she jumped.

"What is it? What is the problem between you and my brother?"

Kate looked at Tariq, troubled. She visualized Nasreen crying in her bedroom back home, fearing she may be pregnant.

"I can't...say."

"Oh," he said, dejected. "Well, finally dinner is served! I have been starving all night waiting for these two to be married!"

Tariq turned his back to Kate and headed toward the dinner line. Kate wanted to call out to him. Tell him everything. Be comforted by his touch.

Suddenly, Nasreen pulled at Kate's thick salwar sleeve.

"It's time for family pictures," she announced.

"Me?"

"You are part of the family now. You followed us across the world!" Nasreen laughed, spreading her arms wide. "You too, Tariq. Picture time."

Tariq moaned, realizing dinner would still have to wait.

Kate followed Nasreen's lead and stepped onto the platform. She walked around the arm of the sofa where Nanima remained sitting. Nanima reached out and touched her hand like the brush of a fluttering dupatta. Aunty Samina had the task of holding the bride's dupatta and garlands from her face so she could see. Laila sat between Aunty Samina and Nanima. In the back row stood Arwah, Kate, Yasmine, Nasreen, Azra, and Sana on one side and Sameer, Tariq, Max, Hari, and Anees on the other side. The young men all wore golden cream sherwani coats matching the groom. Yasmine's salwar was fuchsia, Nasreen's midnight blue, and Arwah wore dark purple. The girls' dupattas were folded and pinned high on their shoulders and all were adorned in full jewels, *chintaaks*, kanphools, and *satladas*. Kate posed with this Indian and Pakistani family for a photograph, her body wrapped in a thousand strands of silken gold and tattooed with mehendi in peacock pattern.

When it was time for the *rukhsati*, Haseena's family surrounded her, bidding her farewell through smiles and tears. Her garlands were removed, and Kate could see for the first time that evening the beautiful tikka suspended on her forehead and the magnificent two-tiered *jhoomar* piece pinned in her dark hair.

The couple, in formless radiance, came down from the stage and moved toward the exit. Anees wrapped his arm underneath Haseena's dupatta and all but carried her out of the marriage hall. Haseena's father paced behind them, holding the Qur'an over their heads as a blessing to their future. They paraded slowly in this way—bride, groom, and creed—through the glass doors and into the flower-decorated town car.

$$* \; * \; * \; * \; *$$

AT MUMANIJAN'S HOUSE, all of the cousins darted to the bedroom door to block it as Rahim escorted his bride toward their matrimonial quarters. Only after he relinquished a wad of rupees to the gleeful younger cousins was he allowed to carry his bride into the room. Kate stood to the side but was eventually pushed into the intimate bedroom.

Aunty Zehba and Mumanijan helped Haseena remove her jewelry, bracelets, and bridal dupatta. Haseena sat demurely like a swan in the middle of the bed, her petticoat fanned around her. Mumanijan placed a sheer veil over her head so that it fell feathery across her shoulders. The Qur'an was placed at the bedside sanctifying the consummation.

Rahim broke free from the younger cousins' grasps, stifling their giggles. Haseena raised her eyes to finally look straight at her new family. Arwah, Nasreen, and Yasmine took turns gently embracing Haseena. Then Kate found herself next to the bed. She was so close to Haseena she could see her porcelain-colored skin and large tear-shaped eyes accentuated with coral rose shading. Her mouth was dainty and almost too small for her long, pointed face. Haseena had a look of quiet resolve. Kate thought she was simply a girl, a classmate, a friend.

"Okay. Out you go!" Aunty Zehba demanded, pushing the girls out of the nuptial bedroom and slowly shut the door behind her.

Chapter 21
Silk Lining

Chicago 1998

A PHOTO OF a jackwood-constructed houseboat slipping along a sepia-toned sliver of backwater in Kerala hung above the mantel and was illuminated by a row of diya lamps. Krishna had discovered the original photo stuck between the pages of her mother's favorite book. She enlarged the picture, framed it, and hung it there as her father had looked on without a word. She had found several other photos of her mother that she reprinted and bound into books.

It was Diwali, and Krishna wore a lavender satin salwar and light-silver sweater. Her hair was cropped in a straight bob that brushed her jawline. Relatives on her mother's side had come from South India to stay for the month of November, including her grandmother and her mother's sister and brother. She had invited Nasreen and Kate but not Raji.

"For you, Nani," she said, handing the booklet bound in cloth and tied with a yellow satin ribbon to her grandmother, who received the photo book as a delicate blessing.

Her aunt sat on a cushion on the floor and her uncle stood. Both held their copies and with utmost care untied the ribbon and began to flip through the photos as if bending a photo meant disrupting a memory of their deceased sibling.

"Happy Diwali," she announced.

"Happy Diwali," her relatives echoed.

"Enjoy these memories of her," Krishna said softly.

Kate and Nasreen huddled over Krishna's aunt and uncle to glimpse the photos. Suneel sat quiet in his favorite reading chair. His young grandnieces had climbed onto each arm of the chair. Mani and Sabreena were sitting on the soft elephant blanket on the floor, entertained by a cousin's daughter who seemed to thoroughly enjoy playing the doting role of mother to two curious eight-month-olds.

Krishna's aunt held up a photo of her sister dressed in her nursing uniform surrounded by the medical staff.

"Saritha called me this day," Krishna's aunt reminisced. "It was her first day. She was nervous. So proud of my sister."

Her grandmother pointed and smiled to the photo of a teenage Saritha standing with her siblings in the lush mountainous backdrop of Kerala. Houses stacked one on top of each other appeared to grow out of the hillside. The young Saritha held her arms outstretched.

"Yes, this one is my favorite too, Nani," Krishna said in a loud voice so her grandmother could hear. "It reminds me of Julie Andrews swirling on top of the Swiss Alps in *The Sound of Music*."

Krishna seemed to be in high spirits or at least trying hard to remember the blissful stories of her mother.

"Ha. This one is the best!" her uncle bellowed, slapping his knee. "Do you agree?" he said, holding up the photo of Saritha caught in mid-laugh.

"Oh, yes. Very good indeed," agreed his wife standing next to him.

Krishna's aunt mused over Saritha's wedding photo.

"So beautiful," she said, admiring the photo.

"Can you see the spinach *dahl* in her hair?" Suneel said, breaking his silence.

"What did you say?" Krishna's uncle asked, bemused.

"It's there, the dahl," Suneel confirmed. "Before our wedding, Saritha was cooking spinach dahl," he began the story. "I was urging her, 'Stop cooking. We are getting married!' But she was *still* cooking, stirring the spinach dahl. She was very nervous and ran her fingers through her hair. Green slime from the spoon spread all across!" Suneel pretended to groom his hair. "I didn't know what to do!"

The room gasped amused listening to Suneel's wedding tale. Saritha's sister peered closer to the photo searching for the evidence.

"I was rubbing and licking my fingers trying to get the dahl out. But I was messing up the little comb in her hair. She hit my hand." Suneel slapped his own hand acting astonished. "'Stop,' she yelled at me. 'It's a sign of good luck. Let's get married now!'"

Krishna's aunt and uncle laughed jovially. Her uncle was short and stout. His stomach rolled as he laughed, his white salwar shirt stretched taunt across its roundness. His wife was petite with a narrow jaw. She slapped her hands together and squealed with glee having thoroughly enjoyed the story.

"Mom never told me that story!" Krishna exulted.

Suneel grinned, pleased with his tale.

"She never in her life seemed nervous to me," Krishna refuted.

"I am sure she was very, very nervous at her wedding," Krishna's aunt said, repositioning herself on the cushion. "Ammi did not approve of this wedding. No." Her aunt waved her finger back and forth in taboo.

Nani shook her head.

"She was so very defiant, *bhaanjii*. But so very in love. And now, we too love her Suneel. He was very good to her." Krishna's aunt eyed her brother-in-law affectionately.

Nani rocked her head side to side, confirming.

Suddenly, Krishna bent forward overcome with emotion. She covered her mouth with her hands and gasped sharply, her eyes filling with tears.

"Oh gosh," she trembled.

"Tee-k, tee-k," her aunt said, shaking her head side to side as her uncle looked to the floor and began shuffling from foot to foot. "We miss her too."

"Excuse me," Krishna said as she walked out of the room.

Kate and Nasreen jumped up from the cushions and followed Krishna to the bathroom.

"Hey," Nasreen said, entering the bathroom. "Are you alright?"

Krishna reached for a tissue on the vanity and blew her nose loudly. "I promised not to cry today. Not during Diwali."

"Don't worry," Nasreen consoled.

Kate closed the bathroom door to make room for the three of them to stand. Aroma from the burning vanilla incense filled the small space.

"You look beautiful, Krish," Kate said, attempting to uplift Krishna's spirits. She stood behind Krishna and could see their reflections in the vanity mirror. "Your necklace matches the salwar perfectly!"

As soon as Kate mentioned the necklace that Raji had given Krishna, she recoiled, realizing it might not be best to bring up the gift.

Krishna studied her reflection in the vanity and placed her hand over the purple heart charm. She shifted her gaze to Kate.

"Raji wanted to be here. To meet my family."

"You don't have to say anything," Kate said.

"Say what?" Nasreen asked suspiciously.

For a long moment, Krishna looked at herself in the mirror. She took a long breath.

"I like women."

Another long moment of silence filled the cramped space. Kate took a deep breath and released it. Nasreen folded her right arm over her left and turned to Kate anxiously.

Grimacing, Krishna put her hand over her eyes.

"Raji is more than a friend. We've been seeing each other for a bit."

"What can I say, Krish? I have known you for so long." Nasreen finally uttered.

"I like her," Kate stated.

"Bhaanjii? Are you in there?" Krishna's aunt rapped intrudingly on the door.

Krishna gasped and slowly opened the door, her eyes still damp and reddened.

"So sorry," her aunt apologized. "The food is almost ready. Do you have a whisk to mix the yogurt? We cannot find one anywhere."

"I will show you," Krishna sighed, abruptly walking out of the bathroom.

When Kate and Nasreen slowly entered the kitchen, they found Krishna's aunt whipping yogurt and honey together in a tin cup, having found the whisk. Nani fidgeted over a tray of potato samosas and a woman from the neighborhood, a close friend of Saritha's and an emigrant herself from South India stood over a large gurgling pot of chicken vindaloo, stirring the contents of the pot with the strength of her entire arm.

"Just an extra splash of palm vinegar," the neighbor said, reaching for the bottle. "And a dash of brown sugar," she added with a final brush of her hands.

"It smells delicious!" Nasreen exclaimed from the doorway.

"Oh, yes. Such a tasty dish," the neighbor said, licking her fingers.

"You are making me hungry," announced Krishna. "I do so miss my mother's home-cooked meals."

"We are ready to eat," Krishna's aunt said triumphantly as she carried the tray of samosas to the dining room.

"Kate and I will help serve," Nasreen insisted as she quickly began the task of carrying plates and serving trays out to the table.

They enjoyed the festive meal of vindaloo, chickpea and potato curry, salad with spiced yogurt sauce and fried *gujia*, small sweet balls with chopped almonds.

Before the evening prayers, Nasreen and Kate turned to leave.

"We have Mona's niece's wedding tomorrow, remember Kate?"

She smiled. "Yes. I am wearing my sari and the new bangles you bought."

"Thanks for being here," Krishna said. "Sorry for dropping a bombshell. I know there is still a lot to say."

"I will call tomorrow, Krish." Nasreen squeezed Krishna's arm in comfort.

Kate put on her navy ski jacket. She dug a hand into her pocket hoping to find a pair of gloves but instead pulled out a crumpled red cocktail napkin. The color drained from her face as it dawned on her that the last time she wore the jacket was after meeting Tariq for breakfast following Eid last March. She had tucked the napkin with Tariq's number scribbled on it into her pocket.

"Did you find money in your pocket?" Nasreen said, attempting a light joke. "I love when I find money in my pocket from last season."

"No, just trash," Kate responded, not amused.

"I will throw it away," Krishna said, holding out her hand.

She shoved the pen-inscribed napkin in her sweater pocket and wrapped the sweater around herself, suddenly cold standing in the foyer.

"Nice sweater. Is it new?" Nasreen asked.

Krishna shook her head and looked to the floor. "It's Raji's sweater."

Nasreen sighed.

"Grab your coat, Krish."

"Why? Where are we going?"

"To Raji's. She invited us, all. It's still early. C'mon!"

* * * * *

THE EXCITEMENT OF Raji's voice bellowed through the intercom followed by a long, intruding buzz. The door clicked open.

Nasreen looked apprehensively up and down the dark block on the near south side close to Chinatown.

"The building is a little rundown but her studio is very nice. I promise you," Krishna reassured.

Their footsteps echoed as they climbed the stairwell to Raji's apartment. A baby's cries drifted from the floor above. Someone was shouting. A teenager rushed down the stairs, nearly crashing into Krishna, who led the way. She clasped the handrail for support.

"Come up! Come up!" came a voice from above.

Raji was leaning over the railing two floors up, waving ecstatically.

"I am so excited you came!" Raji grabbed Krishna's hand as soon as she stepped onto the third-floor platform. "Come in. The party is still going."

"Wow!" Kate said in awe as she entered the small apartment.

"Told you her place was nice."

"You should be an interior designer," Kate added.

From the gritty and musty, dark stairwell, they had stepped inside a subdued but joyful French style studio. The walls were painted a chalky gray accented with black and white still photographs illuminated by a row of hanging pendant lights. In the corner was a daybed covered with a striped linen duvet beside an antique white armoire. A single picture window was dressed with white drapes that puddled onto the floor. The large gilded mirror over the fireplace enlarged the sitting area decorated with a bold blue couch and orange pillows. A vase of pink roses set atop a light blue-gray antique desk next to the door.

"I feel like I am in a room in a chateau," Nasreen added. "Well done."

"You are so nice," Raji said, smiling. "It's such a depressing building and small space, I had to make it a fun place to come home to."

Raji's guests were dancing to a rhumba-rock fusion coming from a CD player on the coffee table that had been moved out of the way.

Raji introduced a young man with a goatee. "This is my little brother, Nishi. He is visiting me for the weekend from Canada."

Nishi waved hello. He was dancing with two men named Ricardo and Rob and an African-American woman named Denise. Silke, a student from Germany, lounged on the blue couch sipping a caipirinha.

"The others had to take off. Now it is not as crowded," Raji said cheerfully. "What can I get you? There is plenty of food left over. Everyone chipped in and brought something."

"Oh, thanks but we ate at home," Krishna responded. "My family cooked a ton of food. I'm so full."

Raji walked into the tiny kitchen big enough for a stove, refrigerator, sink, and breakfast bar. Across the countertop was a trail of brown sugar leading to a pile of lime rinds in the sink.

"Silke has made a mess of my kitchen with her caipirinha concoctions! I'm sure she would make you a drink if you like."

"Not for me. Thanks," Nasreen responded.

"Dessert then? I made traditional American apple pie," Raji said, beaming proudly. "I wanted to make something besides Indian food."

"Got ice cream?" Kate asked.

"Of course."

"Always room for apple pie," Nasreen chimed in as she slid off her coat and hung it by the door.

"I'm so excited you all decided to come. Did I already say that?" Raji grinned brightly as she served dessert.

With homemade pie and ice cream on a platter, Kate admired the prints on the wall.

"Raji, are these photographs ones that you took?"

"Yes! I photographed these from my mother's boutique. She sold a lot of vintage clothes, towel racks, pillows, and stuff. I loved these French country towel racks she had with different slogans on them," Raji said, pointing to one of her favorites on the wall. "My mother inspired me. I am hoping my parents will come for a visit one of these days. They are traveling in Delhi right now."

"The photos are really impressive," Kate remarked, her mouth full of warm apple pie.

"My sister was always taking pictures," said Nishi, still dancing with the others.

Denise turned the volume higher on the CD player.

"I started played with lighting and setting," Raji said loudly to be heard over the music. "Then submitted a few photos to local competitions, and that's how it all started! I got a small scholarship to come to Chicago. Oh, speaking of scholarships, Krishna, I picked up an application for you!"

"I'm not sure I will apply," Krishna responded.

"We talked about this," Raji said, disappointed.

"Application for what?" Nasreen asked.

"To submit a series of photos that tell a story. The winners receive a scholarship and the opportunity to showcase their work at a downtown gallery," Raji explained. "Why would you not apply, Krishna?"

"Why wouldn't you apply, Raji?" Kate interjected.

"It's only for first-year students to the program, and I won last year." She beamed.

"Really? Did you show your work downtown?"

Raji nodded, confirming.

"If I knew you, I would have gone for sure," Kate said apologetically.

"Do you have the album? Can we look at it?" Nasreen asked.

"Absolutely!" Raji clapped and stepped toward the armoire. "I keep my photos in a fireproof safe in here. I don't trust this old building."

Kate and Nasreen took a seat on the couch, balanced the apple pie on their laps, and began to flip through Raji's album.

Raji looked at Krishna standing in the center of the studio and recognized Krishna was wearing her sweater.

"Think about applying, Krish."

"I'll think about it." Krishna smiled for the first time that evening.

* * * * *

THE NEXT EVENING, Kate hurried toward the hotel elevator, as much as she could hurry wearing a sari. She was late meeting Nasreen at Mona's niece's wedding. A man in a sports coat braced the door open for her.

"Thank you. Three please," she said, hopping into the elevator.

With her left hand, Kate held the loose end of the sari at her shoulder and gathered the material at her hip with the right hand. It had taken her longer to get ready than she anticipated, and her sari had loosened from the walk through the parking garage and hotel lobby. The material didn't feel tight enough around her, not like when Aunty Samina and Nanima had helped her dress for the wedding in Pakistan.

The elevator beeped and opened. Kate jumped out immediately scanning the mezzanine for Nasreen.

"Kate! Over here." Nasreen waved from the entrance to the ballroom. "Finally, you're here."

"Sorry. I'm a little late," she said breathlessly. "Which is ironic, right? That an American is late to a Pakistani wedding?" she snickered as she let Nasreen hug her, her own hands still holding the sari.

Nasreen stepped back and eyed her suspiciously.

"Why are you clutching yourself?" she asked.

"This sari isn't tight enough. I must not have remembered how to wrap it right."

"Did you pin it to the petticoat? That always helps if you can't pleat it tight enough."

"Petticoat?" Kate asked, confused.

It was only a moment before the girls looked at each other with widened eyes.

"Oh, gosh! I forgot the petticoat!" Kate exclaimed, horrified.

Nasreen was already doubled over holding her stomach as if in pain, laughing without sound. A few moments later, she came up for breath, her face red.

"You don't have a…you didn't wear a…"

She covered her mouth to keep from bursting. The tears started to flow.

"Nasreen! I need your help," Kate cried urgently.

This only made Nasreen convulse into another fit of hysteria. A young Indian couple strolled past them into the ballroom and looked at them oddly.

Kate smiled and shrugged her shoulders as if to say she had no idea why her friend was acting this way.

"It's not that funny!" She stomped her foot as soon as the couple was out of range.

"Yes. Yes, it is." Nasreen wiped her eyes and tried to regain her breath. "Oh gosh." She pressed her hand to her chest to steady its heaving. "I haven't laughed that hard for…for so long. Thank you."

"Glad it was so amusing. Now what do I do? I'm unraveling here."

Nasreen fell forward in laughter again.

"Pretty soon, I will be standing here in my…"

"Okay. Okay." Nasreen held up her hand in surrender. "Umm. Let me see. Wait here."

"Where are you going?"

"I'll be right back. Just hold yourself together. Literally," she giggled as she hustled into the ballroom.

Kate paced the mezzanine nonchalantly. Nasreen returned shortly, clutching something under her arm.

"C'mon. To the bathroom. I borrowed a petticoat. Someone always carries an extra."

Kate jogged alongside. "What did you say to explain?"

"That yours ripped. Don't worry."

Once inside the bathroom, Kate let go of her sari and immediately the material fell to her feet like a simple sheet. She jumped over the mound of material and into the stall, closing the door.

"Hand me the petticoat."

"Just a minute," Nasreen responded as she gathered the silk sari off the bathroom floor as quickly and neatly as she could.

As soon as Kate put on the petticoat, she stepped out of the stall.

"Okay. Hold up your arms."

Kate followed directions. Nasreen expertly wrapped the sari tightly around her, pleating it as she went.

"Here, grab a pin from my purse."

With her arms still raised, Kate felt around for a pin. There wasn't one.

"It should hold without the pin," Nasreen assured. "Hopefully."

An older woman wearing an elegant green and silver sari, her hair tightly wound and pinned in a bun, entered the bathroom.

"Pardon us," Nasreen reassured. "Technical difficulties."

"Oh. It happens to the best of us," the woman said, grinning. "It's a beautiful sari. And you have the most wonderful red hair."

"Thank you," Kate sighed deeply, finally starting to relax.

Ten minutes later, Nasreen and Kate strolled like young princesses into the ballroom just as they had ten years ago at Rahim's wedding.

More than four hundred guests filled the ballroom decorated in Pakistani wedding style with the nuptial platforms draped with streams of crepe georgette and roses. The room danced as couples moved among the white-clothed tables with large flower centerpieces made of tiger lilies and burgundy roses. The women's saris twirled in exotic colors, their jewelry collectively brightened the dimly lit ballroom, and their bracelets chimed as loud as their voices did in earnest conversations.

Confident that the sari would remain wound to her body, Kate followed Nasreen around the room after an American dinner of picante chicken, asparagus with almond sauce, and rice. Nasreen mingled with friends and acquaintances with natural ease despite the many questions acquiring after her absent husband. Apparently news of Nasreen and Mustafa's temporary separation had snaked its way through the community. Nasreen simply replied that Mustafa was traveling for work, which was true. Her parents were watching the twins. Mani and Sabreena were both growing strong, she told them all with a confident smile.

Nasreen and Kate congratulated Mona's niece, the bride, after the nuptials.

"Marriage is an experience," the bride's mother, Mona's sister-in-law, lectured.

"An experience?" the young bride laughed. "Sounds so romantic."

"Marriage is hard work. You have to be mentally prepared for that. You have to make sacrifices for your family. Wouldn't you say, Nasreen?"

"Absolutely! You have to communicate a lot, listen to your spouse, and sometimes you just have to take a time-out and trust marriage works out," Nasreen remarked. "Congratulations again," she said and walked away.

"The nerve!" Nasreen huffed as soon as Kate was beside her.

"I get so many people, who barely know me, tell me how to be the proper wife and mother. Doesn't every couple have rocky times? Don't tell me about sacrifices! Nobody knows what I have been through."

"You rescued Mani and Sabreena from an orphanage in Islamabad. One parent or two, the twins have more than they would ever hope to have," Kate said sincerely.

Nasreen smiled faintly. "Mustafa and I started marriage counseling."

"Really?" Kate's interest sparked.

"Honestly, it did scare me when he said he couldn't do 'this' meaning this marriage and parenting...with me. I don't want to lose him. We had our first session. I survived," Nasreen confessed. "We agreed to be open and honest."

"It's a start," Kate encouraged.

Nasreen shook her head, remembering she was at a wedding; no place for talking therapy.

"Mona!" Nasreen yelled across the dance floor.

Mona waved for them to join her dancing. She seemed to be enjoying the evening, however hard it was to watch her young niece wed when she was still clinging to the hope of marriage. But Kate learned that Mona had moved out of her parents' house and bought a new car.

Suddenly, music filled the ballroom. The bride's closest friends stepped onto the dance floor to loud cheers from guests. With their hands behind their backs, they rolled their shoulders as the classic Pakistani music flowed through the hall. The guests clapped, encouraging the women to dance. In synchronicity, the girls waved their hips rhythmically side to side in traditional spirit. As the music reached a crescendo of cymbals, the girls crossed their wrists together high over their heads and snapped their hands to the cymbal's tenor. They hopped from foot to foot and spun low to the ground.

Once the South Asian-style dance was over and the bride and groom danced together, the floor opened in a fusion of Pakistani sounds, American rap, and pop hits. Several of the girls flipped off their heels at the edge of the dance floor and danced.

Kate and Nasreen danced late into the evening until the guests thinned. They plopped down in the chairs to rest, perspiring and breathing steadily.

"I haven't stayed out and danced like this in forever," Kate remarked with enthusiasm.

"I certainly have not been out since I arrived back home with the twins."

"Look, my sari stayed together." Kate opened her arms to display the dress still in good form.

"I need that petticoat back."

They both laughed.

"Are you going to call Krishna tonight?" Kate asked.

"I told her I would."

Kate watched the guests move about on the dance floor.

"What do you think about…about Krishna and Raji together?" Kate asked.

"I'm not sure what to think. Krishna and I have been best friends since we were toddlers."

"I remember Krishna made the odd comment back in January when we sat in the French café," Kate recalled. "She said she wanted to freeze her eggs. I had no idea what she meant, really," Kate stated. "I wonder how long she has wanted to tell us but felt she couldn't. I was just thinking about it."

"It takes guts to tell us," Nasreen said.

"I really like Raji," Kate continued. "She is so…joyful. I feel like it's an effort sometimes to feel joyful."

"You will be fine. You will get through this slump," Nasreen assured. She watched the bridal party dance to The Beatles song "Twist and Shout."

"I did the genetic testing," Kate blurted.

Nasreen turned her full attention to Kate. "And…?"

"I didn't inherit the mutations my mother had."

"Told you!"

"Now I just need to graduate!"

"And fall in love," Nasreen poked.

"Like I did in India," Kate whispered, looking down at her lap at the red and golden paisleys in her sari. "I wore this sari at the wedding in Pakistan," she said softly. "And I danced with Tariq for not more than a moment under a canopy of moonlit trees. He kissed me on the lips for the first time, the only time. I never told you that."

Nasreen's expression turned serious as she listened to Kate reminisce.

"Seeing Tariq at your house at Eid brought back memories. So many memories. Krishna said I won't admit how I feel. She's right. I still feel the same about him now as I did then."

Suddenly Nasreen clasped her hand over her mouth.

"What?" Kate exclaimed, flabbergasted

"I didn't know," she choked. "I didn't know how much…"

"What? You're covering your mouth. I can't understand," Kate said, alarmed.

"I didn't send your letters," Nasreen blurted. "Then he wrote to you. To me. To give to you."

Kate was stunned.

"I thought the relationship was an impossibility," Nasreen defended. "I didn't want you to get hurt," she tried to explain.

"You never sent my letters to him?" Kate's voice filled with anger. "You didn't want to hurt me? Nasreen, I was heartbroken! You never approved! You never approved of the thought of me with him!"

"I'm sorry, Kate!" Nasreen cried. She grabbed a cocktail napkin with names of the bride and groom scripted in golden lettering and wiped her nose.

"What gives you the right to decide love?" Kate yelled.

Some of the guests turned to stare.

"I'll call him." Nasreen sounded desperate. "I will explain."

"No!" Kate snapped. "You've done enough!"

"Kate! Wait!"

Kate fled to the door, grasping the sari that loosened from her waist and billowed behind her like a silken red tide as she ran through the hotel lobby. The bellman hurried to open the door for her as she and the fury of material flew out the door.

She sped from the hotel to her apartment. She was thinking of the box Tariq had given her. He said to open the box later but why? The box was empty.

Kate ran up the stairs of the complex, the sari dragging behind. Her heart was pounding as she fiddled with the key in the lock and flung open the front door. She knocked into the doorway of her bedroom and let go of the material, as much as was still clutched in her hand. The sari twirled around her as it descended to the floor and lay in a shimmery ribbon, extending from the front door through the living room and into the bedroom.

Standing in her undergarments shivering, Kate found her jacket and pulled the pocket inside out. Nothing. She tried the other pocket. A rose-colored strip of paper floated to the floor. It had fallen out of the silk-lined box Tariq had given her and must have been under the cocktail napkin. She read the note:

To the girl with mehendi hair,
The one who captured my heart.

Chapter 22

RETURNING HOME

Karachi 1987

The unlined salwar irritated her skin. The outfit—brown with gold leaves outlined with tinsel and tassels that felt like wire netting against her forearms—had been handpicked by Aunty Zehba. There were eighteen women wearing the same glittery saris and eight girls dressed in purple, red, and brown salwars with matching leaf motif.

It was the making of a bad Bollywood chorus line, Kate thought, as she watched Aunty Zehba's uncomely fashion designs on the other girls as they clustered together among the banquet tables, gossiping about the wedding night. Rahim and Haseena sat on the platform, but this time together as a married couple, liberated from the ceremonial garments, abdicated of jinn, and impregnated with blessings for a fertile marriage.

Tonight was the walima and the last of the wedding celebrations. It was also Anees and Rayah's official engagement. The couple sat beside Rahim and Haseena looking like centerpieces, subdued and bored.

Kate stood alone at the edge of the lawn absorbing the scene that, five weeks ago, seemed so foreign but now was commonplace. She was fatigued beyond her own comprehension. So many parties—parties for the newlyweds and fiancés, parties for relatives returning from other places or departing for faraway cities, and parties for small achievements—Kate sometimes did not remember what or for whom they were celebrating.

So many evenings prior, Kate and Nasreen escaped Aunty Zehba's watchful eye; sometimes Mumanijan distracted her with idle talk. The girls joined the cousins for cold drinks and ice cream on the terrace of one of the hotels. When they returned home, they gossiped and played cards until early morning, then fell asleep scattered on the floor, the boys in one room and the girls in another to sleep for a few hours before they were awakened by the heel of a chappal as family stepped over them and assembled for prayer.

But things were changing between Kate and Nasreen. This morning, Nasreen was up early for prayer, and Kate wondered if she had even gone to bed. She observed Nasreen meander through the day quietly, lost in thought.

Kate asked Nasreen if she wanted to sit on the terrace, have a soda at the nearby hotel, or buy fruit from the merchant who passed by the house leading a camel-drawn cart full of ripe fruit bursting in the sun.

Nasreen declined Kate's invitations and instead read a book under the fan. Kate amused herself by playing with a trained monkey that appeared in the street tethered to his master by a rope around his neck. The monkey sported a sparkled gold hat with a red and green pom-pom, wore large green sunglasses, and posed cross-legged on a can for photos. The charming animal grabbed Kate's hand, played dead, held a rifle, and danced to the chimes of his master, attracting gleeful smiles and a handful of rupees from his audience.

"Those poor monkeys are slaves," Nasreen said when Kate came inside and the master and his monkey continued down the road to entertain other patrons.

"What is wrong, Nasreen?" Kate asked. "Is it Anees? The engagement ceremony tonight?"

Nasreen shrugged. "No. I'm over it," she said flatly.

"Well, Faiz seems to really like you."

"Faiz is very immature. We are leaving for home soon." Nasreen's tone sounded more of a warning rather than a statement. "You should cut things off with Tariq," she said. "No reason to drag things out. You will only be hurt."

Nasreen's words still stung in Kate's chest as she watched family and friends congratulate Rahim and Haseena and Anees and Rayah. It seemed to Kate that Nasreen embraced the freedoms of America when it came to social relationships and dating but was quick to criticize her male cousins for straying away from religious doctrine. Kate watched Nasreen approach Anees and Rayah. She wore a headscarf, and if Kate hadn't known which of Aunty Zehba's tinsel and tassel colored salwar kameez Nasreen wore, then Kate may not have recognized her in the fading light.

Kate gazed down at her mehendi-painted feet. The dye appeared mud-brown against her pale skin, the same mud-brown color as her leaf cutout salwar. She and Nasreen had the mehendi designs reapplied, telling the girl to make the dye even darker so it would last until after they had returned home. The girl never looked up as she applied thick threads in swirls and lattice patterns to Kate's hands, squeezing the cone filled with green mehendi paste with artful speed; every few strokes she pinched off the excess dye at the tip of the cone and resumed work without pause. Her fingers were permanently yellowed from her trade. Hours later the stain finally dried a dark red-brown, and Kate brushed off the excess dried dye in large chunks into the wastebasket. The tattooed designs extended past her wrist onto her forearm in a V-shape pattern with three dots and a quick swirl. She rubbed one palm over the ingrained pigment on the other arm. It would take forever for the dye to fade, she thought. *What would her dad think? Would he find it strange?*

"Why are you standing here alone?" Tariq leaned close to Kate and whispered in her ear.

"Just taking it all in," she said, happy that he sought her out. "Really, I'm exhausted." She smiled faintly at him.

"You should feel proud that you survived nearly eight weeks—the redheaded girl in India and Pakistan," Tariq laughed. "And you managed to look pretty despite having to wear Indian clothing picked by my mother."

Kate laughed out loud.

"Enough family and enough drama!" Tariq chuckled. "I'm looking forward to starting college in Chennai in a few weeks."

Kate looked seriously at Tariq.

"That sounds exciting," she said, hiding her disappointment.

Of course the summer must end, she thought. Nasreen's right.

"You must miss your family."

"Yes. I miss my dad."

"Are you excited about your senior year in high school?"

High school was the farthest thing from her mind.

"Not really. Besides, Nasreen is spending the first semester at a law firm," Kate pouted. "I will have to get used to her not being at school."

"If I forget to say later, I am glad you were here this summer. My uncles are staring at me standing with you," Tariq added under his breath. "I have to walk away."

Kate watched Tariq walk toward his uncles.

"Guess what?" Nasreen asked, startling Kate, who had not noticed her approaching. "Aunty Zehba is letting us keep the salwars she made for us. Isn't that great? Now I have to find room in my suitcase for this thing," Nasreen remarked sarcastically.

Kate smiled faintly.

"What's up? My family is worried you aren't enjoying yourself standing here alone."

"I'm tired. It's been a lot of parties."

"I know. It's exhausting," Nasreen said, placing a hand on her glistening forehead.

A few strands of soft hair had escaped her dupatta and clung to the side of her cheeks.

"That's why we get married as teenagers so we have enough stamina to withstand all the wedding ceremonies."

Kate snickered at the joke.

"I hope we can get out of here soon. And certainly get out of these outfits." Nasreen glanced down at her chest. "I don't know what would feel more awkward, standing here in a slip or wearing this hideous attire."

"Now I am imagining you in a slip and a dupatta." Kate muffled a laugh, her mehendi-painted fingers pressed against her lips. "Faiz might never leave you alone then."

Nasreen rolled her eyes. "Speaking of…" she began. "Faiz planned a day at Clifton Beach day after next. I told him it wasn't a good idea, that we were leaving in a few days and I would probably be engaged soon."

"Why would you say that? Are you planning to get engaged when we return?" Kate asked, dismayed by Nasreen's attitude.

"No. Just ending any hope he had that there might be a future, which there is not."

As the walima ceremony dragged, Faiz started the rumor that Nasreen was getting engaged, which spread through the under-twenty guest list quickly before the end of the evening prayer. Faiz seemed to have dismissed Nasreen and was flirting with the sisters who danced at the wedding, which made Nasreen even more furious.

"What is this nonsense that you are to be engaged?" Laila hissed at Nasreen. "Sana says everyone is talking about it."

"Sana is a child. She must have heard wrong," Nasreen snapped back at her mother.

"You are also a child may I remind you!" Laila scolded.

Nasreen glanced across the room at Haseena, a girl of seventeen, sitting beside her husband—a glittering princess, her hands still clasping her matching clutch.

"Yes, a child in waiting," Nasreen responded.

*****

IN THE MORNING, the girls dressed slowly, their bones stiff from the floorboards. Kate watched in silence as Nasreen wrapped a black scarf around her head, meticulously tucking each strand of hair under the cloth. She scrutinized her work in the mirror. Kate thought Nasreen's face looked puffy, unframed by her long dark curls, and was confused why Nasreen had decided to cover her hair. What did it mean? Would she continue to wear the headscarf after they returned home?

Mumanijan must have sensed that the girls needed fresh air and a break from the formality and monotony of social engagements. She asked Mamujan to take the girls, Sameer, and Laila sightseeing. He abided by his wife's wishes and drove the group to the outskirts of the city. Nasreen, Kate, Sana, and Laila were packed in the backseat of the Toyota, half sitting on each other's laps, their bodies knocking together as the car jerked and weaved through the congestive streets. Even Nasreen's dainty perfume could not hide the smell of Pakistan oozing from her pores. Every time Nasreen turned her head, the tail of the scarf brushed against Kate's neck.

Kate gazed out the window at the broken landscape, trying to fight the stupor of sleep hanging over her. Finally, Nasreen's uncle stopped at Mazar-e-Quaid, the tomb of Quaid-e-Azam.

Kate followed Nasreen at a distance around the four-sided National Mausoleum, an architectural icon merging Moorish arches with modern geometry. Inside, the girls leaned against the steel frame protecting the central casket. Here, visitors lingered to pay tribute to the Father of Pakistan.

The tomb's white marbled walls shouldered its massive dome. From the high platform, Kate had her first full view of the city. In the past five weeks, she had seen fragments of the city through car windows; whereas in India she had walked the streets daily, visited evey historical landmark, breathed the grit and dust, and listened to the moans of the city and various spoken dialetcs.

Pakistani city life, on the other hand, Kate experienced at night at elaborate parties in ballrooms and from afar overlooking hotel terraces. It was a place mixed with deep religion, culture, and tradition, a place where an ancient people transported themselves into a modern city.

The steps to the tomb were dotted with locals lounging, their chappals removed and set to one side. At the base of the stairs was a wide promenade bordered by palm trees that swayed in the unobstructed winds. The palms were lined in a row leading to the parliament building that appeared so small from Kate's perspective that she could pinch the building between her thumb and forefinger.

All Kate could think about as she gazed at the scene was their adventure in the Indian countryside, running through the murky lake and climbing the boulders. She thought about meandering around Fort Golconda and, most of all, sitting in the garden with Tariq at the tombs. Part of her longed to stay and be with Tariq, but the other part knew it was time to say goodbye and return home.

Suddenly from behind, Kate heard the rhythmic pounding of boots. She walked under the arched passageway into the scorching sun. Sana ran up behind her and took Kate's hand.

The guards marched from the corners of the mausoleum into line formation. Nine guards and one soldier—who was branded with a red sash across his chest and a series of colorful badges pinned over his heart—stood forward from the line. The soldiers wore khaki uniforms with a wide white belt and red trim, a green plume struck forth from the red emblem on their green berets.

Standing at attention, the men's laced black boots pointed outward in a V. Each guard clasped his rifle firmly against his right pant leg, the open end pointing to the sky. For several minutes, the guards stood in formation. Time seemed to hover, suspended. Finally, the guards lifted their guns and marched back to their assigned stations around the perimeter of the tomb.

"Get together," Nasreen's uncle said from the steps, a camera in his hand and waving for Nasreen and Kate to stand together for a photograph.

He held his camera high in the air and motioned for them to stand beside the soldier. Nasreen sighed and looked casually back at Kate. The two cautiously strolled to stand on either side of the tall young soldier, who did not appear to be much older than they were. He continued to gaze straight ahead. His boots looked oversized compared to the girls' slender bare feet.

Nasreen's uncle continued to wave excitedly while adjusting his camera. Kate had chosen to not wear a salwar kameez today, but instead wore a pink blouse and khaki pants; her hair blew wildly about and whipped across her cheeks.

Nasreen stood poised in a light-blue salwar. Her black headdress was bound tightly around her face. Not a strand of hair blew in the wind.

* * * * *

THE TIME HAD come, and the servants were busy packing the girls' suitcases for their return trip to the States.

It seemed to Kate that she had been away far longer than seven and a half weeks. What she had experienced during the summer, many Americans would never experience in a lifetime. She passed the time before dinner parties alone writing in her journal, trying to capture every experience lest she forget, and trying to make sense of her weary teenage thoughts.

"My uncle wants to take us to his farm. One last outing before we go," Nasreen said as Kate was curled up on a cushion writing.

"Your uncle has a farm in Karachi?" Kate asked.

"Apparently," Nasreen responded. "I have no idea who takes care of it as I'm sure it's not Mumanijan," she laughed.

Mamujan borrowed a van that could seat up to twenty people and gathered the relatives for the trip to his farm in the country.

"Are there animals on the farm?" Kate asked.

"I don't know," Nasreen said, shrugging.

Nasreen, Kate, Sameer, and the older cousins rode on the roof of the van. The aunts, uncles, and younger cousins sat inside. There were twenty-three people total. Three extra didn't matter.

"In India, you can always fit more people," Nasreen said.

During the drive to the farm, all Kate saw was sand in every direction. Tariq sat opposite her, the soles of their sandals touching. Outside the sprawling city of Karachi, they passed a shipping port at high tide. After a couple hours, the buildings and coastline disappeared, and the desert stretched for miles. Villages with houses made of tattered rags spotted the desolate landscape. Half-clothed children ran with sticks among a herd of cows, goats, and skinny dogs.

Tariq pointed out a group of women and girls, their heads wrapped in scarves that extended long behind them. The ends of the scarves snapped in the whipping winds. Donkeys pulled two-wheeled trailers stacked with jugs.

"They are getting water for the day," he shouted above the sputtering of the diesel engine and the flapping rooftop tarp.

"Where are they getting water?" Kate asked.

"The rains fill pockets in the dunes. They collect what water they can," he answered.

The van labored along the sand-filled lane until the sand covered the road so high, the van came to a halt, its rear wheels sunk in a dune.

The group piled out. The uncles investigated. The aunts and the girls stood in a circle except for Azra and Sana, who plopped down in the soft earth and drew lines in the sand. The women's saris snapped in the persistent wind and darkened the sandy landscape.

Kate dug her toes in the warm sand patterned in rifts by the winds coming down from Afghanistan, swirling angrily with winds from the Arabian Sea. She looked across the sand to see a man guiding his camel across the desert.

One can vanish here, she thought. *Just disappear into the blinding gray.*

The men, after much debating, pushed the van around the thickest part of the dune back onto the road. They congratulated themselves for a good effort and invited everyone to get back into the van.

"Chelo," Mamujan called.

Eventually they reached the farm. Kate's bones were rattled from sitting on the roof of the van as it dipped and veered through the potholes and sand dunes. She enjoyed sitting with Tariq even though they could not speak above the noise of the engine. He extended a hand to help her down.

The small farm development had two cows, a hen, a rooster, three chicks, several short coconut trees, a large stone well, and a three-room hut made of thick burlap.

Mamujan proudly showed them the chicken coop, a small barn, and a patch of herbs, cowpeas, and peppers. They picnicked under the large tamarind tree and the watchful eye of the hen and ate mangoes off the rind, the juice dripping down their chins. Nasreen and Kate reverted to wearing jeans and T-shirts. Nasreen had even forgone the headdress and laughed freely with her cousins while sucking mango juice.

Sameer started a muddy water fight by hurling a bucket of cool well water at the group. The hen and her chicks fled the scene, balking loudly at the disruption. The thin dogs barked, excited to join. No one could resist the cool muddy water. The adults dodged away as the younger ones battled in the mud.

After weeks of dressing in glitter and jewels, every strand of hair curled, twisted, braided, and pinned in place, the feel of the raw elements to Kate was a welcomed sense of youth and freedom. She playfully flung a handful of mud at Tariq, splattering it across his chest. He looked at her with shock and intrigue before flicking her with cloudy water from a bucket that a feral cat had happily lapped before scattering away. Kate hid her face and shrieked as the water sprayed her. Nasreen kicked the ground, spurting Sameer with chunks of mud, then ran for cover behind the tamarind tree as Sameer came after her with the pail of water he grabbed from Tariq.

A truce was called after everyone was soaked and spitting grit.

The van headed back to Karachi, bouncing along the sand-covered road. Kate rocked to the rhythm of the van. Tariq sat next to her on the ride back and her head rested gently on his shoulder. In her relaxed state, Kate didn't notice a truck thundering toward them on the narrow lane. Their van veered to avoid a head-on collision, sending Kate teetering vicariously over the railing of the vehicle. Tariq quickly braced himself and grabbed her by the shoulders as the truck passed, its horn blaring. Kate clung to Tariq's strong arms, her eyes wide with fear.

"I got you," he assured.

✳ ✳ ✳ ✳ ✳

"WRITE TO ME," Tariq said to Kate.

Kate stood in the shadows behind the front gate as the uncles loaded the suitcases into the van. Tariq straddled an idling motorbike. He held his helmet under his arm and squinted in the sun.

"I start college at the University of Madras in Chennai next week," Tariq said. "I don't have an address. Ask Nasreen to mail your letter to my mother. I will get them."

He looked at her intently.

"Yes!" she blurted. "I will write, Tariq," Kate confirmed.

"I'll write back, I promise," he said, smiling.

He took her hand and her pulse quickened.

"Good luck, girl with mehendi hair," he said, leaning forward and kissing her gently on the cheek. "They are watching us," he whispered in her ear.

Kate shifted her eyes to the second-floor window and saw the curtains flutter.

"Goodbye, Tariq," she said. "I really…"

He had pulled his helmet over his head and surely couldn't hear her.

He waved to her as the engine revved and spurted.

In a moment, he was gone.

Kate went inside and up the stairs to the main room where the aunts, uncles, and cousins were waiting to say goodbye.

"Your father will be happy to see his daughter," Aunty Samina remarked.

"I'll miss you," Yasmine said, embracing Kate. "I will come to America someday to visit you."

Azra grabbed Kate's leg and didn't let go. Nanima touched Kate's cheeks as she always did, and Kate bowed so the old women could kiss the top of her head. When Kate raised her head, tears streamed down her face.

"My family will never forget you," Nasreen said.

"Thank you for sharing them," she said, hugging Nasreen tighter than she ever had.

She couldn't feel Nasreen's hair, only her dupatta.

She knew they were different girls returning home.

Chapter 23

LEGACY

Chicago 1998

November brought a new purpose. Kate spent long hours in the lab. During the weeks following her transfer out of Dr. Schwitz's lab, she was timid to walk the halls or attend seminars for fear of running into him. Eventually routine returned, driven by grant deadlines, class exams, and looming thesis defenses, and no one seemed to care whose lab she was in. The feelings of dread dissipated as she focused on the looming task ahead—to graduate.

Kate had not spoken to Nasreen in two weeks since she ran from the wedding as her sari unfurled. She could hear Nasreen calling her name as she bolted out of the ballroom. The knowledge that Tariq had always cared for her brought a sense of peace. But he was to be married. At least she convinced herself in her mind that there was nothing to be done and focused instead on her research. Her heart still ached.

Her new advisor, Dr. Crone, was an exuberant man. He was boisterous and cracked crass jokes. He prompted Kate to think on her feet. While her heart raced every time he caught her off guard, she felt purposeful and part of a team. Dr. Crone's favorite pastimes included drinking pints of lager and playing pool. This meant lab meetings were held at the local grill called the Ravenwood on the corner of the pedestrian square. The bar had a dark decaying façade but was never as ominous as its name implied, constantly brimming with students, locals, and university professionals.

At the Ravenwood, all the members of the Crone lab sat at one of the long wooden benches, the planks of the table warped from spilled beer. They went through stacks of napkins, using them as writing pads to jot down equations and schemes. When brainstorming and beer came to odds, the group turned to a game of pool.

Kate enjoyed the camaraderie at the Ravenwood. It was cold outside and the gray city streets called for new snow. The Ravenwood's windows were festively covered with frosty snowflakes and hanging red bulbs, smoked over from warm bodies and chatter inside. Kate procrastinated leaving but finally walked with a colleague back to her frozen car. It was a dark, cold night. After several attempts to start her car, the engine finally turned over.

When she returned to her apartment, her roommate had left a sticky note on the answering machine.

"Message for you! Urgent."

She dropped her bag and launched toward the machine and pressed the flashing, angry button.

"Kate. It's me, Nasreen!" the recorder sounded. "I'm heading to Chicago General emergency room. Krishna and Raji were in an accident. That's all I know. Come quick!"

Kate drove her ratty car with speed through the winter slush and past the decorative holiday lights wrapped around the street lamps. She prayed that her car wouldn't stall and cursed the trickle of heat through the vent. She drove one-handed and rubbed her free hand on her thigh for warmth.

What kind of an accident?

A pang of guilt emerged in her chest. She had not reached out to Krishna since Diwali. She assumed her days were filled with school and being with Raji.

Kate headed in a beeline for the information desk in the emergency room. Whines, moans, and chatter echoed across the linoleum floor. The back of Nasreen came into focus.

"Nasreen!"

Nasreen swirled around.

"Kate!" She rushed to embrace her.

Kate was apprehensive.

"I don't know what happened," Nasreen said as she backed away. "I had to drop off the twins at my mother's. Mustafa is out of town. I just arrived."

"Are you family of the patient?" the attendant asked from behind the desk.

"Yes, I'm her sister," Nasreen lied. "Kate is a very close friend of the family." Her eyes pleaded with the attendant. "Can we see her please?"

The attendant led Nasreen and Kate along a hallway away from the commotion of the emergency area to a smaller waiting room where they waited an hour before Krishna was discharged and appeared in a dried blood-soaked shirt and a bandage wrapped around her head.

"Krishna!" Nasreen shouted. "What happened to you?"

Both Nasreen and Kate stood in shock at the door.

Krishna buried her face in her hands and heaved in sobs.

Nasreen encircled Krishna's head in her arms, not caring about the blood.

"Your head?" Kate asked, noticing Krishna's hair was matted with dried blood around the bandage.

Krishna stood in shock.

"What happened?" Nasreen said desperately. "Tell us, please!"

Krishna tried to regain her breath. Her eyes were swollen and raw.

"It's senseless. It's so senseless," Krishna cried. "It's a blur. Things happened so fast. And then she was lying in the street."

Nasreen looked at Kate confused, but Kate only shook her head, equally as lost. They both took a seat on the bench in the small dull room. A poster of Lake Michigan with a poetic verse written across the sky was tacked to the wall.

"Start at the beginning," Nasreen said. "We're here now."

Krishna took a deep, quivering breath.

"We were studying in one of the studios near campus," Krishna began. "It got late, later than we planned to stay. We should have waited for the campus bus, but it was cold and dark and Raji's apartment isn't that far from there, so we decided to walk home."

Nasreen pressed her fingers to her lips and closed her eyes as Krishna's story unraveled in her head. Kate knew Nasreen was picturing it as she was—two girls at night in the city.

"I know it was stupid to be out alone. There have been a lot of incidents lately," Krishna said, guilt seeping in her voice.

"What happened then?" Nasreen asked calmly.

"We were hurrying to get to Raji's apartment. She was holding my hand. We came around the corner and these men, these thugs, they called us names as we passed. They said things I never even heard before, so vile and hateful. I kept walking. I didn't care what they said. But Raji…"

Krishna pressed her brow in her palm, bracing against the pain of the memory.

"Raji what? What did she do?" Nasreen asked.

"She stood up to them, yelled back, told them to piss off."

"I tried to pull her away. Then one of them shoved us. I fell back on the concrete and hit my head."

Krishna touched the back part of her head, as if she remembered she was hurt, and squinted in pain as she touched the bandage.

"Raji told me to run! I got up and I ran across the street. I thought she was right behind me!" Krishna's eyes were filled with grief.

Nasreen panicked. "What happened to Raji?"

"When I looked back, one of the men had grabbed her arm and the other brandished a knife. They were taunting her. Raji kicked the man in the crotch hard. He doubled over and she rushed into the street." Krishna started to heave. She could barely speak. "I saw the car lights and heard this horrible screech as the car slid and then a thump."

Nasreen and Kate sat horrified, their hands covering their mouths.

"She wasn't moving. She had a gash across her face and arm. I started screaming. I screamed until I heard people running toward me.

"Is Raji…?" Kate said, struggling to speak

"She's in surgery," Krishna cried. "The driver tried to stop. It was too late. The car slid and hit her. I don't know what happened to the men. They ran off I guess. Why did they have to harass us like that? Why?" Krishna's eyes pleaded with Nasreen's to turn back time.

Nasreen shook her head. Tears rolled down her cheeks.

"Did you call Raji's parents?" Nasreen asked.

"I called her brother, Nishi," she sobbed. "Her parents are visiting relatives in Delhi. I don't know how fast Nishi can get here from Montreal, but I told him to come as fast as he can. He was just here visiting her!"

Krishna looked at Nasreen and Kate.

There wasn't anything else to do but wait for the doctor.

✳ ✳ ✳ ✳ ✳

THE HOURS PASSED in the dreary waiting room. Around two in the morning, Nasreen and Kate raided the vending machines for bitter-tasting coffee and cheese crackers.

"I know we have a lot to work out," Nasreen said, broaching the topic of their confrontation at the wedding.

Kate nodded. She wanted to tell Nasreen about the gift and the note Tariq had given her, but she said nothing.

Back in the waiting room, Nasreen and Kate sat on the floor with their backs to the wall and didn't mention their dispute at the wedding but instead focused on Krishna and let her talk.

"Tell us more about Raji," Kate said. "She has the coolest apartment."

"She sends me notes in class," Krishna said, smiling tiredly. "Some funny, some private." Krishna blushed. "She writes just a sentence or two, simple. We started studying together, and I felt happy. For the first time since my mother's death, I felt like I was going to make it."

Krishna's voice cracked from the emotion.

"Raji gave me things, a flower here and there, the purple heart necklace."

Krishna placed her hand over her neck feeling for the necklace. It was there.

"You bumped into Raji and me at the café on Devon Avenue. I thought everything was going to fall apart."

"But it didn't," Nasreen stated firmly. "It didn't."

"I feared you wouldn't understand. It goes against what we're taught...what we believe," she said.

"Like Raji said, friends like you are a blessing. That is what I believe in," Nasreen said.

The doctor came into the waiting room and the girls scrambled to their feet. The doctor stood before them, his surgical mask and hood crumpled in his hand. His face was bloated with stress and fatigue and his hair was disheveled.

Krishna started screaming. Nasreen and Kate stood on each side in a half circle, holding her from collapsing on the floor.

✳ ✳ ✳ ✳ ✳

RAJI'S INJURIES PROVED too grave. The surgeon explained that there was too much internal bleeding and trauma to the head. She didn't make it out of surgery.

"We tried everything we could," he consoled.

Nishi arrived that evening, too late to see his sister before she died. He refused Krishna's offer to stay at her home but said he preferred to go to Raji's apartment and wait for his parents to arrive from India. Then the three of them would clear out Raji's apartment and take her ashes back to India for a formal memorial when the family could gather.

"Nishi told me it's best if I don't go to the memorial," Krishna told Nasreen and Kate in the days following Raji's death. "I know he is right, but it doesn't stop the pain. I feel so helpless."

Krishna sat stoically on the couch in the family room. Kate slouched in the armchair and Nasreen knelt on the floor with Mani and Sabreena. Sabreena had fallen asleep in the bouncy chair, and Mani drooled on a teething toy.

There were more framed photos, Kate noticed, that lined the piano's ledge, now a display case, and extended along the staircase wall to the landing. Krishna had framed many of the photos she had distributed to her relatives during Diwali. There were other photos she had not seen before, photographs of Krishna's mother as a volunteer at a food bank and with friends at a special event where she wore a mint sari covered in rhinestones. In the middle of the wall where the staircase curved hung a beautiful photo of Saritha visibly pregnant with Krishna. She was laughing with one hand resting on her swollen belly. Krishna must have found the old photos in her mother's things along with the seascape picture of the boat in Kerala that still hung above the mantel.

"I just want to sleep," Krishna stated.

Suddenly, Mani let out a piercing cry.

Krishna was unfazed by the noise.

"Oh, he is hungry," Nasreen said, jumping up and swooping Mani into her arms. She carried him into the kitchen for a snack of crackers and milk.

Kate fidgeted in the chair and spied a book on the coffee table partly covered by Suneel's magazines and newspapers.

"I heard this was a good book," Kate said, picking up the novel, thankful for a distraction.

Krishna shrugged. "I haven't read it. It's Raji's book."

Kate flipped through the pages. The book opened where a red napkin was inserted between the pages.

Kate pulled out the smoothed cocktail napkin and paused.

"Oh my gosh," Kate said, surprised. "This napkin with Tariq's number on it. How is it in Raji's book?"

Krishna looked confused.

"I gave it to you at Diwali to throw away, remember, at the door?"

"Oh, yeah," Krishna recalled unemotionally. "I put it in my pocket. I was wearing Raji's sweater. Obviously, I forgot about it and Raji found it. Why would you throw it away if it had Tariq's number on it?"

Nasreen had entered the living room with Mani, bits of crackers stuck to his puffy cheeks. Kate locked eyes with Nasreen.

"Honestly, I don't know anymore! Tariq and I had breakfast together the morning after Eid," Kate explained. "He talked about his upcoming engagement and finishing his master's and returning to India. He seemed to have everything worked out. I can't expect him to feel the same about me ten years later. We were just kids then. But he gave me his number on this napkin and he gave me this beautiful jewelry box with a note inside that said, 'To the one that captured my heart.' I didn't know about the note for the longest time until, Nasreen, you confessed about the letters that you never sent. I rushed home and remembered that the box had been open in my pocket and I found the note."

"Raji saved his number for you, so maybe you should call him," Krishna said.

"Just call him," Nasreen added.

"He is arranged to be married!" Kate said, irritated.

"He obviously still cares," Krishna argued. "You're being pitiful! Raji always sent me notes," she said. "Little notes. Some were funny and some were so full of heart. There are a bunch of papers in that box." Krishna motioned toward the plain cardboard box by the fireplace. "Nishi saved some of Raji's possessions for me. The ones he thought I might want to hold onto. I don't know if I will find another note in that box full of her personal things or if I have read the last one." Krishna choked back tears. "I never sent her notes. I don't know if she knew how much I cared. But, if I had a second chance," she heaved, "I wouldn't hesitate to call her and tell her how I feel!"

Both Nasreen and Kate were overcome with emotion.

"I loved her," Krishna sobbed. "That is all that matters."

Krishna's father had at some point entered the room to stand in front of the window and was staring blankly out at the lonely trees standing as stripped stalks in the December haze.

"Raji died protecting you, Krishna. I think she knew you loved her," Nasreen said.

✶ ✶ ✶ ✶ ✶

KRISHNA SANK DEEPER into a depression. She didn't return to the photojournalism program for the new semester but took a leave of absence. Losing Raji within a year of losing her mother proved to be too much for her soul.

Kate hurried to Krishna's home after she left the lab like she did many nights a week since Raji's death. Nasreen was there with the twins. Suneel cooked them dinner—a delicious fusion of South Indian and Bangladeshi cuisine. Krishna's father seemed more lively and cooked with new purpose.

The young women sat together in the warm dining room under the low light of the chandelier, snow falling outside. Since Krishna remained quiet, Nasreen started talking to fill the stillness.

"Marriage counseling hasn't been as awful as I anticipated it would be. Mustafa is a good father," she said, pausing to look at her plate full of food, the steam rising off the rice. "He told me he wants to be a good husband, but I don't let him in." Nasreen ate a spoonful of rice pulao. "This is excellent by the way," she remarked as she savored the Bangladeshi recipe. "I don't know if the counselor can save our marriage."

"Have faith," Kate said.

Krishna poked at the food with her fork.

"I talked about the rape," Nasreen revealed.

Kate stopped eating and placed her fork down on the plate to listen.

"Once I spoke the words there was no going back," she continued. "I was angry. So angry that I was cussing at my abuser wherever he is. Then I fell apart. It was like a monster erupted inside."

Kate placed her hand over her mouth.

"When I regained some control," Nasreen laughed, nervously, "I could see the relief in Mustafa's eyes."

"It takes courage," Kate said.

"I think of Raji, the victim of this hate crime, and I know I can't be silent anymore."

Krishna looked at Nasreen with pain and admiration. The room was growing dimmer as dusk diffused through the large front windows.

Suneel entered the dining room with a teapot. "I thought you girls would like some tea," he said with a meek smile. "Darjeeling, Krishna's favorite from India."

"I would love some," Nasreen answered brightly. "Thanks for going through the trouble."

"No, no trouble," Suneel said and then turned to his daughter. "I added cardamom like your mother used to do."

Suneel wore a light-colored oxford shirt that tinted his freshly shaven chin a healthy glow. He reached over to set the tray of tea on the table.

"Your father seems to be coping better?" Kate said after Suneel had left the dining room.

"He is quiet most days, reflecting on a past memory. He started cooking my mother's favorite recipes, and we both remember the last time we enjoyed the dish with her." Krishna smiled faintly.

"Have you talked to him about Raji?"

Krishna looked pained.

"He looks at me confused," she responded, "like he doesn't know quite who his daughter is. I haven't exactly lived up to what my parents envisioned for me—a lesbian artist."

Krishna looked at the floor. No one spoke. Even the twins, strapped in their seats, sucked in their breath and blinked.

"The closest my father and I came to talking was a few nights ago," she began. "I came home and heard flute music coming from the basement. I found my father sitting on the floor next to an old dusty leather case. He was playing 'Moon Dance,' my favorite song. Apparently, he used to play the flute next to my crib when I was a baby to get me to sleep. I never knew he played!"

Krishna looked bewildered at Kate and Nasreen as they listened intently to her story.

"He played the flute so wonderfully, the sound was a mix of joy and nostalgia. I waited for him to finish the song. He knew I was standing behind him, and without turning around he told me he always wanted to be a professional flutist. I asked him, 'Dad, why did you stop playing the flute if it's what you wanted to do?' He told me because his parents wanted him to focus on his studies. By the time he went to graduate school in physics, he played so infrequently that he packed it in the back of a closet until I was born and he was inspired to play again. But by the time I was three or four years old, he'd packed the instrument away again."

Krishna paused and took a deep breath.

"Then he turned to me and said, 'I dream now of your mother, and in my dreams I am playing the flute.'"

The doorbell rang, startling them. Suneel appeared in the room, surprised by the thought of a visitor.

"I'll get it," Krishna said, grateful for the distraction.

"I'm glad you, my daughter's friends, are here," Suneel said in an attempt to fill the silence after Krishna had left the dining room.

Krishna returned holding an envelope and looking confused.

"This came, certified mail for me," she said as she pulled out the letter and began to read.

Suneel sat at the table with Nasreen and Kate and poured himself a cup of tea.

"It is notification for a scholarship. But I don't understand."

"Scholarship for what?" asked Nasreen.

"Says I won a scholarship to make a photo documentary for the category entitled 'Voices of Asian Immigrant Women.' What is this?" Krishna looked up, confused.

"Did you submit something?" Nasreen asked.

"No."

Krishna scanned the next page of the letter and continued reading aloud.

"'Student portfolios will undergo a panel review, and selected collections will debut at a gallery in the Chicago arts district in fall next year.' This must be a mistake."

"How can it be a mistake?" Kate questioned.

"I don't know. Raji developed the black and white photos of India, and she reprinted the photos of my mother that I made into the booklets that I gave my relatives at Diwali. She kept pushing me to apply. I told her I wasn't ready to exhibit. We had a fight about it, actually. Then, in her apartment, you two were there. She had the application. I said I would think about it."

Suddenly, Krishna dropped the papers at her side. Her mouth hung open in shock.

"What?" Nasreen asked.

"Raji had your photos," Kate realized.

"It doesn't make sense. She couldn't have just submitted on my behalf," Krishna debated. "Raji would have needed my signature and information."

"Did she forge your signature?" Nasreen asked, intrigued.

Krishna flipped to the last page of the letter and found the signature line. She looked at her father, astonished.

"Yes, I signed it," Suneel confessed.

The young women turned their full attention to Suneel, awestruck.

"Raji asked me to fill it out for you. I didn't want to at first, but she kept coming to the house. She was very persistent."

"Why?"

"Because she thought you had a good chance, I suppose."

"No. Why did you sign it, Dad? You didn't want me to go into the arts!" Krishna snapped. "You and mom wanted me to get an MD and be a doctor and get married."

Krishna realized she was yelling. She paused and saw the pain in her father's eyes.

"I never said I didn't want you to pursue a career in the arts," Suneel said calmly.

"I want you to be happy, *beti*. That is all I ever wanted, for you to pursue your dreams in this country," he said with resolution. "I know she was hard on you. I know her expectations were different from yours but..."

Large tears filled Krishna's eyes.

"I lost my wife, and I will not lose my daughter!"

"I don't know what to say," Krishna said, crying.

"What is there to say, beti?

"Raji left you a gift, Krishna," Kate said.

Suneel reached up to grab his daughter's shoulder. For more than a year, he had huddled in the shadows of being a widower. Now, in the dim light of a new moon, his expression was hardened, resolved.

"Tell your story, beti."

Chapter 24

of

souls

Chicago 1998

Kate hurried out the double doors of the science building and braced against the north December wind that caught the door as she exited. She pulled her scarf up over her chin and jumped two steps at a time down the front steps and onto the footpath. The lawn was spotted with fresh snow and sparkled in the sunlight.

She hurried along the path and glanced at her watch. It was a quarter to two on Saturday. If she missed the bus, she would have to wait an hour in the cold or go back to the lab.

Nasreen had called and requested she meet her tomorrow in Pepperwood Grove but wouldn't say anything else.

"It's a surprise," she told Kate over the phone.

She was curious to know what Nasreen was up to.

Suddenly Kate noticed a man in a black double-breasted trench coat, gray hat and scarf, and nice shoes standing on the path in front of her. He was looking down at a piece of paper, turning it in various orientations.

"Can I help you find something?" Kate asked.

He turned around and looked up.

"I think I found it," the man said.

"Tariq?"

He smiled.

"I went to your apartment and your roommate said I would find you in the Basic Science Building. It has taken me awhile to figure out what that building is, but I presume it's this concrete block." He motioned with his hand.

Kate laughed, releasing her breath.

"What are you doing here, Tariq?" she asked.

"I wanted to talk to you."

"I don't understand," she said, bewildered by the fact he was standing before her.

"You're cold," he replied. "Can we go somewhere for tea?"

"Across the quad, there is a place," she answered cautiously, adjusting her scarf.

Kate glanced at him as they walked.

"You flew here from New York?"

"Yes."

"To see me?"

"Yes," he confirmed.

She brushed her hair from her face with a mitten-clad hand and quickened her step. They crossed the street and walked toward the entrance to the Aero Club bar and grill.

The Aero Club was sparsely occupied and smelled of fried food but was warm.

"Do you often work on Saturday?" Tariq asked as he removed his thick coat and hung it on the hook at the side of the booth.

Kate slid across the booth still wearing her ski jacket.

"Yes. I am trying to finish my thesis. You flew here to see me?" she questioned again, trying to make sense of his sudden appearance.

"Nasreen called me," he sighed. "She told me everything. The letters. Not sending them."

"I got upset at her about that," Kate said. "She felt guilty."

"I am not thinking about the letters, Kate. I never forgot about you. I always wondered about us."

"Really?" she asked, intrigued.

"Yes."

"You wrote your number on the napkin, and I wanted to call," she began.

"Why didn't you?"

"Because you're engaged," she accused.

"No. I'm not."

"You talked about the woman you are arranged to marry," she said, not letting her guard down. "You mentioned her when we met for breakfast last spring. You met her. She is nice and beautiful, you said."

"Indian mothers arrange their son's marriage from the time they are eighteen. When have I listened to my mother?"

She smirked. "I should have known."

He looked at her with a steady gaze.

"Kate," he said in a voice that made her heart pound. "I am here to see about us. If there is an 'us' after all. You are very determined and courageous. You go after what you want. I don't want to hold you back."

"Hold me back?" she said, astonished. "You are the uninhibited one, free to roam the world."

"I always come home."

"You said that before," Kate responded, remembering their time in the café.

"It's true."

"I don't know what to say. It is amazing you are here sitting across from me. But how does this work? Aren't you returning to India after New York? Your life is there or wherever you end up traveling. I live here," she stated rationally.

"I'm here. I don't know where this is going. But I know I am happy here."

* * * * *

TARIQ DROPPED KATE off at her apartment.

"I am staying at Sameer's through tomorrow, then going back to New York," he said as Kate opened the car door.

She looked back at him.

"I have been wanting to see inside the Bahá'í House," he continued. "I will be there tomorrow morning…at ten. Will you meet me?"

She lingered for a moment then gave him a half-smile and got out of the car. After looking back, she let herself into her apartment complex and went inside.

That night, she listened to the subtle sound of new snow falling against the gutters. At her bedside, she stared at the jewelry box with Tariq's note to her inside.

✳ ✳ ✳ ✳ ✳

THE BAHÁ'Í HOUSE of Worship appeared as an ice crystal palace against the snowy landscape with its lace dome and intricate columns. In the summers, Kate biked past the white beauty situated peacefully on a hill located just north of campus but had never come inside.

The building was inviting with its perfect symmetry of nine dome sections, nine fountains in the garden, and nine pillars, each harmoniously inscribed with symbols of each of nine religions.

The inside was intimate and simple, a place for reflection. Kate walked under an alcove and studied the writings. She moved out of the path of a small girl of Chinese descent who ran ahead of her mother and into the auditorium.

The auditorium hummed with low voices in prayer. A man she thought might have been Tariq but wasn't looked up at the ceiling deep in thought. A Hispanic family huddled together, their heads bowed, and a group of co-ed friends whispered to each other enjoying the escape.

Tariq wasn't there.

Kate took a seat near the back and listened to the whispers drift past her ears. Her eyes scanned the tall columns. Finally, she stood and walked out of the auditorium. She stopped. In the foyer, his back to her, stood Tariq. He was looking up. The morning light filtered through the dome and rained down on him. She followed his gaze. In the center of the ceiling, she could see the Arabic inscription.

"What does it mean?" she asked.

Tariq spun around. His blue-gray eyes danced as he realized she was there.

"O Thou Glory of Glories," he answered in a low voice.

"Thanks for showing me this place," she said, stepping toward him. "I've never been inside."

"There is lots to discover," he said.

"I'm not predictable."

"Thank Allah for that," he said, laughing. "And you're not mysterious either. You're independent and beautiful."

She extended her arm and he pulled her toward him.

Kate rested her head on his chest softly.

✳ ✳ ✳ ✳ ✳

A "FOR LEASE" sign hung in the dark window at 725 Lynn Street. The address Nasreen had given Kate appeared to be an empty office building in the business district in downtown Pepperwood Grove.

The awning was faded and needed replacement. The door had wood splinters showing through the cracks in the chipped white paint, and the windows cried for a good washing. Had she remembered the number correctly?

She placed her gloved hands against the window and peered inside, but a curtain was drawn across the window. Her breath vaporized against the cold exterior.

"Kate!"

Hearing her name, Kate looked down the block. She saw Nasreen pushing the twins, swaddled in the double stroller. She walked at a pace past the dry cleaners, ice cream shop, and deli to where Kate stood, fidgeting in the cold.

"You look…happy," Nasreen said, catching her breath in the frigid air.

Kate looked down and waved at the twins in the stroller. Mani's large brown eyes were the only visible part of him under his blue hat. His nose and chin were bundled with a matching scarf. Sabreena was stuffed in a fluffy yellow snowsuit. She squirmed in her seat and pulled at the tassel of her hood.

"I saw Tariq," she said.

Nasreen's face lit up with surprise. "He's here?"

"We have a date tonight." Kate grinned.

Nasreen gave her a look of relief and joy. There was nothing for her to say.

"There's Krishna." Nasreen waved to Krishna as she approached from the other direction.

"Hi," Krishna greeted. "It's always so cold in Chicago," she complained. "Here, Nasreen, I found these when I went through Raji's things in the box." Krishna pulled out two hardback children's books from her satchel. "Raji wrote Sabreena's name in this one and Mani's in this one along with a cute note. I'm sure she meant to wrap them."

The twins squealed as they reached for the colorful books.

Nasreen laughed. "Raji left us each something. Do you realize that? Amazing."

"Speaking of which," Kate added, "how is the documentary coming along?"

Krishna was back in the photography program at Columbia College full time and had accepted the scholarship to produce her photo documentary.

"It's a little challenging, a good challenge," she said. "I am meeting my deadlines. I will be doing some traveling around the US later this month to photograph and interview female immigrants from India."

"That's awesome," Kate said with enthusiasm.

"Okay," Krishna said shivering. "Nasreen, you brought us here. Now, what is this place?" She pointed to the "For Lease" sign.

"This…" Nasreen presented, "is mine."

Krishna's eyes grew wide.

"Really? You bought this?"

"Yes," Nasreen confirmed. "I am officially a business owner of a yoga and Pilates studio." She smiled proudly.

"It's got great potential," Kate said.

"Needs a little TLC," Nasreen added, shrugging.

"But it's yours."

"That it is! Want to look inside?"

"Definitely!" Krishna exclaimed, walking toward the door, eager to get out of the brutal Chicago wind.

Nasreen turned the key in the rusty lock and wiggled it back and forth until it gave and the door swung open. She plopped the keys on the front desk.

The space smelled like adhesive and fresh paint.

"Over there is the group co-ed exercise room. And on this side is a smaller room for women's-only yoga and Pilates."

Kate peered into the room.

"A yoga and Pilates studio, huh?" Krishna pondered, looking around the room imagining the finished product. "You did it!"

"I want to make it more than a studio—a place where women come to commensurate and be healthy," Nasreen stated with resolution. "There will be a meditation room, and I am bringing in yoga and Pilates instructors and nutritionists," she explained.

Nasreen led the girls to a back room and switched on the light. The room was painted yellow, and in the middle was a circular rug with pictures of building blocks and a table and chair for crafts and coloring. A few toys were scattered around the edge of the rug.

"This will be my childcare room," she said proudly. "Moms won't have an excuse not to get out for physical and mental therapy! I can also bring Mani and Sabreena to work with me."

Both Mani and Sabreena had enough of being confined in their winter attire and squirmed in the stroller and reached out for the bright-colored objects. Nasreen unstrapped both of them, stripped off the layers of clothing, and set them free to play. The twins tumbled toward the toys, squealing happily.

Kate watched Mani run to the table and grab the crayons, and Sabreena picked up the blocks. Nasreen had found the solution to being a business owner and mother.

"I'm proud of you," Krishna said. "How did you pull it off?"

"Mustafa and I sold some investments we made shortly after we got married," she said. "My parents kicked in a loan as well."

Kate sat down on one of the green circular ottomans placed around the perimeter of the room. Krishna followed and sat on a red cushion, and Nasreen sighed before plunging down into a blue beanbag.

"Mustafa is thinking of taking a position in California with the new firm," Nasreen announced.

"What?" Krishna and Kate said in shocked unison.

"Did he ask you to go with him?" Kate asked.

Nasreen shook her head.

"I don't understand," Krishna said, visibly upset. "I thought you were in counseling and working through everything."

"We are. I have told him everything. I know I shut him out all these years. I buried my feelings about the rape. I was afraid. I married Mustafa in part to hide behind the marriage as if the traumatic event would dissolve away after we were married. When I couldn't get pregnant, the shame and anger turned into resentment toward Mustafa."

"Isn't the counseling helping get that all out and talk through it?" Kate asked.

"The question is, where do we go from here, and do we go together?"

"How do you answer the question?" Krishna asked.

"Mustafa has to decide what he wants to do, and I have to figure a few things out on my own too. I'm no longer interested in law school but I am thinking to get my MBA. Mustafa and I are not seeing or speaking to each other for three full weeks, and then we will meet in Grant Park at a certain time if we want to continue together."

"And if only one of you or neither of you shows up?" Krishna asked, knowing the answer.

"Then it's over."

Nasreen watched the twins playing.

"I told my parents that Mustafa is thinking of going to California," Nasreen continued. "My mom cried all week. She worries about me being alone. How can I be alone? I have twin toddlers! I am too exhausted to feel alone." She laughed.

Nasreen rose up from her beanbag seat. "There is still more to see," she announced.

They left Mani busy pushing a dump truck across the letters on the rug and Sabreena stacking blocks and walked into the adjoining room.

"This is my favorite room over here," Nasreen said.

She flicked on a lamp with four colored lights that hung down in an umbrella arrangement. The centerpiece of the room was a beautiful medallion motif oriental rug. The lights from the umbrella lamp created a relaxed ambience.

Nasreen removed her shoes, left them at the doorway, and walked to the middle of the rug. She dug her toes into the plushness and spread her arms in a yoga pose. Oversized orange and red cushions still in their wrappings were stacked in the corner.

"This is the meditation-slash-stretching room," Nasreen said, stretching her arms out even wider to showcase the space.

Krishna joined Nasreen on the rug, linking her arm with Nasreen's.

"A meditation room is important for the soul," Krishna said.

Kate noticed the vase then, in the opposite corner from the wrapped cushions. It was Nanima's vase with its fluted top and etched golden half-moon carvings.

"I finally found a place for it," Nasreen said, following Kate's gaze. "I think it works here. Don't you think?"

"Yes. It is the soul of your business."

Chapter 25

DEBUT

One Year Later • Chicago 1999

There was a crowd of people outside the contemporary gallery named Roots located in the west loop on Washington and Logan. The gallery's name in black bold letters was bordered by white Edison bulbs that illuminated the block from the art supply store to the Chinese restaurant that looked out of place despite having the best lo mein noodles this side of Chicago.

It was the night of the Asian-American photojournalism exhibit, and Krishna's portfolio, "Women from the Spice Garden," was debuting.

Through the spring and summer semesters, Krishna worked arduously on interviewing and photographing the lives of women from a similar region in southwest India as her mother. The region surrounding Kerala was known as the land of the spices. Krishna restored and reprinted old photographs of her mother and the other women and returned in July to India to interview and photograph the women's family members. Nishi visited Krishna on her trip and helped set up photo shoots and interviews, happy to be working on a project that captured his sister Raji's spirit.

Nishi had brought with him a box containing a portion of Raji's ashes that he was able to harbor away unnoticed. When Krishna returned to Chicago, she, Nasreen, and Kate sprinkled Raji's remaining ashes under a tree in a simple park with a bench and an old swing set not far from the photography store where Raji worked.

"Raji and I met here for lunch sometimes. I took the photos of her with my new camera that I had bought to take to India," Krishna told Nasreen and Kate. "This is the place that reminds me of her."

Krishna printed and framed twenty-seven photographs retelling and retracing the story of her mother and three women of the same generation, from their professional careers as a nurse, a musician, a business owner, and a history professor, back to their villages on the Indian spice route. Krishna finished just ahead of the August submission deadline to the gallery exhibition.

The gallery showcased three student portfolios. Krishna's photos made the cut. Everyone intended to be here for her photojournalism debut; even Kate's father was attending with the woman he'd started dating recently after so many years since Kate's mother's death.

Kate jaywalked across Washington Street toward the theater, her scarf wound snugly around her and tucked into her caramel-colored cashmere coat. Tariq had insisted that she buy the coat, and although it was more than she wanted to spend, she adored how sleek it made her feel. The plush collar and wool scarf offered a thick barrier from the December winds sweeping across Lake Michigan. For the first time since starting graduate school, winter in Chicago didn't feel nearly as harsh and merciless.

She admired the marquee, feeling the incandescent warmth from so many bulbs radiating all the way to the middle of the street. Kate had not expected a crowd. She glanced at her watch. She was running slightly behind.

Then she saw him.

Tariq was standing at the entrance waiting for her. He was wearing a tuxedo with a thick wool scarf wrapped around his neck. He shuffled in the cold waiting for her. He looked dashing. For a moment she remembered him, an eighteen-year-old dressed in a white satin sherwani suit, waiting in the path for her outside the

Sheraton Hotel in Karachi. The night he kissed her for the first time. She smiled and hurried across the street toward him.

For as many years as they had thought about each other worlds apart, they discovered each other anew, meeting every other month and meandering the streets of New York and Chicago. Over the summer, she stayed in New York in his tiny apartment and wrote her thesis. They explored the intriguing nooks of the city and explored each other at night as they lay in each other's arms. Making love with Tariq awakened every dream she had of him over the years and flooded her with desire.

Tariq returned to Chicago last week for her graduation. He was in the audience along with her father, Nasreen, Krishna, and colleagues from the department. Dr. Crone stood behind her on stage and lowered the red and yellow scholarly hood over her head and placed it across her breastbone, letting the hood drape down her back. The weight of it and the years of perseverance it held in its threads made her stumble backward. She placed her hand on the satin hood, breathing deeply and bracing herself. She heard her father's cheer loud and clear from the audience as she accepted her doctorate degree.

A taxi beeped at her as she stepped onto the curb and ran to Tariq. He caught her as she fell into him, her lips pressed with his. His scent flowed over her, and he embraced her tightly and responded hungrily until she released him.

"Did you hand in your thesis?" he asked.

"Final copy. I'm done!"

"Congratulations." He smiled at her.

"I've got tickets to a gallery showing," he said, holding up two stubs. "I hear it is all the Chicago rave."

Kate laughed. "Anyone who is anyone is here!"

"They even have the red carpet laid out," he said as he offered Kate his arm. "Ready?"

Kate linked her arm around his and they passed through the entrance into the warmth of the gallery.

Nishi stood inside the entrance and handed Kate a brochure with a wide smile. He looked handsome in a dark sherwani coat. Kate noticed a purple pendant pinned over his heart in memory of his sister.

The gallery was crowded. Men suited up and women dressed in classic attire mingled, nibbled on hors d'oeuvres, and admired the life-sized black and white photographs that lined the white linen-colored walls.

"Kate!"

Kate turned to find Krishna, dressed in a midnight-blue satin salwar kameez and black billowing chiffon scarf, rushing toward her.

"You made it!" Krishna exclaimed happily. "Come over here," she said, grabbing Kate's arm and leading her to the student exhibits. "Start here and walk this way. That is how I designed it," she explained gleefully, leaving Kate and Tariq standing in front of the large photo of sari-clad women sitting in a circle on the earthen floor sharing a laugh.

"Krishna's work is…good," Tariq said in awe as he studied the women's expressions.

"Look, there is Nasreen." Kate pointed across the way.

Nasreen was chatting with Mona, Shabana, and Sara. Nasreen seemed content, Kate noticed. Her yoga and Pilates studio was steadily building its clientele, mainly women, some looking to get into shape, lose weight, meditate, or find strength in being with other women.

"You two made it," Nasreen said enthusiastically. "Krishna is flitting around like a butterfly. Have you seen her?"

"Yes," Kate answered. "She explained how to view the sequence of photographs. Everything is quite inspiring."

Suddenly, Kate felt something around her leg and heard a squeal. She grabbed Tariq's arm for stability. Mani was pressed against her coat, enjoying the plushness as if she were an oversized teddy bear.

"Hi, Mani," Kate said, smiling.

Mani flashed a grin, showing his new tooth.

"As-salaam-alaikum," she greeted Laila, who was holding Sabreena's hand. "Nice to see you."

"Wa-alaikum-salaam," Nasreen's mother responded.

"Kate, your father is here, over by the cocktail bar." Nasreen nodded toward the back of the gallery. "I met your father's girlfriend. She is very nice."

Without letting go of Tariq's arm, Kate quickly walked to where her father stood, enjoying a light beer.

"Dad!" Kate grinned widely.

She was engulfed in his embrace.

Kate greeted her father's new girlfriend, who had auburn hair like her mother's. She was softspoken and even-tempered like an evening breeze. Kate liked her unassuming nature and the fact that her father was completely enamored.

Kate's dad shook Tariq's hand and patted him on the back.

"My daughter, the PhD?" Ian said proudly.

"Dad." Kate rolled her eyes.

"Hey. Get used to it. I deserve to be a proud dad after all." He squeezed her shoulder. "Now she is off to France on a fellowship."

"Dad, what do you think about Krishna's photographs?"

"Very impressive," he said. "I think I see a little of what attracted you to India."

Kate slipped off her coat and handed it to Tariq. She was wearing a classic black dress with lace neckline and sleeves that showed off her shapely swimming arms.

"You look beautiful and happy," her father whispered when Tariq was out of earshot walking toward the coat check.

"I am happy," Kate confirmed confidently.

From the west wing of the gallery, instrumental music resonated through the gallery. A woodwind quartet had started playing, and Kate heard the softened strings of a cello, violin, and viola and the poetic tune of a flute wafting. Standing tall and waving his flute with passion as he blew into the windpipe was Krishna's father. Kate watched the ensemble play in synchronicity until Tariq reappeared at her side.

"Look, Suneel is playing the flute!" Kate exclaimed. "Krishna said he always wanted to play a gig."

Enjoying the melody diffusing through the picture gallery, Kate and Tariq followed Krishna's photojournalistic story. Kate stopped in front of a photo of two women walking hand-in-hand beside a reflection pond, dotted like a painting with the colors and faces of the people strolling alongside. The Taj Mahal filled the sky behind her with its pure white radiance. The music from the quartet rose to an ethereal crescendo.

Krishna's photos transported Kate into the pandemonium of Indian street life and into the intimate earthly homes of the women whose lives she traced. Kate could hear the sounds of revving engines, incessant honking, and foreign voices irradiating from the photos and mixing with the shrill of Suneel's flute.

"I love this black and white photo," Kate said to Tariq. "It could be taken during wartime or peace. The message is the same."

She admired the scene showing a young woman on the train, her hand pressed against the window. Haze from the locomotive filled the corner of the photo giving it that timeless look. Three women huddled together on the platform and reached out over the tracks waving farewell in the moments before the train pulled away.

The last photo of Krishna's series was the picture of Raji looking passionately at the camera. The photo was the one Krishna developed in the basement darkroom, the one that captured Raji's essence. Above the portrait, in dark bold letters, were the words, "TO RAJI, IN LASTING MEMORY."

Krishna strolled among the guests, who clapped softly as she walked past. She had a look of relief and humble gratitude. Nasreen was holding Sabreena in her arms. The child was clapping her hands together, enamored with her new talent. Suddenly she squirmed and Nasreen put the youngster down.

"Bapa!" Sabreena squealed.

Mustafa barely caught his daughter as she barreled into his legs. He swung her up into his arms. Mustafa grinned as he approached Nasreen and took her hand. Their silhouettes were illuminated by the black and white photograph of Krishna and her mother blowing dandelions in the lawn of their simple Midwestern home. Mustafa never accepted the position in California but instead showed up in Grant Park at the designated time after their three weeks of separation. Nasreen was there too, walking around Buckingham Fountain until they were standing face-to-face. "My life is with you and our twins," he told Nasreen.

A cameraman hunched over and angled his camera at Krishna, who stood framed by her photos.

"Wait!" she exclaimed.

Krishna motioned to Nasreen and Kate.

"I could not have done it without you two," she said. "Friends like you are a blessing."

"Okay, I'm ready now," Krishna said, and the cameraman took the photo of Kate and Nasreen standing on either side of Krishna.

"I was accepted as a transfer student to NYU," Krishna whispered once the cameraman was finished taking photos. "I will enroll in spring semester."

"I knew you would get in," Nasreen said.

"Congratulations!" Kate exclaimed.

"It will be amazing to live in New York."

"Amazing and expensive," Kate interjected.

"In New York, I will continue to tell our stories of being Indian-American."

"Just remember us little people," Nasreen quipped.

"This may be it for a while," Krishna said seriously. "Us, together."

"When do you leave for France?" Nasreen asked Kate.

"In January. I have a month of language classes and then a year of research," Kate added.

Kate had received a fellowship to study at the Institute Pasteur in Molecular Genetics. She was going to study the disease that killed her mother to someday help design the drugs that could save someone like her mother.

"And Tariq?"

"He is coming to Europe in spring. We are going to travel in France," she said, her eyes lighting up. "I hope I can speak a little of the language by then. That is all we planned so far," Kate said, telling herself that it was only for a year.

"If you can survive the year apart and still be strong, then it would be a relationship worth holding onto," Nasreen said. "You'll know."

"Like the three of us," Kate said. "We have survived a lot, and here we are embarking on the new millennium with great potential!"

"Remember when we sat on the black stone bench at Mecca Masjid?" Nasreen asked.

"Yes," Kate said, and Krishna nodded.

"And how the legend says that whoever sits will return to sit there again?"

"Yes."

"Wherever we go, we will come back to sit together."

Glossary of Terms

Ammi:	mother
Allah:	God
As-salaam-alaikum:	common Muslim greeting in Urdu
Bahu:	daughter-in-law
Banarasi:	fine silk from the city Varanasi
Banyan:	fig; national tree of the Republic of India
Baraat:	bridegroom's wedding procession
Bas:	enough
Betel:	leaf of a vine; consumed in paan as a stimulant
Beti:	daughter
Bhaanjii:	niece
Biryani:	mixed rice dish
Chaachaa:	uncle in Hindi
Chaachii:	aunt in Hindi
Chappals:	Indian handcrafted leather slippers
Chintaak:	choker with precious jewels
Choli:	midriff-baring blouse worn with a sari
Churidar:	tightly fitting trousers
Chelo:	"Let's go" in Urdu
Dahl:	lentils
Diwali:	Hindu festival of lights

Dholak:	drum with a leather head
Dupatta:	long, multi-purpose scarf and a symbol of modesty
Eid (Eid Mubarak):	festival that marks the end of Ramadan (Blessed Eid)
Feringhee:	foreigner, especially one with white skin
Ganesha:	Hindu deity in a human form but with head of an elephant
Garam Masala	blend of Indian spices
Ghee:	clarified butter
Gulab jamun:	milk-solids-based sweet soaked in sugar syrup
Gujia:	sweet dumpling
Henna:	dye from the henna tree used as temporary body art
Howdah:	carriage on the back of a camel or elephant
Jhoomar:	elaborate pendant; hairpiece
Japa mala:	string of prayer beads
Jinn:	demon
Jutti:	traditional ethnic heavily embroidered footwear
Kanphool:	ornate earrings that cover the outer ear and extend down
Kameeze:	loose long-sleeved top worn over a salwar
Khalajan:	respectful title for eldest maternal aunt
Khara:	traditional wedding dress of Hyderabadi Muslim brides
Kohl:	cosmetic applied to infants to strengthen the eyes
Kurta:	loose shirt falling just above or somewhere below the knees
Lute:	plucked string instrument
Lehengas:	long, embroidered and pleated skirt
Mamujan:	respectful title for eldest maternal uncle
Masoor dal:	dish containing split red lentils
Mayoon:	Pakistani pre-wedding, during which the bride goes into seclusion before the wedding
Mehendi:	pre-wedding ceremony; reddish-brown paste applied as skin decoration during weddings
Mecca:	holiest city of Islam
Mumanijan:	respectful title for eldest maternal uncle's wife
Muburak:	congratulations
Turmeric	ginger plant native to South India

Naan:	oven baked flatbread
Neem:	native tree to India; its seeds and fruits produce neem oil
Nikah:	Marriage contract in Islam
Paan:	preparation combining betel leaf with areca nut; chewed for its psychoactive effects
Roti:	flatbread
Ramadan:	month of fasting; ninth month in the Islamic calendar
Rukhsati:	time when groom and family leave together with the bride
Salaam:	gesture of respect
Salwar:	loose trousers gathered at the ankles and worn with kameez
Sanskrit:	sacred language of Hinduism
Sari:	traditional drape worn in Asia that is 5-9 yards in length
Satladas:	Seven-stringed pearl necklace
Sherwani:	a long coat-like garment worn over a *kurta*
Supari:	areca nuts chewed with betel leaves
Tamarind:	tree cultivated in India and produces pod-like fruit
Thawb:	ankle-length Arab garment
Tikka:	traditional forehead jewelry that attaches in hair with pins
Urdu:	national language of Pakistan
Vindaloo:	Indian curry dish
Wa-alaikum-salaam:	response greeting in Urdu
Wallah:	person concerned with a business
Walima:	marriage banquet in an Islamic wedding
zardozi:	metal embroidery
Zari:	thread traditionally made of fine gold or silver

About the Author

SIOBHAN MALANY holds a PhD in chemistry from the University of Iowa and was trained in pharmacology at the University of California, San Diego. She works in the biotechnology sector and pursues creative writing. She is an accomplished grant writer and has published over forty scientific articles and articles for *The San Diego Woman* magazine and for the Association for Women in Science. She is an avid cyclist and enjoys kayaking, hiking, and travel. She lives with her husband and two sons in Orlando, Florida. *Mehendi Tides* is her first novel.

Morgan James
Speakers Group

We connect Morgan James published authors with live and online events and audiences whom will benefit from their expertise.